T0148066

Victoria's Peace

Thomas J. Koelsch

authorHOUSE®

AuthorHouse™
1663 Liberty Drive
Bloomington, IN 47403
www.authorhouse.com
Phone: 1 (800) 839-8640

© 2015 Thomas J. Koelsch. All rights reserved.

No part of this book may be reproduced, stored in a retrieval system, or transmitted by any means without the written permission of the author.

Published by AuthorHouse 10/29/2015

ISBN: 978-1-5049-5087-9 (sc)
ISBN: 978-1-5049-5086-2 (e)

Print information available on the last page.

Any people depicted in stock imagery provided by Thinkstock are models, and such images are being used for illustrative purposes only. Certain stock imagery © Thinkstock.

This book is printed on acid-free paper.

Because of the dynamic nature of the Internet, any web addresses or links contained in this book may have changed since publication and may no longer be valid. The views expressed in this work are solely those of the author and do not necessarily reflect the views of the publisher, and the publisher hereby disclaims any responsibility for them.

DEDICATION

For the Children

You may give them your love but not your thoughts,
For they have their own thoughts.

You may house their bodies but not their souls,
For their souls dwell in the house of tomorrow,
Which you cannot visit,
Not even in your dreams.

You may strive to be like them,
But seek not to make them like you.
For life goes not backward nor tarries with yesterday.

From The Prophet "On Children"
by Kahlil Gibran

THE DEBUT

"Mayday! Mayday! Mayday!"

There was crackling static on the radio.

"Mayday! Mayday! This is Blue Fox! Does anyone copy?"

Crackling static again.

"This is Blue Fox! Mayday! Mayday! Someone answer for Pete's sake!"

"Stay on it, Steiger!"

"Morris's dead, major. So's Starky'n TJ. Bobby's real bad, sir!"

"Get back on the radio, Steiger, and keep callin' our position!"

"But, captain…"

"Do it, Steiger! I'm gonna ditch!"

"What!"

"The radio, Steiger! There's two bogies on our tail!"

"Okay, okay…Mayday! Mayday! This here's Blue Fox. Come in? Does anyone copy? Call on channel two. Mayday!"

There was a burst of static and then a high-pitched squeal.

"Mayday! Mayday! Mayday! Blue Fox's on fire'n dustin' it! Coordinates: V-5, H-4! Mayday! Mayday! V-5, H-4! You ain't never gonna see that baby, sir!"

"Shut up! I'm put'n 'er in!"

"But, sir, in the middle of the…"

There was another burst of static and a loud whine on the radio.

"She's droppin' too fast, sir! Jesus-H-Christ! May…"

There was a violent explosion several hundred feet above the Pacific, and a fireball could be seen by the men on the aircraft carrier ten miles to the east.

Simultaneously, at St. Joseph's Hospital, stateside, over five thousand miles away, there was a terrifying scream. It was a scream of such intensity that people walking in the out-patient ward on the floor below stopped for a moment, tilted their heads upward, and looked toward the ceiling, their mouths slack and their eyes apprehensive as the sharp edge of the scream tore their hopes of immortality in two. It was an outburst so full of terror, affliction, surprise, and absolute horror that Margaret Demarest, a veteran obstetrics nurse, peeled the picture of a handsome air force officer from the death grip of the woman on the delivery table and stepped back, her fingers splayed against her breast. Undaunted, Doctor Peter Finch reached between the legs of the woman on the delivery table as a pinkish-white, wriggling infant plopped into his palms, its tiny fists jabbing at the air with little boxer movements as if it were frantically trying to ward off an unseen enemy.

* * * * * * *

2

THE INCARCERATION

The room was cold and dark. Outside, the wind wailed in the trees, and frigid branches rapped the frosted windowpanes. Shrill, sharply honed cries rose from a white crib set on casters in one corner of the room. Like an invisible shield, the smell of urine surrounded the crib, and two tiny fists reached between the high wooden slats that enclosed it. The fists stabbed at the darkness with short, jerky movements, and the cries ascended to a high-pitched squeal.

Suddenly, a rectangular square of light opened in one wall. Two quivering black shadows slithered, like garden snakes, beneath the crib. Then there were garbled noises:

"What're we going to do, daddy?"

"Stop calling me that! You was the one who wanted it. A status symbol, you said. Buy one on the underground market, you said, like he's a commodity on Wall Street."

"Children are God's messengers. Isn't that what the bishop told you, daddy?"

"Don't get sarcastic. Besides, how many kids does the dad-blamed bishop have? Can't you stick a bottle in its mouth or something? I've got to be at the office early."

"There you go again. Stick a bottle in its mouth. Stick a bottle in its mouth. As if that's all there is to it! Maybe the bishop or Father Devine would like to roll up their sleeves'n change one of these, whew!"

"For God's sake, Pickle Puss, what're we paying a maid for?"

"I fired her. She was stealing the sterling silverware. Now, go back to bed. Your mother always said you were a crybaby."

"Aren't you coming?"

"In a minute."

Momentarily, the pungent odor disappeared, the tiny fists relaxed, and the garbled noises trailed off as the rectangular square of light disappeared behind a black wall. A purplish pall descended over the crib like a coffin drape, and there was an intermittent rapping on the window. From the crib, a muffled, blanket-muted cry punctuated the dank gloom with an unspoken question: "Are the snakes still under the bed?"

*   *   *   *   *   *   *

PART I

On the second floor landing outside the freshman dormitory of Loyola Hall, a skinny, dark-haired kid, wearing a bright red, Hawaiian print silk shirt, shinnied up one of the iron poles which held a metal, latticed grating in place on all four sides of an old elevator shaft. The elevator itself had long since been removed, leaving a gaping fifteen-foot wide empty shaft which dropped two floors into the basement where there was a laundry room.

Craning their necks to see upward through the openings in the grating, several boys watched the wiry kid who was edging his way along the narrow rim of the grating six feet above them. One of the boys, a fat, freckle faced kid who wore a white shirt, a thin black tie, and black double-knit pants, grabbed hold of the grating and shouted, "Come on, Reicharte, bet you can't do it, chicken breath!"

"Dagnabbit, Snyder, cut it out!" a gangly, walleyed kid with coke-bottle glasses broke in. "You'll distract 'em?"

"Who asked you, four eyes," Snyder replied and twisted his pug nose disgustedly.

"I'm tellin' you anyways, fatso!"

"Who're you callin' fatso, tapeworm?"

Webber took a threatening step toward Snyder who shrank away and yelled, "I'm tellin' if you take one step closer!"

"Cut it out, you guys!" a little Italian kid exclaimed. "Dittman'll hear us!"

"Nobody asked you, dip stick!" Snyder sneered at the little kid who was wearing the school's black blazer with a red shield sewn on the breast pocket. The shield was decorated with a quill pen and Latin textbook with the words Ora Pro Nobis[1] stenciled beneath. "Anyways, he's always reading his vespers in his room 'til the bell rings for Mass!

Go on, Reicharte! Do it like you said, Mr. Biggedy!"

One foot in front of the other, the skinny kid was balancing, precariously, on the narrow, top edge of the grating. He had his hands outstretched like a tightrope walker's, and the rubber soles of his black and white, high top Ked basketball shoes seemed to be the only thing between him and a long fall.

"You'd better not try it, Christian!" Webber yelled and nervously pushed his horn-rimmed glasses up on the bridge of his long nose. Then he stuck his big hands deeply into the side pockets of a black silk athletic jacket which bore the red school shield with its bold, black-lettered request. He shrugged his shoulders and peered through the grating into the laundry bay far below.

"Fifty bucks says you can't do it!" Snyder taunted, his fat face pressed against the metal grate.

"He'll never pay you, Christian!" the little Italian kid yelled, while anxiously peering through the triangular openings in the grating.

---

[1]   Pray for us.

"Shut up, grease ball!" Synder snapped and punched the little kid's shoulder with his pink knuckles.

From his precarious perch on the top rim of the grating, Christian could vaguely hear the boys arguing below him. He could see a pile of laundry bags at the bottom of the shaft. He knew they were full and at least waist deep because on Mondays everyone in the whole dormitory building tossed their stuffed bags over the high, metal grating into the empty shaft where they tumbled into the basement. Snyder had once told him that they'd put the wire gratings up along the stairways and landings right after a senior had tried to make the jump from the third floor and had broken his neck in spite of the laundry bags piled up at the bottom of the shaft. Snyder was a card-carrying liar though. Besides, he was only jumping from the second floor, and he could easily break the fall by landing at a slight angle with his feet first, then his butt, and finally, his hands. The bags stuffed with dirty clothes would cushion his weight as he fell through them. When he looked down, his heart leaped, and he felt as if he'd been plugged into a wall socket. Even the peach fuzz on his forearms bristled.

"Dittman'll be out in a few minutes for roll call!" Snyder shouted. "Come on, chicken bones!"

All the boys had their fingers laced through the openings in the grating while they anxiously peered upward. Christian's footing slipped in spite of his basketball shoes, and he teetered, momentarily, before he regained his balance. Feeling the cowlick in the crown of his head rise like a divining rod, he took a deep breath and slowly exhaled. Then, almost as if he'd been pushed by some daredevil shadow, he lowered his weight over the toes of his Keds and sprang into the air.

Going down, his Hawaiian print billowed out like a bright red parachute, his stomach sank as if lead-weighted, and he had the heady sensation that he was falling in slow motion. Finally, like a thin slab of cement, he hit the laundry bags feet first, plummeted through several layers, and disappeared completely.

"Dagnabbit!" Webber exclaimed as he peered downward, his beak sticking through one of the openings in the metal grating. "He's done gone right to China!"

"Bull frogs!" Snyder apprehensively replied, straining to see. "There's a million bags down there to break his fall."

"He's right, Webb," the little kid piped in, his brown eyes the size of half dollars as he searched the bags at the bottom of the shaft for a sign of Christian. "Look!"

Just then, the top layer of laundry bags began to move as an arm pushed through. Next, you could see the top of Christian's head, a bushy shock of dark brown hair with a cowlick that curved upward from the crown like an Indian feather. He crawled over the top layer of bags toward a cement ramp at the rear of the laundry bay. First rubbing one shoulder and then his leg he winced, pulled himself onto the ramp, and waved at the boys who were looking down from above.

"Son-of-a-gun made it," Snyder hissed under his breath.

"You owe 'em!" the wavy-haired Italian kid piped in.

"Forget it, peanut head!" Snyder shot back. "You have to be nuts to try that!"

Webber yelled, "You done it! You done it!" and Christian smiled up at him from the loading dock in the laundry room. Turning abruptly on Snyder, he said, "Nobody better tell, Snyder!"

Suddenly, a deafening bell went off, and all the boys scurried down three flights of stairs and out a side door to a long, tree-lined sidewalk. A motley crew of boys ran up from all directions to join them. Some wore parkas, some had on athletic jackets, others wore black blazers with colorful stocking caps, and some had on expensive overcoats with fur collars.

"Sui generis!"[2] Snyder exclaimed while pulling on a leather pilot's cap and Fox Brothers' overcoat. "Reicharte jumped!"

"Sui bull crap!" a kid with a suede overcoat and his hair swept back in ducktails hollered. "Talk English, butterball! Everyone knows your Dittman's suck!"

"What floor?" another kid yelled. "Who saw it? I don't believe you guys."

"He did! From the second floor landing!" Snyder shot back while giving Webber the finger.

"Holy Toledo!" a tall kid wearing an overcoat, ear muffs, and leather gloves blurted out.

"Hey, here comes Polinski!" Webber interrupted the others. "See if he'll do the hula thing, Snyder!"

"Yeah, give 'em some of them foreign cigs, Snyder," Valeno piped in.

Out of breath, Christian joined the group of boys who were lining up along the edge of the sidewalk. One of them asked, "Did you really do it, Christian?" and, while zipping up a fur-collared, brown leather, air force jacket he'd found one day while rummaging through the attic with the family maid, Christian surprised himself

---

[2]   Of its own kind, unique

by replying, in an awkward voice, with a Latin expression he had heretofore been unable to even translate: "In vino veritas."[3] Then he jumped in line next to Valeno and glanced for the hundredth time at the mysterious name stenciled on the left breast of his oversized jacket: Major Culpepper.

"You's guys better snap to," Polinski, the Polish custodian, badgered. He was coming up the walk with a snow shovel in his hand. "Dittman's peeoed 'bout somethin'."

"Do it, will yah, Mr. Polinski?" a kid asked.

"Yeah, please, Mr. Polinski," Snyder pleaded, his round, clerk's head bobbing out of line, and the pilot's cap strapped under his chin.

"Come on, Mr. Polinski, PLEASE," the dark Italian kid begged, his eyes raised imploringly.

"Come o-n-n-n," everyone joined in.

Palming a pack of cigarettes while glancing, defensively, over his shoulder toward the side door of the dormitory building, Snyder reached out and dropped the cigarettes into the custodian's open hand. With a flick of his wrist akin to sleight of hand, the custodian shuffled the package into his pants pocket. Then, leaning his shovel against a tree, Polinski, a short, stocky man with a bull dog's face and a locomotive's build, took off his parka which exposed a soiled, cigar-burned, army green, sleeveless undershirt. Hanging the hood of his parka over the handle of the shovel, he took several sharp bites on the cigar butt he always had in the corner of his mouth, grabbed his left wrist with his right hand, and tautly flexed the bulging muscles of his left arm. This made a large tattoo of a half-naked

---

[3]   In wine is truth.

hula dancer undulate between the biceps and elbow. Each time he flexed, the hula dancer's hips swiveled.

"Holy cow!" Valeno yelped, his eyes popping.

"She ain't got no bra on" Webber pointed out. The other boys were breaking ranks and crowding around.

Polinski, a lordly smirk on his face, chewed vigorously on his cigar and flexed his arm while commenting to Snyder, "Got any a dem imported cigars left, sonny?"

Snyder, his eyes glued to the hula dancer, absent-mindedly reached into his leather overcoat, pulled out three cellophane-wrapped cigars, and handed them to the custodian.

"Let's see it again!" a kid yelled as he pushed through the throng.

Bending his left fist while opening and closing it, Polinski flexed his arm. The cigar butt wiggled in the corner of his mouth. "Dem's knockers!" he exclaimed.

"Can I touch 'em?" Snyder asked, tentatively sticking a finger out.

"I dare yah!" someone hollered.

Polinski took out a Zippo lighter with a Marine's emblem on the side, lit his cigar, and drew heavily on the tip. Then he casually stuck his arm in front of Snyder's face and flexed while Snyder reached forward, his hand hesitating over the tattoo.

"Chicken!" several boys hollered.

"Watch out, Snyder, she'll bite your hand off!" a kid yelled.

Snyder, looking like he'd eaten a canary, tentatively touched the tattoo as if he were testing a hot stove, and everyone, including Polinski who was flexing all over the place, laughed. Just then, a tall, gaunt priest with a severe, gray-walled crew cut came out of the dorm building and headed toward the group of boys. He was dressed in a drab, black cassock which hung over his pointy shoulders like a blanket over a broomstick. Because his feet were hidden beneath the long cassock, he seemed to glide along the icy sidewalk as if he were on casters. Hawk-eyed, he looked down his sharp, witch's beak and suspiciously eyeballed the group of boys.

"Dittman's comin'!" the cry went up as if someone were announcing the onslaught of a freight train.

Polinski quickly grabbed his parka and shovel and remarked to Snyder, "You owe me some more a dem zotic smokes, sonny."

"Hold on there, Mr. Polinski!" Dittman demanded as he walked up. "What's going on here?"

"Ah, nuttin, Fadder," Polinski replied with a look of mock surprise.

Pointing with the edge of a clipboard at the boys who had quickly lined up along the edge of the sidewalk, Dittman pursued, "What were they all excited about then?"

"Beats me," Polinski said with a shrug of his big shoulder.

"Have you been showing off again, Ivan?" Dittman persisted. There was a hush along the line of boys, and Snyder snickered when Polinski, looking sheepishly down at his worn combat boots, stuck both hands into his trouser pockets.

"What's so funny, Snyder?" Dittman barked.

"Nothing."

"Nothing what, Norman?"

"Nothing, Father."

"Are you sure?" Dittman coaxed and added in a syrupy voice, "Norman?"

"Well..." Snyder hesitated while nervously glancing along the line of boys whose eyes were throwing daggers at him.

"Lying's a mortal sin, Norman," Dittman argued as he stepped up to Snyder, his beak almost touching Snyder's pug nose when he leaned down.

"Well, he, uh, just let us peek."

"Is that so, Mr. Polinski?" Dittman asked, turning on the custodian.

"Awe, geeze, Snyder," Webber cut in, sticking his goose neck way out of line. "You asked 'em to."

"This is not a matter that concerns you, Webber!" Dittman snapped, waving a corner of his clipboard at Webber and then addressing Mr. Polinski: "I've spoken to you about this before haven't I, Ivan?"

"Vut eats only a lass," Polinski shrugged.

"She's naked!" Father Dittman exclaimed.

"So vas she when she ver borned."

All of the boys laughed while Dittman glared huffily at Polinski and asked, "Are you talking back to me, Ivan?"

"I ain't talkin' to nobody in particular, but you asked me," Polinski shortly replied and zipped up his parka.

"Maybe I'll mention this to the rector this time," Dittman threatened while making a note on his clipboard, his chin cocked imperiously.

"Do vhat yah have to, Fadder," Polinski evenly responded as he walked away.

"He didn't do nothin', Father," Valeno vouched for Polinski and snapped his fingertips under his chin at Snyder who stuck his tongue out in retaliation.

"Nobody asked you for your opinion, Mr. Valeno," Dittman remarked and added with an angry head shaking in the direction of Polinski, "I've never seen such insubordination. A janitor, mind you."

With that, Polinski, not turning around or even slowing down, reached behind his back, raised one buttock higher than the other, and pulled the seam of his khakis out from between his cheeks with a flip of his fingertips.

"That's a Polish dirty gesture!" Snyder exclaimed when the boys in line laughed.

"Polinski!" Dittman interjected, but the custodian had disappeared into the dormitory building.

"He's probably been drinking again, Father," Snyder put in.

"Non compos mentis[4]," Dittman angrily added.

"In toto![5]" Snyder whinnied in his choir boy's voice. "Can I take roll, Father?"

"Snyder's a tattletale!" Webber hollered.

"Where's your school blazer, Mr. Loudmouth?" Father Dittman retaliated. "Button up that coat'n tuck in that shirttail!"

Webber's head recoiled back in line.

"Where's your tie?" Dittman pursued.

"I couldn't find it."

"Five demerits!" Dittman remarked and wrote a note on a yellow sheet of paper attached to his clipboard.

"But Snyder didn't wear his neither."

"Ad nauseam[6]," Dittman shot back. Then, referring to a list on his board, he hollered, "Moffitt!"

"Here!" a lop-eared towhead answered while looking guiltily at his shoes.

"Got your lines, Howard?"

"Ah, no, I forgot 'em."

"No, what?"

---

[4]   Not of sound mind.
[5]   In full; wholly
[6]   To the point of nausea

"No, Father."

"Why'd you forget 'em?"

"I don't know."

"I don't know, what?"

"I don't know, Father."

"Double it!"

"But..."

"Krowell!"

"Here!" a tall, flat-topped kid yelped. He was wearing a black jacket with the school shield sewn on the breast, and St. Xavier's inscribed in bold, red cursive letters on the back.

"J.V. going to win this week?" Dittman asked the boy as he checked his name off his list.

"Heck, yeah," the handsome, dark-eyed kid cockily replied, "we got Boyle goal tending'n Scott's on right wing again."

"See that you do then," Dittman said. "It'd be a nice change of pace."

Everyone in line laughed.

"He ain't got no tie on!" Webber suddenly exclaimed.

"I don't remember asking you, Webber," Dittman responded, adding, in an offhanded manner, "And besides, why aren't you out there?"

"My grades ain't good enough," Webber added, hanging his head.

"And whose fault is that, Mr. Webber?"

Webber peered over the top of his horn rims, but didn't reply.

"Daugherty!" Dittman continued roll.

"Here!"

"Snyder!"

"Here, Father Dittman," Snyder cooed. He emphasized the priest's name with a syrupy inflection.

"Here, Father's fine, Norman," Dittman quipped and checked off Snyder's name.

With that, someone in line broke wind. Everyone laughed, except Father Dittman, and they all looked at Snyder.

"I didn't do it, Father!" Snyder defensively exclaimed. "It was Reicharte, I think. He thinks he's a big shot circus performer."

"Slow down, Norman. He thinks what?"

"Ah, nothing, Father," Snyder replied, deferring to the glowering faces of his classmates.

"We'll see about 'nothing'," Dittman scolded. "Do you think Christ was concerned about what people thought of him, Norman?"

"Wouldn't know, Father. That was a long time ago before me."

"That's not what I mean," Dittman snapped and waved Snyder off when he started to say something else. "More to the point, there's an element around here who need their ears pinned back, and I think I know just the way to do it."

"How's that, Father?" Snyder whined.

"Leave that to me, Norman," Dittman casually replied and briskly walked along the line of boys, his cassock swirling around his ankles. When he passed by, each boy stiffened and then craned his neck out of line to see where he was going to stop. At the end of the line, he stopped in front of a skinny kid whose eyes conveyed a puzzled, faraway, thousand yard stare as if his mind were traveling at the speed of light to some exotic, out-of-this-world destination. The long tail of a bright red shirt was hanging out beneath the boy's flight jacket. A pair of fuzzy, black ear muffs with a metal band that stretched over the top of his head, accentuated a feather-like cowlick which curved upward from the crown of the boy's head. With his hands and clipboard held stiffly behind his back, Father Dittman put his face directly into the boy's and tried to stare him down. The boy's eyes didn't waver. Instead, they seemed to absorb the priest's glare like a blotter absorbs ink. Father Dittman backed off, gave the boy an inquisitive double take, and handed his clipboard to one of the boys in line. Then he smugly reached into the long slit at the side of his cassock and pulled out a glossy but tattered copy of Playboy which he unrolled and held in the upward turned palms of his hands like a sacrificial lamb.

"Would this happen to be yours, Mr. Reicharte?" he dryly asked with a complacent smile.

"Huh?" the surprised boy replied, blinking his eyes as if startled from a dream.

"Is this yours?" the priest coldly repeated.

Crippled with astonishment at the sight of the magazine displayed in front of everyone, the boy was speechless.

"I found it during dorm inspection," Dittman continued and raised both eyebrows accusingly. "Behind your dresser."

The other boys in line whispered behind their hands, and Snyder pointed an accusing finger at the magazine.

Watching the dog-eared pages of the magazine flutter in the brisk wind, Christian felt as if a jagged shard of glass were slowly being shoved into his gut, and everyone in line was waiting for him to bleed to death.

"How come it was ditched behind your dresser?" Dittman persisted.

The boys in line nervously laughed as if they were somehow guilty by association.

"I don't know," Christian weakly replied, his throat dry as burned toast and his face in flames.

Shaking his head and making little clicking sounds with his tongue, Dittman said, with a withering look and lowered voice, "You should be ashamed of yourself."

Christian felt as if he were sinking in quicksand.

"I'll bet he's got glaucoma," Snyder popped in, and the other boys chuckled in a muted, guarded fashion while giving one another evasive, sidelong glances.

"You guys get over to Mass," Dittman ordered, "while I finish with our little acrobat here. And I don't want to see anyone cutting through the cafeteria."

The boys broke ranks and headed across the football field, a few of them glancing over their shoulders before cutting through the side door of the cafeteria.

With his hands on his hips, Dittman gave Christian a censuring look and bluntly asked, "Do you want it to shrivel up and snap off like a dead twig?"

Christian stared at the toes of his black-and-white high tops.

"You'd better start praying to the Blessed Virgin, young man," Dittman pursued while he carefully rolled the magazine up and stuck it through the long slit in his cassock.

"I'll throw it away," Christian managed to squeak as the evidence disappeared beneath the black cloth of the priest's cassock.

"Sed libera nos a malo![7]" the priest shot back, perturbed.

"Pardon me?" Christian replied.

"You heard me. Now, get to Mass before you end up with demerits from Father Oxley. I don't ever want to see you showing off again. I could get you expelled for even thinking about jumping into that shaft. A boy was killed once." He possessively patted the side slit of his cassock where the incriminating magazine had disappeared. As if an afterthought, and with a quizzical look at the name printed in black letters on the breast pocket of Christian's flight jacket, he added, "By the way, I've been meaning to ask you

---

[7] Deliver us from evil.

about that jacket. There's no one by that name around here and it's way too big for you. Where'd you get it?"

Christian distractedly replied, "In the attic," and shuffled away. His legs felt hollow, and it seemed as if an invisible imp were stealing his breath. Feeling the hair on the back of his neck prickle, he glanced over his shoulder. Father Dittman was staring after him like a suspicious guard, and he was hollering, "I thought I told you not to wear that silly beach shirt! This is Wisconsin, not Miami Beach!"

Feeling like a drowning sailor slipping away from his life preserver, Christian zipped the flight jacket up to his throat so Father Oxley wouldn't see his shirt. He cut across the football field to the sidewalk which led to the cathedral. Black, crippled branches from overhanging tree limbs seemed to reach out for him, and Dittman's words jangled in his ears like a primitive voodoo chant: Sed libera nos a malo.

Racking his brains, he tried to figure out what Dittman had said. Libera he remembered from Latin class. He reviewed his conjugations: Libera, liberae, liberam, libera. He pondered, and the translation gradually worked its way out of his memory like a snake out of a basket: Deliver...us...from...evil, the words coiled upward as he approached the cathedral which loomed in front of him like an ancient monolith. The steeple bells suddenly tolled startling him. He pulled hard on the handle of one of the two iron-bound oak doors which led into the church and slipped in, the heavy door closing behind him with a loud sucking sound while a dank, silent, tomb-like atmosphere enveloped him.

"You're late," Father Oxley, a hoary hunchback, cackled as he came down a narrow, circular, metal staircase which descended from the bell tower. His words resonated like fire crackers from the foyer's vaulted ceiling. "Mass's started! Didn't you hear the bells? Where've you been? Do you want demerits? "Taedet me; pudet me.[8]"

"But I was with..."

"Shhh," the hunchback shushed, holding a crooked finger to his lips. "Ten demerits in loco parentis.[9]"

"But Father Dittman..."

"Ave atque vale![10]" Oxley shushed in a muted exclamation while pointing toward the interior of the church. "Persona non grata![11]"

All the seniors in the rear pews turned around to see what was going on. Christian, taking off his jacket, zipped by them, his Hawaiian print shirt billowing as he headed for the freshman section at the front of the church near the communion railing. Genuflecting abruptly and getting back up all in one motion, almost as if he'd tripped, he squeezed by several boys who were kneeling near the left arm rest of the pew, and stumbled into his assigned place at the far end of the pew next to Webber. On his right, only a few feet away, a slick, pink-and-purple veined, marble column thrust upward like a pillar of ice. Similar columns were spaced at regular intervals along the side aisles. Like petrified Atlases, they supported on their shoulders the soaring, vaulted arches of the towering ceiling. Recessed high above his head, stained-glass windows transmuted in-flowing light into fluctuating patterns of light and shadow. Perhaps from the lackluster affect the lead, bottle-glass windows had on the light, or because Snyder had suggested there were priests and nuns buried behind them, the walls seemed to bulge and a rust colored moisture appeared to trickle from the cracks between the bricks.

---

[8] It wearies me. It shames me.
[9] In the place of a parent.
[10] Hail and farewell!
[11] An unacceptable person.

"Dominus vobiscum" the priest chanted, his voice echoing from the altar.

"Et cum spiritu tuo," the altar boys, kneeling at the foot of the altar like black and white ceramic sentries, responded in the effeminate voices of freshmen.

When Webber made a snoring sound, Christian poked him in the side, but Webber only snuffled and went back to sleep. Others in the pews around him were either nodding off or squirming around like trapped animals looking for more comfortable perches. A few twisted their rosaries into knots or stared blankly at the open page of a prayer book.

Momentarily, he was distracted by the plaster tablets hanging at regular intervals on the side walls. The tablet to his immediate right worried him. It depicted Jesus struggling with the weight of a cross. Some of the paint had chipped off leaving exposed portions of white plaster, but one could still imagine the dimensions of the cross which appeared to be too much to carry for any man. Once, before retiring to bell ringing in the cathedral tower, Father Oxley had stopped during a Sunday sermon from the pulpit, pointed directly to the tablet and cried out: "He died on the cross for your sins!" The words, like a false accusation, had smoldered in his mind for days, finally sinking into his unconscious where they still burned without flame.

As if searching for an escape hatch in a sinking ship, his eyes were drawn toward the sanctuary where a mighty dome rose to dizzying heights. The dome was decorated with gray cumulus clouds out of which silver bolts of lightning flashed. Beneath this, as if lightning had made contact, gigantic tongues of flame engulfed the tangled torsos of writhing human beings. A Gothic rose window, above and behind the altar, dimly illuminated the dome. Once, when serving Mass, he'd peered up into the dome and, to his dismay, had seen himself in the dome fires. When he'd told Snyder about it, Snyder had squealed and called him a dumb cluck because there were mirrors in the dome.

Suddenly, Webber woke himself up by breaking wind. Boys in the pew ahead turned around scowling and Snyder, his eyes slits, peered around one of the marble columns where he'd been posted. The comb tracks in his red, pomade-slicked hair were visible as well as his right hand which hovered a pencil over a pad that he was taking names on.

"Per omnia saecula saeculorum," the priest chanted while one of the altar boys rang a rack of bells. This brought Christian's attention back to the altar. Webber's too. It was the consecration of the host and for as long as he could remember, he had been waiting, right after the bells, for the miracle Sister Mary Margaret had told them about in fourth grade. Webber had scoffed, but she'd even shown a black-and-white movie of it where a priest was standing at an altar with his back to the congregation. He wore a white linen gown and poncho. Right after the bells rang, he put both hands around the stem of a chalice and raised it above his head. When his arms were fully extended, he dropped to one knee, and all of a sudden, bloody wounds opened in the backs of his hands. Sister Mary Margaret had told everyone in the class that the black holes were absolutely just like the crucifixion wounds of Jesus and that what was happening to the priest on the screen was called stigmata. When Willy Orenbach asked her how she knew the wounds were just like the ones Jesus had had when she wasn't even there, she'd hushed him up with a squinty-eyed-deep-inhaling glare. Now, just as he'd been doing ever since grade school, he watched closely as the priest's white, blue-veined hands lifted the chalice upward while he dropped to one knee like the priest in the movie had done. He could clearly see the priest's hands, raised as they were, but no wounds appeared. He began to wonder again if the nun had been putting them on. She'd always told them that faith was the willing suspension of disbelief.

"I told you so," Webber whispered.

"But she said the movie was a documentary," Christian whispered while keeping a sharp eye out for Snyder whose red head occasionally darted out from behind the column.

"Documentary, my ass. Them things're rigged all the time just like the movies."

"Shhhhhhh," Christian whispered, shading his mouth and glancing toward the marble column where, sure enough, Snyder was taking down their names.

There were more bells, and groups of boys left their pews to line up at the communion railing which separated the sanctuary from the congregation. Letting a kid by, Christian ducked down and leaned back against the sharp edge of the wooden bench. He was glad to give his knees a rest, and guys always looked at you funny if you didn't go to communion. They knew, like a silent conspiracy of fraternity brothers, that you were not in the state of grace, probably from lustful conduct of one kind or another. A couple of seniors who were waiting in the center-aisle line to receive communion gave him censuring glances. Hands prayerfully folded against their chests, they had smug looks on their faces, looks of sly respectability as if they were about to sprout white wings. He wondered how much such a look could hide.

The priest, wearing a floor-length white gown beneath a glittering, green, silk poncho, with the letters IHS embroidered in gold and silver filigree on the front and back, came down from the altar, a little altar boy trailing behind. He held a shiny gold chalice in one hand and a white, thinly sliced wafer between the thumb and index finger of the other.

The communicants knelt along the railing which made a semicircle around the plush, red-carpeted sanctuary. The altar boy walked at the priest's side. He held a gold plate beneath the chin of each communicant so the body of Jesus would not fall on the floor if it missed the receiver's tongue. "Dominus vobiscum," the priest said each time he deposited a wafer on a recipient's tongue, and the recipients made the sign of the cross over their faces so fast that it looked like they were swatting gnats.

Tranquilized by the heat, candle smoke, and burning incense, Christian let his eyes wander upward where there were leaping flames and yawning infernos with semi-nudes clinging to thunderheads. An iron-muscled nude man was painted between the great wooden buttresses. His naked torso writhed out of a swirling black cloud which floated inches above a flaming abyss. Mesmerized, Christian wondered if he would someday be painted across a cathedral ceiling, in memoriam[12]. Hadn't Snyder told a story once about a kid who'd jumped to his death from the bell tower?

Some of the communicants were coming back, straggling along the center aisle between the pews. Webber, shifty-eyed behind his goggles, had his hands tightly folded against his chest, and his long neck stuck out in front of him like a hungry bird's. Snyder, cherub-faced, like the angels hanging lifelessly from the cornice, was a few feet behind Webber. He had the palms of his hands pressed tightly together with the fingertips extended straight upward and his elbows stuck out from his obese body. The metal cleats on the heels of his Wingtips clicked. Suddenly, with a quick jump forward, he caught the heel of Webber's loafer with his toe. Webber walked out of the shoe, then stopped and went back to put his shoe on, showing Snyder

---

[12]   In memory of.

a big fist. Wearing a shiny, red and black varsity football jacket, Greenley, a tough, burly senior with a flattop haircut, lunged, head lowered, down the aisle. He looked fiercely into the freshman pews as if challenging anyone who might dare to mock his prayerfully folded hands. No one looked back as Greenley was known as the "locomotive", and he was the star fullback on the school football team. Valeno, unable to find the pew he'd been kneeling in, dodged back and forth while his classmates in the pew acted as if they didn't know him. Others, their eyes nervously flitting to and fro, and their heads and shoulders severely bowed, shuffled along the aisle as if being prodded from behind by the stiff rod of an invisible tyrant. Each one wore a long-sleeved, white shirt with a thin black tie.

Christian let his eyes wander toward an alcove in the front corner of the church where there was a black, wrought-iron, vigil light rack. The rack displayed flickering candles which were set in small, colored glass containers. If one slipped a donation in a slot at the bottom of the rack, one could get a blessing for someone. Snyder had once done a whole day's kitchen duty for lighting all fifty candles and not paying. Tiny flickering flames from a dozen candles cast flitting shadows over a life-size statue which stood on a platform above the vigil lights. The statue depicted a man who wore sandals and a long robe with a white rope tied around the waist. Small white birds were nesting in the folds of the robe. The man's left hand reached out invitingly.

"Dominus vobiscum," the priest canted as he set the glittering chalice behind the revolving doors in the tabernacle, the gold doors clicking shut like a bank vault.

"Et cum spiritu tuo," the altar boys responded.

"Deo gratias," the congregation concluded in unison as the priest and altar boys disappeared into the vestry.

"P-s-s-t," Snyder signaled from the monitor's post behind the marble pillar.

Startled, Christian jumped, his heart steeled. For a split second, he'd thought it was the statue.

"Centerfolds?" Snyder sneered as he motioned for Christian to exit the pew and get in the line forming down the center aisle.

"What do you mean?" Christian bluffed as he put on his flight jacket and left the pew.

"You know exactly what I mean and so does that pervert, Webber."

Stung, Christian shuffled down the aisle behind Snyder whose red head was cocked jauntily to one side. Just as Snyder passed through the huge, iron-bound oak doors which led from the foyer to the outside, Christian had an irresistible urge to look back into the eyes of the bearded bird man. Letting the boys behind him pass out the doors first, he turned around and looked into the distant alcove. The bearded man's face was animated by the flickering candles at his feet. His eyes, like metallic buttons, peered inquisitively toward the foyer, and it seemed as if the wings of the little birds, which were nesting in the folds of his brown cassock, fluttered. The ponderous doors sucked shut behind him, and the bright, snow-reflected light of the outdoors blinded him just long enough for him to see, on the darkened stage behind his eyes, a flock of silver birds which appeared like darting fire flies.

*   *   *   *   *   *

"Keep your hands out of your pockets!" Father Oxley ordered. The blatant exclamation cut sharply into Christian's daydream, and jolted him upward in the folding metal chair which was set a few rows back from the stage from which Oxley was speaking. There was a buzz in his ears, and Father Oxley's shrill voice slowly faded into a distant drone as his mind drifted away again, fifteen-hundred miles away where the Florida sun was close and very hot, and a sea breeze swept ashore, bending the tall palms and brushing everything in its path with a salty freshness.

Sitting on a sea wall with his legs dangling over the edge just above the water line, he watched a sea gull soundlessly glide over the blue-green water. Swooping suddenly, it plummeted into the water with a big splash and came up with a long, green pin fish which wiggled in its beak. He was wearing a new shirt. It was a red Hawaiian print which depicted a foaming seascape, a pearl-white beach, towering palms with long, drooping leaves and puffy clouds. Made of silk, it felt airy and cool on his back, and because it was oversized, it kind of billowed in a light breeze. Sometimes, in a stiff breeze when the wind got under the hem, he felt as if it would lift him right off the ground.

"Sins of the flesh are the most despicable of all sins!" Father Oxley's voice scattered his thoughts like broken glass. "Allow the flesh to dominate, and your souls will be devoured by the most carnivorous cannibal ever to creep across the face of the earth!"

Christian squirmed in the metal folding chair as the beach of his daydream dissolved into a desert of black sand with scattered stands of thorny cactus. A flock of white birds flew suddenly upward from the black sand, their wings on fire.

"Lust," the hunchback Jesuit cried out while peering from under bushy eyebrows and waiting a few moments before continuing in a well-modulated, softer voice, "the savage cannibal of the human spirit! Caveat emptor[13]! Sanctum sanctorum[14]!"

Taking a white-knuckled grip on the sides of his chair, Christian tried to ignore the carnage taking place on the black desert of his conscience. Snyder, Valeno, and Moffitt were apprehensively glancing over their shoulders as if they thought someone were stalking them. Webber, in the row ahead, was picking a festering whitehead on the back of his neck. Everyone was wiggling nervously, and the chairs were making a racket on the wooden gym floor.

"Lust," the ancient priest reiterated and hitched up his over-long cassock with the sides of his wrists as he peered out at the assembly from his bent posture, "is the most insidious of all desires! It feeds on itself, never satisfied! It lives, like a poison, in the darkened corners of the mind!"

Reeling beneath the verbal deluge, Christian crumpled in his seat like a discarded puppet. The black desert had become a heaving bog of bubbling, sucking hot gases and molten rock. Dead birds fell from the dark sky like white bean bags.

Meanwhile, with the hem of his cassock dusting the floor, Father Oxley reached into the long slit at the side of his robe and took out a copy of the National Geographic which he unrolled and waved in the air like a flag. Then he stepped toward the edge of the stage and used the magazine as a pointer: "These are to remain in the library!" he shouted at his cringing freshman audience. They are intended for research, not prurient interest!"

Prefects, who wore cassocks without white collars, walked up and down the side aisles watching for boys who were not paying

---

[13]   Let the buyer beware.
[14]   Holy of holies.

attention. They always walked with their hands behind their backs and looked sideways. The whole place was quiet except for squeaks and rattles from the folding chairs. Father Oxley, his bushy eyebrows raised quizzically in the direction of the first few rows of boys, asked, in a warm, syrupy voice, "Who among you would trade a few moments selfish pleasure for an eternity in hell? Vae victus[15]! The thought's the deed, lads."

Swallowing a big lump in his throat, Christian could see Snyder mopping his brow with a monogrammed handkerchief, and Webber, next to Snyder, was nervously picking at another pimple. Valeno and the kid next to him had their chins on their chests while secretly peeking at one another as if looking for a clue to the other's thoughts.

"Eternity, lads," Oxley persisted, pacing back and forth across the stage now, his hands tightly clasped behind his back. "Count every grain of sand on every beach in the world, and you haven't begun to measure the years of eternity. Have you ever burned a fingertip on a stove? Agonizing, wasn't it? Verbum sapienti[16], imagine that pain intensified an infinite number of times."

As if shot in the back, Christian bolted upright. The screen had lit up in his mind again; the camera flickered a moment, and then wide-angled into the vast desert with the black sand. This time, he was running across it. His Hawaiian print fluttered out behind him like a red flag, and a blazing fire tumbled after him.

"Now, lads," Oxley's voice caressed as if he had his arm around each and every one of them, "why not, before going home for Christmas vacation, day after tomorrow, rid yourselves of this selfish pleasure. Doesn't your conscience nag? Why not pray to

---

[15]   Woe to the vanquished!

[16]   Word to the wise.

the Blessed Virgin for the courage to confess your indiscretions? Requiescat in pace[17]."

The fire was catching up and flames licked at his extremities. In a few seconds nothing was left but a black stump with smoldering appendages like a burned out cactus plant.

"Wake up, Reicharte!" someone shouted, stumbling past him.

Mesmerized, he stared at the smoking stump. He could still see the vague outline of a human being, one leg out in front of the other and both arms stuck out at right angles, frozen in the final stride.

"Must be some daydream, Reicharte," a prefect said. He was standing above Christian, the long, wide sleeves of his black cassock flapping like vulture's wings.

"What?" Christian blurted out as if just awakened, Father Oxley's words clicking in his head like castanets, and the black desert shimmering.

"Is anything wrong? Everyone's gone to church."

"No, I--a--nothing," Christian stammered and rubbed his eyes.

"You'd better scat then," the prefect encouraged. "Polinski's already taking up chairs."

Mr. Polinski, who wore a sleeveless sweatshirt which exposed the infamous tattoo, was rapidly folding up chairs and loading them, four at a time, onto a cart. Out of the corner of one eye, he watched as Christian came down the aisle. When Christian passed, he flexed a few times. Trying not to look, Christian tripped on one of the cart's castor wheels, and Polinski, hands on his knees, laughed so

---

[17] Rest in peace.

hard that he almost bit his cigar stub in two while the prefect gave them both a quizzical look from the rear exit.

Embarrassed, Christian pulled on his flight jacket and hurried outside, the janitor's laughter, like a devil's shriek, pealing in his blossoming ears. There was a freezing wind and a dull, gray sky overhead. The black, frozen trees appeared rigid as deformed corpses. He pulled the lamb's wool collar of his jacket up and buried his hands in the deep side pockets. Oxley's words snapped between his temples like static discharges: Who among you would trade a few moments selfish pleasure for an eternity in the fires of hell? Eternity was forever, and forever was a long time. The punishment and the crime seemed absurdly disproportionate but so was life and death. And why was pleasure selfish?

Walking along, he noticed how his jacket smelled of aged wood and moth balls. It had been kept in storage in the attic, a short flight of stairs above the maid's third floor room. While cleaning the attic, Rose had found it one day. He recalled how they'd go up to the attic every fall and unpack the winter coats. They'd go through the ancient, wooden trunks and pull out old books, magazines, clothes, artifacts, and assorted costume jewelry. Sometimes, they'd even use old costumes to role play. One time she found a brittle copy of a book called Catcher in the Rye. The cover had been torn off, and someone had cryptically written on the yellowed flyleaf in red letters: Throw out. Rose had told him it was a classic that'd disappeared from her room a while back, and she'd stuck it in the hip pocket of her jeans. She always wore a baggy pair of blue jeans, rolled up at the cuffs, a man's flannel shirt, rolled up at the sleeves and open at the throat, and a dilapidated pair of tennis shoes which she referred to as her mud shoes. When she put her long, auburn hair in a ponytail, she reminded him of one of those teeny boppers on the cover of Look. He'd recently tried to find the Catcher book in the school library, but it wasn't there. Neither was Huckleberry Finn for that matter. The librarian, Father Beckley, had shrugged it off and suggested Sixty Saints for Boys. No matter, Snyder had copies of almost anything, even Playboy, hidden in the laundry room. He rented them for cash or cigarettes.

Bending into the wind, he reluctantly aimed himself toward the cathedral which loomed like a dark fortress on the horizon of his muddled consciousness. He recalled the time Rose and he had found the cigar box with the mysterious war medals. The box was in the attic at the bottom of an old foot locker under some blankets right next to his father's civil defense helmet. Having been flat-footed and registered 4-F, his father had never gone to war and had only had to wear the helmet and stand on top of the Sears building to scan for enemy planes with a pair of camouflage binoculars he'd bought at Sears. (Ironically, from what he'd observed on a Florida vacation beach, which was the only time he'd ever seen his father without shoes and socks, he was positive his father's feet had high arches.) Inside the cigar box, they'd found the war medals, a grainy picture of a dashing, uniformed pilot, and a gold watch with the inscription, USAF, Love, Molly, '42 etched on the back. The pilot was standing next to a B-29 bomber and was pointing to a name painted on the plane's nose. The name was stenciled beneath a caricature of a well-endowed blonde in white shorts, midriff, and spiked heels. It said: Molly's Bee. The black and white picture was dull, grainy, and yellowed with age, and neither he nor Rose had been able to recognize the man in it, although he recalled having had a goose-bumpy feeling when looking at the man. The foot locker had also contained a brown leather flight jacket with the name, Major Culpepper, stenciled on the left breast.

"Hey, Christian, what's your hurry?" someone shouted, scattering the pieces of his daydream like a dropped jigsaw puzzle.

"I'm late!" Christian hollered back as he approached the wide stairway leading up to the cathedral. Above the huge doors in the brick facade, an arched window, with bottle-glass, stained panels, glimmered. Holding open one of the doors which led into the darkened foyer, he spotted Snyder coming out of the side, altar boys' entrance. He was fiddling with the zipper of his fly as if he'd just gone to the bathroom. His cheeks were bright pink, and he was walking with his feet splayed as if he were going up a hill on skis. He had on a WW1 leather pilot's cap with a chin strap and was stuffing a carton of cigarettes inside the overcoat he was wearing. A few seconds later a burly senior with a severe flattop haircut came out the same door. Zipping up a varsity football jacket, he warily looked over his shoulder as he scuttled in the opposite direction from Snyder. Over the senior's head, a flock of birds appeared, just black dots in a scudding gray sky, and then the enormous door closed behind Christian, making a loud sucking sound like a dying man's last breath.

The church smelled like snuffed out candles, and only a dim glow emanated from the stained glass, arched windows which were recessed in high, narrow niches. Towering marble columns stood along the aisles like fossilized sentries. In the far corners near the sanctuary, candles flickered in multi-colored glass bowls which were set on tiered racks beneath life-size statues. Saint Francis, like a resurrected mummy, stood inert in a concave wall recess. His eyes were cloaked in shadows, and the birds that'd been nesting in the folds of his brown cassock were mysteriously gone. Only jagged spots of exposed white mortar remained as if a fraternity prankster had hacked the birds off with an ax.

A tomb-like silence filled the cavernous edifice. Mortar corpses remained in resurrecting poses along the cornices which trimmed the high walls, and the painted eye of a naked man on the frescoed ceiling appeared transfixed in horror, his lower body in flames. A few boys, severely bent over in penance, knelt apart at the communion railing, and some others, heads bowed, were scattered about the church pews. Along opposite side aisles, against the walls, and about halfway between the foyer and the sanctuary, there were two tall boxes with thick purple curtains which hung over entrances located on each side of a wooden door. On opposite sides of each of the boxes, a number of boys stood in lines. Some of them stood cross-armed with their hands clasping their shoulders as if from the dank chill or from apprehension.

Skulking into one of the lines, Christian tried to go over his list which flickered through his mind like a blue movie: there were, of course, the National Geographic photos, especially the one with the native girl in it; the tattoo; (Maybe he'd get one when he went into the air force.) the erotic dreams; the Playboy confiscated by Dittman; (Did a peek count mortal or venial?) the extra cookies he'd palmed in the cafeteria; the...the...he couldn't say it as the number of times had multiplied exponentially; the profanity; the cigarettes; the jump, and a dozen other infractions that shuffled through his mind like Snyder's pornographic playing cards. His heart raced because he had to do it this time, or the number of times would be impossible to repeat to anyone.

A boy came out of the box, and the purple curtain flopped back over the dark entrance. Another boy went in, so he moved forward a few feet behind the kid in front of him. Greenley, the crew-cut senior who'd come out the altar boys' entrance behind Snyder, came down the center aisle. He had closely set, withering, dark eyes which condemned any freshman they looked at. Christian ducked behind the tall kid in front of him while Oxley's words rebounded around the walls of his mind like a handball: Who among you would trade an eternity in hell for a few moments selfish pleasure? He glanced up at the nude man on the ceiling. The fires were licking at his limbs, and the devils were hungrily clutching at his feet while he struggled to get to the upper air. He died on the cross for your sins! the priest's vehement accusation recoiled off the front wall of his mind like a kill shot.

A boy came out of the box, leaving the purple curtain swinging back and forth, and he was next. With his heart fluttering like the wings of a bird in a cage too small, he hesitated on the balls of his feet in a confused quandary of fight or flight. Peering around to see if anyone were watching, he slipped into the box, unconsciously feeling the texture of the crushed velvet curtain on his way. As the curtain swung back shutting out the light, he knelt on a wooden kneeler in front of a wire screen and rehearsed in a whisper, "Bless me Father, for I have sinned. I haven't been to confession in ah-- about a....a few weeks." Suddenly, the purple curtain rustled, and someone's shuffling feet appeared beneath the hem. He had the peculiar feeling that he was hiding in a closet with only a thin strip of light beneath the door. He could hear indistinct murmurs coming from the other side of the screen, and he wondered if the priest could see through. Suddenly, a wooden door set behind the screen clacked open startling him. "Dominus vobiscum," a rasping voice emanated from a profile silhouetted on the other side of the screen.

"Bless me Fa--" his voice stuck in his throat like a peach pit when he recognized the rector's smoker's voice.

"Dominus vobiscum," the hoarse voice repeated as if speaking from behind a shade.

"Ah, bless me Father for I have sinned, ah..."

"Go on," the profile said and coughed, loudly.

"My ah--last confession was ah--ah--."

"Approximately's good enough."

"Well--ah, about a few weeks."

"Yes," the silhouette replied, quivering behind the screen, and the purple curtain rustled as someone wearing Wingtips with scuffed toes went by.

"Ah--ah-umm..."

"Go on, son."

"I--ah--used bad language, mostly to myself though. God'n damn'n such."

"How many times?"

"A lot."

"Pardon me?"

"Too many, Father."

"All right," the profile interrupted while having a coughing spasm.

"And I cheated off Valen...this guy, once."

The silhouette wheezed.

"And I didn't--ah--do my class work in study hall a number of times," he stammered, losing control, his mind reluctantly reeling in the big ones. "And I peeked at these dirty pictures ah--five, no, a few times or so'n had some impure thoughts too."

"Where'd you get them?"

"The thoughts?"

"No, for heaven's sake, the pictures!"

"Oh, Snyd--I mean--ah--well, in the library."

"Impossible! This isn't a public school."

"National Geographic, Father."

"But those are for educational purposes."

"A lot of the teachers are butt naked though."

"Excuse me?"

"Sorry, Father."

"All right, get on with it then," the phantom profile mused, his breath passing through the screen like an invisible nerve gas.

"Ah--," Christian hesitated a moment, struggling to reel in the fleeing big one, "to tell the truth, I ah--I ah--."

"How many times?"

"I lost count."

A few moments of silence ensued. The profile dropped his rosary on the floor where several beads broke off and rolled around. Then the shadow behind the screen hissed: "How many times?"

Christian opened his mouth, but no sound would come forth.

"You'd better tie a knot in it, mister," the profile continued in a muted voice, his words coming through the screen like tongues of flame, and the purple curtain rustling as if blown by the devil's breath. "You will say ten rosaries for your penance, and you'd better start praying to the Blessed Virgin."

"Just one more thing, Father. I dressed up like a girl. Is that a sin too?"

"What do you think?"

"But she said it was only role playing."

"She? Role playing? You were with a woman?"

"Our maid."

"Jesus, Mary'n Joseph! I don't want to hear any more of this twisted soap opera! I've a mind to breach my vows and report this! This is an all boys' school! Why I never..."

The wooden panel behind the screen clacked shut in Christian's face. His heartbeat was almost audible, and his first impulse was to run, but the curtain was the only way out, unless he broke through the mesh ceiling screen which covered the box. Then where would he go? Up into the ceiling vault to be pulled into the fire like the naked man? Or snatched by one of the zombies who were cavorting in the coffins around the cornices? He imagined an angry mob, led by Snyder and some seniors, waiting outside the curtain with a cat-o'-nine-tails. Hearing movement on the other side of the screen, he pulled the curtain aside and peered around the church. Pale bars of mote-filled light filtered through the recessed, stained glass windows on the opposite wall, and several boys were kneeling at the communion railing. He heard the wooden panel on the other side of the box clack, and a boy came out, so he bolted through the curtain and ran down the aisle into the foyer. The door was sealed like a tomb, so he had to push it with his shoulder to get it to open enough for him to slip through.

Outside, the sunlight was blinding, the wind bit into his cheeks, and the tears in his eyes felt like frozen flecks of ice. He ran down the steps in front of the church and cut across the football field to the field house. There were a few guys ice skating on a nearby rink, and a couple of boys, pulling a toboggan behind them, climbed a distant snow-banked hill. While one part of him longed to be with them, the other part, forlornly, buckled beneath the weight of his muddled conscience. He went into the field house to the locker room, hurried into one of the stalls in the restroom, and locked the door behind him. Taking off his jacket and pulling down his pants, he sat down on the toilet, resting his boiling face in the palms of his hands with his elbows on his knees. His guts felt as if they were being squeezed through a vegetable grater, and he figured maybe a good, clean evacuation would somehow discharge the whole humiliating episode. A few minutes of silence ensued, but then his composure was interrupted by the sound of heavy breathing and a drawn out moan followed by the strike of a match. Curious, he peered under the partition of the stall but saw nothing.

"What's the matter?" a snotty voice with an accusing lilt in it came from above.

Startled, he pulled his pants above his knees with one hand, quickly wiped the other across his eyes, and looked up.

"What happened?" Snyder insisted, his pale, round, freckled face appearing specter-like behind a billowing cloud of smoke. A Lucky Strike dangled loosely from his mouth.

"Nothin'."

"Why you cryin' then?"

"I wasn't."

"You were too!" Snyder carped and took a deep drag on the Lucky Strike while reflecting: "Greenley saw you comin' out of church like a cannon ball. What'd the old sop rector give you? A bunch of Hail Marys, I bet." Snyder hesitated and took a long, thoughtful drag before adding, in a confidential tone, "Bet he told you to hog tie that libido, huh? Lot a good that'll do. It's kind of like tryin' to stop the blink of an eye or a nervous tick, ain't it?"

"I wouldn't know," Christian defensively replied, his face starting to boil again.

"Liar."

"Who you callin' names?" Christian barked halfheartedly.

"Sorry," Snyder interjected in an injured tone. "You don't have to be so sensitive. You going to tell 'bout me smokin' in here?"

Christian shook his head.

"Dittman already found 'em in my foot locker'n called my old man. Trouble is he was out of town'n my mom won't tell. I traded my portable radio for ten cartons from Greenley. He gets 'em from some guy he knows in town, and I can sell 'em for black market prices. That's what my old man's always sayin'. Hey, you want to buy a couple of packs?"

"I guess."

The restroom door suddenly opened, and Snyder's red head disappeared, leaving a cloud of blue smoke circling above the stall.

"Snyder?" someone questioned in a hushed voice.

"In here," Snyder whispered, and Christian, looking under the stall door, saw Webber's big feet and dirty tennis shoes shuffling across the floor. Snyder's stall door opened, slammed shut, and a match was struck creating a sudden acrid smell. A few moments later, Snyder and Webber peered over the top of the partition, cigarettes dangling loosely from the corners of their mouths.

"He was cryin'," Snyder said and pointed at Christian.

"I wasn't!"

"Were too!"

"Who gives a witch's teat!" Webber snarled while he peeled the cigarette paper away from his upper lip. "We're going to get caught if you guys don't clam up!"

"You're lippin' it, dummy. Do it like this." Snyder cocked his head to one side, took a long draw on the Lucky, casually blew another perfect smoke ring, and withdrew the cigarette from his mouth with his thumb and index finger which left his other three fingers gracefully extended.

"You look like a girl," Webber said.

"Crater face!" Snyder shot back.

"Same to you, lardo. At least I can sit down without bustin' the furniture!"

"At least I can see without wearin' frogman's goggles!"

"At least I ain't Dittman's suck running around in a pilot's cap when I ain't even been in a plane for a ride!"

"Bull frogs! I took a plane to get here!"

Suddenly, the restroom door flew open and banged against the wall. Snyder and Webber ducked down and squatted on top of the toilet tank, while Christian peeked under the stall door. A black cassock swished by and stopped by the sink. A bar of sunlight slanted through a crack in an overhead window. Its rays landed on a pair of black shoes which appeared beneath the hem of a black cassock. There wasn't a sound in the room for several minutes, just a thin haze hovering above the stalls and an acrid smell. Then, like a thunderclap, all hell broke loose: "You've got exactly one minute to come out!" Father Dittman exclaimed, his voice resonating in the tiled bathroom. A few moments of dead silence ensued, and then Dittman hollered, "Thirty seconds!"

"I got a wipe, Father," Christian croaked, sticking his own pack of cigarettes into his underpants.

"Hurry up!"

He flushed the toilet, came out, and zipped his fly so fast that his shirttail caught outside the zipper.

"Give--me--the--cigarettes!" Dittman demanded. He paused for emphasis between each word and held his hand out.

"I don't have any on me," Christian replied while pulling on his flight jacket. "See," he added and pulled out the lining of both jacket pockets.

"Flushed 'em, huh?" Dittman said. Then he put his hands on his knees and bent over to look beneath the stall door. "Who's with you?"

"Nobody," Christian earnestly replied with an involuntary glance toward the stall doors.

Ignoring the remark, the priest walked to one of the stalls, reached out and swung the door open with his fingertips while asking Christian, "Are you sure no one was in here with you?"

"No, Father," Christian hedged.

"Get down to the office then!" the priest snapped.

Hurrying toward the exit, Christian noticed a shadow wavering on the floor in front of him as if displaced there by a body of intercepting light. The shadow stretched itself out like a two-dimensional cutout filled in with black. When he reached the door, the shadow slipped off the floor into the exit so that when he went through, it was like stepping into a tailor-made suit. A couple of guys went by. They were passing a basketball back and forth as they ran along the drab corridor. As if pushed from behind, he cut off the ball and dribbled it between his legs and down the hallway a few yards. At the fire exit, he shot it back to the guys by bouncing it off the metal cage that covered the ceiling light. It felt as if his body had been suddenly and mysteriously invaded by an irascible spirit, a shadow which would lie dormant until he shed the mask he wore like a sheep sheds its wool.

*   *   *   *   *   *   *

"What happened yesterday?" Snyder asked as he turned around in his desk and shaded his mouth with his hand.

"Yeah, what'd he do?" Webber joined in from across the aisle.

"No rec. for a week, and I got a clean the bathrooms for a week with Polinski.."

"During rec.?" Webber asked.

"Yeah."

"Did you tell?" Snyder asked.

"Tellin's for pantywaists."

"Oh, yeah?" Snyder challenged. "What 'cha mean by that, Reicharte?"

"Yah didn't tell?" Webber interrupted, flabbergasted.

"Who's waggling his tongue back there?" Father Dittman questioned without turning around, his back to the class as he declined some Latin nouns on the blackboard.

"Not me, Father!" Snyder ejaculated while pointing his thumb at his chest and vigorously shaking his head from side to side.

"Webber?"

"Ah, no, Father. I'm, ah, takin' notes as fast as I can."

Webber and Christian, sitting across the aisle from one another, leaned over their Latin texts and looked very busy. Snyder looked over his shoulder and stuck his tongue out at Webber.

"Mr. Snyder," Dittman reported, "please decline land."

Snyder's neck snapped around as if he'd just been lassoed and he cawed: "Terra, terrae, terrae, terr...am..."

"Go ahead," the priest urged as he wrote Snyder's answers on the board, his back still to the class.

"Terram, terra, terrae, terrarum..." Snyder thoughtfully hesitated.

Webber reached across the aisle and flicked a pencil tip on the back of Snyder's head.

"Yes, Norman?"

Terrae, terrarum, terris, terras, terr..."

Webber snapped the pencil on the back of Snyder's head again.

"Webber's flickin' me, Father!" Snyder yelped, turning around and giving Webber a fierce glare, his lips pursed in the exaggerated manner of a dandy.

"I saw 'em, Norman," Dittman replied as he slowly turned around and faced the class. His tongue was deeply inserted in his cheek.

"But he did it while you were writing on the board."

"Jesuits have eyes in the backs of their heads, Norman. I just wanted to see how far our little welfare recipient would go."

Everyone sat perfectly still while Dittman carefully set the chalk on the rail beneath the board, tapped his fingertips against one another, which sent up a cloud of chalk dust, and walked slowly toward Webber's desk. His cloudy eyes, set closely to the bridge of his beaked nose, were tucked below his eyebrows, and his tall, emaciated torso was bowed as if he were stalking a very dangerous prey. Stopping next to Webber's desk, he glanced around the room with a smug look and then peered down at the top of Webber's greasy head. "What's going on back here?" he asked while the class poised on the edges of their seats.

"Nothin'," Webber answered, not looking up.

"Look at me when I'm talking to you!"

"I didn't do nothin'," Webber said and kept his eyes on the desk in spite of the priest's demand.

"I didn't do nothin'," Dittman mocked. Then he added, in a flat, stern voice, "I saw you."

"But you were turned around."

"Didn't you hear what I told Norman? Take off those glasses!"

"But I was only playin' around," Webber rationalized while removing his glasses.

"Put your hands flat on the desk and look up here," Dittman demanded while rolling up the right sleeve of his cassock.

"I was only..."

"Now!" the priest exploded, his chiseled face becoming very red.

The class was hushed with anticipation. Christian huddled in his desk across from Webber. His eyes were trained on the priest's exposed forearm. It was long, unnaturally thin, and hairless with blue veins crisscrossing beneath transparent, brown-spotted skin.

Without warning, the arm, as if released from a tightly coiled spring, swung back and snapped forward, the priest's open hand swiping across Webber's cheek with a loud smacking sound. Momentarily, the boy's cheek blossomed, and he bolted upright in his desk, covered his ear and cheek with one hand, and tried to blink away the tears which threaded their way along his sharply defined cheek bones.

Taking a deep breath, Dittman rolled the sleeve of his cassock down over his wrist and hissed, "In loco parentis[18]."

"What?" Webber sobbed, cupping his ear.

"In loco parentis, ah, that means in the place of a parent," Snyder blurted out as he rapidly translated the priest's remark on a scratch pad.

"That's right, Norman. Why can't the rest of you backsliders be more like Norman here? He's a good boy. He follows the rules to the letter, does exactly as he's told, follows directions, and, if my eyes aren't deceiving me, goes to communion regularly."

"Every single day, Father," Snyder boasted.

"Me too," a weasel-faced kid shouted.

"Nobody asked you, Dwayne," Dittman scolded, and the kid tried to make himself disappear.

"I can't hear nothin'," Webber half-heartedly remarked under his breath, one hand still cupping his ear.

"Pardon me?" Dittman responded, turning sharply on Webber with a dangerous glint in his eye.

---

[18]   In place of a parent.

"Nothin', Father."

"Let me see your work then."

Webber handed over his paper, and Father Dittman gave it the once over, remarking, "It looks like you spilled your lunch on it. I can't even read it."

The class laughed, guardedly.

"Pardon me," Webber stated while bending the rim of his ear with his fingertips.

"Cut that out, Webber!" Dittman ordered when the class snickered. "Wipe up those crocodile tears'n put your nose to the grindstone for a change. This isn't a public school, young man."

"What?" Webber replied with a sly look for Christian.

"You heard me!" Dittman's voice reported like a shotgun blast as he caught the object of Webber's glance and turned to Christian with the remark, "How 'bout you, Mr. Reicharte. Are you of Snyder's ilk?"

Christian's pulse quickened unnaturally as the priest's drooping black sleeves flapped near his head. The man was peering at him along the curved bridge of his nose as if he were sighting a gun. He managed to weakly reply, "Probably not, Father."

"Decline war," Dittman snapped, "and keep your eyes off the board."

Squirming in his desk, Christian offered, "Bella, bellae, bell..."

"Go on."

"Bellis, bellarum, bellis?"

"Balderdash!"

The class laughed.

"Bella, bellae, bellis, bellarum, bellae, bell...ah...bellus?"

"Are you bloody daft?" Dittman exclaimed as he flicked Christian's ear lobe with his fingertips while the class laughed. Then he checked his watch and walked back up to the blackboard.

The rim of his ear sharply stinging, Christian clenched his fists and hunched over his text where there was a picture of a Roman gladiator fighting a naked man while an arena full of white-robed spectators looked on, their faces rabid. Snyder was moving an index finger back and forth across the other one while pointing at him, and the rest of the class were staring.

The bell suddenly rang, and Dittman, at the board, wrote down the assignment and then turned to the class with an angry scowl on his face. The only sounds in the room were the distant clicking of the big clock above the blackboard and a sputtering sound from an old radiator which was bolted to the floor along the back wall. "If you've learned nothing else today," Dittman addressed the entire transfixed class, "I hope you've learned that you can't put one over on a Jesuit. Like the pagan Indians, we've developed a sixth sense, eyes in the backs of our heads if you will."

"Nemo est qui hoc putet[19]," Snyder mumbled under his breath, just loud enough for the boys around him to hear.

---

[19]   There is no one who thinks this.

"Pax vobiscum[20]," Dittman concluded with a snappy up-and-down-and-across mid-air wave which was his way of dismissing the class with a blessing.

Everyone scurried out of the room, and Webber, cupping his ear, ran down the hallway followed by Christian who, trying to keep up with Webber, bolted out of the crowd, his black and white basketball shoes digging in for speed. Flying down the rear stairwell, he shadowed Webber out of the building and down a curved driveway to the field house. By the time he caught up, he found Webber in the main locker room. He'd thrown off his threadbare overcoat and was sitting on one of the long benches in front of the lockers. Clad in brown cords and a turtleneck sweater, he was holding his ear with his left hand while trying to wipe off his glasses with the other. There were tear tracks on his pimpled cheeks, and one cheek was blooming.

"Dagnabbit!" Webber shouted as if he were unaware of Christian's presence. "I'll get that SOB if it takes me the rest of my life. I'll kill 'em with my bare hands. He's nothin' but a alcoholic anyways! Snyder seen wine bottles in that coffin he calls a room up there by the freshman dorm."

Tongue-tied, Christian observed Webber as if for the first time. He looked different with his glasses off, more frail and vulnerable. For one thing, his dull eyes were pitifully crossed. His floppy ears and crooked nose were more sharply outlined. Tall and gangly, his arms and legs hung so long and loosely that he looked like a lab skeleton. Snyder once said that he'd heard the secretary in admissions say that Webber's mother had had polio when he was born. Christian handed him a handkerchief which Webber took without looking up and used it to wipe his glasses. Then he wiped his nose along the length of his shirt sleeve. "Why'd he single me out? Snyder's always mouthin' off'n never gets nothin'."

---

[20]   Peace with you.

"Cannibals only shrink the best heads," Christian replied, surprised at his own uncalculated response which sounded strangely alien, echoing as it did in the empty locker and shower room.

"Yeah, good one, Christian," Webber responded with a slight peel of laughter. "Why don't Dittman get a real job?"

"Beats me."

"Probably 'cause alls he can do is talk that Latin mumbo jumbo. Maybe we should a saved them Indians from him."

Christian laughed and picked up Webber's books which were scattered on the floor. "You ain't so dumb, Web," he commented. "You just think outside their books is all."

"Dagnabbit, dumb's Snyder suckin' up to Greenley'n Dittman all the time. Dittman even knows Snyder's gettin' cigs from Greenley, but Snyder's ole man's a mobster. Least that's what everyone says. He gave this dump big bucks. My ole man's a plumber." Taking a breath, Webber hesitated and then added, with a confidential glance at Christian, "Hey, don't tell nobody will yah? Our pastor got me in here for nothin'. My ole man put in the new plumbin' at the rectory. You should see the place. Looks like that there Taj Mahal. I helped a couple days'n them priests'n nuns just stood 'round gawkin' like a bunch a old maids. My old man says they don't even have to pay taxes'n he can't even get a contractor's license 'cause it costs too much. Christian handed Webber his books neatly stacked, and Webber jumped up and kicked a locker with the toe of his shoe. The blow severely dented the metal door. "Dagnabbit!" he exclaimed and grabbed the toe of his tennis shoe while jumping around on one foot and grimacing with pain. As if an afterthought, he added, while sitting down and rubbing his foot, "I built me a hot rod last summer from junk yard parts'n never once looked into one a them there Latin books. I'd like to see Dittman do that. It's got a four barrel, overhead cam, three-fifty-seven'n it'll do a hundred-twenty on a straightaway. Holy smokes, we'd better get to study hall!"

"Can I ride in it sometime?" Christian asked as he and Webber opened their lockers.

"Does a penguin have a cold butt?"

Laughing, Christian added, "Here, better put your overcoat back on."

"Dagnabbit, give me that. My mom sewed it up three times."

Heading out of the field house, they chatted like two soldiers from different planets, Webber, tall and spidery, his big hands flapping below his hips, and Christian, wiry and cat-like, his basketball shoes barely touching the ground. At Loyola Hall they cut through a side door, ran up two flights of stairs, and went into a large study hall with long strips of bright fluorescent lights flickering and buzzing above ten rows of wooden school desks which were bolted to the floor. Splitting up, they silently slipped into their desks, and Christian furtively lifted the desk top, shoved his books inside, and withdrew a sheet of paper and an envelope. Now and then, someone coughed, and you could hear the sound of paper rustling when a student went into his desk for something. Father Oxley snoozed at a desk set on a platform in front of the students' desks. His gray hair was a wild tangle of greasy threads, and there were patches of hair growing randomly on his craggy face. He had unruly tufts of white hair sticking out of his nose and ears. Occasionally, his over-large head would bolt upright momentarily and then droop, causing his chin to drop against his chest. Keeping one eye on Father Oxley, Christian set an open Latin text on its spine and placed the writing paper and envelope behind it. Glancing around the room, he confirmed that Snyder was busy working at his desk in row one, and the other students appeared to be reading Latin texts or grimly working on written homework assignments. Checking out Father Oxley one more time, he began writing:

12-15-55

Dear Rose,

How are you? I am fine. (I guess.) I'm in study hall. Father Oxleys's sleeping at the proctor's desk on a platform in front which overlooks our desks which are bolted to the floor. The guys here call him Snowflake because he's always got piles of dandruff on his shoulders from his wild hair. It even grows out of his nose and ears like weeds or something. He's about a hundred and all humped over and knobby like an old tree. He talks Latin a lot and can hardly hear from ringing the cathedral bells so long. This place is really boring. Everything's beige on top and dark brown on the bottom. All the walls and stuff. We sleep in these cubicles with partitions and no ceilings. All the priests and prefects (Prefects are becoming priests.) wear these long, fluttery black cassocks with long slits on the sides. (They put their hands into these slits and you wonder where they go. Webber, my friend, says they're holding up their socks.) I'll be home Saturday on the bus for Christmas vacation. I guess it's better than being here but I wouldn't want to have to prove it. Watch out for my mother. She listens to your phone calls on the upstairs phone, and sneaks up to your room and looks at your books and then tells my father that you read obscene literature. Those books you showed me aren't even in this library and it's huge.

You should see the church here! The walls (big blocks) seem like they're swelling up and it looks like blood's trickling from the cracks. Snyder - this busybody here - says this place used to be a monastery and they buried dead monks and nuns behind the walls to keep out evil spirits. Everyone's has to go into these tall black boxes and say their sins to a shadow behind a screen. It makes you feel kind of like you're in a crowded restroom without a door on your stall. Snyder says it's how they keep tabs on what's going on around here. Just a sec Oxley woke up.

Okay, I'm back with my Latin text turned to Rome for cover. We're supposed to be studying. Caesar's friend's talking. I'll write you the translation: "If Caesar, for all his genius, could not find a way out, who is going to find one now?" See, this jealous idiot Brutus and his gang killed Caesar because they thought the people would elect him king and Caesar always put honor before anything. This stuff is like breaking brainy secret codes. Just a second.

Oxley's asleep again. What else? Oh, my friend Webber got slapped in class because he was flicking Snyder behind the ear. Snyder deserved it but I felt sorry for Webber because he never gets picked for anything like Snyder and he's got acne to boot. He's acting now like he can't hear. Pretty sly, huh?"

Last thing. I got caught smoking but I really wasn't. Not then at least. Can we go up to the attic and get those medals sometime? I could wear them on my flight jacket and be somebody. Oh, oh, Oxley's up doing a homework check. Please write back! I never get a letter like everyone else even Webber and Snyder. Feels like someone's shadowing me sometimes, like a spy. And my voice is changing too. I don't know, but once when I was serving mass I looked up into the ceiling dome and saw MYSELF in the painted fires. Snyder says there's mirrors up there. For my sake, I hope so. I have to go. Bye! Write!

Signed,
Christian

When Father Oxley stopped to look over Valeno's work, Christian slipped the letter into the envelope he'd set out and stuck it into his desk under some books. Then he picked up his Latin text and began to studiously examine the black and white drawings of Roman culture.

"P-s-s-t," the boy on Christian's left signaled as he reached out with a folded sheet of paper.

Christian snatched the paper out of the kid's hand, but kept a sharp eye on Oxley who was still at Valeno's desk. Opening it, he recognized Webber's sloppy scrawl: Do you wanna dig out some a my shots later? I don't have a handball though.

Suddenly, the note was snatched out of his hand from above. He'd underestimated the Jesuits again. Father Oxley was reading the note, his bleary eyes almost touching the paper. When he finished, he crumpled it in his gnarled paw, slipped it into the side slit of his cassock, and went back to the platform where he fastidiously lifted the hem of his cassock with his fingertips as he approached the first step. Going up the wooden steps of the platform, he stumbled on the top step and turned around to frown at the step as if it'd moved. As if scolding the step, he absent mindedly commented, "Parturi unt montes nascetur ridiculous mus[21]," and a number of students, including Christian, scrambled for scratch paper so they could attempt a translation. A subdued laughter rose from several desks

---

[21]   There will be born a ridiculous little mouse.

around the study hall as translations were exchanged, and then the dismissal bell rang with a clatter because someone had bent the metal bell cover just enough to subdue its usual fierce, inanimate clang of authority. Picking up a ruler from his desk, Father Oxley, his silver-gray shock of wiry hair, thatched eyebrows, and humpback making him appear like a fairy-tale wizard, slapped it on his desk like a magic wand as the boys headed for the exit. "Just a minute, Mr. Reicharte," he cackled, "and you too, Webber! I see you ducking there! What do you think? I'm blind? Do you two think you can put one over on me? The rest of you get to your classes!"

Christian and Webber, who were ahead of the others, stopped, gaped at one another in mock innocence, and walked back to the priest who was trying to find the study hall door key among a dozen others attached to a huge key ring. Fumbling with the keys, he addressed the boys as they reluctantly approached, "You two've got detentions Saturday afternoon."

"What for?" Webber sulked.

"You know what for, Webber. You've been caught with notes before. I've warned you, ad nauseam[22]. My goodness, I can't seem to find the key. Taedet me. Taedet me[23]."

"But Christian didn't do nothin'!"

"Don't holler at me, Webber! He's guilty by association, ipso facto[24]."

"Huh?" Webber queried with a bewildered look for Christian.

---

[22]   To the point of nausea.
[23]   It wearies me. It wearies me.
[24]   By virtue of the same fact.

Finding the right key, Father Oxley ignored Webber's retort and commented on the key instead. "Sanctum sanctorum[25], here it 'tis. I've got to do something about these keys, Dei gratia[26]."

"But Christian was only..."

"He's supposed to be wearing a white shirt and tie, not that... what kind of shirt is that for goodness sake?" Oxley interrupted.

"Hawaiian, Father," Christian said with a self-conscious glance at his shirt.

"Hawaiian? I've a mind to send you to the rector. Where's your blazer?"

"No one's been enforcin' the shirt'n tie," Webber cut in. "Half the seniors're runnin' round with hockey sweats."

"What about the game Saturday?" Christian interrupted.

"Deus ex machina[27]," the hunchback carped as he locked the study hall door.

"Huh?" Webber said.

"My opinion of hockey, Webber, but don't worry over it. You two won't be participating in Saturday's masquerade. Be in study hall at two with plenty of paper and a couple of pencils in case one breaks."

"But the game starts at two," Webber whined.

---

[25] Holy of holies.
[26] By the grace of God.
[27] A contrived instrumentality.

"Two sharp," Oxley reiterated over his rounded shoulder as he shuffled away, the hem of his over-long cassock dragging a crumpled piece of paper along beneath it for a few yards before it rolled away.

"Non compos mentis[28]," Christian heard himself articulate his worst subject as if he were a ventriloquist's dummy. He watched the hunchback's black cassock flutter, like a phantom's cape, into the shadows of the dimly lit corridor.

"Say what?" Webber asked as he threw a notebook at the wall. "I didn't know you knew that junk, and your voice."

"Me neither," Christian said with a shoulder shrug. "Caesar's creepin' into me like a morphine injection."

Crestfallen, they went down the stairs to the first floor and out a side exit. It was a clear, keenly cold day with long, thin clouds, like vapor trails, streaking the sky. Boys' voices echoed from the hockey rink where the varsity team, mostly seniors like Greenley, was practicing for the homecoming game on Saturday. On the way into the field house, Webber ripped a Christmas wreath off the door and threw it into a nearby trash barrel with the tirade: "Bah, humbug, I ain't gettin' nothin' but a whippin' anyways. They'll be tellin' me all over the place what a privilege it is for me to be going to an exclusive - they say exclusive as if I shouldn't be here - private school when they can't 'ford it. I don't even want to be here, dagnabbit! All my friends're goin' to Ridgemont. They've got shop, agriculture, mechanic's class'n babes all over the place. I mean real women if they ain't wearin' them falsies."

"Falsies? You mean those pointy things?"

---

[28] Not of sound mind.

"Yeah, and watch out 'cause they can poke an eye out in a heartbeat."

"Will they do it?" Christian asked as he pulled a red Duncan Imperial yo-yo out of his jacket pocket, the field house door shutting behind them.

"All over the place," Webber shot back. "What do you think it's for anyways? They do it in drive-ins, parties, back seats, in the woods, their house, anywheres."

Christian put the yo-yo's string loop around his finger and snapped his wrist. The yo-yo had a single diamond rhinestone centered in each spool, and the diamonds sparkled like the real thing as the spools spun down the string and stalled at the bottom before snapping back up the string into Christian's palm.

Webber's eyes followed the yo-yo's antics. "How come you don't say much?" he asked Christian in an off-hand manner.

"Would it make any difference?" Christian indifferently replied as the yo-yo shot out of his palm all the way down to the end of the string where it stalled a second and then flipped three times around-the-world before it smacked back into his palm.

"Dagnabbit!" Webber shouted. "How many can you do?"

"Four times with my other yo-yo. It's got six diamonds, three on each side. It's got better balance too," Christian replied, his concentration on the yo-yo as it shot straight up in the air. "The string's gotta have just the right tension. This one's a touch loose."

"Dag-double- nabbit!" Webber repeated, impressed. "I seen this demonstrator once who could only do two."

The yo-yo reeled out, stalled at the bottom, crawled along the hallway floor a few feet, climbed back up the string, and then zipped straight out along the string into a pair of perfect three-sixties.

"Wow!" Webber commented, mesmerized by the yo-yo and pandering to a gathering crowd of boys by loudly inquiring, "Can you do the baby's cradle?"

The yo-yo shot out of Christian's palm, reeled down the string and stalled. The polished spools rapidly spun as Christian shaped the string into a triangle where the yo-yo, swinging back and forth, magically appeared, diamonds flashing.

"Do it again!" Webber shouted when several boys in the crowd clapped.

"I have to piss," Christian remarked as the yo-yo snapped back into his palm with a loud smack.

"Me too," Webber asserted as the crowd broke up. "Cut through the lockers. There's one in the weight room hardly no one uses."

With Webber on his tail, kicking lockers as he passed, Christian cut through the locker rooms, dodged a couple guys who were lifting weights in the weight room, and pushed open the restroom door. Anxious, he yanked open one of the stall doors and bolted in only to be stopped cold in his tracks by the sight of Greenley, the senior with the sidewall flattop he'd seen following Snyder out of the side door of the cathedral. There were cartons of Lucky Strikes, Playboy magazines, and a few boxes of cigarillo cigars piled on top of the toilet tank. Greenley, his letter jacket on the floor, was facing the toilet tank and straddling the toilet while Snyder, like a football trainer in a Fox Brother's overcoat, rubbed his back.

*   *   *   *   *   *   *

As the Greyhound bus ticked off the miles between Oakland and Milwaukee, Christian settled in his seat and watched the white-carpeted landscape go by in undulating waves. He counted the telephone poles as they flickered by the window. The middle finger of his right hand had an ugly callous from writing Latin passages during and after the homecoming game. Before it was over, he'd written twenty-one pages of his Latin text, and St. Xavier's had lost miserably to Wolcott, a small school in the local farm community.

Father Oxley, harboring a grudge against Webber for cutting the bell rope in the cathedral so he couldn't reach it one Sunday morning, fiercely scolded them both and sent them to bed early despite their pleas to be allowed to go to the homecoming bonfire.

The Greyhound's wheels hissed on the wet pavement, and the snow glittered brightly as it flashed by the windows. A mental picture of Snyder and Greenley's little commissary in the toilet stall still occasionally snapped on in his mind like a sudden light in a cave of bats. Greenley had threatened his life, and Snyder had begged, on his knees, for silence even offering cigarettes, clothes, candy, radios, watches, skis, Playboys and money as incentives. Recalling Caesar's plight, he'd declined everything and gone on his way without one word said, but Snyder and Greenley still looked at him with the pleading eyes of a beggar. After all, their entire black market was at stake and the rest could easily be misunderstood.

There was a blast on the Greyhound's horn, and the lady across the aisle looked up from the magazine she was reading through the bottom half of a pair of bifocals. She smiled at him, adjusted her glasses, and went back to her magazine. As no one was sitting next to him, he moved over by the window and started to count telephone poles again in order to drive the bats out of his mind.

Before long he found himself thinking about Rose. He hoped she'd still be there. Most of the maids never lasted more than a few months. His mother always told her friends in the bingo club that maids were no good transients looking for a meal ticket. Rose was different though. Somehow, she managed to simultaneously convey an air of absolute indifference and utter concern which kept his mother off balance. About twenty, she was no more than five feet tall with the compact, athletic build of a gymnast. She had reddish-brown hair which she kept in a ponytail unless they were rummaging in the attic. Then she'd let her hair down, and they'd put on old costumes and cross dress. Role playing she called it. One time she'd even given him a wet French kiss while admiring how cute he was in a blonde wig, white cashmere sweater, red poodle skirt, and saddle shoes. She had small sculpted features with chestnut eyes, a lush mouth, and glistening red lips. She was bold and had once told his mother that she wouldn't work in a uniform unless it was a special occasion. She always wore a jade necklace which depicted Buddha, and she was never without a paperback novel which she kept tucked in the hip pocket of her baggy jeans like a scuffed and tattered wallet. Sometimes, she'd borrow his Latin text and study it while she was working. She'd hold it out in front of her and push the vacuum with the other hand. When his mother and father were out, she'd come down from her attic room and sit with a book at the breakfast room table. She'd read to him if he hung around, and he'd try to understand brain teasers like Wordsworth's, "The child is father of the man."

The driver's voice suddenly cut across his daydream like a sharp knife through a clean sheet: "Milwaukee, folks! We'll be arriving at the depot in about five minutes. Please stay seated 'til the bus arrives and stops inside the depot. It's been a pleasure for Greyhound."

There was some commotion around him as people reached for carry-on luggage on the metal racks above their heads so he put on his coat and gloves and reached for his own luggage. There was a lot of traffic outside, cabs honking, and police sirens. He noticed the overhead Christmas decorations and a Santa Claus in front of a department store.

"Downtown terminal!" the driver called over his shoulder, and there was the sound of air brakes as the bus went down a ramp and descended into a basement depot. The bus door hissed open so he followed the crowd out the door, letting the elderly ladies go first.

Once he arrived in the lobby, he looked over the crowd that was waiting at the turnstile, but he didn't recognize anyone. There were loud greetings as people from the bus went through the turnstile, and there was a lot of hugging and kissing until the crowd dispersed, exiting up a nearby stairway. Heavy-hearted, he set down his duffel bag and skates and took out his wallet for cab fare. Dim, fluorescent lights flickered above him casting twitching shadows on the black-and-white tile walls. There were a few weather beaten, unshaven vagrants with threadbare overcoats, ragged mittens, and black stocking caps pulled down over their ears. Their eyes were sodden with booze and rejection. A bleary-eyed man in a grease-stained, ankle-length, khaki overcoat held up the wall next to a rusty coke machine, and an ancient ticket agent, wearing a green eyeshade, slumped over the counter behind an arched window at the rear of the waiting area. The whole place had the poisonous smell of a poorly maintained lavatory.

"Hey, kid, yah got any money in that fat leather wallet?" someone hissed.

Christian snatched the wallet back into his pocket with a start, for it seemed like the voice had emerged directly from a shadow on the wall. Turning around, he looked at a tall woman with a face like a theater mask. Her toothy grin exposed a gold eyetooth, and she had straight, platinum hair which fell, in oily strands, over the shoulders of an old raincoat. Because the coat was thrown open and slightly back over her shoulders, he could see right down the plunging bodice of her red dress.

"Pardon me?" he managed to reply, his eyes transfixed.

"If you got some money, you can have some fun, baby," she said with a glance over her shoulder at the dozing ticket agent.

Embarrassed, Christian looked around for help.

"How 'bout it, kid?" she asked, peering at him, the gold eye tooth gleaming. "Yah wear a nice overcoat with a corduroy suit and get off a bus so swell. I bet you're one a them rich, boarding school kids home on Christmas vacation, huh?"

"How'd you know?" Christian naively replied, the woman's red dress shimmering with silver sequins.

"Experience, sonny. I don't see no folks though."

"Me neither. I guess I'll just have to get a cab."

"How 'bout it?" she repeated, tapping the toe of a red pump on the floor while casting furtive glances around the terminal. "Bet your little girls friends don't look this good."

"No, I mean--ah, well, I never even, ah..."

"What's the matter?" she interrupted. "Can't yah talk and stare at the same time?"

Christian's face lit up like a flare.

"Twenty bucks," she pursued while reaching into a small black purse and retrieving a cigarette which she hastily lit with an old Zippo lighter.

Impulsively, Christian blurted out, "Does that include the luxury tax, ma'am?"

"Very funny," she hissed, swinging the little opera purse over her shoulder. "If I had my man here, I'd give you a spanking. All you rich brats are the same!"

Pulling out his wallet, Christian took out a twenty from the secret compartment under the dollar bill flap and held it out to her with an appeasing look in his eyes. "I didn't mean anything by it, really."

Surprised, she snapped the bill out of his hand and stuffed it down the front of her dress commenting, "That's more like it. Maybe you ain't a little pussy after all." Pinching his coat sleeve, she added, "Come on."

Having the uncanny sensation of walking beside himself, almost as if a sidekick were pushing him along, he grabbed his skates and duffel bag and went with her up the stairs. They walked several blocks due east of the bus station into a rundown section of town which he'd only heard of in wild stories from older guys at the skating rink. There were bars on every corner. Empty beer cans and cigarette packs cluttered the streets and gutters. Slack-jawed bums loitered on the bottom steps of old buildings which had broken windows and rusty fire escapes. They passed a dilapidated movie theater with an elderly red-headed Negro lady sitting in the ticket cage. To his utter amazement, he even saw a prophylactic, like the one Snyder had shown everyone, floating in a clogged curb-side gutter.

Feeling like a skulking shadow of himself, he followed her up several flights of steep stairs which led into an old building above a bar. The long, narrow hallway upstairs was lit by one, naked, seventy-five watt light bulb which hung loosely from an outlet connected to an extension cord. Glancing furtively over both shoulders in turn, she took a small key from her purse, opened one of several doors along the corridor and beckoned him in with her fingertips. When he hesitated at the threshold, she pursed her lips and shook her head back and forth with the comment, "We're not going to be a little mama's boy now are we? She took his arm and yanked him into the room, closing the door and locking it. She hung the key on a peg next to the door and went over to a curtained alcove where she hung up her raincoat. As if he weren't even in the room, she pulled the red dress over her head, threw it over the back of the only chair in the room, kicked off her heels, and stood there, lighting a cigarette, in nothing but a huge, underwire black brassiere, red panties, black garter belt and stockings: "You a virgin?" she asked, taking a long, casual drag from the cigarette and then setting it in an ashtray on a night stand next to what looked like an overnight cot with a thin mattress and springs.

"No," he sharply asserted, his eyes shyly darting away from the sight of her exposed undergarments.

"I thought so," she affirmed. "Give me your stuff'n take off them clothes."

"Everything?"

"This ain't no doctor's office, sonny."

Gulping down an intense impulse to run, he hesitantly stuck his leather gloves into his coat pocket and handed her his coat, duffel, and skates while he nervously peered around the room. The cot had dirty sheets on it, and there was an exposed light bulb, like the one in the corridor, right above a small kitchen table which was set on an oval throw rug in the middle of the room.

"Come on," she pleaded. "I ain't got all day, you know."

"Is the door locked?" he asked, stalling for time.

"Don't be such a scaredy-cat and come here. I'm not going to take out your appendix or nothin' but I hope you've got a squeaky."

"Squeaky?" Christian summarily questioned just as someone pounded on the door.

"Oh, shucks, no, it's Sid!" she exclaimed while grabbing for her dress and putting it on in one practiced motion. "Get out on the fire escape! The window!"

Everything went crazy in his head as he looked out the window where a rusty fire escape hung loosely against the wall. Beyond the fire escape, there were rooftops and a huge clock hung on the side of an office building. Just as someone pounded on the door again, the clock tolled with slow regular strokes like a funeral summons, and, almost as if he were standing outside the window looking in, he heard himself, or what sounded like a loose assembly of himself, inexplicably shout, "Yeow! Alea iacta est[29]!"

"Candy!" someone yelled through the door and pounded some more. "You'd better not have another one of them minors in there! It's back to the salt mines this time, lady!"

Feeling his legs buckle beneath him, Christian grabbed his overcoat, duffel, and skates and opened the window. A string of purple, rhinestone beads fell out of his coat pocket just as he raised one leg up on the window sill.

"Just a minute, Sid!" Candy shouted as she picked up the beads and fondled them as if she'd found a string of pearls. "What're these, worry beads?"

---

[29] The die is cast!

"Kind of. It's a rosary," Christian replied as he climbed unto the fire escape. You use it to say penance and stuff. You can have it if you stall that guy until I get down."

"Geeze, thanks, kid. I can sure use 'em 'cause if Sid finds out he's gonna kill me!"

"What about me?" Christian said as he slammed the window down behind him and started to climb backwards down the rusty stairs. Just as his head was about to disappear beneath the windowsill, he saw her put the rosary around her neck like a necklace and look in the mirror while admiringly touching the beads. Then she opened the door to reveal a guy who looked like he'd just been dipped in a vat of grease. Unshaven, he had a sharp jaw and cruel eyes. He had on a black stocking cap, a black leather jacket, blue jeans and black boots. Warily, he looked around the room and then toward the window just as Christian hit the ground and began running for his life.

Desperately trying to translate the spontaneous Latin phrase he'd involuntarily uttered at the window and run at the same time, he repeatedly glanced over his shoulder with the paranoia of an escaped convict. After a couple of blocks, he gained control of his emotions and realized that his comment at the window had something to do with him. Based on his limited experience translating Cicero and Caesar, it was some kind of expression of doom, probably a result of feeling so much beside himself throughout the whole ordeal. It was almost as if he'd been remotely controlled during the entire escapade like an actor simply blocking out his moves for a script on a stage, and his own voice had sounded strangely affected, almost effeminate.

What was unnerving though was who or what was at the control panel? Maybe, like Caesar, they were following him. He'd always had a vague feeling of displacement as if he weren't quite himself.

He wished he still had his rosary. He used it a couple times to say a penance, but it was really more like a talisman or lucky charm like the maid's Buddha.

At Fifth and Lake, just out of skid row, he waved down a cab and breathed a sigh of relief when it accelerated into a busy street where a myriad of colors immediately impinged upon him, calming his anxiety with the tinsel of civilization: there were Christmas tree lights blinking off and on in all the department store windows. Norwegian pines stood in front of many department stores like tiny forests in the midst of a granite labyrinth. There were green wreaths hanging at regular intervals above the streets, and every few blocks a costumed Santa Claus stood ringing a bell for passersby to drop their change into his coffer. The cab raced by throngs of brightly dressed shoppers as it dodged and weaved its way into the suburbs.

Going by Taylor Park, he noticed, among the people skating around the rink, a tall man who was wearing black ski pants, a bright red turtleneck sweater, and a long, white scarf. The man was bent low over a pair of speed skates, his arms rhythmically swinging behind his back. Recognizing the man's short, salt-and-pepper beard and his trademark baseball cap with over-lapping ear muffs, Christian asked the driver to stop, paid his fare, and gave the driver a couple dollars extra. Luckily, he'd kept some money in the toe of his shoe, something Webber had shown him. Then, forgetting himself, he buttoned up his coat, grabbed his duffel and skates, and ran headlong toward the rink like a sailor jumping ship.

Seeing Christian approach, Coach Wrigley skidded to a stop which caused ice to spray in a wide arc over the snow-banked border of the rink. "Hello!" he shouted with a broad smile and a wave. "Where've you been?"

Out of breath, Christian commented, "Boarding school. We got two weeks for Christmas."

"Boarding school. Like all boys and ROTC?"

"Yeah, and no little league."

"Too bad. I'm coaching at Lincoln."

"You got the job?"

"Yeah, let's see what you remember from little league."

Christian took his skates from around his neck and sat down at the edge of the rink to put them on. He laced the rawhide tightly and wrapped the excess lacing around his tendon guards. He went into his duffel bag for a heavy sweater and his flight jacket which he exchanged for his overcoat and corduroy sport coat. He wasn't in any hurry to get home.

"Nice jacket," the coach commented while lacing up a speed skate. "Who's Culpepper?"

"Beats me. Found it in our attic. It's warm as heck."

"I know. It's the leather. First rule of holes?"

Christian remembered their near loss in the finals. They were down three- zero, but Wrigley always had a prompt: "When in one, stop digging!"

"Nice recall."

"I liked the one where Johnson missed that slap shot'n asked you what you thought of 'em at half time. You said, 'I don't.' He made four saves the second half."

"Inside out motivation. Let's go."

They skated up to the boarded hockey rink where a pair of goals was set up at opposite ends. They picked up a couple of beat up hockey sticks someone had left behind and skated into the rink.

"See if you can get it by me," Wrigley said as he threw a puck down and back skated into the goal at one end.

Dribbling the puck down the court, Christian skated straight for Wrigley who feinted left and right. In an instant, Wrigley's stick was under his, and the puck disappeared as the coach skated away with it toward the opposite goal where he slap shot it into the center of the crease. "You're rusty!" he hollered as he gathered the puck from the goal. "What've you been doing?"

"Latin conjugations!"

With a flip of his wrist, Wrigley sent the puck zipping over the ice. Christian caught it on his stick, clenched his teeth, and skated toward Wrigley. Faking a slap shot, he gave Wrigley, who'd come out of the cage, the slip, but when he glanced over his shoulder to see where the man was, he missed a step, and in that moment of indecision, Wrigley snatched the puck from behind and was gone. His long-limbed stride transported him over the ice in a red blur. At the opposite goal, he casually flipped the puck in and skated back to Christian.

"What'd I do wrong?" Christian asked.

"Get out of your own way."

"What do you mean?"

"You're tripping over your own shadow."

"But she's a spy."

"Pardon me."

Just then, two teenage girls approached the hockey boards. One of them was a tall, skinny brunette in a fuzzy white cap with ear flaps, a blue skating skirt with a matching turtleneck, white hose, and white figure skates. The other one was heavily made up with thick, blue eye shadow and red lipstick. Short in stature, she had long brown hair, which tumbled to her shoulders from beneath a red stocking cap. She had a saucy ski-jump nose, and a heart-shaped face with bright, bold eyes. Beneath her wide open Lincoln High football jacket, she wore a pink cashmere sweater which had a deep depression between two sharply projecting cones. Between the cones, a small, silver cross hung from a sterling silver neck chain. She wore tight jeans over a pair of boy's hockey skates with tendon guards. Christian remembered her from the eighth grade. At little league practice, she used to write him silly notes laced with abbreviated codes like S.W.A.K. Her real name was Anne Baxter.

"Remember them?" the coach asked.

"They used to hang around little league."

"Yeah, pains in the butt too. I told that little one not to smoke around the boys. Here, take the puck up."

Christian caught the puck on his stick and dribbled it toward the goal at the other end of the rink. At about mid-rink, he passed it back to Wrigley and then skated around his back. He angled toward the side where he knew Wrigley would pass the puck to him by rebounding it from the boards. He picked it up right after it caromed from the top edge of the side boards, and then, with a long backswing, he zipped it into the goal.

"That's more like it!" Wrigley hollered. When he saw the two girls climb over the side boards and skate in their direction, he added, "Oh, oh, here comes the Bopsy twins!"

Christian skated up to the coach, but when he saw the girls, he stuck his neck into his collar and started to leave.

"Stuck up!" the little one hollered.

"What's your hurry?" the coach called after him.

Feeling the nape of his neck turn bright red, Christian hesitated and then turned around and walked back in spite of an overwhelming shyness.

"Too much Latin and not enough Greek, huh," Wrigley teased and gave Christian a playful punch on the shoulder which only made him shrink away, eyes downcast.

"Didn't you used to coach the little league?" the tall one asked the coach as she approached.

"Still do. Whatever happened to that cheerleading idea you had for the team?"

"Oh, we're still practicing, but we need to get a sponsor to buy us the outfits."

"How about Meyer's Real Estate? They're always looking for ads."

Out of the conversation, Anne Baxter and Christian shyly stabbed the ice with the toes of their skates until Anne finally took the initiative.

"'Member my notes?" she asked Christian who was studying the toe of one skate as if a snake had come to rest on it.

"Yeah."

"How come you're not going to Lincoln like everybody else?"

"'Cause."

"'Cause why?"

"Just 'cause. I don't know. My parents."

"What's your last name?" she asked and lit up a Marlboro like an old pro, inhaling deeply while sticking the half empty pack into the hip pocket of her jeans.

"Reicharte."

"Reicharte? You don't look like that name. Sounds like a foreign name."

"What do you mean by that?" Christian snapped, unable to avoid staring at the pointy cones which stretched the girl's cashmere sweater to its absolute limits when she pulled the shoulders of her jacket back and stuck out her chest as if posing for a camera.

"Geeze, you don't have to be so touchy! I'm just saying you look more like a Cobb or Sanders or something. Your name doesn't fit your looks."

Christian saw her lips moving but was unable to comprehend what she was saying. His eyes were glued to the silver cross which flickered, like an occult charm, in the unnaturally deep valley between the cones. "I'm supposed to be home by now," he said with embarrassment, his voice sounding like a girl's.

Working her thumbs through the belt loops of her jeans like a cowboy and taking a drag on her Marlboro, Anne, with an exasperated expression, tilted her head slightly and appealed, "Don't be a big baby. Let's get some hot chocolate in the warming house. You look awful."

"I gotta go," Christian shyly squeaked, his cheeks bristling with the heat of his blood as he skulked away, ashamed of his own timidity.

"I'll run you home, Christian," the coach intervened when the girls started chattering like a pair of rhesus monkeys. He followed Christian to the edge of the rink where he'd left his gear.

"See yah around, Christian!" Anne hollered, waving, "I'll call you."

Christian managed a robotic wave and the coach, putting his hand on Christian's shoulder, remarked, "You've got to break out of that shell, son."

"But it's safe," Christian blurted.

"It's a dungeon."

"How do you get out?"

"You've got to do the hardest thing there is to do in life."

"What's that?"

"Be yourself."

"But she only speaks in Latin."

"Say what?"

"See what I mean."

* * * * * * * * *

"How much is that dog-gy in the win-dow?" Rose sang out in a throaty, unself-conscious voice, her dark pony tail tied with a yellow ribbon and highlighted by sunlight cascading through the French windows behind the piano.

"Arf! Arf!" Christian responded in his best puppy's bark.

"The one with the wag-ged-y tail," Rose continued as Christian played the baby grand, catching, in his peripheral vision, the jade Buddha she always wore. It was suspended from a gold chain and hung, like a bewitching talisman, between the open folds of a baggy, man's flannel hunting shirt she loved to wear. "I must take a trip to Cal-i-for-nia and leave my poor sweet-heart-a-lone," she continued as she reached for a peppermint in a long, thin box next to a clicking metronome.

"Arf! Arf!", Christian responded, and they both laughed. Then she carelessly put her hand on his thigh and squeezed just below his jean pocket while huskily singing: "If she has a dog, she won't be lone-some, and the dog-gy will have a good home."

"Ahhruff!" Christian barked like a sick puppy, covering his mouth with his hand in embarrassment as his secret life snapped up like a suddenly opened switch blade.

"What's going on down there?" a nasal twang reported from the top of the red-carpeted, circular staircase which ascended from the piano platform in the living room.

There were a few moments of silence while Christian and Rose fidgeted and exchanged fearful glances.

"You heard me!" the voice cracked like a whip on a marble floor.

"Nothing, Mrs. Reicharte," Rose finally responded. Then she shut off the metronome and reached for the box of Brach's peppermints which she hastily slipped under the piano bench.

"It doesn't sound like nothing to me!" the shrill voice lashed back. "Is he there with you?"

"Yes, ma'am," Rose said with an impish look for Christian who was warily peering up the stairs.

"Haven't you got anything to do, Rose? Father Devine's coming for dinner, you know. I want everything spic and span."

"Yes, ma'am."

"Is the table set?"

"No, ma'am."

"Use the sterling silver and china."

"Yes, ma'am."

"And tell him to take a bath and get dressed up and not in that ridiculous shirt he's been wearing."

"I'll tell 'em," Rose answered. She glanced at Christian's Hawaiian print shirt and winked.

"Check the turkey too."

"I've been keeping an eye on it."

"See that you do. And don't forget to dust my glass elephants in the china hutch."

"I did 'em. The ceramic frogs too," Rose said as Mrs. Reicharte's open-toed, backless, silk slippers loudly flip-flopped along the upstairs hallway, marking her passage to her bedroom.

When they heard Mrs. Reicharte's bedroom door close behind her, Christian and Rose jumped up from the piano bench. As Rose leaned over to put away the sheet music and retrieve the peppermints from inside the piano bench, Christian caught his breath at the accidental sight of her naked breasts which, unencumbered by a brassiere, swayed freely beneath her partially unbuttoned shirt. Momentarily transfixed, he barely noticed her eyes which caught his and then dropped to her chest as she remarked: "My, my, you've really grown up since September."

Snapping out of it, he blushed all the way to his toes and bolted upstairs to his bedroom. He closed and locked the door. Flustered, he sat on the edge of the bed and contemplated her remark. It was the way she'd emphasized grown up as if she were really impressed with him. Maybe, though, she really thought he was stealing a peek down her shirt which may, in fact, have been the case. He wasn't sure, but she seemed to like it. Somehow, she didn't look as old as she used to. He'd never noticed her skin texture before. It was very smooth and shiny. It was dark brown, darker than he'd ever perceived as if his vision were improving. Her teeth were pearl white, and she always smelled like a newly dug garden, fresh, damp, and earthy. He liked the way she always looked right at him when she spoke. She didn't have those nervous, accusing eyes which looked right through him while conveying secret unsharing thoughts like the eyes of Snyder, Dittman, and especially his mother.

In the blink of an eye, as if stepping out of one character and into another, he reached beneath his mattress where he'd hidden the National Geographic he'd purloined from school. Flipping through the dog-eared pages, he found the place: there was a lush jungle with emerald-green foliage swaying in a tropical breeze. A line of coconut palms encroached upon a broad beach with sand as white as the inside of a clam shell. Beyond the beach, a blue-green sea sparkled like a suddenly opened chest of jewels, its foamy fringes lapping lazily along the shore. Above, there was a blue sky, dotted with clumps of cumulus clouds. Naked children with dark skin and hard, round bottoms ran along the beach. Native women with long, tapering legs, drooping breasts, and sharply jutting bottoms, covered only with thin loin cloths, danced around a drummer. Feeling his own heart beating like a war drum, he searched for the native girl who was partially obscured by a palm tree at the edge of the beach. She had long black hair which cascaded between her shoulder blades all the way to her bottom which was sparsely covered with a tattered loin cloth. She had a wide nose with large brown eyes and thick ruby lips. She was skinny with dark brown skin and narrow, boyish hips. Her small breasts glistened with beads of sweat. Settling back on the bed and letting his face rest on the cool white sheet, he wondered if only he, maybe not even the photographer, knew she was there. Letting the magazine slip from his fingers, he closed his eyes and listened to the drum beating. It was like a heartbeat in its regularity. It pounded in his breast making him hot and sweaty.

"Christian!" Mrs. Reicharte's voice shrieked at the door.

Racing through the jungle, he felt the dense foliage whip his back, and he could feel her breath on his neck.

"I'm coming!" he managed to holler, his voice breaking hideously.

"Don't holler at me, young man! I don't know why you're locking this door lately!"

He slipped the magazine under his mattress.

"Open this door!"

"Yes, mother," he said, holding his pants up with one hand while opening the door a crack with the other.

"What's going on in here?" his mother, clad in a pink terry cloth bathrobe, asked as she pushed the door open and peered around the room. A goiter protruded from her neck. She wore a thick mask of cold cream, and a white towel, like a turban, was wound above her head.

"Nothing," he squeaked.

"Nothing what?"

"Nothing, mother."

"What's the matter with your voice then? Sounds like you ate a canary."

Staring guiltily at the floor, he noticed how his mother's toes, with their long, talon-like nails, stuck through the open toes of her satin slippers like dragon's claws.

"Well?"

"Yes, mother. I guess there's something wrong with my voice, mother. It's changing or something, mother."

"Don't get sarcastic with me," she quipped and looked suspiciously around the room. "I want you to get dressed up for Father Devine. He's coming...what's that smell? Smells like an animal's in here."

Clasping his hands behind his back, Christian gaped around the room and innocently remarked, "I don't smell anything."

"Don't put an act on for me, snot nose. You can't pull the wool over my eyes. Now wipe that nose and get rid of that garish Hawaiian thing. Put on something presentable. Turning to leave but stalled by an afterthought, she added, "Where'd you get that shirt? It looks like you've been sleeping in it."

"When we went to Florida."

"I suppose you traded your radio for it."

"No, I..."

"Don't argue with me! We've caught you trading your things before. Like that St. Christopher's medal you traded for a kite."

"But it was a Japanese box kite."

"Foolishness. Haven't you got any sense of value? That kite was nothing but paper, and the medal was sterling silver. Besides, your Aunt Louise gave it to you for your birthday."

"But I asked for a Duncan Imperial yo-yo."

"Don't talk back! I've told you that 'til I'm blue in the face! Haven't I?"

"Yes, mother."

"That's better. Now get ready and come downstairs like a little gentleman. Your father's counting on this dinner so behave yourself...and comb that haystack."

She left the door open as she lumbered down the front stairs, her double-wide bottom quivering beneath her beige, terry cloth bathrobe. The heels of her backless slippers smoked with talcum powder residue and slapped on the stairs.

A few minutes later Christian heard the doorbell ringing so he peeked out the bedroom door and over the landing of the living room downstairs. The front door in the foyer opened, and there was a brilliant flash of winter sunshine reflected from the snow outside. It was followed by a frigid draught of air that reached all the way up to his bedroom and down the collar of his Hawaiian print shirt. Then, like a sudden eclipse, there was a burst of black, the door was shut, and Father Devine ambled in. He handed a black felt hat to Rose who hung it, along with his black overcoat, on a brass coat rack.

"Mother of mercy," he commented, rubbing his hands together. "It's cold outside. Am I early?"

"They're not down yet, but make yourself at home," Rose replied and twitched her nose as if smelling something.

Still peering over the landing, Christian remembered serving Mass for the priest. He always smelled as if he'd spilled a bottle of cologne on himself, and he made servers help put on his vestments when he prepared for Mass. The altar boys called him pixie dust because when he talked, he often emphasized his words by holding one hand cocked back with his thumb pressed against his second and third fingers as if he were pinching magic dust. He was a soft, obese, middle-aged fellow. He had a round face, very pale skin, curly, light-brown hair which formed ringlets over his forehead and beady blue eyes. He had short arms, like stumps attached to his torso. His hands were noticeably small with long shiny fingernails manicured to unusually sharp points.

With a saccharine smile which exposed a distinct overbite, Father Devine followed Rose into the living room while anointing his lips from a lip gloss tube.

"Mr. Reicharte'll be down shortly," Rose said. "Can I get you anything, sir?"

With a surprised, questioning glance in her direction, the priest replied, "A toddy might be nice. To take the chill off, mind you."

"Of course," Rose quipped, unconsciously pulling at the hem of her maid's costume to avoid the priest's surreptitious glances as she departed.

Just then, Mr. Reicharte, balancing a pair of rim-full crystal cocktail glasses on a tray, rushed in through an archway from the dining room. He was a stout man with vague, gray eyes, and a nose too big for his face. He had wiry, upward-slanting eyebrows, and matted, yellowish-gray hair with a severe part down the left side. He wore wire-rimmed spectacles, brown suit pants, a striped tie, and black, slightly scuffed Cordovans. His white dress shirt was transparent allowing a scooped undershirt with thin shoulder straps to show through. With a broad salesman's smile, he thrust one of the high balls in front of Father Devine's face: "Rum'n coke, Father?" he said, smugly tilting his head and peering over the top of his glasses.

"God bless you, Walter. How'd you remember?"

"The Matson's funeral reception."

"I dare say. You've got the memory of an elephant. That was a year ago."

"I never forget a name neither. Not good for business. You never know when an insurance premium'll depend on it. Let's take a load off our feet."

"Good idea. I've had early Mass all week. The pastor'n me alternate." The priest sipped his drink as if it were a cup of hot tea and added, in the manner of an afterthought, "Incidentally, Walter, before I forget, isn't that maid of yours a bit upbeat?"

"How do you mean?" Mr. Reicharte replied as he directed the priest past the fireplace where a log burned. There was a large recliner near the piano, and the priest sat down next to a fragrant, seven-foot pine Christmas tree which was over-decorated with multi-colored tinsel, blinking lights, tin foil figures, colored balls, and a six-inch angel on top with wings that flapped every thirty seconds.

"Don't get me wrong now, but I was sure she referred to me as sir," the priest commented with a surprised look when the chair cushion gave way beneath him and made a loud sucking sound, like a gasp.

Acknowledging the priest's chagrin, Mr. Reicharte said, "We call it the behemoth, Father. It's a hand-me-down from Ethel's mother who passed away last fall."

With that consolation, the priest relaxed and held on to the arm rests as he sank into the framework of the chair, commenting, "Lord, have mercy. Is it trying to eat me?"

They both laughed as Mr. Reicharte sat down in an overstuffed armchair by the fireplace and put his black shoes up on an ottoman. There were circular rings on the soles of each shoe where they'd scuffed through the leather. Then he stretched his legs out until the hem of his pants hiked up, and a pair of black garters could be seen holding up his long black support hose. "So she referred to you as sir did she? A good worker, but one of these new-fangled liberals. I'll have a talk with her."

"And that Buddha necklace," Father Devine cut in.

"She claims it's a good luck charm. We gave her a fourteen karat crucifix, but she wasn't interested. There's no respect anymore. They're either listening to that racket they call music, or they're watchin' that dad blamed TV. I wish I'd never got one. That American Bandstand should be put on the Legion of Decency list if you ask me. The way they gyrate around with each other right in front of God'n everybody's a disgrace. Why, gosh darn it, I'd be ashamed of myself. I should write Bishop Sheen a letter."

"Why don't you, Walter," the priest interjected between sips of his high ball.

"Look at this," Mr. Reicharte continued as he reached into a brass magazine rack, pulled out a copy of Look, and held it up. "She might'nt be wearing a dress at all. It's blowed up over her knees on purpose. "Why, you can see her panties for heaven's sake! I'm about to cancel my subscription!"

"Now, now, Walter, don't get your dander up," Father Devine advised, self-consciously averting his eyes from the cover picture. "I didn't want to get anyone in trouble. It's Christmas, mind you."

"Why, hello, Father," Mrs. Reicharte said as she passed beneath the dining room archway into the living room, adding, with a frown and a bite in her voice, "Why didn't you call me, Walter?"

"I thought Rose did."

"You shouldn't have presumed."

"Who made you head coach around here, Pickle Puss?"

Mrs. Reicharte glared at her husband, her chubby pink face a mask of suppressed tight-lipped anger. Struggling to free himself from the behemoth's grasp, Father Devine scolded them with a "Now, now," and added, in reference to the chair's tenacity, "Mercy, is this thing holding a grudge, Walter?" Finally on his feet, he shook Mrs. Reicharte's hand while trying not to stare at the frosted-pink hairdo piled, beehive fashion, four inches above her head.

The priest's reaction to his wife's new hairdo wasn't lost on Mr. Reicharte who interjected, "It takes a lot of gettin' used to, Father, like buttermilk."

Mrs. Reicharte glowered at her husband and the priest ignored Mr. Reicharte's remark. "I didn't get a chance to speak after Mass," he said, almost dropping his empty high ball glass. "Mrs. Overbee was..."

"Mrs. Overbee's a nuisance," Mrs. Reicharte interrupted.

"If you say so" the priest replied, slightly taken aback.

"Never mind then. We enjoyed your sermon, Father.

"Indeed? Why thank you, Mrs. Reicharte. It often seems no one's listening. Sometimes, I even get the feeling I'm looking out at a sea of eyes. No heads. Just eyes."

"It ain't exactly an open forum, Father," Mr. Reicharte commented as the priest sat down, the spongy old cushion gasping and embracing him like a man-eating plant.

"I've asked you to get that cushion replaced, Walter. You're such a scrooge sometimes," Mrs. Reicharte carped. Then she reached for the priest's empty tumbler and asked, "Can I get you another?"

"Oh, I shouldn't, really," the priest replied, handing her the empty high ball glass.

"Go ahead," Mr. Reicharte prodded. "Let your hair down. It'll do yah good besides helpin' yah. There's no teetotalers around here 'cept maybe this here maid with no respect for the cloth. She's one of them health nuts. Don't even eat meat, mind you."

"I guess another won't hurt," the priest replied, his palms up as if helplessly capitulating. "It's Christmas after all."

"That's the spirit," Mr. Reicharte emphasized as he thrust his own tumbler out for his wife to take.

"Rose!" Mrs. Reicharte hollered as she snatched the glass out of her husband's hand.

"Another rum'n coke's fine," the priest put in with an annoyed tug at the stiff white collar around his neck.

"Same as usual for me, Pickle Puss," Mr. Reicharte sniped with a wink and a broad, ingratiating smile for his wife who huffily turned her back on him and went into the dining room with the tumblers. Her broad bottom bounced in a waistless, floral-print sack dress which hung over her stout frame like a furniture drape.

Christian closed his bedroom door which shut off the landing overlooking the living room. He lay in bed and put his hands beneath his head. His thoughts threaded along a ribbon of sunshine which streamed through a white-curtained, arched window on the opposite side of the room. Another week and he'd be back at school. He'd probably be standing in one of Dittman's roll calls or sitting in study hall staring at the beige and dark brown walls while wrestling with the mice in Latin conjugations: "Edi-mus, bibi-mus, viv-mus, ore-mus," he heard his own voice, in a higher, more effeminate register than he was used to, conjugating the verbs. He thought it was only hormones, but he felt fractured anyway. The weird Latin conjugations, like cryptic codes, wrinkled his brow with their puzzling riddles, and an uncomfortable feeling of sadness and alienation would always overcome him when she spoke. It was like he lived with a stranger who loved him and was trying, in her own way, to offset his loneliness. Even now she murmured under his breath with a comprehension of Latin well beyond his own experience: "Per Ardua ad astra[30]."

"Christian, are you almost ready?" Rose called through the door. She's on the warpath. Who're you talking to?"

"Ah, no one! I'm coming!" he hollered as he picked up his sneakers. Then he changed his clothes and smoothed out his Hawaiian print. He looked in the mirror above his dresser to comb his hair. For a split second he thought the reflection was that of the Roman kid in the picture on page seventy-two of his Latin text. The kid had wavy blonde hair and wore a toga and sandals. He rode a huge, barrel-chested, white horse. Then the outrageous cowlick in the crown of his unruly, dark brown hair popped up, like a rooster's cockscomb, and the illusion in the mirror disappeared. Opening a jar of pomade, he plastered the cowlick down with the sticky substance and slicked the sides of his hair ducktail fashion. Then he dashed out of the room and down the back stairs which led into the butler's pantry between the kitchen and dining room.

"I thought I told you not to wear that silly shirt," Mrs. Reicharte scolded as he passed her in the pantry. She was anxiously

---

[30]   Through hardship to the stars.

supervising Rose who was carrying food between the kitchen and dining room: "Don't spill that gravy," she warned. "Where'd you put the cloth napkins? I told you I wanted to use the monogrammed, cloth napkins didn't I? Where's my highball?"

"Right there on the counter where you left it, Mrs. Reicharte," Rose replied. She winked at Christian and reached into a cupboard with one hand to pull out a stack of cloth napkins which she handed to Mrs. Reicharte who was peering into her empty high ball tumbler.

"Who's been sipping my drink?" Mrs. Reicharte barked, holding up the empty glass.

Christian was out the pantry door in a flash and Rose quietly replied, "You're the only one I've seen around it, Mrs. Reicharte."

"Well, don't just stand there," Mrs. Reicharte snapped back. "Get me another and bring the turkey into the dining room. Use the silver platter."

"Where've you been?" Mr. Reicharte questioned Christian as he slid, round-shouldered and doe-eyed, into a high-backed chair across from Father Devine. His mother placed a cloth napkin at the side of each plate. Then, with a directorial wag of her finger at Rose, who was balancing a large turkey platter on the palm of one hand, sat down opposite Mr. Reicharte at one end of the long dining room table.

"The platter's hot, Mr. Reicharte," Rose said as she set the sterling silver platter of turkey next to Mr. Reicharte who put his nose right over the platter, sniffing.

"Walter!" Mrs. Reicharte protested.

"I was just checking it, Ethel," Mr. Reicharte shot back.

"With the end of your nose? What's the matter with you?"

"Now, now," Father Devine intervened. "Shall we say grace?"

"Christian," Mr. Reicharte summoned. He peered over the tops of his bifocals at Christian and nodded like a funeral parlor director.

Stiffening for the ritual, Christian hesitantly began. Mr. and Mrs. Reicharte both glared at him. Their eyes were glassy. Half way through, his mind went blank, and he stumbled over the words.

"For heaven's sake, Christian," Mrs. Reicharte interrupted.

"He can't learn, Ethel," Mr. Reicharte remarked as if it were a foregone conclusion.

"Now, now, it's to be expected," Father Devine interceded, adding, with a schoolmaster's oblique glance at Christian, "It's from thy bounty, through Christ our Lord, amen, son."

Christian stared at his plate while Rose, wearing a black and white maid's costume she'd been ordered to wear for the occasion, went around the table and filled wine glasses at the adult's plates. At Christian's place she poured a tall glass of milk, reaching out and adjusting his shirt collar with her free hand. Father Devine sipped his wine, dabbed his lips, and then shook open the cloth napkin which he fastidiously tucked into the white collar around his neck. Holding his wine glass with his baby finger extended, he looked across the table at Christian. "That's quite a bold shirt, lad" he observed, tilting his head as if to get a better view.

Christian kept his eyes on the tablecloth and didn't reply as he reached for the potatoes.

"What do you say, Christian?" Mrs. Reicharte asked.

"Thank you."

"Thank you what?" Mr. Reicharte barked. "Don't they teach you no respect up there? I'm payin' 'em an arm'n leg for heaven's sake."

"Thank you, Father, father," Christian replied.

"We've got 'em in St. Xavier's, Father, the boarding school," Mr. Reicharte informed the priest. "Is this the wine I've been saving, Pickle Puss?"

By way of reply, Mrs. Reicharte just folded her arms across her chest, pursed her lips, and went squinty-eyed livid. Meanwhile, Father Devine asked, "Isn't that the exclusive Jesuit school where the young man committed suicide?"

"Shore is. Saint Ignatius Loyola's crew. Give 'em a boy'n they'll send back a man. Even if it takes a few black'n blue marks."

"I see," the priest replied with a tentative inflection as he topped off his potatoes with a ladle full of gravy. Then, unaware of Mrs. Reicharte's expression of horror, he picked up his silverware, the knife, fork, and the spoon, and carefully wiped off each implement with the corner of the monogrammed table napkin.

"George Webber's kid got in on a welfare scholarship," Mr. Reicharte commented with a side-long glance and shoulder shrug for his wife whose mouth was stuck wide open. "I expect we'll be tithing that tab for years to..."

"Walter, you didn't pass Father Devine any cranberries," Mrs. Reicharte, recovering her composure, interrupted with a cautionary glint in her eyes.

Mr. Reicharte passed the cranberries which added another serving dish to the several which were already crowding the priest's plate.

"Christian, your elbow's," Mrs. Reicharte snapped as she handed a dish of pickles to the priest whose hands were full.

"Woe, slow down, folks!" Father Devine protested.

"Can I have some more potatoes?" Christian murmured.

"Say please," Mr. Reicharte ordered.

"Can or may?" Mrs. Reicharte questioned.

"I don't want any," Christian blurted out.

Angrily pointing his fork at Christian, Mr. Reicharte, with gravy dripping down his chin, lashed back, "What did you say?"

"Now, now, it's Christmas, Walter," Father Devine interrupted as he passed the potatoes to Christian. "Besides, they're good for growing boys. Aren't they Christian?"

Christian didn't respond, and Mrs. Reicharte shot a conspiring glance directly at her husband who recoiled, his head drooping over his plate as he stabbed a thick piece of turkey breast with his fork.

"What's your favorite subject?" the priest pursued.

"Hockey."

"Indeed, do you have a girlfriend?"

"How can I in an all boys' school?"

"I dare say," the priest acknowledged, taken aback.

"Don't be a wise acre," Mr. Reicharte admonished.

"Some more gravy, Father?" Mrs. Reicharte asked. She passed a green and brown duck-shaped gravy boat to the priest and added, "It's made from scratch."

"My, my," Father Devine asserted and accentuated his words by holding up his left hand slightly bent at the wrist with the thumb pressed against the tips of the second and third fingers. "My mother makes everything from scratch, even ice cream. We lived on a dairy farm."

"Is that a fact?" Mr. Reicharte said as he swished a mouthful of wine around in his mouth. "Ethel did too. She used to milk..."

"Walter!" Mrs. Reicharte angrily cut off her husband.

"But you did, Pickle Puss! I ought a know!"

Mrs. Reicharte's goiter bobbed, and there was a blast of music from the kitchen so loud that the lead crystal tear drops hanging from the glass chandelier above the table tinkled.

Mr. Reicharte looked over his shoulder toward the pantry and exclaimed, "Turn off that Communist propaganda, Rose!" and the music faded out. Then, setting his wine glass down like a judge's gavel, he contemplatively began picking his teeth with his fork while deliberating, "Whatever happened to Dorsey'n Como? Como could put a guy to sleep lookin' at 'em, but at least it was music, not dadblamed noise. More wine, Father, or maybe another high ball?"

"Times change, Walter," Father Devine replied, holding out his wine glass. His cheeks were a rosy pink which gave his face a cherub-like radiance beneath the ringlets of hair which curled over his forehead. (At a glance, Christian thought the priest's face reminded him of a picture of Julius Caesar in his Latin text or was it Nero?) "Just a dab now," the priest cautioned Mr. Reicharte by fluttering his pointy fingernails at his wine glass as Mr. Reicharte poured.

"Maybe so," Mr. Reicharte continued as he topped off the priest's glass, spilling some when he noticed his wife mouthing the word NOW at him. "But if you ask me, that Presley's another Commie pinko with a Jewish agent."

"I don't think so," the priest replied as he patted his lips with the tip of a chap stick. "I think he's like a freak hail storm in the summer. Here one minute and gone the next."

"Couldn't you say that for anybody?" Christian said without thinking, the sound of his own trilling voice making him cower.

With a razor-sharp glance for Christian and an appeasing eye for Father Devine, Mrs. Reicharte retaliated: "Children are to be seen and not heard, Christian."

Ignoring everyone, Mr. Reicharte cut in. "Did you see where Ed Sullivan had to cut 'em off at the waist 'cause a those nasty gyrations? Mary Mother of God, they're singin' about everything from doin' it in movie balconies and with hound dogs to havin' your balls on fire!"

"For God's sake, Walter!" Mrs. Reicharte exclaimed, her face a contortion of anger and disgust.

"Calm down, Walter," Father Devine added with a consoling look for Mrs. Reicharte who was draining her wine glass. "I don't think it's worth getting your blood pressure all out of whack. I think

Bishop Sheen had the right idea on his telecast the other night. Did you see it, folks?"

"Oh, well, yes..." Mrs. Reicharte stuttered.

"No, the fight was on," Mr. Reicharte contradicted.

"Indeed," the priest commented just as Christian dropped a fork full of peas on the tablecloth.

"Now look what you've done," Mrs. Reicharte barked.

"As I was saying, the bishop..."

"Some more turkey, Father?" Mrs. Reicharte interrupted with a venomous look for her husband.

"How 'bout some dressing?" Mr. Reicharte added, passing the plate.

Father Devine irritably held out his hand like a stop sign and snapped, "No, I'm fine. If I may finish for heaven's sake!"

Taken up short, Mr. and Mrs. Reicharte, their noses bulbous and red, exchanged shocked glances and took long pulls on their wine, immediately refilling their glasses from nearby bottles.

With an exasperated sigh, Father Devine continued, "As I was trying to say, the bishop remarked about how young people today have a spirit of sacrifice and surrender that comes from the knowledge that their own sins were the cause of the crucifixion.

"Amen," Mr. Reicharte flatly replied. Then he raised his wine glass in salute, put it down with a thud, and proceeded to blow his nose into his monogrammed cloth table napkin.

"Caveat emptor[31]," Christian heard a strong soprano voice unaccountably leap from his throat before he could stop it. Beside himself, he glued his eyes to his plate.

"Pardon me?" Father Devine challenged with a withering look for Christian.

"Mea culpa[32]," Christian, blushing deeply, involuntarily replied.

Mrs. Reicharte cut in, "Clean you plate, Christian. And don't talk with your mouth full. How many times have I told you that?"

"Don't you want to belong to the clean plate club?" Father Devine intervened, dressing his query in a church-door smile, and a wink for Mrs. Reicharte.

"No."

"I don't think that was an appropriate response, young man," Mrs. Reicharte quipped.

"The Jesuits'll clip that tongue," Mr. Reicharte offered.

"It's Christmas, folks," Father Devine reminded them, while tugging on his clerical collar as he held his glass out toward Mrs. Reichart who was already pouring.

"Me too, Pickle Puss," Mr. Reicharte said, holding out his glass.

With an intimidating glare, Mrs. Reicharte filled her husband's wine glass to the brim and then, turning her back slightly toward the priest, mouthed the word NOW. Her face was florid, and her porcelain-blue eyes had an unnatural shine in them.

---

[31]   Let the buyer beware.
[32]   My fault.

Discomposed, Father Devine commented, "This collar's a nuisance sometimes," and unsnapped a silver tab behind his neck which made the starched collar flap outward.

"Is it too hot, Father?" Mrs. Reicharte said, abruptly getting up. "Let me get the thermostat." Rushing to the thermostat which was on the wall behind the priest's chair, she feigned to adjust the temperature, and squinted at her husband while again mouthing the word NOW, her mouth like a black abyss.

Cowed, Mr. Reicharte drained his wine glass, loosened his tie, and unbuttoned the two top buttons of his shirt which exposed brown moles on his bumpy, hairless chest and a St. Christopher's medal. Then he ventured, "I've, ah, been meaning to ask you, Father..." He hesitated distracted by his wife's challenging, hands-on-her-hips demeanor behind the priest.

"Yes, Walter?" Father Devine asked. He caught Mr. Reicharte's eyes and glanced over his shoulder at Mrs. Reicharte who instantly began fiddling with the thermostat, her face a mask of concern.

Rose looked in from the butler's pantry, and Mrs. Reicharte motioned for her to clear the table, excused herself, and went into the pantry, nudging Mr. Reicharte's shoulder as she went by.

"What's for dessert, Ethel?" Mr. Reicharte asked over his shoulder.

"It's a surprise," Rose interceded and briskly walked out with a tray full of dirty dishes, the short skirt of her maid's costume revealing a pair of athletic legs which were not lost on Mr. Reicharte nor the priest, both of whose eyes were riveted on her mid-thigh hem line.

Clearing his throat, Mr. Reicharte took off his glasses and wiped the lenses with his table napkin. "I hope Ethel didn't make it," he absently commented.

"Now, now, Walter," the priest scolded and wagged his finger at Mr. Reicharte. "You were meaning to ask..."

Mrs. Reicharte suddenly appeared with a tray of pudding dishes filled to the brim with the surprise. It was a thick, creamy substance mixed with a dark, wrinkled fruit.

"What is it?" Mr. Reicharte asked while holding the dish he was handed right beneath his nose and sniffing.

"I slaved over a hot stove all morning," Mrs. Reicharte answered. The front of her bulky sack dress dropped exposing patches of talcum powder which stuck to her ample cleavage.

Mr. Reicharte poked a fingertip in his surprise and then licked his finger with an approving nod.

"Walter!" Mrs. Reicharte protested.

Father Devine fastidiously tasted a bit of the surprise on the end of a teaspoon. "Summa cum laude[33]," he commented and smacked his lips with satisfaction.

Christian picked at his surprise. He was wary of the black pieces which poked through the surface of the pudding. Mr. Reicharte and Father Devine ate greedily. Mrs. Reicharte sat straight up in her chair and shot perturbed glances at her husband at the other end of the table.

---

[33]   With (the highest) praise.

"What was that you started to ask about, Walter?" the priest commented between bites.

"Oh yeah," Mr. Reicharte said as if he'd forgotten. He licked his fingers and glanced at his wife whose face was livid. "I was wondering if I could have a list of all the parishioners at the church? You know. Phone numbers, addresses, and so forth."

With a barely perceptible glint of recognition in his eyes and a remote tremor in his voice, the priest cautiously replied, "That might be arranged, but I'd have to consult with the bishop about the ethics."

"Ethics?" Mr. Reicharte questioned, slugging down half a glass of wine.

"That's fine," Mrs. Reicharte interjected just as her husband was about to continue, "How about some more dessert, Father?"

"No, I don't think so."

"Oh, come on, Father. Don't be a poor sport."

"Oh, all right. If you insist."

"Walter?" Mrs. Reicharte questioned her husband with a Cheshire cat's grin on her face.

"Don't mind if I do," Mr. Reicharte replied with a wink for his wife. His big ears were bright red around the rims.

Mrs. Reicharte stepped on a button which was beneath the carpet under the table, and a few seconds later the door of the butler's pantry burst open and Rose came around the table with more servings of the surprise.

Digging into his second dish, Father Devine filled a conspiratorial lull in the conversation by instinctively changing the subject. "I hope you folks'll come over for bingo Wednesday nights," he said between bites. "We're going to start holding it in the new church annex."

"Wouldn't miss it for the world," Mr. Reicharte replied. He talked with a mouthful of the surprise while keeping his head bent over the dish. "Ethel walked away with fifty bucks last week. Did you know I donated the new bingo board? The numbers'll flash right up after you call 'em."

"It's lovely, Walter. I was there, remember? Business must be good."

Mr. Reicharte licked his fingers and wiped them on a corner of the tablecloth. "Just a second," he said. "I'll show you." He took out his wallet, opened it, and let an accordion of credit cards flip-flop to the floor. A dozen credit cards could be seen through the clear plastic windows.

"I dare say," Father Devine commented, raising an eyebrow, "you must have lots of lists."

"Your elbows, Christian," Mrs. Reicharte scolded and then said to the priest, "Mrs. Dillon donated a TV."

"She can afford it," Mr. Reicharte added.

"Is her husband still in real estate?" the priest asked.

"Yeah, he's got his own office now. I sold 'em life insurance years ago. He should be excommunicated by now. Third marriage'n all."

The numbers on the bingo board his father had donated blinked on an off in Christian's mind like an arcade bumper game, and the voices at the table faded away. On the first bingo night after the installation, his father and several others had worn their Knights of Columbus costumes. His father had worn his three-cornered hat with the plume, a tux with tails, a red sash, and first degree medals even though he'd only been an air raid spotter on Saturday afternoons. Christian remembered how his father had made him go along that night. His dry, cold hand had collared him behind the neck as he touted his personal code of ethics: "It's not what you know. It's who you know." The wool suit had made his skin literally crawl, not to mention the noose-like knot in the tie he was ordered to wear. When they entered the new bingo annex, the colored lights on the bingo board were blinking on and off illuminating the numbers already called for the bingo cards. Father Devine, who was wearing a green eyeshade and leather apron, turned the handle of a round, metal cage. The cage contained numbered balls which flew out of an opening. The priest called out, B-51, I-14, G-21, while ushers, wearing green money-changers' aprons, rushed among rows of tables to collect money from silver-haired ladies and gentlemen. Hanging on a front wall above a speaker's platform, there was a huge crucifix which bore the tortured body of Jesus, a gift donated by the Knights to venerate the opening of the new bingo annex which was joined to the church like an arm to a torso.

"We've got company, Christian."

Christian's ears popped, and there was a rush of air between them. The sounds in the room became exaggerated. Silverware clinked, his mother's voice twanged, and he could distinctly hear his father's lips smacking the surprise.

"Do you mind if I inquire as to what the surprise is, Mrs. Reicharte," the priest asked, gulping down some wine with a mouthful of the surprise. "Is it your own recipe? I've never tasted anything like it."

"It's prune whip, Father."

"Prune what?"

"Whip."

"I dare say. You certainly put in a lot of prunes."

"I call it creative cooking, ad libbing the recipes."

"Indeed, but prunes?"

"Did you see my four door, V-eight out front, Father?" Mr. Reicharte interrupted as he noisily scraped the bottom of his surprise dish.

"Indeed, but shouldn't it be in the garage?"

"Later, let 'em gawk for a while. Especially that Jew next door. Damn thing cost me an arm'n leg, but, like I tell my customers, charity begins at home."

"Oh," the priest countered, "I thought it began in church, Walter."

"Touché," Mr. Reicharte responded, holding up his wine glass in a toast, and then swilling what was left in the glass.

Their attention was suddenly distracted by Christian who self-consciously muttered, "Rose said," he paused, his ears turning shell pink, "'Charity begins in the heart.'"

A few moments of silence ensued while the adults exchanged bewildered glances, and then Mrs. Reicharte countered, "What would Rose know about it? She's never seen the inside of a church in her life."

Then it happened, the surprise: Ppppwwwwiit. Mr. Reicharte, listing noticeably to port, cracked wind, a noxious burst which left a stubborn odor.

"Bingo," Christian impulsively remarked under his breath.

Inhaling deeply, Mrs. Reicharte gave her husband, who was sheepishly staring at the tablecloth, a fierce glare and suggested that Christian take the priest to the amusement room to show him his electric train.

"That sounds feasible," Father Devine listlessly added, his eyes dull and his loose collar flapping beneath his jowls. "Coming, Walter?"

"Uh, I'll catch up later. Them prunes're attacking me already."

"You're excused, Christian," Mrs. Reicharte ordered.

Struggling up from the table with a double-fisted push, Father Devine tripped on a chair leg, recovered his balance, and wryly commented, "You're not planning on ad libbing any cakes for the church bazaar are you, Mrs. Reicharte?"

Peeved, but showing only a hint of anger in her small, round eyes, Mrs. Reicharte managed a strained smile and a curt reply. "Why, I hadn't intended to. Let Mrs. Overbee."

*   *   *   *   *   *   *

The amusement room was located in the basement at the end of a long, cement-floored hallway from which doors opened into a furnace room, storage room, laundry room, and canning room. It had black and white linoleum tiles on the floor and recessed fluorescent lights in the ceiling. A well-stocked bar made of oak stood along one wall. There was an old Spinet piano against another wall. A poker table with a green, felt top stood in the center of the room. An electric train rested on top of a long table next to the bar.

Father Devine came out of a corner bathroom. His face was ashen and sweaty, and his black suit coat, carelessly thrown over one arm, was severely wrinkled. His clerical collar flapped loosely around his neck. As if to himself, he observed, "Ad libbing with prunes, mind you."

"Rose tried to tell her," Christian remarked as the priest walked over and sat down on a stool next to Christian at the end of the train layout. Christian had removed his sport coat and was pushing the throttle of a large transformer. The HO gauge engine started down the looping figure-eight track while pulling some brightly colored box cars, flat cars, tankers, and a caboose. They both watched as the train moved around the track, through a tunnel, and over a plaster mountain. There was a loader, switches, a remote coupler, and a little two story station house with a tiny, plastic station master who went up and down the outside stairway when the train went by. Christian blew the whistle as the train chugged along the split-level layout and, keeping his eyes on the engine, bashfully commented, "I can make it smoke. Want to see it?"

"I dare say," Father Devine responded with a grimace. "I'd like to see that, but would you excuse me again? It's those darn prunes! I'll be right back."

"Maybe the booze too," Christian added as he uncoupled a flat car.

"Nonsense," the priest snapped as he scuttled into the bathroom.

Christian let the train fly around the tracks, and when the priest returned, his face livid, he asked, "Are you okay, Father? Your collar's falling off."

"I've gotta breathe, thank you," the priest snarled. Then, catching himself, he added, "The smoke's lovely. Perfect rings. I always wanted one of these things when I was a boy, but we couldn't afford it."

"Maybe you could get one now," Christian replied. He stopped the train and put another smoke pellet into the steam engine's smokestack.

"I don't know. They may frown on that at the rectory."

"Why?"

"Well, because, I don't know."

"You want to try it?"

"Me? No, you go ahead. Anyway, I didn't bring my engineer's cap."

"Here," Christian said. He handed a striped replica of an engineer's cap to the priest.

"No, no," Father Devine retorted and shooed the cap away with his fingertips as if it were a crown of thorns. "You wear it. It'll muss my hair."

Putting the cap on and flipping a switch, Christian unloaded a flat car and then started the train down the tracks. As the station master shot up the stairs and disappeared into the station, he asked, "Do you want to play a game or something?"

"That's a good idea. Do you have Chinese checkers or a jigsaw puzzle?"

"Jigsaws take too long, and I don't know where the checkers are. I know a neat mind-reading game though."

"Mind reading? I'm not sure if that's something you should be doing even if it were possible."

"But it's neat. It's only make believe. Come on."

The priest applied a dose of lip gloss. "I don't know..."

"Rose played."

"Yes, but your parents said she's a bit off base."

"My parents're off base."

"Oh, all right. As long as it's not a Ouija board or Tarot cards."

"I have to get some stuff," Christian interrupted. He ducked behind the bar on the other side of the room where he opened a couple drawers, rattled some plates around, and mysteriously lit several matches while popping his head up and down over the bar to see if the priest were watching. As he came out from behind the bar, he was carrying a couple of china plates. "Let's sit at the poker table across from each other," he said.

"Fine by me," Father Devine responded. They both sat down opposite one another. Christian put one end of a long piece of string into his mouth and held the other end out to the priest. "You have to put that end in your mouth," he said.

"What for?" Father Devine asked and lurched backward as if the end of the string were a viper's head.

"It's to keep our eyes connected. You've got to look right into my eyes all the time so I can see into your brain."

Father Devine assumed a pose of eternal patience. "Sure," he skeptically said and reluctantly clenched the end of the string between his front teeth. The string stretched across the table between them, each one holding one end of it between his teeth.

"Now," Christian said, handing the priest a plate, "hold this plate out in front of you. Keep the bottom facing me, and remember, you've got to keep eye contact all the time or it won't work."

With upward-rolling eyes, the priest snatched the plate as if he were only tolerating a child's whim out of the goodness of his heart.

"No, hold it by the edges, out in front of you just below eye level'n use both hands," Christian instructed.

Father Devine adjusted his plate and held it by the edges with both arms extended so the plate was out in front of him and just below eye level. The back of the plate faced Christian, and the back of Christian's plate faced the priest.

"Okay, keep lookin' into my eyes and concentrate hard on an object."

"Anything? Like a boot or whip or something?"

"Yeah, but don't say it out loud. Just think it."

"Okay, I'm thinking of something, but I don't believe I'm doing this. If the pastor saw me, he'd think I'd been drink...well, it's Christmas after all."

"I understand, Father. Can you see the object clearly in your head?"

"Indeed, but this is silly. Hurry up. My head's spinning."

"You've got to give me some clues. With your index finger, reach around and draw on the back of your plate the first letter of the object you're thinking of. No! You can't look 'cause we have to keep eye contact, remember?"

Shrugging his shoulders, the priest reached around to the back of his plate which faced Christian, and with his index finger, drew a large "A" on it. Christian simultaneously reached around and traced the shape of the same letter on the back of his plate which faced the priest.

Staring intently into the priest's bloodshot eyes, Christian exclaimed, "I think I'm getting it!"

"Come on then. I'm getting the hiccups," the priest snapped, burping.

"Okay, okay, trace the shape of the "A" on your cheek."

"What?"

"Like this," Christian said and used the tip of his index finger to trace the letter on his cheek.

Almost out of patience, Father Devine sighed deeply, pursed his lips around the string in his mouth, and drew the letter on his cheek with the comment, "This is ridiculous."

"Now the other one. Like this," Christian said, and the priest followed along, his face florid. "Now down your nose like this and across your forehead."

Squinting inquisitively from beneath his eyebrows as if something were dawning on him, Father Devine brushed his index finger over his cheek, nose, and forehead exactly the way Christian had done.

"Touch the end of your nose like this," Christian said, his cheeks puffing out like an exotic fish's.

Sighing and shaking his head back and forth, Father Devine mimicked Christian. Then, with the abruptness of someone who has just heard a strange sound in a dark room, his entire body stiffened, the string dropped from his mouth, and his head canted slightly to one side while his eyes converged on his index finger which he held in front of his face as if testing for wind direction. "Saints above!" he shouted as he peered back and forth between the pad of his index finger and the inscrutable balloon-fish smile on Christian's face. "What's this smudge?"

Mrs. Reicharte suddenly interrupted from the doorway. "What's going on down here?" she asked while giving Father Devine an inquisitive once over.

Both Christian and the priest looked toward the door where Mrs. Reicharte's girth blotted out the light in the hallway.

"Holy Mother of God!" Mrs. Reicharte exclaimed. She was staring, thunderstruck, at Father Devine.

With a withering look at Christian, Father Devine got up from the table and went over to the bar where there was a mirror behind some bottles on a shelf. Putting his hands on his hips, he puffed his chest out, tilted his head at a slight angle, and looked into the mirror. His face rapidly changed colors from hangover pale, to pink, to scarlet. There were black streaks and smudges on his cheeks, nose and forehead. "Why you little...little...devil in disguise!" he stammered as he gaped at his reflection, his eyes rimmed with fluid.

Outraged, Mrs. Reicharte ambled over to Christian, grabbed the rim of his ear, and dragged him out of his chair and over to the priest. "You should be ashamed of yourself!" she exclaimed. "I told you never to do that trick again! My good chinaware too!"

"But Rose laughed for a week," Christian replied, trying to pull his ear away from his mother's grasp.

"Apologize this instant!"

"But I didn't mean..."

"Take off that cap and apologize!"

"I'm sorry."

"I'm sorry what?" she wailed and tugged on Christian's ear while he cringed in agony, his eyes involuntarily tearing.

"I'm sorry, Father," he said, dropping the engineer's cap on the floor.

Staring into the mirror, the priest angrily remarked, "I can't believe I fell for this tomfoolery," and wiped his face with a white handkerchief which only smeared the sooty residue. "By Jesus, would you look at this mess?" he said to Mrs. Reicharte and held out his soiled handkerchief which hung from the tips of his thumb and index finger.

"Let's go upstairs, Father," Mrs. Reicharte said while still holding on to Christian's cauliflowered ear, "and I'll get you a washcloth."

"And let Walter see this?" the priest interjected. "Not on your life! The Knights'll be joshin' me for life. The bishop might even find out. It could get all the way to the archbishop for Pete's sake!"

"Walter's been in the bathroom all afternoon. I told him he should be down here. But don't worry Father..."

"Don't worry?"

"No, I'll make sure he doesn't mention this to anyone. The list, you know."

"List? That's another thing I'd..."

"We'll have another high ball after we get cleaned up."

"Don't patronize me, and I don't want another high ball," the priest snarled and sheepishly looked at his reflection again as if he were unable to comprehend the reality of his situation. Then, with his fists clenched at his sides, and his blue eyes turning yellow as if he were fighting an interior battle with the devil, he snapped his clerical collar back on and walked out the door.

"You stay right here, young man!" Mrs. Reicharte exclaimed with a sharp tug on Christian's ear. "Your father's going to be hysterical. Don't you have any sense at all? Do you think I cater 'til I'm blue in the face because it's a pleasure? I'm sick'n tired of kowtowing." Her jowls quivered, and her lips were severely drawn downward as she let go of Christian's ear. With her slip showing beneath the irregular hem of her sack dress, she waddled out of the room and slammed the door.

Christian cupped his ear in one hand and took several deep breaths to dam the tears. He ran out of the room, down the hallway, and up the stairs to the landing by the first floor door which had been left open: "He was Ethel's idea, Father," he overheard his father say. "I don't know what gets into him. Sometimes I think he's one a them paranoid schizophrenics. You know, two or three people bottled up in one. There's no hurry, Father. Here, let me help you with that overcoat. There now. Are you sure you won't stay for the game? There's more wine."

"I've had quite enough of your brand of hospitality, Mr. Reicharte."

"Let me get you one for the road at least. I was counting on you for the game."

"The game or the list?"

"Oh, I'd forgotten. What about the list?"

"What list? My hat, please."

When he heard the door close behind the priest, Christian cringed at the hysteria in his father's voice: "Ethel!"

"For heaven's sake, stop yelling," Mrs. Reicharte said as she lumbered out of the dining room into the living room where she pulled back a front window drape. "He's not even to his car yet."

"But the list!"

"I heard him! Why didn't you just say it was for Christmas cards?"

"You were eavesdropping again? What if he seen you? I've asked you not to do that a dozen times, Ethel!"

"Don't you yell at me, Walter Joseph!"

"Don't call me that! Where the hell did you get that hairdo?"

"Don't you dare take it out on me, Mr. Reicharte!"

"But it looks like cotton candy, God dammit! He was staring at it!"

"I'll have you know it cost you twenty dollars, and it's the latest thing! If you read something besides the Wall Street Journal, you'd 'ave seen it! It's a beehive."

"A what? Maybe on a thirteen year old. And that dress looks like a flour sack for Christ's sake!"

"Well, I never...just who do you think you're talking to? Your sister's a shining example of fashion I suppose."

"Don't even mention..."

"You'd think she was born on skid row the way she wears those hand-me-downs. Besides, it's that waif you should be taking it out on not me, Mr. Big Shot with the credit cards!"

"You're the one who suggested the underground network, mommy."

"Stop calling me that! Children are God's messengers, you said."

"What will people think, you said."

"Someone to hit baseballs to, you said. Why, you couldn't run to third base without having a heart attack! I've never seen you lift a finger..."

"I'm gonna beat the daylights out of 'em right now!"

Christian shut the door and bolted back down the stairs and into the amusement room. A few minutes later his father came in. Wearing only a pair of slippers and an undershirt tucked into a loosely hanging pair of slacks, he hefted a belt in one hand and hitched up his pants with the wrist of his other hand. "You've managed to embarrass us good this time," he said. "Do you have any God damned idea how much this will cost me in premiums, schlemiel?"

Christian cowered, and for a split second he thought he saw Father Dittman's scarecrow face reflected in his father's bloodshot eyes.

"You should be ashamed of yourself! Money don't grow on trees you know! Do you think we had that gilded lily over here for our health? Why, I could buy'n sell 'em in a minute. Walkin' out on me, God dammit! Look at me, you little bastard!"

With that Mr. Reicharte lashed out with the belt. Christian instinctively put a hand out and backed into the train table which caused the engine's whistle to mysteriously make a short burst. "Stand still, you little devil!" Mr. Reicharte hollered and lashed out again. Christian pivoted, and the belt looped around and missed him by a mile. Mr. Reicharte, potbellied, and tipsy, lost his balance and fell into the train table which caused the engine's whistle to sound off again. Glasses askew, he lashed out several times with the belt, but Christian deftly feinted this way and that which caused Mr.

Reicharte to miss his mark and finally strike a direct hit on the train depot. The station master shot down the steps and back up again, and a little red door slammed shut behind him. "Get over here!" Mr. Reicharte screeched as he clumsily shuffled around in his slippers while holding his drooping pants up with his wrist. "Stop dancing around like a peacock and take your punishment like a man!" Then, with his left hand, he suddenly reached out and grabbed Christian's nose between his knuckles. Firmly knuckling the nose, he jerked Christian's head back and forth while hollering, "Don't ever let me catch you doing something like that again! Do-you-hear-me? That was your meal ticket that walked out the door, moron!"

Christina's knees buckled beneath him as Mr. Reicharte squeezed his nose in a vice-like grip. He jerked it for emphasis: "Do-you-hear-me?"

"Yeah," Christian answered and sunk to his knees as jolts of pain shot through his head.

"Yeah, what?" and another jerk for good measure.

"Yeah, Father," Christian replied, backing into the train table.

Mr. Reicharte lashed out at the engine and it toppled, taking a few cars with it. And get rid of that shirt! You look like a God damned faggot!" he exclaimed as he walked out and slammed the door so hard that a piece of plaster fell from the ceiling.

Sinking to the floor in a trembling heap, Christian felt his nose. It was numb, and some blood oozed from one nostril. An all-consuming mortification sent chills shuddering through his body. His chest heaved in dry sobs as he tried to dam the tears.

"Christian?" Rose queried as she opened the door a crack and peered into the room.

"I'm over here."

"What happened? Rose commented as she walked over to where Chrisitan was slumped on a stool. She did a deep knee bend in front of him and took his chin in her hand, the hem of her maid's uniform hiking up to mid-thigh.

Shocked by the sight of her red panties," Christian involuntarily barked, "Arf!"

"Cute," she giggled. "I was in the laundry room. It sounded like a cock fight in here and they're fighting cats'n dogs upstairs. The priest left in a snit. Here, wipe your nose with this Kleenex. It's bleeding. What'd you do to 'em anyway?"

"The mind-reading game."

"Fortuna favet fortibus[34]," she said, emphasizing each word.

"Tacticus," Christian replied and wiped his eyes on the short sleeve of his Hawaiian print shirt, the tears blending with the blue sea at the foot of a swaying palm tree.

"Mentum mortalia tangunt[35]," Rose added as she swept the hair out of Christian's eyes with a soft caress. "I've been reading your textbooks."

"You should be taking my Latin tests."

"Here," she said and handed him a peppermint patty from her apron pocket. She popped one into her own mouth and commented, "Look, you've got to savor it. Let the chocolate bleed all over your teeth like this."

---

[34] Fortune favors the brave.
[35] Mortal things touch the heart.

"Ummm," Christian commented while licking the chocolate from his front teeth and eyeballing the books under Rose's arm. He thought he smelled a trace of alcohol too, not to mention his mother's perfume. "What're you reading now? Something for your night class?"

"Yeah," she replied and took the paperbacks from under her arm. "I almost forgot about 'em. One of your Latin books and Jung."

"Jung?"

"Yeah, for my psyche class.

"What's it about?

"Shadows."

"Really? I have one. She's a Roman spy I think."

"We've all got someone under lock and key. Oh, speaking of shadows. Guess what's on? She went over to a small radio on the bar. She turned it on and tuned it while commenting over her shoulder, "It's just about time."

"Is it Wednesday?" Christian asked.

"Yeah'n seven o'clock."

The radio buzzed as she adjusted the tuner, and then you could hear the omniscient, cynical laugh of the Shadow. It was followed by his deep, measured voice: "The Shadow knows," the voice echoed and then there was a haunting laugh which sent chills down the backs of gangsters. The announcer's voice came on, and Rose went over to the poker table. She set the Latin text and the dog-eared copy of Jung on the green surface and sat down. Christian sat down beside her. The announcer was saying: "Lou Cole presents the mystery man who strikes terror into the hearts of sharpsters, law breakers, and criminals." Rose took out a pack of Lucky Strikes and plucked two out of the pack, handing one to Christian and lighting them both.

"Guess you found 'em," Christian abstractly commented, taking a shallow puff.

"The Shadow knows," Rose replied, blowing a perfect smoke ring which undulated in the air.

They split the mints and listened to the radio program wherein the Shadow deftly trapped the bad guy inside the very safe the gangster intended to rob. When the cops opened the safe, the bad guy, gasping for breath, was lying in a crumpled heap on the floor, and the Shadow's ominous baritone emanated from the walls: "You cannot run from your shadow, Mr. Duvall. This the Shadow knows." This was followed with the Shadow's spine-tingling laugh, and Rose got up and turned off the radio while asking, "Do you want to play the piano? Your nose's stopped bleeding."

Feeling his nose with his fingertips, Christian said, "I guess so," and went over and sat down with her at an old Spinet upright. He played and she sang:

> How much is that dog-gy in the window?
> I do hope that dog-gy's for sale.
> (Christian: Arf! Arf!)
> I read in the pap-ers there are rob-bers
>
> With flash-lights that shine in the dark;
> My love needs a dog-gy to protect him
> And scare them a-way with one bark.
> (Christian: Arf! Arf!)

When she kissed him, it was like a freshly watered, unopened rose had been placed in his mouth and gently rotated. For a moment he couldn't breathe, but then she released him, and he managed one more feeble, not very believable, bark.

*   *   *   *   *   *   *   *

It was a bitterly cold afternoon. The sky was pale and sagging like a wet blanket. The wind whipped the snow into swirling eddies from the tops of snow banks. Sharp, dagger-shaped icicles hung from the coving around the rooftop of the brown-brick dormitory building. Huddled in the doorway, Webber and Snyder were arguing, and boys milled restlessly about on the sidewalk. Half listening to the boys argue, Christian shuffled aimlessly around the fringe of the group. A vague feeling of unease clutched at his gut as he pulled up the fur collar of his flight jacket. He thought the feeling might be the result of the bleak weather, but when his eyes wandered toward a row of shimmering third-floor dormitory windows, he saw the real source of his jitters. Father Dittman, both hands tucked into the waist sash of his cassock, was studying him with a fierce stare that reached right into his pockets. Unnerved, he looked away and when he stole a return glance the priest was gone.

"He can too!" Webber's voice nudged Christian.

"He can't!" Snyder rebuffed.

"Can too."

"How much yah wanna put on it, four eyes?"

"You never paid me for the pool game, whale bait."

"The bursar's not open, dim wit."

"Who you callin' a dim wit?"

"I'm lookin' at you ain't I, Webber?"

"You'd better take it back, or I'll slug yah, Snyder!"

"You do'n I'll tell Father Dittman soon as he comes to take roll. Nobody can do a flip off that elevator shaft. Only one guy ever tried it'n he broke his neck. My father said!"

"How's your daddy know anything 'bout it?"

"He went here, dummy. Everybody knows he's on the board of directors. S.L. Snyder of Snyder and Cohen Chemicals."

"Whoop-dee-doo!" Webber mocked and snapped the hood of his parka over his head. "What's he make? Toilet bowl cleaner?"

Making a perfectly round hole between his lips, Snyder stuck his tongue out at Webber and whined, "You'd better shut your trap. I could get you expelled, you know. My father gives this school buckets a money! He used to be senior class president when he went here, bub."

"I'm shakin' all over, bub," Webber retaliated. He held his hands out and shook them and pretzeled his double-jointed, gangly body until it looked like it was going to fall apart. "Did daddy wear that pilot's cap too?"

Crowding around, the boys laughed at Webber's antics, and Snyder, pulling on the unbuckled chin straps of his pilot's cap, stuck his double-chinned face up toward Webber's and cried out, "This cap was my father's in the war, bub! I'll thank you not to make fun of it or..."

"Or what, bub?"

"Or else," Snyder backed down.

"Twenty bucks says he can do it, daddy-o, Webber persisted.

"I'll back 'em" Valeno, a runty Italian kid put in.

"Me too," Moffitt, a lop-eared lad added.

"He'll bust his ass," Snyder charged.

"Bull shit, fatty," Moffitt exploded. "He made the other jump look easy didn't he?"

"I could've done that," Snyder bragged with a sing-song cockiness.

"Vat? You couldn't get out've a sandbox widout bustin' yer butt!" Polinski, the custodian, yelled from the outer edge of the group and everyone roared with laughter.

"Enim suae est virtutis[36]!" Christian impulsively shouted, the words sounding as if they'd sprung from a shadow at his side like a ventriloquist's. It was her again.

Everyone stopped talking and turned around to stare at Christian who'd been standing quietly at the rear of the group. By the looks of anticipation in the boys' eyes, Mr. Polinski's too, Christian knew his fate was already sealed, and the words he'd heard spoken from the prostitute's windowsill echoed in his mind: Alea iacta est, the die is cast.

"Valor my ass!" Snyder bellowed. It's suicide'n you sound like a little girl."

"In vino veritas[37]," the words involuntarily sprang from Christian's mouth, and everyone looked at one another with expressions of amazement.

---

[36] It is of my valor!
[37] In wine is truth.

"Sui generous[38]," Snyder misquoted and shrugged his shoulders while giving Christian a look of disbelief. "It's your Latinate girlfriend's ass in a sling, not mine, show off."

"Sui generous up your Latinate ass, egghead," Webber squawked.

Just then the ear-splitting sound of the school bell which was hung on the brick facade of the dormitory building jarred the daylights out of everybody. Father Dittman, the deep sleeves of his black cassock flapping like wings, flew out of the dorm with a clipboard which had a stubby pencil attached to it by a piece of string. Waving the clipboard, he held up the hem of his cassock with the other hand and yelled, "Line up!" as the boys scrambled into place for roll call.

"Can we see the tattoo after?" Snyder pleaded with Polinski who was hurrying away. "Can we? Can we?"

"Haven't you got work to do, Mr. Polinski?" Dittman hollered as he rushed up like a military advisor, his attention focused on some papers attached to his clipboard.

"He didn't show it, Father!" Snyder yelped.

Polinski, wearing a green military fatigue jacket, continued on, but when he got behind Father Dittman, he stopped and pointed to his upper arm. Then he pulled out a cigar stub and waved it. Snyder made an okay circle with his thumb and index finger and held it up to Polinski who nodded and hurried away.

Unseeing, the man with eyes in the back of his head, flipped some papers over on his clipboard and barked, "Krowell!"

"Here!" a boy in line responded. He was a tall, athletic boy with black, greased ducktails sweeping behind his ears.

---

[38]   Of its own kind, unique. (Correct form: Sui generis)

"Moffitt!"

"Here!"

"Got your lines?"

"No, Father."

"Double 'em! Valeno?"

"Here!"

"Dunbar!"

"Here!"

"Walsh!"

"Here!"

"Reicharte!"

"President!"

There was a snicker along the line of boys. They were craning their necks out of line to look at Christian who was biting his lower lip in misgiving. The word, to his chagrin, had shot from his mouth like a silver bullet.

Shushing the boys with an evil-eyed look down the end of his beaked nose, Dittman retaliated with: "Maybe you'd like to attend comedian's class in the rector's office, Reicharte? We could even invite your parents to come for the show."

With sagging shoulders, Christian stuck his hands into his trouser pockets and stared at the ground.

"I thought not," Dittman carped and referred back to his clipboard. "Webber!"

"Ah, here," Webber replied, his long neck withdrawing into his collar like a frightened turtle's.

"Cat got your tongue, Webber?"

"Ah, no, Father, I ah, ah, well..."

"Conscience, Webber? Maybe it's the overdue lines."

"Yes, Father, but I had to do a detention for Father..."

"Triple 'em!"

"But..."

"Snyder!"

"I'm here, Father Dittman," Snyder whinnied.

Father Dittman read the rest of the names on his list, checking names off as the boys responded. In spite of the cold, he walked along the line of boys like a drill sergeant and had several boys open their coats so he could check for black ties and white button-down shirts. He gave Valeno three demerits for no tie, and Christian got five for wearing his Hawaiian print shirt. Dunbar got five for not having his prayer beads at Mass. Finally, he dismissed everyone with a warning to go directly to study hall. As the students pulled parka hoods over their heads and hurried away, he exclaimed, "Not you, Reicharte! You're going to stay here and run ten laps around the football field! President notwithstanding!

*   *   *   *   *   *   *

With an over-sized head set directly on top of his stooped shoulders Father Oxley, bent almost in half like a serf paying homage, rolled out, as if on castors, from behind his desk. His feet were hidden by the hem of his cassock which dusted the floor of the elevated platform that overlooked the neon-lighted study hall. According to Snyder, Oxley's back had once been broken by a bell which broke loose in the cathedral bell tower and grazed his back on its plunge to the floor. Snyder had also claimed that the priest's hair had turned stark white on the day he'd seen blood squirting from the cathedral walls. Just as the hunchback was about to speak, Christian ducked into his desk in row five.

"You're tardy, Mr. Reicharte!" the ancient bell ringer cackled, his thatched head cocked sharply upward. The students responded to the priest's admonition by turning around in their desks which were bolted to the floor.

"But I was running laps for Father..."

"Tardy's tardy! You should know better by now! Why were you late? Never mind. Late's late! Sed fugit interea, fugit irreparabile tempus[39]!"

"But I had to run ten..."

"Ten demerits," Oxley interrupted and waved the gnarled stub of his hand like a club.

"Sonus ad aurem[40]," Christian snapped before he could get his hand over his mouth.

"Pardon me?" the startled priest asked when everyone laughed.

---

[39]   But meanwhile time flies, time the irrevocable.
[40]   You make a noise in my ear.

Helplessly, Christian replied, "Lapsus linguae[41]."

Taken aback, Father Oxley noted, "Seems you know your Latin a might better'n your F average shows, Mr. Reicharte. Why not let the rest of the world benefit from your genius? Like translating Cicero from page six."

Snyder laughed out loud, and the rest of the class smothered giggles. Snyder crossed one index finger over the other and moved it back and forth while smugly pointing toward Christian who was rushing to page six of his Latin text.

"Mind your own business, Norman!" Father Oxley snarled at Snyder. Then he ambled across the lecturer's platform, and sat down behind his desk. Taking out a large handkerchief, he mopped his forehead and blew his nose loudly which caused a round of snickers from the back of the room. With a long, withering stare, he snapped the boys back to attention and continued: "I want you all to buckle down and start paying more attention to your spiritual obligations. There's a certain element around here sui generis[42]." He hesitated as if trying to recall his place, and flakes of dandruff fell on his shoulder when he scratched the side of his head.

"A certain element, Father," Snyder piped in from row three, seat one, right in front of the speaker's platform.

"Indeed, thank you, Norman. A certain element who may not be in the state of grace. Carpe diem[43]. Verbum sapiente[44], the Lord doesn't take us away at our convenience, you know."

---

[41]   A slip of the tongue.
[42]   Of its own kind, unique.
[43]   Make use of the day.
[44]   A word to the wise.

Many of the boys secretly glanced at the others. Some lifted their desk tops and ducked behind them while shuffling books around. Like an ancient owl on a tree limb, Father Oxley tilted his enormous head almost to his left shoulder, stood up, and glared at the boys while tapping his fingertips together just beneath his thick nose. Then, in a soft, maternal tone, he continued, "If you think you can put a hood over God's eyes, you've got another thing coming. Put that desk top down, and pay attention, Moffitt! You too, Valeno! Sed libera nos a malo[45]. Where're your manners. Now, where was I? Oh, rigor mortis[46]!"

"The part about making use of the day, carpe diem, and verbum sapiente, a word to the wise, Father," Snyder highhandedly commented while rubbing his knuckles on his chest.

"Yes, I remember now. The deus ex machina's[47] next." He held his forehead with his fingertips and absently mumbled to himself. Then he approached the front of the platform and continued, "Verbum sapiente, indeed. Some sick person is cutting pictures out of the National Geographic in the library. A number of back issues featuring Africa and New Guinea are missing in toto[48]."

When the priest paused and peered around the room, a bloated silence ensued. There was only the faint buzz of the long, overhead, neon light strips. Boys' eyes guardedly flitted left and right. Others had their noses down on their desks as if ducking gunfire. Seizing the moment, Oxley retired to his desk and resolutely added, "God does not pay weekly. He pays at the end. Ora pro nobis[49]."

---

[45]   Deliver us from evil.
[46]   The stiffness of death.
[47]   An artificial device.
[48]   In full, wholly.
[49]   Pray for us.

With that, the priest sat down and began reading from his breviary, but not without gazing over the top of his book at the new Latin scholar in row three who was busily writing from his Latin text. He recalled giving Reicharte an F for the semester in Latin. The boy had a wild cowlick and oddly mismatched eyes, one violet and one hazel. He puzzled at the boy's sudden Latin proficiency and summarily fell asleep.

"P-s-s-t," someone whispered across the aisle as he kicked a note across the floor toward Christian's desk.

Keeping one eye on Father Oxley, Christian cautiously leaned out from his desk, picked up the note, and unfolded it behind his Latin text which was opened to his favorite page with the picture of a Roman kid riding a great white stallion. The note read: Five more purgatory certificates if you do it, wise acre. After lights out.

Feeling the contradictory impulses of flight or fight, Christian thoughtfully turned the note over and over in his hands. He could still get out of it. He was beside himself when he said he'd do it. It was impulsive and careless of him. She'd spoken through him again: It is of my valor, indeed. He wished she'd speak for herself next time. He took one of Snyder's certificates out of his desk. To keep him quiet about the restroom incident, Snyder had added free purgatory certificates as payoffs. Krowell and Moffitt had bought some, and Webber was indebted for a dozen. Crude drawings of angels drinking malted milks at a soda fountain in the clouds adorned the top of the certificate, and at the bottom there were blazing fires with arms and legs sticking out of the flames. In between the drawings, Snyder had neatly printed a title: Certificate of Reduced Time In Purgatory. Then he spelled out the terms of the certificate: For the price of one dollar or one dessert, this certifies that the bearer shall receive a one year reduction in purgatory time in the event of his death. The bearer signed it, and Snyder co-signed it like this:

Norman Snyder, Broker. Christian took a long look at his certificate and another look at Snyder's note. Then, in spite of himself, he tore the certificate in half and wrote a note back to Snyder: Put your money where your mouth is.

Just then, Snyder turned around in his seat and leaned out of it. Holding on to a long piece of string with a piece of chewed gum attached, he threw the gum down the aisle. When the gum reached the foot of his desk, Christian folded his note and attached it to the gum. Snyder reeled the string in and retrieved the note just as Oxley's enormous head bobbed up. Rubbing his eyes with both fists, he hollered, "Are you sending notes again, Norman?"

"Who me, Father?" Snyder asked and pointed at his chest with a look of utter bewilderment.

"Is there anyone else here by that name?"

"No."

"Well?"

Snyder opened both hands palms up and shrugged, his face a perfect mask of innocence.

"Your father's endowments won't keep you out of hell, Norman. Remember that. How 'bout you Webber?"

"I don't have no notes," Webber replied and self-consciously pushed his horn-rimmed glasses up on his nose when everyone snickered.

"Any notes, Mr. Webber. How can you expect to learn Latin if you can't speak English?"

Webber just shrugged his shoulders and refused to look up.

"If I catch anyone in here passing notes," Father Oxley continued, losing his balance when he got up from the chair but catching himself, "I'll have him translating Cicero all night long. Deus Vuet[50]! Now, put up your books. The bell's about to ring."

The bell rang, and Christian stuck his fingers into his ears to stifle the piercing clang. He hurried down the aisle, but Oxley spotted him just as he was going through the double doors at the rear of the study hall.

"Sanctum, sanctorum[51]!" Father Oxley blurted out. "I almost forgot. I want to see you a minute, Mr. Reicharte!"

Christian stopped at the doorway, and Father Oxley came up to him as boys pushed by into the hallway. The priest's hair stood on end like an electric shock victim's, and his wrinkled face was a mask of arthritic pain. When the last student disappeared out the exit, he cackled, "I've been meaning to ask you about these demerits you've been collecting. Twenty-five to date. That's almost one per diem[52] this month. Tardies, homework, overdue lines, attire..."

"Seniors wear turtlenecks."

"I know. Against my expressed wishes, the rector's relaxed the dress code. I opposed this khaki and dress shirt thing ab initio[53]. Where's your tie?"

"I don't know. The seniors aren't wearin' 'em."

---

[50] God wills it!

[51] Holy of holies!

[52] By the day.

[53] From the beginning.

"No one's wearing gaudy painted shirts either," Oxley replied, his voice brittle with suppressed pain. "Why, they used to wear full ROTC uniforms around here before they started these so-called endowments. Now, the parents're running things, not the rector. Private rooms for seniors no less. And televisions. Monks ears! Next, they'll be bringing girls up, and you're not winning any popularity contests around here, Mr. Reicharte. Sometimes I feel you're not altogether. Why can't you behave?"

"I'm not altogether."

"Ha, right. Maybe I should get down on my knees'n pay homage. Your grades aren't altogether either. They're infra dignitatem[54]. What do you have to say for yourself?"

"Nolo contendere[55]."

"No contest?"

"Ipso facto[56]."

"What? Are you making fun of us now.

"Non sequitur[57]."

"Pardon me?"

"Obiter dictum[58],"

The Latin phrases reflexively leaped from Christian's mouth like frogs into a pond. They were out of his mouth and gone before

---

[54]   Beneath one's dignity.
[55]   No contest.
[56]   By virtue of the same fact.
[57]   It does not follow.
[58]   A passing remark.

he'd been able to translate them as if he were possessed by some silver-tongued banshee.

"A passing remark, is it, Reicharte?" the priest countered, his voice a shrill crescendo, and his expression a tangled web of bewilderment, anger, curiosity, and apprehension. "What I say does not follow, Mr. Reicharte? By all means, Mr. Reicharte, maybe you should be teaching seniors' Latin instead of me. Get out before I run you off to the rector's. Why, I declare, non sequitur. Obiter dictum. Ipso facto, monk's ears!" Christian took off, lickety-split, but not fast enough to avoid hearing Father Oxley's admonishment which followed him down the corridor like a communicable disease: "Sed libera nos a malo[59]!"

At the end of the hallway on the landing next to the elevator shaft Webber, Valeno, Moffitt, and a couple of other boys guys were arguing about who was cutting up the National Geographic. Snyder was selling purgatory certificates to a couple of guys. When Christian approached, Webber wanted to know if he was kidding about the flip down the elevator shaft. Valeno was afraid they'd all get expelled. Snyder cut in, "Right after lights out, buddy boy. Fifty bucks." His friends folded their arms across their chests and displayed the smug smiles of soothsayers.

A reply flew out of Christian's mouth like a perfectly pitched note from an opera singer, "Vici![60]"

Aghast, Snyder glared at Christian, and the smirks of his friends caved into slack-jawed expressions of surprise. Suddenly, a voice boomed down the elevator shaft from an upper floor: "Why are you boys malingering?"

---

[59] Deliver us from evil!
[60] I conquered!

"I'm not, Father!" Snyder whinnied as he scurried up the stairs. "I was tryin' to find out who's takin' the National Geographic!"

"God already knows!" echoed down the shaft.

They all bolted up the stairs. Webber tripped on one of the steps and lost his glasses. When Christian stopped to pick them up, he was knocked down from behind but still managed to recover the glasses unbroken. He gave them back to Webber at the second-floor landing where Dittman, wearing a threadbare black cassock which drooped over his shoulders, stood with his hands on his hips. He had a thick black prayer book stuck in the black sash around his waist, and he stood beneath a dim light bulb which hung from the ceiling by a tangled cord. His elongated shadow bobbed on the wall behind him as he monitored the boys on their way into the dormitory.

In the dormitory, boys were standing around the narrow aisles between curtained alcoves. Everyone was talking about Christian's chances of surviving a flip down the elevator shaft, and some were making side bets. The idea of someone doing a somersault into the abyss, falling all the way to the basement, and landing on a huge pile of laundry bags was unheard of. A plain jump was one thing, but a flip was out of the question from two stories up.

When the lights blinked on and off, signaling the three-minute warning, Christian pulled his curtain shut and slipped under the covers with his cords, shirt, and tennis shoes still on. Feeling a lump beneath his pillow, he reached beneath it and pulled out a copy of the National Geographic. He'd have to be more careful and make sure he taped it behind the dresser as there could be an alcove or locker search any day now. He quickly flipped to the dog-eared page. She was still there, peeking out from behind the palm tree, her dark brown eyes staring right at him and her head slightly tilted as if she were trying to signal him. Her swarthy skin glistened in the tropical sunlight which flickered between palm trees. The lights went out suddenly so he got up, taped the magazine behind the dresser, and pushed the dresser into the wall.

Back in bed, his thoughts shifted quickly to the elevator shaft. Appearing in his mind's eye like a long, thick, coiling cobra, the narrow shaft swayed from side to side, opening its mouth wide as if to swallow him. The idea of the flip had come about almost in spite of himself. He'd mentioned it to Webber who said it was a daredevil stunt. Like the first jump, it was as if another self were taking over and he was just a frightened spectator. Backing out now was out of the question. His fear was profound, but the compulsion was diabolical, almost as if he were possessed by a fearless demon, not a little Latin wizard. Suddenly, the curtain of his alcove rustled, and he could hear the faint, intermittent sound of Dittman's breath being exhaled from his nose as he lurked in the dark aisle between alcoves. He heard a long, low moan from Webber's alcove next door. It was followed by the sound of stifled giggling across the aisle. Then the curtain next door snapped open, and Dittman hollered: "Take your hand out from under those covers this instant!"

Webber groaned, and everyone in the dorm laughed behind their curtains. Dittman hollered again, "No wonder you're blind as a bat, Webber!" Webber's curtain snapped shut, and Dittman's flashlight scuttled across the ceiling which could be seen through the open tops of the alcoves. The laughter faded, and the flashlight went out. For a long while, there was absolute silence in the dorm as the boys listened for Dittman to double back, but there was nary a footstep nor the click of rosary beads. Christian could hear the palpitations of his own heart which was pounding like a bongo drum.

"P-s-s-t," Webber signaled from the narrow ledge which ran along the top of the wooden partition which separated the alcoves. "That was close. Hey, are yah still gonna do it?"

"Nihil agendo homines male agere doscunt[61]," Christian heard himself say in a sultry voice unlike his own. Then he sprang from the cot as if pulled by a ghost.

"I failed Latin, Christian. But are you? Hey, wait for me to get down."

Stopping a moment to double-knot his high-top, black-and-white basketball shoes, Christian opened his curtain. He could see several shadows skulking toward the doorway, and then Webber, squinting through his coke glasses, came up behind him. Slinking along the wall, they worked their way in the dark toward the corridor.

There was a dim emergency light burning in a wire cage on the ceiling above the elevator shaft. The landing light had been turned off. The stairway was dark, and the boys' shadows wavered over the linoleum floor and wire screen that surrounded the deep shaft. Snyder had on his lime-green terry cloth bathrobe with a pair of backless leather slippers. Huddled together, Moffitt and Valeno looked vulnerable in their pajamas, open bathrobes, and stocking feet. Webber, looking like a flamingo in his pink pajamas and black slippers, craned his rubber neck around the corner and looked down the dark hallway where Dittman's room was. Making a time-out signal with his fingers and palm, he snaked along the corridor toward Dittman's room, his pajama bottoms reaching only to mid-calf which exposed white, almost hairless bird legs.

Dittman's apartment door suddenly opened, and Webber ducked into a nearby doorway while the others darted down several steps off the landing. Taking a swig out of a pint-sized bottle and wiping his mouth on the scooped sleeve of his cassock, Dittman stepped into the middle of the corridor and looked up and down. Then, lowering the bottle to his side and mumbling under his breath, he

---

[61] By doing nothing men learn to act wickedly.

went back into his room and closed the door behind him. The boys waited. A few moments later, the door opened again. This time, the priest took one long, neck-stretching look toward the landing while thoughtfully scratching his nose and then went back into his room and closed the door.

After breathlessly waiting several minutes, Webber made his way back to the landing where the boys were waiting. He told them he'd seen Dittman's light go out beneath the door, and he'd heard the recoil of cot springs. Snyder glared at Christian. His chubby arms were folded across his chest, and the big sleeves of his bathrobe dangled. Webber and the other boys peered through the grating which enclosed the gaping elevator shaft. Christian was already climbing the wire screen by sticking the toes of his basketball shoes into the metal openwork. Finally balanced on the narrow, top edge of the grating six feet above the landing, he slowly turned around so his back was facing the empty elevator shaft.

"My God, he's gonna do a back flip!" someone whispered.

"I don't believe it!" another guy replied, stifling his voice with his hand.

Taking a deep breath, Christian flexed his knees, relaxed, brought his arms straight over his head, pushed off hard, and somersaulted backward toward the deep pile of laundry bags below, his Hawaiian print shirt billowing out like a multi-colored sailboat spinnaker. Straightening out in the nick of time, he plummeted into the pile of stuffed laundry bags feet first with his arms at his sides.

"Dagnabbit!" Webber intoned. "He done it, Snyder! He done it! And a back flip to boot!"

"Shut up, cretin!" Snyder belted back as he stared through the grating disbelievingly. "Dittman'll hear us. Besides, he ain't walked out yet. Maybe he busted a leg or somethin'. I don't see 'em."

"Stop blabberin', you spastic!" Webber blasted. "He done it'n you know it. Pay up, butterball."

"Cool it, you'se guys," Valeno cut in. "I seen an arm movin'."

"You're blind shorty." Snyder snarled. He had his pug nose stuck right through a hole in the grating's openwork. "He's broke his neck. I just know it. I told 'em so. Just like the senior's."

They all peered through the wire as Christian slowly crawled out from beneath the laundry bags and waved up at them. The white birds on his shirt flashed beneath a bright light bulb which hung from a single cord above the loading dock.

Suddenly, like a clap of thunder in the night, a voice cracked: "Sed libera nos a malo[62]!"

They all jumped back from the grating as if it'd been electrified.

"What, in the name of St. Xavier, is going on here?" Father Dittman exclaimed. He was standing right behind the boys. His hands were thrust in the broad, black sash he wore around the waist of his cassock. Red flecks streaked the whites of his eyes, and he appeared like a silhouette in the shadows of the dim emergency light.

"I was only on my way to the bathroom, Father," Snyder squeaked as he thrust one hand over his groin and boldly started toward the corridor. With the speed of a boxer's jab, Dittman's claw shot out and grabbed him by the collar.

---

[62] Deliver us from evil!

"Just a holy minute, Norman," Dittman urged. "I demand to know what's going on here."

"I didn't flip down it." Snyder snorted.

"Flip? What are you talking about?"

All the boys sheepishly glanced toward the fence, and Father Dittman, drawn by their looks, went over to the grating. Peering through the openwork, he exclaimed, "Blood of the saints!" The red Hawaiian print was rippling on Christian's back as he climbed out of the deep laundry bay up onto the loading platform.

"He flipped off the top of the grating, Father." Snyder blurted out as he tried to pull his collar out of the priest's clutches.

"Flipped?" Dittman asked, flabbergasted.

"As in somersaulted. My collar!"

"Somersaulted, but that's thirty feet."

"Forty. Head over heels from the top edge of the grating. My collar!"

Peering up at the top edge of the fence, Father Dittman let go of Snyder's collar and screamed, "Holy Mother of God! How'd he get up there? There's no footholds in the new grating the rector had installed after the accident."

"Climbed, Father. He thinks he's a cat."

Father Dittman peered down the shaft and shouted, "Reicharte, get your bloody tail up here right now! Persona non grata, prima facia[63]!"

Christian ascended the several flights of stairs from the basement to the second-floor landing as slowly as he could so he could catch his breath. Although the impact had knocked the wind out of him, he now felt as if every fiber of his being were electrified. He could even feel faint static discharges in his shirt as it rippled over his back. When he arrived on the landing, the priest had sent the others to bed, but he could see Snyder and Webber peering toward the landing from the door of the dorm. Dittman was standing, spread-eagled, with his long, bony hands, like a pair of dueling pistols, resting in the wide black sash around his waist. His flecked eyes smoldered, and his emaciated face was taut with crows' feet around the eyes and deep ravines in the cheeks. "Persona non grata[64]!" he barked.

"Non sequitur[65]," Christian snapped back without thinking, his voice inflamed and passionate, but without ill will.

"It does follow!" Dittman shouted, sticking his neck out, his prominent Adam's apple quivering. "Don't try any of your linguistic gymnastics on me, Mr. Reicharte. Look at me when I'm talking. Father Oxley's told me about your smart aleck Latin charade. Who do you think you are? Some kind of high wire act?"

"Rara avis[66]?"

"A rare bird? My Aunt Matilda!"

---

[63]   An unacceptable person at first sight!
[64]   An unacceptable person.
[65]   It does not follow.
[66]   A rare bird.

"Stella duce[67]."

"Stop that! You're under the leadership of the devil, and you're certainly not pulling the wool over my eyes, Mr. Latin scholar. You've got "F's" on your last five Latin exams. You may've impressed Father Oxley, but I'm nobody's fool."

Christian stared at his sneakers and endured the priest's anger. He was still flushed from the powerful adrenaline surge of the jump, and he felt a touch dizzy, and strangely giddy.

"I've a mind to send you directly to the rector's where an expulsion would be in order. How'd you like that?"

"Deus vuet[68]."

"All right. That's it! Forget the rector. I'll take care of this myself. A little good old-fashioned discipline should straighten you out, Dr. Spock and Mr. Freud notwithstanding. You be in my room tomorrow afternoon at two o'clock sharp. I think I'll let you stew awhile. Two o'clock."

Beside himself, Christian hurried away. His feet felt as if they'd sprouted wings, and the tail of his Hawaiian print filled with air, giving him a trace of lift. The dorm was moon-lit now, and the white alcove curtains rustled as if from an unseen wind. Shadows scuttled over the ceiling as peeping Toms opened and closed their curtains. At his back, he heard a cork pop from a bottle and Father Dittman talking out loud to himself: "Rara avis, my ass," was clear, followed by what sounded like: "Stella duce? My Aunt Matilda's ass."

*　　*　　*　　*　　*　　*　　*

---

[67]   Under the leadership of a star.
[68]   If God wills it.

Sitting on the steps behind the cafeteria, Christian felt as if a tiny crab were leisurely crawling down the back of his shirt. Two o'clock sharp. Dittman's words echoed in his mind. Straighten you out. He recalled having felt a similar, nauseating apprehension somewhere before. It was a blurred, fragmented, nearly unconscious reminiscence still thriving on the very edge of his memory: There were rows of white bars, like crib slats, jittering shadows on a white wall, and growling voices which leaped from gaping holes in the black-tongued shadows. A little old-fashioned discipline. The priest's words rattled around in his memory like a witch's hex.

"What's the matter, Christian?" someone yelled from another planet.

Barely aware of the other's presence, Christian stared as the boy shrugged and disappeared around the corner. His mind raced in and out of dead ends. He could hide in the bell tower, but he'd probably end up deaf after Oxley got done ringing them every morning. He could run into the hills beyond the football field. He could even commit suicide like Johnny Moreno had done when he'd jumped from the bell tower after his father, a Mafia Don according to Snyder's grapevine, had told him not to come home after he'd been expelled for suspicion of homosexuality. The hands on the Mickey Mouse watch Rose had given him pointed to one-forty-five. He wished he were in the watch with happy-go-lucky M-I-C-K-E-Y. He put the wristwatch to his ear and listened as Mickey's chubby mitts marked off the instants of eternity.

"Look, you guys," Snyder sniped as he came out the rear door of the cafeteria with a couple of his overfed buddies," he's talking to the garbage cans."

"I wasn't," Christian squawked, caught off guard.

"You were too! That jump must've scrambled your brains, ole buddy. What'd Dittman do anyways?"

"None of your business, lard ass!" Christian heard himself holler in a voice which seemed to come from another's throat.

Taken aback, Snyder gave his friends a quizzical look and timidly took a step toward Christian with his friends on his heels. "What'd you call me?" he asked in a doll's voice while twisting his pug nose upward for emphasis.

"Your first name!" Christian shot back, springing to his feet as if a devil had yanked him by his shirt collar He stuck his face right into Snyder's, clenched his fists at his sides, and added, "You wanna hear the second one?"

Warily eyeing Christian's queerly mismatched eyes, Snyder recoiled a couple of steps backward. "Let's go, you guys," he said to his bloated friends. "He's not altogether."

"Give me my money, Snyder. Right now! I can still tell, you know."

"Okay, okay, old buddy," Snyder replied and took out a thick wallet. "You don't have to get your panties in a knot. Here, buy yourself a new shirt."

After the boys had gone, Christian pocketed the cash and watched Mickey's mitts inexorably creep toward two o'clock. The voice had surprised him and Snyder too. Something like shape-shifting, he guessed. Maybe hormones, male and female, struggling for dominance. At five of two, he zipped up his parka, and walked steadily toward the brownstone dormitory building. The air was cold, and the sky looked like a slate ceiling. The barren tree branches were crooked and coated with thin layers of ice. Two boys with skis over their shoulders were crossing the football field on their way into the hills that rose like camels' backs beyond the field. Webber called to him from the hockey rink so he waved. When he glanced at a second-floor freshman dorm window, he spotted the silhouette of Dittman who appeared to be flapping the scooped sleeves of his cassock.

Hurrying into the dorm, Christian ran upstairs and went to Dittman's door where he stopped to collect himself. He experienced a moment of vertigo as if he were peering over the edge of a deep ravine. Reaching out, he knocked on the door. His heart leaped when he heard water splashing in a sink, and Dittman mumbling something in Latin. He waited a minute and knocked again, tentatively, as if tapping on the lid of a coffin.

"Yes?" a veiled voice answered from within.

"It's me."

"Who's me?"

"Me, Christian Reicharte."

"The president? What do you want?"

"Two o'clock. Remember?"

"Oh, yes, just a minute."

Christian waited, catching his breath. The door knob began to turn, very slowly, and the door opened a crack. Father Dittman peered out. His face was ruddy and creased with a frown which accentuated the crow's feet around his eyes and the deep ravines of his cheeks. His flecked eyes were filmed, and he had dark bags beneath them. He blew his beak into a soiled handkerchief and stuffed it into the long slit at the side of his cassock.

"I'm here," Christian said, struggling to keep his voice from breaking.

"Come in," the priest acknowledged in a hoarse voice. "Two o'clock. Ah, huh. I was just getting ready."

Just getting ready for what? Christian thought as he stepped past the priest into the room which had a stale, moldy smell and a stifling lack of oxygen. It was an unusually long, narrow room which tapered at the far end toward a tall window covered with a thick velvet curtain. A thin band of pale light escaped at the bottom of the curtain where the frayed hem was too short. Beneath the window a radiator hissed, emitting a thin, almost invisible jet of steam from a shut-off valve. A worn oriental carpet covered the floor. It depicted intertwining snakes and was spotted with what looked like cigarette burns. Along one bare wall, there was a cot. It was covered with a threadbare army blanket. On the wall above the cot, there was a large wooden crucifix. It bore a delicately wrought porcelain statuette of Jesus. The hands, feet, and abdomen of the statue were pierced with gruesome black holes. Thick droplets of fire-engine red paint oozed from the wounds, and a ghastly crown of thorns pierced the statue's skull. In front of the radiator, there was a card table and folding chair. An ashtray full of cigarette butts rested on the table next to a deck of Bicycle playing cards arranged in the shape of a pyramid for solitaire. In a walk-in closet covered with a partially open curtain, Christian spotted a wooden Coke case filled with empty wine bottles.

"I'm going to give you a little taste of an old-fashioned medicine, Mr. Reicharte," Dittman off-handedly commented as he washed his hands in a sink and carefully toweled them off as if preparing for surgery.

A solitary bead of urine dropped into Christian's underpants.

"It worked on Mr. Snyder and a couple others who thought they were better than the rest of us."

Dismayed, Christian knitted his eyebrows and stared at the snakes in the rug. They were black with red eyes and green tongues. Then he was startled by the sound of his own voice, she was back and full of herself: "Inimicis ignoscere debumus[69]."

"Indeed, I think you're making fun of us in a very sarcastic manner, Mr. Reicharte. Would you like to translate this off the top of your head, Mr. President? Into Greek, mind you: Spare the rod and spoil the child."

"Humanum est errare[70]."

"Not even close. See, there it is again. The sarcasm. And that shirt's part of the charade. The rector's backed off a little on the blazers, but this isn't a beach party yet." He stopped a moment and pulled out a folding chair which was tucked under the card table. "I haven't forgotten about those pajamas either," he continued. "Disgraceful. What's more, and I shouldn't be telling you this, but you're on the list of suspects in the National Geographic caper." Hesitating, he sat on the wooden chair and smoothed out the lap of his black cassock with fastidious strokes of his long hands. "Well, don't just stand there gaping at the floor," he continued. "What do you have to say for yourself?"

"Nolo contendere[71]."

"See what I mean?" Dittman replied. "That's the devil-may-care sarcasm I'm talking about. No contest, huh? We'll see about that. Remove that coat and take down your pants."

---

[69] We ought to pardon our enemies.
[70] It is a human thing to error.
[71] No contest.

"Huh?"

"You heard me. Take them down and come over here. This'll straighten you out, believe me."

Christian hesitated. He was repelled by the deep hollows in the priest's cheeks and the red, feverish look of his complexion, not to mention the bloodshot eyes set closely together alongside the narrow bridge of his sharply curved nose. The man could easily pilot a broomstick, he thought.

"Stop stalling. Take them down and come over here. Maybe you'd rather I report the elevator incident to the rector. You'd be looking at nothing less than an expulsion with your academic record."

Abashed, Christian dropped his air force jacket on the floor, unbuckled his belt, and let his trousers drop to the floor.

"What in God's name! Aren't those panties?"

"Ah, well, I didn't notice. The maid probably accidentally put them in my luggage."

"I see, but you didn't have to wear them! Take them down."

Mortified, Christian pulled his underpants down.

"Come here."

With his trousers and underpants around his ankles, Christian blushed from ear to ear and shuffled toward the priest who pointed toward his lap while commenting, "Now lay over my lap."

Stricken, Christian sprawled over the priest's lap, his head almost touching the floor.

"Don't move."

For a split second, Christian saw himself, unaccountably, as a baby peering through the stiff white slats of a crib. Bats were darting overhead, and their shadows fluttered over the crib. He felt the cold pad of a clammy paw caress his bare buttocks very softly as if it were smoothing a sheet, and then a succession of sharp, smarting pains shot through him. Like the bends, the stinging pain spread to every joint and muscle in his body. Clenching his teeth, he fought off a barrage of tears. He closed his eyes tightly as a huge wave engulfed him and held him down. After what seemed like an eternity, Dittman, breathing rapidly and heavily, commented, "Quid pro quo[72], Mr. Latin scholar. That should teach you some respect. Now, pull up your pants, and I don't want to see any crocodile tears nor hear a word about this from anyone. Keep your mouth shut. Mandatory expulsion, remember. And I'm not going to forget those panties. Very strange to say the least, but we'll give you the benefit of the doubt for now."

Feeling like a cat suddenly let out of a gunny sack, Christian sprang from the priest's lap. In one swift motion, he pulled up his underwear and pants. Holding his trousers up with one hand, he picked up his coat from the floor with the other and ran from the room, down the long corridor, and into the dorm where he collided with a couple of boys who were on their way out. They stared after him and hollered something he didn't hear. At his alcove, he snapped the curtain shut so hard he tore off a few of the hooks which held it on a metal rod. Sprawling across his bed, he buried his face in his pillow and cried. His chest heaved, and his breath came in short, painful sobs. After a short time, he leaned back on his heels and

---

[72] Something in return.

began beating the pillow with his fists. He pummeled it repeatedly until a hoarse, guttural sound rose out of his chest like the bestial howl of a wounded animal: "Excrucior[73]!"

Exhausted, he fell across the bed and curled up with his knees against his chest. Momentarily, he drifted into a fitful sleep where his body, like a detached organism, involuntarily twitched, and his mind, like a rabid dog's, beat itself against the inside walls of a long black box which was tumbling end-over-end. Through a wire screen at the top of the box, he could see stained-glass windows which swirled by like images at the end of a kaleidoscope, and there were flying coffins. Corpses were struggling to get out of them. A white-robed, pale-faced youth with curly red hair, a bloated stomach, and a pug nose flew by. His white wings flapped between his shoulder blades as he strummed a harp. He wore the sly smile of a circus sideshow attendant.

Suddenly, a cold, metallic hand reached into the dream box and clutched the nape of his neck. It yanked him out and dragged him down a long, undulating red carpet which was lined with majestic, blue-veined, marble columns. In an instant, the pillars turned into black, hooded angels with sleek, blue-black crows' wings which rhythmically flapped between their shoulder blades. The angels' skeletal arms reached out from inside the wide, dangling black sleeves of their robes and tore his Hawaiian print shirt from his back, tossing it in the air where it burst into flames. The birds in the fabric flew upward into a huge dome where they battered themselves to death against thick, lead-framed, stained-glass windows, their bodies falling like spent missiles. There was a sizzling sound, like frying bacon, followed by a sustained shriek as a firebrand was pressed against his chest, branding it with the letters OS.

---

[73]   I am being tortured!

"Stigmata[74]!" he heard his own voice crying out in tongue..

"Christian!"

"Excrucior[75]!"

"For Christ's sake, wake up! Christian!"

"Nunc aut nunquam[76]!"

"You're floppin' 'round in here like a fish out'a water," Webber said, his goggled eyes lit with curiosity as he peered around the edge of the alcove curtain. "Was you dreamin' or somethin'? You should of heard them weird words you was yellin'. Stigma somethin' and some other Latin stuff. Roll's in a few minutes. Hurry up. Dittman's still on the warpath."

"I had a nightmare. They were branding me with the letters OS."

"OS? What's that mean?"

"The black book, man. They're throw'n the book at me. "Member the black dot in Treasure Island? This's a whole book, Webber."

"Black book? Black dot? Hey, wake up, Christian. You slept right through supper. The table captain took down your name."

Twin storms poured into Christian's mismatched eyes. The look startled Webber, but not as much as the depth, resonance, and conviction of Christian's reply: "My name's always been down ."

*   *   *   *   *   *   *   *   *

---

[74]   Mark of disgrace.
[75]   I am being tortured!
[76]   Now or never!

"Snyder!" Father Dittman's voice cracked like a slap shot.

"I was early, Father," Snyder squealed, his breath vaporizing in the frigid early morning air.

"Moffitt!"

"Here!"

"Krowell!"

"Here!

"Valeno!"

"Here."

"Speak up, Dominic!"

"Here!"

"Reicharte!"

There was no reply, and the boys looked inquisitively up and down the line.

"Christian Reicharte!"

The wind whistled like a ship-board summons.

"Where is he?" Dittman snapped while peering over the top of the clipboard, the hem of his dingy cassock whipping around his ankles.

"He wasn't at lunch, Father, Snyder put in. "Baldwin took his name down."

"He wasn't at rec. either!" a boy at the end of the line shouted.

"Have you seen 'em, Webber?" the priest asked, a trace of anxiety in his voice.

"Pardon me," Webber said, cupping the flap of his ear.

"Cut that out, Webber. You heard me. Did you see 'em?"

"Ah, no," Webber replied, his eyes flitting back and forth between Father Dittman and the distant hills which appeared on the other side of the football field behind the priest. "I ain't seen nobody."

"Are you sure, Webber? the priest challenged. He caught Webber's eyes and looked toward the faraway, snow-blanketed hills. There was a black shape visible, like a black pawn on a white square.

"Maybe he ran away like Moreno did," Snyder mused, his button eyes trained on the hills.

"Don't butt in where it doesn't concern you, Mr. Snyder!" Dittman fumed. Then, as if shadowed by a bird's wing, his emaciated face darkened and his voice quivered: "The little devil can't do this."

The wind whistled, the boys speculated noisily, and the blot on the snowy hill moved a square, like a passed pawn.

*   *   *   *   *   *   *   *   *

PART II

The third pickup truck that passed skidded to a stop fifty yards beyond where Christian was standing at the side of the two lane highway. He had run like mad down the blacktop road before he climbed in. "Thanks for stopping, sir!" he shouted, out of breath. Then he took a last look across a wide field toward the red barn he'd stayed in the night before.

The driver grunted and shifted into first gear, gunning the engine loudly. His head was small and shaven to the bone. There were pouches under his eyes, a lump, like a swollen tooth, bulged in one cheek, and thick reddish-brown stubble grew on his cheeks like rust on a tin roof. He wore a tattered, black-and-red checked hunting jacket which hung loosely over a pair of grease-stained bib overalls. Feeling a shiver of panic, Christian felt like leaping out.

"You over from dat boarding school?" the man asked and jerked the wheel when a rear tire slipped off the road.

Grabbing the dashboard, Christian managed to reply, "Yeah."

"Kinda early to be hitchin' ain't it?" the man continued with a sidelong glance at Christian.

"Yeah, I guess."

"What 'cha up to then?"

"Nothing."

"Ain't ya cold?" the stranger pursued. He opened the window and spit out a long stream of amber spittle. "It's below zero this mornin'. Ain't that one of them air force jackets?"

"Yeah, and it's warm'n these gloves're lined. I've got sweaters on too'n more stuff's in my duffel bag."

Unconsciously picking a tiny piece of green slime from his nose and wiping it on his bibbed overalls, the stranger continued, "Where ya headin'?"

"Town."

"Yah quit school or somethin'?"

"No, my grandmother's dying. She's about a hundred."

"Sure, kid, and my cat ain't got no bum hole neither," the stranger replied with a sneering, sidelong appraisal of Christian.

Feeling beads of sweat break out on his forehead, Christian ignored the remark but took a death grip on the door handle as the truck raced by a road sign which read: Huntington - Five Miles. Then, quite unexpectedly, the man swung the wheel hard. The sudden turn threw Christian almost into the man's lap as the truck fish-tailed off the highway onto a dirt road which led into a thicket of pine trees laden with snow.

"That there's a C-O-D turn, kiddo," the man squealed as Christian struggled to regain his posture in spite of the careening truck which bounced all over the place as it hit ruts in the dirt road.

"C-O-D?"

"Come over, darlin'!" the man shouted. "C-O-D!"

Stunned, Christian grabbed the door handle with both hands as the stranger spun a doughnut in the middle of a small clearing of pines. He slammed the brakes on, turned off the engine, and opened the window to spit out another long stream of spittle. In a flash the window was up, and the man slid over. He put his arm over the back of the seat behind Christian and grinned like a Cheshire cat, one gold tooth shining at the back of his mouth. "Yah wanna rub backs?" he bluntly asked. "I'll do yours if you do mine."

Freezing stiff as a saint's statue, Christian managed to grunt, "Huh?"

"Backs! Do you wanna rub 'em?"

"No--I--well-I--a--don't..."

"Don't be so gosh awful shy. I ain't gonna hurt ya. You can even ask that fat little rich punk, Snyder. I picked 'em up last time he sneaked into town."

"What?" Christian replied in shock, his eyes darting back and forth between the stranger's gold-tooth smile and the door. "My parents're waiting for me in Huntington. My big brother's there too. He's a policeman."

Scratching his bare skull, the man ruminated a few moments. Christian held his breath. Then, quite unpredictably, the man shouted, "All you snotty punks at that richy school're a bunch of pricks! Get the Sam Hill out'a here 'fore I punk yah like I done Snyder!"

Christian scrambled out. He dragged his duffel bag after him, and the stranger gunned the engine. With both rear wheels spinning, he pulled out onto the road, rolled down the passenger-side window, and spit while yelling, "Shit-faced prick!" Thick brown spittle blew away from his cheeks like root beer. Screeching like a banshee, he rolled up the window and sped down the road. Slush sprayed out from behind the rear wheels and the vehicle slipped on and off the shoulder of the dirt road.

"Holy scum bags!" Christian exclaimed as he dropped his duffel bag and eyeballed the rear end of the truck which was fish-tailing up onto the main highway. "Cave canem[77]!" he shouted. "Ave atque vale[78], slime worm!" Warmed up, he slammed his hand into the crook of his left arm and raised his fist while shouting, "Up yours, flea bag! "Quid pro quo[79]!" The Latin oaths had exploded from his mouth like sailors' curses, and he felt quite beside himself when he noticed his own fist waving wildly in the air. With an involuntary shudder, he picked up his duffel, shouldered it, and headed for a nearby hill. From the hilltop, he got a clear view of Huntington which was silently sleeping, like a storybook village, at the bottom of a long, curving ribbon of blacktop. He trained his eyes on a glimmering copper steeple that rose above the slanted rooftops. The steeple flashed in the rising sun like reflecting mirrors, and he imagined someone was sending him signals. He remembered reading The Hunchback of Notre Dame. In the story a church was considered a refuge. A renegade could hold up in a church without reprisal. Sanctuary they called it.

After a long, freezing cold trek across an open field, over an old railroad trestle, and through some backyards, he arrived at the church with the copper steeple. It was white with red, green, and blue stained glass windows. No one was around so he opened one of the double doors at the top of a short flight of shallow steps

---

[77] Beware the dog!
[78] Hail and farewell!
[79] Something in return!

and walked in. He unzipped his jacket, cupped his ears to warm them, and looked around. It was gravely cold inside. Slanted bars of sunlight pierced the stained glass windows which were spaced along the walls at regular intervals. Ceramic stations of the cross, depicting gruesome scenes of Christ's torture and sculpted in bas-relief for a three-dimensional effect, hung on the walls between the windows. There were two wide rows of wooden pews with a green carpet between them and two narrow side aisles next to the walls. Midway along the wall aisles there were two confessionals with tavern doors in the middle and curtained entrances on each side. A wooden railing traversed the front. It separated rows of pews from a linen covered altar which was set back a distance from the railing and centered upon a raised platform. Behind the altar there was an inward curving wall that extended from one side of the church to the other. A mural depicting the Last Supper covered the wall.

Spotting a metal votive candle stand by the wall near one end of the communion railings, he walked over and shook a metal coin box which hung from a bracket attached to the front of the tiered stand. The cover of the box was locked with a large padlock as if it were full of gold instead of five and ten cent offerings. Taking out his Boy Scout pocket knife, he opened the big blade and used it to pry open the bottom edge of the cover. Nickels and dimes fell to the carpet so he picked them up, counted them, and put them into his pocket. Then he picked up a long wooden match from a container attached to the stand, scratched it on the stand, and fired every candle. He warmed his hands over the flames for a few minutes, picked up his duffel bag, genuflected, and headed for the altar.

Jumping over the communion railing, he cut across the carpeted altar apron, and went through a door which led into a side room off the altar. The room was a small sacristy where the clergy put on their costumes. There was a toilet and sink in a curtained alcove so he went in and sat down. A few minutes later, he heard the front door of the church open. Startled, he quickly got up, pulled up his trousers, grabbed his duffel bag, and ran into the sacristy. Someone was coming up the center aisle so he frantically searched for a place to hide. Next to a tall vesting table he saw a wall panel with a small handle screwed into it. He ran over and pulled on the handle but the panel wouldn't budge. The voices were coming from the altar apron so he tried pushing on the handle, and the panel opened slightly, swinging inward like a secret panel. He jumped through and carefully pushed the panel back in place as pitch darkness enveloped him. Holding his breath, he listened through the wall.

"I wanna serve the bell side. It's my turn to ring 'em 'cause you done it last time. Hey, someone's lit up candles already."

"So what, scuz! I seen 'em lit this early."

"Not all of 'em."

Christian let out a stream of breath when he suddenly realized that it was Sunday, and a couple of altar boys were in the sacristy putting on their costumes to serve early Mass. Everyone always wanted to ring the sterling silver cluster of bells. He took a flashlight out of his duffel bag and switched it on. A sharp light speared the darkness. It illuminated a narrow passageway which was just wide enough for a single person to walk through. The ceiling was only a few feet above his head. He walked along the passage which curved around toward the other side of the church where there was another paneled wall section with a little knob screwed into it. When he pulled on the knob, the panel opened a crack and revealed another sacristy exactly like the other one except it didn't have a curtained lavatory. He pushed the panel closed and started back. There were built-in shelves along one wall of the passage. The shelves were laden with colorful vestments embroidered in gold filigree. There were black cassocks and white surplices which were folded and neatly stacked. There were candles, gold incense pots with long chains attached, gleaming gold chalices, missals and hymnals, wooden racks stacked with unlabeled bottles of wine, and small cardboard boxes full of round, quarter-size white discs of unleavened bread.

Feeling hunger and thirst for the first time since he'd run away the night before, he grabbed a box of the communion discs and a bottle of wine from the shelf, positioned the flashlight on top of his duffel bag, and spread his jacket out on the floor. With his Boy Scout knife, he pried out the cork in the wine bottle and took a long swig, wiping his mouth with the back of his hand. Then he snatched one of the chalices from the shelf and filled it with wine. Thrusting it out in front of his face, he toasted, "Et tu, Brutus[80]," and tipped the chalice to his lips. The cool, biting liquid went down like apple cider, and for the first time since he'd left school, he felt warm all over. Opening the cardboard box, he took out a handful of the hosts and stuffed them into his mouth. It wasn't a sacrilege because the hosts weren't blessed yet. Tilting his head way back, he poured another gurgling stream of wine down his throat, grabbed another handful of unleavened bread discs, and sat down on his coat for breakfast.

"In nomine Patri, et Filii, et Spiritus Sanctus, amen," a dull, muffled voice came from the other side of the wall like a voice from inside an ancient crypt. Startled, Christian recognized the incantation: In the name of the Father, the Son, and the Holy Ghost. It was followed by Latinate incantations in boyish soprano voices. A Mass was starting.

"What the heck?" Christian questioned the wall, taking a swig of unblessed wine for good measure. He got up and listened at the wall. It was definitely a Mass. He was right behind the altar. He picked up the wine bottle and took another deep draught, most of which ran down his chin. There was a fluttering above him, like a bat had passed overhead. He frantically waved his hands back and

---

[80]   You too, Brutus?

forth above his head. Snatching up the flashlight, he peered around the narrow passageway for signs of life. Seeing and hearing nothing, he took another swig from the bottle and sagged to the floor like an unattended puppet. Whatever it was made another fluttery pass over his head, and he waved his hands back and forth above his head again. "Arf! Arf!" he impulsively yelped, giggling and sprawling on the floor where his arm knocked out the flashlight. Then, in a low, melancholy tone, he began to softly sing. He punctuated each phrase with a loud hiccup: "How much is that dog-gy in the window? I do hope that dog-gy's for sale. If he has a dog, he won't be lone-some, and the dog-gy will have a good home. Arf! Arf!"

Languishing beneath the mysterious wing-like fluttering which fanned his face, he slowly slipped away, like a dark wave from a sandy shore. He drifted out to a remote tropical island with a broad white beach. There were lofty palm trees which, from afar, appeared like ornate beach umbrellas. One tree, located on a narrow finger of sand, was wind-bent right over the sea so its green fronds touched the water. Gray-white sea gulls hovered, their wings barely moving as they soundlessly coasted down the backs of gathering cumulus clouds. A thin spiral of smoke mysteriously ascended from the lush tropical foliage which gathered from the coastline toward a blue mountain. An on-shore breeze transported the gritty smells of sea weed, salt, and fish, and foamed the surf as it swirled over pink and white seashells on the sandy beach.

Then he saw her. She dashed behind a palm tree, a blur of swarthy nakedness. His blood boiled to the surface of his skin as he tied on a loin cloth and picked up a spear. She was quick as a cougar. He tripped on vines and got his bare foot caught beneath a tree root. He recovered quickly and tossed his spear aside. Branches whipped his back, and he could feel blood trickling from his face where sharp branches had lashed him as he broke through the dense jungle.

Somewhere in the distance, not far from the blue mountain which overshadowed the jungle, he heard the rhythmic beat of a signal drum. His pulse quickened at the sound, for it pounded through the jungle like a giant's footsteps. Suddenly, she materialized from behind a palm. She was cloaked only in her own long black hair, and her lean body glistened in a shimmering sword of sunlight which slashed through the canopy of dark green foliage. Her white teeth flashed and the thick black triangle between her sinewy legs appeared like a panther's pelt. Breathless, he raced toward the tree only to trip and sprawl beneath it, a musky scent the only trace that she'd been there.

"Who is he? I thought I heard something back here."

"Dunno, Father. I didn't know 'bout this here room even. Look out!"

"Jesus, Mary'n Joseph, duck!"

"What was it?"

"A bird for heaven's sake. It's flying into the sanctuary."

"How'd it get in here, Father?"

"He must've let it in, but how'd he get in here?"

"Beats me. I ain't never seen 'em no wheres. Have you, Jeremy?"

"No, I ain't never..."

"He looks rich, Father. Look at that leather jacket. He must've come from over at the boarding school. Is this here one a them secret passages?"

Christian groaned and put up his hand to block the glare which he thought was the sun knifing through the thick canopy of jungle.

"Saints above!" the priest shouted. "I thought I smelled something nasty. He's regurgitated! Look by his coat there!"

"Phew!" the altar boys added.

Christian peered around his outstretched hand. He saw a tall man who was wearing a white cassock, green poncho, and a black, three-sided cap. Next to the man there were two small boys dressed in white surplices and black cassocks. They were all pinching their noses with one hand while holding their arms outstretched like stop signs.

"He's gotta be one a them boarding school snots, Father. I seen a bunch of 'em in town Saturday. This fat red-headed one was buyin' Playboys at Jensen's drug store. I think they hitched a ride from Crazy Banyan."

"You don't say," the priest commented. He poked the toe of his shoe into Christian's side. "What're you doing in my church, young man?"

"Sanctuary," Christian moaned as he tried to sit up. His well-oiled bones collapsed like rubber, and a jolt of pain hit his head like a hammer.

"What in tarnation!" the priest hollered. "Would you look at this! He's been into the wine. Look at the empty bottle and--what the--oh, holy Mother of God, he's been drinking from a chalice. They're direct from Rome, mind you. The Holy Father's heirlooms. Why, I don't believe my own eyes! He's been into the hosts too!"

"Sanctuary," Christian moaned, the syllables spilling from his mouth like sawdust from an old rag doll.

"Mercy, I think he's drunk," the priest speculated while pointing at Christian as if he were a church mouse.

"I got a pee."

"For God's sake, go!" the priest snapped as he stepped aside with his palms against the front of his poncho.

In a state of vertigo, Christian struggled to his feet. He rocked and swayed on his new rubber legs, stumbled past his dumbstruck audience into the alcove, pulled the curtain shut, and lowered his pants just in time before his kidneys exploded in a relentless river of torturous pleasure. Then came Montezuma's revenge. Buckling at the waist, he dry heaved until his guts felt like a stone quarry.

"You'd better have something to say for yourself!" the priest shouted through the curtain. "What in blazes were you doing in there? Who are you? We won't tolerate another suicide around here. Can't they keep you boys under their thumb over there?"

His face the color of wet cement, Christian finally stumbled out, barely able to maintain his balance.

With his arms folded across his chest, the priest blocked Christian's path. "Who are you?" he demanded. "I've a mind to call the sheriff."

"Christian."

"Christian, what?"

"Christian, Father."

"Your last name, numbskull."

"Oh, ah, Reicharte."

"And what exactly are you doing drunk in a church passageway, heaven help us?"

"He busted in, Father!" one altar boy interrupted.

"I didn't," Christian argued. "The door was open."

"It weren't! And you busted into the storeroom."

"I was just looking for sanctuary," Christian appealed to the tall, middle-aged priest who was divesting. "I guess I drank too much of that wine, but I was thirsty and starving when I got here."

"What's he talkin' 'bout, sanctuary?" one altar boy asked.

"He's read too many story books, Jeremy," the priest answered as he handed his poncho and black hat to the crew-cut altar boy who was standing at his side like a valet.

"What kinda shirt's he wearin'? It could blind ya."

"Some kind of imported, citified shirt I guess. Now, mind your own business'n snuff out the altar candles. Both of you. I'll take care of this."

"Well, that's sure a queer shirt, Father," one boy added and the other nodded his head in affirmation. "I'll bet he's ran away like that kid who killed hisself."

"Is that right?" the priest demanded as he shooed the altar boys out of the vestry. "Nobody 'round here'd wear a picture shirt like that. Speak up, boy!"

"Yes, Father," Christian managed to say before grabbing his aching stomach with both hands and adding, with a shrug, "Persona non grata[81]."

"Indeed, you are," the priest replied. He gave Christian a hard stare. "Sacrilegious too. You've eaten hosts. And there's the wine. If that chalice's scratched your father's going to pay the piper a thousand times over."

"Mea culpa[82]. The hosts weren't consecrated though."

"It doesn't matter. You're going to have to be punished for this..."

"Why"

"Because."

"Should I get the sheriff?" one altar boy asked as he and the other boy carried some snuffed candles into the sacristy.

"I thought I told you to mind your own business," the priest scolded as he took the candles from the boys and put them on the vesting table. "Get 'em a bucket of soap'n water and a mop. I'm going to call the boarding school while he cleans that mess up in the storeroom. You boys keep an eye on 'em. And not a word about that passageway to anyone."

"His eyes're funny," one altar boy said.

"Yeah, they're different colors for cripes sake!"

"What about sanctuary?" Christian appealed.

---

[81]   An unacceptable person.
[82]   My fault.

Picking up a telephone from a night stand next to the tall vesting table, the priest glared at Christian and stiffly pointed toward the storeroom as he coldly replied, "Sanctuaries are for birds."

*   *   *   *   *   *   *   *   *

Father Luther, a tall, blonde man with a prominent Adam's apple, sharp, blue eyes, a flat-top haircut, and a basketball player's lean build, was drawing a sketch on the blackboard at the front of the classroom at St. Aloishas, a private school for boys. It was a picture of a stairway going up through some clouds and beyond into the black cosmos of the blackboard. At the foot of the stairway, there was a stick figure of a boy who was crawling on his hands and knees toward the first step. Each step was labeled in ascending order: powerlessness, guilt, reparation, and reconciliation at the top near the clouds.

Slumped in the back of the room near a long, hissing radiator and behind five rows of boys, all of whom were sitting as erect as tombstones, Christian was startled out of a daydream by the voice: "Vae victus[83]." Several boys glanced over their shoulders at him but quickly turned when they heard Father Luther's admonishment to pay attention. Father Luther was drawing a stick-figured devil near the bottom stair and a fluffy angel at the top.

Since his expulsion from St. Xavier's and subsequent return home, the effeminate voice had become embarrassingly clever and unpredictable, not to mention inexplicable. It had started when he was hauled before the St. Xavier's rector for running away and trespassing. The rector had asked him what he had to say for himself, and the sassy voice, with complete disregard for him, had barked "Vero pecarre[84]!"

He recalled how the emaciated rector had sat in a leather swivel chair behind his desk and lit a cigarette. Taking a deep drag, he'd pulled an ashtray over and casually said, "He's disrespectful, Mr. Reicharte. He's irreligious and insubordinate. Why, he wears that silly shirt every single day." To this, the voice had flatly replied:

---

[83] Woe to the vanquished.
[84] I fear to do wrong.

"Quot homines, tot sententiae[85]." Then the rector had squinted over the top of his glasses at Mr. Reicharte as if he suspected a conspiracy. His father had simply raised his palms toward the ceiling with an expression of absolute dismay.

After that, the rector had gotten down to business and accused him of sacrilege, blasphemy, and pornography, the latter with respect to the earmarked centerfold of the Playboy which was openly displayed on the rector's desk.

To these admonishments, the voice had loudly retorted: "Homo sum, et nihil humanum alienum est mihi[86]." It seems the voice liked riddles, but the rector hadn't been in the mood for translating. Ignoring the remark with a severely raised eyebrow for his father, he'd stood up, clasped his hands behind his back, and walked over to a large window which overlooked the football field. With his back toward them, he casually took another drag on his cigarette, stared out the window, and stiffly said, "To put it bluntly, Mr. Reicharte, the little rapscallion won't do it our way. He's just a bit too outspoken and self-ruling, not quite all together if you ask me, but I'm not a psychiatrist am I. I'd suggest St. Aloishas, your own parish. I could even call Father Devine if you wish."

While his father cupped his face in his hands, he'd snatched the cover of the Playboy over the centerfold with a flashy sleight of hand. As if to deflect attention, the effeminate voice teased, "Inimicos vestros amate[87]."

With that, his father had shouted: "What the heck's gotten into you, schmuck?"

---

[85] There are as many opinions as there are men.
[86] I am a man, and nothing human is foreign to me. (Terence)
[87] Love your enemies.

And the sultry voice had retaliated with "Multum in parvo," another one of her riddles which he, for once, had been able to translate: Much in a little.

While he reminisced, the little stick figure on the board had managed to get to the step labeled guilt and was clinging to the edge. Father Luther drew horns on the devil while commenting over his shoulder: "The road to heaven, lads, is not paved with good intentions, but good works. When Adam and Eve ate from the tree of knowledge, we all became part of a whole greater than the sum of its parts." He then wrote Labore est orare beneath the sketch and asked a tall, blonde boy in the front row to translate the message. The boy thoughtfully rubbed his peach-fuzzed chin and squinted at the Latin expression as if it were graffiti on a wall. After what appeared to be a short interior struggle, he pounded his forehead with a clenched fist and replied, "To work is to pray".

Christian, meanwhile, vainly struggled to cover up the impulsive ramblings of his soft spoken shadow: "Cur non mitto meos tibi, Pontiliane, Libellos? Ne mihi tu mittas, Pontilian, tuos." Distracted, several boys nearby looked over their shoulders and stared at him while he earnestly flipped through his Latin-to-English dictionary as if unaware of their concern. When the boys turned back around, he quickly translated the outburst which was strangely out of his depth given its length and complexity: Why do I not send you my books, Pontilianus? Lest you send me yours, Pontilius. Gaping at the mysterious message, Christian was amazed at this inexplicable ability to rapidly decode his worst subject in a voice which was almost, but not quite, prissy. She seemed to like to assert herself on behalf of him as if he were not measuring up to her expectations. Sometimes, he wanted to kick himself for always being one step behind her. He feared she'd leave him in the dust and sweep up after herself.

Father Luther began to draw flames beneath the devil at the bottom of the stairs. One of the flames reached all the way up to the struggling stick figure. The flames reminded Christian of the inferno on the cathedral ceiling back at St. Xavier's. He recalled seeing his own reflection in the dome even though Snyder had said it was only recessed mirrors. Someone threw a tightly folded wad of paper which hit the edge of his desk and fell on the floor. He picked it up, unfolded it, and read: Hey, new kid, try this one if you're so hot: Balnes, vena, Venus corrumpunt corpora nostra. Sed vitam faciunt balnea, vina Venus. Several boys had turned around and were eyeballing him so he checked on Father Luther who had his back to the class while writing a definition of reconciliation on the board. Anxious to show off and make some friends at the same time, Christian got out his dictionary and handbook and went to work. He came up in record time with a clean, but embarrassing, translation: Bathing, drinking, lovemaking corrupt our bodies, but they make life worthwhile. The boys around him started laughing.

"Mr. Bloomfield!" Father Luther barked as he headed toward the blonde kid's desk, his quick eyes darting between the boy and Christian who was way in the back. "What's so blamed funny about reconciliation?"

"Nothing, Father. I was just, ah, well, ah..."

"You were just passing a note to the new boy that's what," Father Luther said as he scooted down the aisle to Christian's desk.

"But it wasn't about anything important" the blonde kid whined as he watched the priest's back and nervously tugged at the knot of his black tie.

His jaw firmly set like a boxer's, the priest ignored Bloomfield's comment and walked to Christian's desk. "Let me see it, mister!" he demanded.

Glancing at the blonde kid whose face turned pale, Christian reluctantly handed the note to the priest who snatched it out of his hand and read it out loud to the class, emphasizing the pronunciations: "Balnes, vina, Venus corrumpunt corpora nostra. Sed vitam faciunt balnea, vina, Venus." Students around the room scribbled translations on pieces of scratch paper, and then the whole class laughed.

Calmly waiting for the guffaws to subside, Father Luther, without taking his eyes off Christian, remarked, "Is that so, Mr. Bloomfield? And just how would you know?"

The class laughed again and stomped their feet while pointing accusingly at Bloomfield whose face turned from pale to pink.

"That's enough!" Luther hollered after a few moments, his eyes glaring into Christian's mismatched pair. Then, stepping behind Christian's desk and speaking in a conspiring tone, he addressed the top of Christian's head where a cowlick, like a curving feather, grew: "Your name's on the black list, mister. Remember that. Your reputation's preceded you, and as far as I'm concerned, that shirt's out of line at St. Aloishas. This isn't a cruise ship. The boys wear dress shirts and ties around here since Father Devine took over the helm."

"De gustifus non disputandum[88]," the words skipped from the tip of Christian's tongue before he could cut them off, and the class, which had turned around to watch, laughed.

"I beg your pardon?" Father Luther replied, taken aback.

Christian's neck retracted into his shirt collar like a turtle's into its shell.

---

[88] There is no arguing about taste.

Thoughtfully pinching his jaw with his right hand for a few moments, Father Luther waved for silence. Then, as if suddenly illuminated, he asked, "There is no arguing about taste is it? Maybe you'd like to decline some fifth declension nouns for us, Mr., ah, what is it? Reicharte? Would that suit your taste?"

Bombarded with the fish-eyed stares of the entire class, Christian clammed up. Father Luther, his dark eyebrows knitted with consternation, went back to Bloomfield's desk. With a fraternal wink for the class, he addressed Bloomfield who had his hands neatly folded on his desk top: "Mr. Bloomfield, why did you include bathing in your little treatise?"

Bloomfield gulped and cautiously looked up at Father Luther whose athletic, six-foot-three bulk was hovering above him like a black-cloaked assassin: "Ah, well, because, ah..."

A few students giggled and Father Luther, smirking conspiratorially around the room, held up his hand like a stop sign. "Because, Bloomfield? Cat got your tongue?"

"No, Father. I think 'cause the Romans didn't like baths 'cause it was against their religion."

Everyone laughed including Father Luther who commented over the racket, "Not bad, Bloomfield. You've been doing your homework I see. That's more than I can say for the rest of these birds."

"Wouldn't that put a wet blanket on the love-making though?" Costello, a fat, moon-faced, J.V. footballer shouted.

The class roared, some of them stomping their feet while others hooted riotously. When Father Luther held up his hand for quiet, everyone ignored him so he went up to his desk and picked up a huge, gold-leafed black book and rapped it on his desk several times.

Then he shouted at the top of his lungs: "That's just about enough! Lord have mercy!"

The whole class fell silent and stiffened in their seats as if rigor mortis had set in. Furious, Father Luther glared at the class a few moments and then snapped: "Who made us?"

"God made us," the class snapped back in unison.

"Who is God?"

"God is our Father," the class chorused.

"Where is God?"

"God is everywhere."

"What is the supreme act?"

"The act of contrition."

"The cardinal sin?"

"Blasphemy."

"The pavement to heaven?"

"Good works."

"The Trinity?"

"Father, Son, and Holy Ghost."

"The eternal holocaust?"

"Hell" was loudly chorused with the exception of one soft voice which was almost lost in the clamor: "Cum grano salis[89]."

"That's more like it, gentleman," Father Luther congratulated, vaguely aware of several boys near the back who had turned around in their seats so they could stare disbelievingly at the new kid who had one hand firmly clamped over his mouth. Wiping his brow with a handkerchief he'd taken out of the long slit in the side of his cassock, the priest continued, "Remember, this isn't a public school. You're to behave in a civilized manner here. Besides, you should be ashamed of yourselves. We've got a new classmate to set an example for. Down to business now and no more foolishness. Twitty, stop staring at the new boy. You too, Sorenson. He's still wet behind the ears. Mr. Twitty, what do you make of the sketch I've drawn on the board?"

Twitty tossed the hair out of his eyes with a sharp jerk of his head and squinted at the sketch on the board as if it were a secret code.

"Mr. Twitty?"

"Ahh..."

"Yes?"

"Let me see, Father. I think it's because the kid's been bad and he's trying to get away from the flames and into them clouds for a breather."

"Them clouds?"

"Those, Father."

---

[89]   With a grain of salt.

"That's better. And how do we know he's bad, Mr. Costello?"

"Impure thoughts, Father?"

There was a barely perceptible chorus of chuckles around the room as the priest spoke, "Not funny, Costello, and not even close. Original sin. We covered this last week, Joe. I gave you the definition to memorize. A natural depravity or tendency to evil innate in mankind and transmitted from Adam to the race in consequence of his sin. Maybe you need to write it fifty times."

"But couldn't he choose not to feel guilty? He's got a natural tendency to do good stuff too, and some of the bad stuff is good as a matter of opinion."

"No, because the sin's there whether you like it or not."

"Like good guilt?"

"Not exactly."

"What exactly, Father?"

"Because original sin's from the beginning. That's why. It's like a birthmark."

"Summum ius summa inuria[90]!" Christian tried to catch the words, but it was like trying to catch fire flies.

"What?" Father Luther asked as he looked around the room for the source of the outburst.

---

[90]   The more law, the less justice.

Christian ducked behind a tall kid in front of him. His heart raced like mad, for he was frightened out of his wits that the reckless voice would assert itself again.

Father Luther glared at the class, his eyes like gas jets. Everyone slumped in his seat or ducked behind someone. Frank Harris turned around to make a for-shame sign at Christian, and Luther unloaded, "Turn around, Harris! You too, Tuttle! I'm just about ready to put this entire class on work details Saturday! The next person who yells out is going to the office. I was trying to use the Aristotelian method, but if you're too immature, we can just write essays for a few days!"

The class remained silent as slaves.

"Mr. Osborne, the sketch. What about powerlessness?"

"I saw this on Bishop Sheen."

There were a few muffled snickers around the room.

"Glad to hear it, Mr. Osborne. Powerlessness?"

Thoughtfully pinching his lips with one hand, Osborne stubbornly shook his head back and forth and replied, "I don't know. Seems kind of unfair him being powerless and guilty too."

"Without even a trial," O'Brien, a pimply-faced kid in row two asserted.

"Mis-ter O'-Bri-en," Father Luther said, emphasizing each syllable. "What have I repeatedly said about interrupting?"

"His father's a lawyer!" Costello exclaimed.

"I don't care if his father's the Pope," Luther shot back.

"Sorry, Father. I was just thinking out loud," O'Brien added. "It doesn't make any sense though. My dad says there's no guilt without will, and I don't see choice here what with the powerlessness and the sin being original and all. The punishment seems so out of proportion to the alleged crimes too."

There were subdued murmurs around the room.

"Maybe your father needs to examine the difference between secular and theological law."

"I can mention that."

"Did you father ever tell you about badgering the witness?"

"But you said you were using Aristotle's method."

"This is religion class, not a courtroom. I think your father would know the difference. He's a Knight of Columbus if I'm not mistaken."

"But what does that have to do with..."

"Faith, Mr. O'Brien."

"My father said never to be absolutely certain of anything."

"Don't make a doubting Thomas out of yourself. We're talking about unquestioning faith in the unknown, not scientific propaganda. Reserve that stuff for the courtroom if you please."

"But how can you prove something exists if it doesn't?" Costello elaborated.

"Faith, Costello, and the willing suspension of disbelief," Father Luther admonished, "just like the soldier in the foxhole under fire. You've heard of the thousand yard stare, I'm sure. Well, that soldier's staring at eternity, believe me." With that, Father Luther waved down Costello's hand and walked up the aisle and over to his desk at the front center of the room. A large, round school clock with a plastic frame hung right above his desk on an otherwise bare wall. Glancing at the time, he picked up a large black book from his desk and gave it a solid rap on his desk as an attention getter. Then he told the class that the assignment would be to write one paragraph about the sketch on the board. He added that the paragraph should contain definitions for each of the words used in the sketch.

Desk tops banged, papers shuffled, and everyone bent over their papers. Father Luther walked up and down the narrow aisles between desks. He had one hand stuck in the black sash around the waist of his cassock, and the other hand held up the black book while he read to himself. Now and then, he lowered the book and peered over the top of it at a student's paper.

After conscientiously printing his name, period number, and Religion 101 in the upper right-hand corner of his paper, Christian was startled by his pencil which began moving across the paper as if seized by invisible gravitational forces. Stopping abruptly in the center of the paper, it shifted back and forth, like a typewriter roller, and then moved a number of spaces left and began printing in a neat Romanesque:

The Prophet

With glowing eyes and
Onion breath, he spoke
Of sin, sorrow and sudden death.

Then he raised his Book and
Shook his fist; stamped his feet
And tossed his head.

But the crowd just frowned and
Turned around,
For the Prophet's pants had
Fallen down.

"Put your papers on my desk before you leave!" Father Luther shouted from behind his desk. "Kennedy, your paper! You too, Morrow!"

As if being shoved from behind, Christian stumbled to the priest's desk and slipped his paper beneath several others while Father Luther was looking into his black briefcase. Then he hurried toward the door.

"Mr. Reicharte!"

Startled, Christian stopped and slowly turned around.

"Are you from Miami?"

"No, Father."

"Hawaii?"

"No."

"Just curious. That shirt."

"Rome," the phantom voice clamored. Christian blushed, feeling as if he'd just broken wind, but the voice reasserted itself, "I just stopped by to check out the gladiators."

Some boys at the door laughed, and Father Luther, with a measured smile, a cocked eyebrow, and both hands bending a pencil almost to the breaking point, replied: "Is that so Mr. Reicharte?"

As if with ghost limbs, Christian did an abrupt, Spartan about-face. Uncontrollably, he lock-stepped down the aisle where he did a tight left-face at the end of the row of desks and a sharp right-face at the door where several boys stood by, their surprise covered by hands over their mouths. All the while, Christian could feel the priest's gas-jet eyes, like boll weevils, drilling the back of his head.

*   *   *   *   *   *   *   *   *

Lying on his bed in his bathrobe, Christian thumbed through the National geographic until he found the dog-eared page. The native girl was still behind the tree. She peered around it with a wide-eyed, inquisitive look. Her long, muscled legs tapered to her bare feet where floral garlands encircled each ankle. A loose string around her waist held up a skimpy loincloth. A dense canopy of green jungle growth hung above her, and spots of light, like silver rain drops, flickered through the cover, dappling her naked torso.

Gazing into her eyes, he was sure he spotted a glimmer of recognition. It appeared as if she were trying to communicate something to him. She might be anticipating a secret rendezvous at the edge of the jungle where the sea spread out toward the horizon like a broad, glittering, sterling silver service tray. He'd get a good tan before they met. The dull, rhythmic thud of drums caught his ear, and the occasional squeal of a wild animal mingled with the rapid beats of his heart. Vaguely, as if it were coming from some remote part of the jungle, he heard a hollow tapping, like successive strikes on a piece of bamboo. He wondered if she were trying to signal him, and unconsciously uttered, "Cupio. Cupio haec cognoscere[91]."

"Christian?" Rose asked as she stuck her head in the door. "I knocked but...oh, golly, 'scuse me. I didn't know you were busy." Quickly closing the door, she spoke through it: "There's a phone call. Should I tell her you're, ah, studying geography?"

Shoving the National Geographic, along with several pages which had fallen out of the layout, under his mattress, Christian breathlessly replied, "No, I'm coming."

A few minutes later, after quickly dressing, he opened the door and stepped out on the landing above the living room where he could hear his mother's cranky voice on the phone:

---

[91] I desire. I desire to know these things.

"Christian? Why, he's in his room studying. Who's this please?"

There was a pause, and Christian cringed.

"A friend's not good enough, my dear. You'll just have to identify yourself if you wish to communicate with anyone in this household."

Christian went to the bottom of the living room stairs and listened, the back of his neck burning. His mother was using the phone in the breakfast room which was just off the living room.

"...and what school do you attend, my dear?"

There was another pause as he crept closer to the breakfast room door.

"...a huh. That's the old public school on Hamilton is it not?"

There was another pause.

"...and what church does your family attend?"

There was another pause, and Rose came by on her way into the dining room. "Studying geography, were you?" she asked with a broad, incriminating smile and a sing-song inflection which made Christian blush from head to toe. Then, from behind her hand, she added, "Be careful. She's in a nasty mood. The goiter's acting up again." Flipping her long ponytail over one shoulder, she went into the kitchen, and Christian peeked around the frame of the breakfast room doorway.

"...a Quaker? Don't get sarcastic with me, young lady, or you won't speak to anyone. What? I don't care if it is the society of friends. Christian!"

Startled, Christian hesitated a few moments and then slinked into the breakfast room and took the phone from his mother's outstretched hand. "It's some snotty little girl for you," she snarled and self-consciously pulled the lapels of her terry cloth bathrobe together.

"Hello," he said with one eye on his mother who sauntered into the kitchen, her broad bottom jiggling, and the heels of her open-toed, backless slippers slapping the waxed floor like seal flippers. "Who's this anyways?"

"Me, Anne. From the rink, remember? Not the tall, skinny one."

"Oh, yeah."

"Who was that on the phone, Godzilla?"

He gulped. "How'd you know my number?"

"Looked it up, dingy. How else? Mr. Wrigley told my mom your last name. They know each other from the cheerleaders."

"You went to all that trouble for me?" Christian asked, his heart skipping a beat when he noticed a little puff of dusting powder near the floor by the kitchen door.

"Why wouldn't I? You're not a werewolf or anything are you?"

"In vino veritas[92]," the voice came as if from his shadow on the wall.

"What?"

---

[92] In wine is truth.

"Ah, nothing," Christian hastily replied. Then he noticed a pair of silk slippers at the bottom of the kitchen door.

"Was that Greek or something?"

"What?"

"In vino, whatever..."

"Ah, no, ah..."

"Can't talk, right? She's listening?"

"Yeah."

"How many humps does she have?"

"One, for real."

"For real?"

"Goiter," he whispered.

"Sounds ghoulish. Look, can you go skating tonight?"

"I guess, maybe."

"You can come over after. My parents're going out."

"They don't care?"

"No, they trust me. I go to the public school, remember? Meet me at the bench by the hot chocolate machine. Okay?"

"Umm, I guess."

"You don't sound too sure. They'll give you a hard time, right? I don't know why I always fall for one of you tight-assed private school guys. They sure keep a tight leash on you."

"No, I can go. It's just that, well, you know how they..."

"Hey, cool it. I'm just raggin' yah. Mine can be old-fashioned as hell too. They tried to get me not to wear makeup once. Just tell 'em you're going to a birthday party or something."

"Yeah, that's a good idea. I'll do that."

"I have to go! Six o'clock. Bye."

"Where do you think you're going?" Mrs. Reicharte snapped as he hung up. She'd materialized in the kitchen doorway like an apparition. Her face was a mask of cold cream, and her hair was bundled in a towel.

"To the rink after supper."

"After supper what?"

"After supper, mother."

"Nobody said you could go, did they? And watch your tone, young man. You're lucky to even have a roof over your head."

"What do you mean?"

"Just what I said. Did you ask your father?"

"No."

"No, what? Stop looking at my goiter."

"I wasn't, mother."

"Yes, you were. Everybody does. It's grotesque, and you know it. I'm seeing Dr. Baldanza about it, and I may have to have an operation. My thyroid's out of whack."

"Quidquid erit, superanda omnis frotuna ferendo est[93]," the silver-tongued shadow asserted herself without regard for Christian who slammed his hand over his mouth too late.

"Pardon me?"

"Nothing."

"It most certainly was something, young man, and I want to know what it was you said to me."

Christian stared at his basketball shoes, stymied.

"You made fun of me, didn't you?"

"No, I..."

"Five thousand a year your father pays them to teach you how to make fun of us in tongue."

"I didn't. It pops out sometimes. "Fortuna favel fortibus[94]. See! It's like somebody else is..."

"Nonsense. You know exactly what you're doing, and I'm going to mention it to your father. If you ask me, you need to see my psychiatrist."

---

[93] Whatever shall be, every fortune must be overcome by bearing it. (Virgil)
[94] Fortune favors the brave.

"Can I go skating in the meantime?"

"Where'd you meet her?"

"At the public rink in the park."

"She's a Quaker for Pete's sake."

"What difference does that make?"

"Don't talk back! How many times've I told you that?"

"Ad nauseam[95]."

"All right, I've had just about enough of that! You're not fooling me one little bit. You're making fun of us. If I hear any more of that speaking in Latin nonsense, I'll call Doctor Wilder and have you committed. Do you understand me? Who made you a priest?"

"Circus plenus, ianuae clausea, clamor ingens[96]," Christian uttered while examining his Keds and secretly praying that the voice would shut up.

"Stop that!"

Christian bit down hard on his lower lip, splitting it slightly. There was a pinpoint of blood.

"That's better. Now, go ask your father."

Carrying one of Christian's Latin grammars in a hip pocket, Rose came into the breakfast room and cut in, "Do you want me to do the kitchen windows?"

---

[95] To the point of nausea.
[96] Circus full, doors shut, great noise.

"Can't you figure that out for yourself?" Mrs. Reicharte snarled. "The bishop will be here for dinner. Did you dust my frogs? And polish up the sterling silver again."

"Mea culpa[97]," Rose replied.

"Not you too!" Mrs. Reicharte exclaimed.

"Just kidding," Rose added as she walked briskly toward the kitchen door where she stopped, dug into her apron pocket, and took out a rabbit's foot which dangled from a gold chain. "Here," she said and handed it to Christian.

Blushing deeply under Mrs. Reicharte's cold stare, Christian took the rabbit's foot Rose had once given him as a present, opened the little chain, and clasped it around a belt loop.

"It almost went in the wash," Rose commented with a wink for Christian as she walked into the kitchen, her long ponytail bouncing on the back of her sweater, and the hem of her panties showing through a pair of skin-tight white pedal pushers.

Watching after Rose, Mrs. Reicharte set her hands firmly on her ample hips and dryly commented to no one in particular, "Why, that huffy little pagan has on my perfume. Rose, isn't that my perfume you're wearing?" When there was no reply, she added, "A lot of nerve if you ask me. She couldn't afford Chanel in her wildest dreams ." Beside herself with consternation, she addressed Christian, "What're you still standing there for? Go ask your father. That young lady's on her way to the unemployment line if she doesn't buckle down. I'll dock the snitty little waif's paycheck, and she won't be so high and mighty."

---

[97]   My fault.

Christian just made it into the dining room out of earshot of Mrs. Reicharte before a suppressed remark sailed from his lips like a sailor's oath: "Iuppiter, excrucior[98]!" Then he tucked in the long tail of his Hawaiian print, took a deep breath, and walked beneath the high, dining room archway toward Mr. Reicharte who was sitting in a large recliner next to the living room fireplace which snapped and crackled over artificial logs. Pope Pius the Twelfth, framed in sterling silver, peered sightlessly outward from behind non-glare glass which hung on the wall above the fireplace. Mr. Reicharte's yellowish-gray, Vaseline-slicked hair glistened above the centerfold of The Wall Street Journal. He had his feet propped up on a hassock. .

Repelled, Christian forced himself to approach the great leather chair and stopped a few feet from it. Self-consciously, as if in the presence of a prelate, he noisily cleared his throat. Mr. Reicharte lowered the paper just enough to reveal the glassy-gray, bespectacled eyes of a bookworm.

"Can I go ska..."

"No. Not until you buckle down. It's a waste of time."

"It's my time."

"Don't talk back. How many times do I have to tell you that? You could fall and get seriously injured, and we'd be stuck with hospital bills. Money don't grow on trees you know. Besides, when I was growing up, there was always a lot of riffraff at them rinks. My mother'd make us stay home and read."

---

[98] Father of the gods, I am being tortured.

"I do. I've read Huckleberry Finn and The Old man and the Sea. Rose gave 'em to me when she was done. She's going to be a psychiatrist or a writer."

"Whoop-dee-do. Those jobs don't make no money and for your information, that Huckleberry wha-cha-ma-call-its been placed on the Legion of Decency black list. My word, the way that boy treated his elders and ran away with a nigger. What kind of reading is that for a boy that studies Latin in a parochial school?"

"But his father's the one who was bad."

"Is that so?"

"He was..."

"Don't interrupt. I always did what I was told, and it paid off in the end because my father once put a hundred dollars under my pillow. My brothers didn't get a dime. They was always talking back."

"Moriturus te saluto[99]."

"Don't dare start that foolishness around here. I thought we'd put that nonsense to rest at St. Xavier's. Do you want me to tell your mother about them pornographic pictures?"

"Mea culpa[100]."

"Mea what? If you're wise cracking me, I'll find out. The bishop's coming for dinner in spite of your shenanigans. All I have to do is ask 'em. He says that gibberish every Sunday at Mass, smarty pants. Do you want me to ask him?"

---

[99]   About to die, I salute you.
[100]   My fault.

"No."

"I'd better not catch you playing any practical jokes this time either."

"Okay, can I go?"

"I'm not finished. Look here...the Reader's Digest, and Post, and here's the Wall Street Journal, and whatever happened to that copy of Sixty Saints for Boys Santa Claus brought you for Christmas a couple of years ago?"

"I think it's in my room, but I like novels like Catcher in the Rye."

"Catcher in the wha-cha-ma-call-it? What kind of tale's that?"

"It means the hero waits by the edge of cliffs and catches little kids running out of the rye grass before they fall off the edge."

"Right, sure. Holy cow, do you think I got to run my own insurance office by reading stuff like that? Catching kids in the rye or whatever ain't going to make you no money, Mr. Latin scholar, and I wouldn't say this in front of the bishop but neither's all that Latin they're teaching you."

"But a lot of words come from..."

"When I was your age, it was the three R's, reading, writing, rithmatic that counted not all this high sounding foreign culture stuff. Why, we could multiply three digit numbers in our heads for Pete's sake. Nowadays, they don't even teach 'em the multiplication tables."

"Sed fugit interea[101]," the bossy voice asserted herself in spite of him.

"Stop that, for crying out loud. That Latin mumbo-jumbo died with Caesar'n Brutus, or was it Nero?"

"Ubi Roman venero Caesarem videbo[102]."

"Cut it out! If you only knew what we've sacrificed for you, you wouldn't be so blamed cocky. Your mother and me stuck our necks way out for you, you know. I've a notion to take you out of that school. Maybe have you committed."

Straining to hold back another Latin quip which was frolicking on the tip of his tongue, Christian's cheeks blew out as he bit down on his unruly tongue.

"I didn't say swallow your tongue, for heaven's sake," Mr. Reicharte cut in. Then he set the newspaper on his lap, folded his hands over it, and gave Christian a down-to-business look, his eyes like tiny pools of dirty water. "What in the devil's wrong with you? Why can't you behave like everyone else? There's snow still on the ground, and you're wearing that silly shirt with birds flying around on the beach. What the devil's gotten into you? We never used to know you were in the same room."

"Alter ego[103]."

"All right, God dammit, that's enough!" Mr. Reicharte exploded and took off his glasses. He gave Christian an intense, falcon-eyed stare. "You know, people are starting to think you're off your rocker.

---

[101]   But meanwhile time flies.
[102]   When I come to Rome, I shall see Caesar
[103]   Another self.

That's not even your normal voice for Christ's sake. It sounds like a girl's."

"In vino veritas[104]. May I go?"

"Who're going to meet?

"Anne something."

"What's Anne something's father do?"

"He's a policeman I think, but what does that have to do with..."

"A flatfoot. They don't make no money."

"What'a yah mean?"

"I mean you've got to associate with the right people in this world. It's not what you know, but who you know. Jesus, Mary and Joseph have you got a lot to learn. Where's your pride, boy? Do you think I send you to an exclusive private school so you can run with the likes of a policeman's daughter? What next? A coal miner's kid?"

"Nil praeter nasum Tongilianus habet[105]."

"All right, wise acre, that's it! What did you say, and I mean business this time?"

"Ah, it was, ah, if I clean my room, may I please go skating with a friend later?"

"It didn't sound like that many words to me."

"'Cause, ah, Latin's concise. It's not strung out like English."

---

[104] In wine is truth.
[105] Tongilianus has nothing but a nose. (Martial)

Mr. Reicharte picked up his newspaper and settled back in the recliner while commenting, "That better be all you said. Go on. You'll never amount to nothing anyways. I don't know why I waste my breath. Get a haircut, God dammit. You're starting to look like one a them fairies over on Michigan Street. Them jeans you're wearin' look like pedal pushers."

Fuming, Christian self-consciously looked down at his shirt and stove pipes, turned around, and walked toward the dining room. With one hand, he felt the soft, furry texture of the rabbit's foot which dangled from the gold chain attached to his belt loop. At his back, he heard his father say, "Catcher in the rye, my eye," and when he glanced over his shoulder, he saw The Wall Street journal, like a black and white death mask, slip over a disdainful smile. Hurrying into the breakfast room, he slammed his hand over his mouth just in time to muffle a sudden exclamation that sailed from his tongue like a witch's curse: "Caesar a Bruto interfectus est[106]!"

*　*　*　*　*　*　*　*　*

---

[106]　Caesar was killed by Brutus.

Christian waited in the small living room of Anne's house. The house was the size of the garage behind his own home and sparsely furnished by Sears and Roebuck catalog items. He felt a strange kind of fluttering anxiety in his stomach. What did he have to worry about other than the fact that he'd never been on a date before or even inside a girl's house, not to mention being alone with one. She seemed awful sassy for her age too.

Anne's father, a tall, well built man with a tanned, robust face, had picked them up at the rink and brought them over to the house. Anne had impressed him with her skating and had even taught him the glide waltz. Her mom, who looked like Anne but was less endowed, had welcomed him, not with the third degree like at his house, but with a broad smile and a coke. The folks were late for the annual policemen's charity ball so they both had excused themselves and gone upstairs to get ready. Anne was in her room changing out of her damp skating clothes because they had both taken a tumble together.

There was a mirror on the wall over a small fireplace so he got up from the couch and went over to check on his cowlick. It'd popped back up in spite of the pomade he'd plastered on it. For a split second he thought he looked like the Roman kid pictured riding a huge white horse in his Latin text, except the kid had thick blonde hair and no cowlick. He poked, pushed, and pressed until he got the stubborn cowlick to lie down. It was hot in the room, which had a space heater attached to the fireplace, so he took off his wool sweater and threw it over his air force jacket on the back of the couch. The tail of his Hawaiian print was out again so he tucked it into his jeans. He retied his Keds and rolled up the cuffs of his pegged fourteens, the new kind of jeans with severely tapered legs and the seat hiked up tight so it didn't sag like pajama bottoms. Rose had given them to him for a birthday present, and they fit like an animal's hide. He felt streamlined and ready for action in them, as if he could move through space with less resistance. If only he could get rid of the cowlick and his wild mop of dark brown hair, he'd be just like the Roman kid who was galloping away on a stallion in the textbook picture.

"Anne'll be down in a minute, Christian," Anne's mother said as she came down the stairway. She looked surprisingly young and beautiful in a low-cut, ballroom gown with a string of pearls which dropped into a modest cleavage. Anne's father was right after her, and he looked tall and regal in a tux and shiny black shoes.

"We've got to hurry along," Annie's mother continued as her husband helped her into a very plain wool coat. "We're running late. Now, you two have fun, and we'll give you a ride home when we get back, Christian. Did you tell your folks you'd be home late?"

"Ah, yeah," Christian hedged. He was supposed to be home by eleven.

"You be sure to call them if we're past midnight so they won't worry. There's plenty of food in the refrigerator and plenty of coke. Upstairs is off limits and don't go out of the house. Anne knows the rules."

"I might let you take a turn at the wheel on the way home, Christian," Anne's father added as he pulled on an overcoat and put his arm around his wife's waist. Then they walked out and closed the door behind them.

Christian went back over to the mirror. The cowlick was back with a vengeance. It stood straight up like a feather in a woman's hat. He smashed it down, and straightened the collar of his Hawaiian print. He checked his zipper. The fly was closed. He took out a handkerchief and popped a tiny pimple which was on the side of his nose. He checked his fly again. It was definitely closed. He went back and sat on the couch where Anne had left him. He picked up a magazine from a long coffee table in front of the couch.

"You wanna commit some mortal sins?"

She questioned him from the arched doorway which opened from the kitchen into the living room. She'd appeared there like a blonde apparition, startling him because he remembered her having brown hair. Her heart-shaped face was heavily made up with thick black eyeliner, blue eye shadow, rouge, and red lipstick.

"Mortal sins?" he asked, his eyes glued to the soft texture of her pink cashmere sweater which was stretched to its absolute limits.

"Isn't that what you boarding school boys call messin' around?" she frankly replied, posing in her skin tight sweater.

"Fortis qui se vincit[107]," Christian heard his shadow's warning, and it felt like a switchblade had opened in his trousers.

"Is that so? Well, sic hoc nunc to you, dingy. Check this out."

"Sanctum sanctorum[108]!" his shadow howled when she held up a bottle of clear liquid. Beside himself, Christian leaned forward and read aloud the label on the bottle: "Vodka!"

"My dad got a case for Christmas," she replied. "He'll never miss a bottle. Get a cigarette out of the wooden box on the coffee table."

When she went back into the kitchen, Christian opened a flat, wooden cigarette box with a policeman's shield embossed on the top. It was full of Camels, the unfiltered kind. He knew they were

---

[107] A brave man is he who conquers himself.
[108] Holy of holies!

stronger than the Lucky Strikes Snyder panhandled, but he took one out and lit it anyway. He could hear cupboards banging and ice cubes clicking in glasses, and then she came into the living room with two ice tea glasses full of a thick, reddish liquid.

"What's that?" he asked, coughing into his fist from the impact of a drag on the Camel.

"It's a Bloody Mary," she commented as she handed him the tall glass while sipping eagerly from her own. Then she set her glass on the coffee table with a bang, and reached for a cigarette. "I seen my dad makin' 'em at a party once. Tomato juice'n Vodka, half-'n-half."

"Ne nunc moriar[109]!"

"Yeah, me too," she replied as she sat down on the couch next to Christian. Then she took a big swallow from her Bloody Mary, lit a cigarette with an unconscious flick of a table lighter, and took a long, deliberate inhalation. "I usually smoke Marlboros, but I ain't got any. Drink up, dingy."

Christian took a big swallow. "Not bad," he commented, puckering his lips and turning up his nose before taking another swallow with his eyes tightly shut.

"You get used to 'em," she said and took another swallow. She moved closer to Christian who was sitting on the edge of the couch. "Relax will yah? I sneak 'em up to my room sometimes if I'm wound up or feelin' kinda down in the dumps. My parents both work so I'm here alone a lot. The public school guys're too immature'n my mom says it's just as easy to marry someone rich as poor."

"Really?" Christian responded with a drag from his Camel and then a big cough. He was slightly repelled by the flaky, blue mascara

---

[109] Let me die now!

she wore on her eyelids, but she smelled wonderful and the sweater was irresistible. He wanted to wear it.

"They want me to meet a nice boy," she said and took another swallow. Then she casually blew a pair of perfect smoke rings. The rings hung in the air like halos and slowly disintegrated. "Are you a nice boy?" she coyly added.

"Ah, my name's on the list if that's what you mean," Christian responded while noting the bright red lipstick marks she'd left on her cigarette and front tooth. He was getting a little skittish. She seemed awfully sophisticated for her age.

"List?"

"The black list."

"Oh, I'm on that all the time. I'm gonna get us another one'n put on some music. They'll be out real late tonight."

"Yeah, ah, good idea," Christian added, suddenly feeling warm and cozy. "Where'd you learn to blow smoke rings?"

"My dad. He does it all the time when he smokes. I'll be right back. Let me have that."

Gulping down what was left of his drink, Christian handed her his ice tea glass and observed, "This stuff works kinda fast doesn't it?"

With a cigarette hanging from one corner of her mouth, she replied, "Naw," and went into the kitchen. She returned with the bottle of Vodka and two high ball tumblers filled with ice cubes. She switched on a table radio, turned off the lights, and topped off both tumblers with pure Vodka.

"Straight booze?" Christian questioned, examining his tumbler by the light from the kitchen.

"Why waste time. Wanna dance?"

"I guess," Christian replied and took an anxious drag from his Camel and a gulp from his tumbler. "Where?"

"Right here, dingy," she quipped and pointed toward the living room rug while taking a swig.

Christian took another swallow and wiped his mouth with the back of his hand. He got up and followed her around the coffee table where he tripped over one of its legs. The music from the radio roared in his ears, and when Chuck Berry screamed, he cringed.

"Dingy," she commented and wrapped his arms around her neck as the song changed to "Smoke Gets In Your Eyes".

"Do you have to call me that silly name?" Christian heard his voice from far away.

"WKRO for rock-'n--roll," the announcer squealed, "brings you the number one hit song in America today!" Then the Platters' voices came on with "The Great Pretender", the lyrics arcing between them like a band of sparks between two electrodes: rocking and swaying their way through the song, they held one another up until Anne, her speech slurred, came up for air, "Leth lie down for a minute. My head's thpinning."

"Thoes mine," Christian replied while peeling her sweaty arms from around his neck. Then he felt her fall on top of him like a sand bag, the old Sears couch squeaking. She began smothering him with kisses and her hands groped.

Christian floundered beneath her like a fish out of water. His head whirred and his hands instinctively strayed beneath her sweater where they tentatively squeezed the conical cup of her brassiere. The cups, as if spring loaded, abruptly recoiled with a pop.

"No, Chrithton, don't. Not there," she breathlessly whispered. "They're falsies."

Thunderstruck, Christian jerked his hand away as if he'd touched a hot wire.

"Goodness gracious, great balls of fire!" Jerry Lee Lewis screamed. over WKRO. The music stampeded over them like wild horses, and someone's foot kicked the coffee table causing the tumblers to fall off. From afar, Christian heard his shadow's voice, echoing, as if coming at once from the floor, walls, and ceiling: "Facilis descendus Averno[110]."

"Don't stop, dingy," was her only reply as the black book slammed shut in his face.

* * * * * * * * *

---

[110] Easy is the descent to Avernus. (The lower world.)

Feeling like the elephant that'd been tied by an unbreakable chain as a baby and by a thin piece of rope as an adult, Christian dutifully stood in line by the side aisle wall of the church. A confessional loomed in the dusky half light like a magician's box. On each side of the box several people waited in line, and in the vestibule behind him, his father stood with his mouth firmly set, and his arms tightly folded across his chest.

Anne's parents had called his father and complained that they'd expected a private school boy to know how to treat a young lady. Ever since, he'd been on the black list. His mother had even threatened to have him committed for therapy with Doctor Wilder, her psychiatrist.

Next to the box there was a pedestal bearing a tall statue of a saint. The saints eyes were vacant. A plaster finger was missing from one of the statue's hands leaving a white, powdery stub. Standing in line on the other side of the box, there was a tiny, white-haired old lady. She wore a long black woolen dress, a black overcoat, black rubber-soled work shoes, and a flat, broad-rimmed, veiled hat. The hat had a partridge seated sedately in its crown. Several ancient men also waited in line on each side of the box. They held their hats in hand, and their clothes were dark, stained, and wrinkled as if they'd slept in them. Glancing over his shoulder, Christian caught the evil eye of his father who was keeping an eye on him from the foyer while wagging a finger at him to get in line.

When he heard the familiar clack of the wooden door over the screen inside the box, Christian's chest tightened because he was next in line. An old man with a long topcoat and severely scuffed brown cordovans came out of the box and hobbled up the aisle to the communion railing which spanned the front of the church.

The old lady with the black bird hat disappeared behind the curtained entrance of the black box when suddenly, with a loud crash, a snowball flew through the stained-glass window above the altar and exploded in mid-air like a white hand grenade. Bits of colored glass flew everywhere. The elderly people who were standing in lines on opposite sides of the black box gaped, with expressions of horror, at the sunlit hole in the window.

There was a clack from within the box, and, to Christian's shocked surprise, Father Devine stepped out. He peered around, and then ambled up the aisle a few feet beyond the tall box so he could get a good view of what the parishioners were gawking at. Sticking his hands deeply into the sleeves of his black cassock, and stepping backward a few paces, he looked up at the bright hole in the window, shook his head at it several times, and exclaimed, as if someone on the other side had stayed around to listen, "Ave Maria! A te peta ne hoc facias[111]!"

Christian glanced over his shoulder hoping that his father may have abandoned his post to run outside and catch the culprits who threw the snowball, but Mr. Reicharte glared back at him and wagged his fingers toward the box. There were two purple curtained entrances to the box, one on each side of a wooden doorway. He went in the entrance on his side, and pulled the purple curtain shut kneeling on the hard wooden kneeler which put his face directly in front of a black screen. He put down a terrible urge to run but there was no way out this time with his father blocking the foyer door.

Suddenly, the wooden door behind the screen opened, and Christian's hands became fists. Father Devine, as if harboring anger about the broken window, snapped, "Pax vobisum[112]," and his silhouette appeared behind the screen. A dim light filtered

---

[111]   Hail Mary! I ask you not to do this!
[112]   Peace with you.

through the screen enabling Christian to see a small plaque hanging on the wall behind the priest's head. Squinting in the shadows of the curtained alcove, he could barely read the words inscribed on the plaque. It was the same expression Father Dittman was fond of using: Sed libera no a malo[113].

"Pax vobiscum" the silhouette repeated.

As if stigmatized by the inscription on the tablet, he involuntarily, like something remotely controlled, sprang upward and bolted through the purple curtain which was left swinging back and forth in the entrance. Feeling his Ked basketball shoes digging in, he held himself back, half running and half walking toward the vestibule where his father was posted, his arms still stiffly folded across his chest like a palace guard's. Ignoring his father's question, "Did you go?", he walked directly out. In a fleeting glance over his shoulder, he caught his father's thunderstruck expression and Father Devine was peering inquisitively around the opened door of the confessional.

Outside, the bright sunlight was blinding, and the cold, fresh air washed over him in liberating waves. Surprised at how fast his heart was beating, he stopped at the foot of the stairs to catch his breath, put on his earmuffs, and zip up his jacket. There was a group of boys hiding behind some trees across the street. The trees' thawing limbs were contorted, and their trunks jutted up from hard patches of snow. One of the kids jumped out and threw a snowball at Christian. When he ducked, the snowball passed over his head and exploded against his father's chest as he came out of the church yelling, "Did you go?" As the boys ran away squealing with laughter, Mr. Reicharte lamely shook his gloved fist and yelled a series of oaths so loudly that several people came out of the church to see what was going on. One of them, the lady in the bird hat,

---

[113]   Deliver us from evil.

gave Mr. Reicharte a severe look of self-righteous indignation and wagged her finger at him.

"Stop laughing like a hyena and get in the God damned car!" Mr. Reicharte yelled at Christian while giving the lady an up yours spearing motion with his right hand. "Dad-blamed brats've got no respect for nobody no more!" With that, he went around the car and got in, started it, and peeled away from the curb with a loud grinding of gears. This made people at the church door cover their mouths with their hands in astonishment. It also emancipated Christian's obnoxious shadow who sat up in her seat and boldly remarked: "Magistro errante, pueri guadebant[114]."

The Latin quip in the car on the way home from church was the last straw. Mr. Reicharte had boxed Christian's ears and sent him to his room until Dr. Wilder could be consulted. Christian stared out the second floor window which overlooked the two-car garage, patio, empty pool, and fenced back yard. Mr. Reicharte had insisted on putting up a six-foot fence right after the Bernsteins moved in next door. It was something about them being Jews. Taking a Lucky Strike out of a pack he'd hidden in his sock, he opened a window, lit the Lucky, took a puff, and blew the smoke out the window. A chilly draft blew in, and from the Bernstein's yard, he heard the first signs of spring. Children's voices wavered over the keen air. There was the smack of a baseball striking oiled leather, and the crack of a baseball against a wooden bat. Reaching into the bottom drawer of his dresser, he pulled out his Japanese box kite which he'd folded up for the winter. He also took out a worn Wilson's fielder's mitt, a can of linseed oil, his Yankee's baseball cap, a baseball, a bat, and a shiny red Duncan Imperial yo-yo with three bright diamonds on each side.

---

[114]   As the master was making a mistake, the boys rejoiced.

With the Lucky dangling from the corner of his mouth, he put on the baseball cap and adjusted the yo-yo string loop on his finger. He flipped his wrist which spun the yo-yo to the bottom of the string where it stalled for several seconds. Then he looped it around-the-world in wide three-sixties until it popped into his palm with a smack. Satisfied, he undid the finger loop and put the yo-yo into the hip pocked of his pegged blue jeans. Then he took a last puff and tossed the cigarette out the window.

Suddenly reminded of something, he half unconsciously wandered over to his bed and lifted the mattress. He reached way under for his National Geographic. Feeling nothing, he lifted the mattress up and peered beneath it, but the magazine wasn't there where he'd left it. Dumbstruck, he dropped the mattress and got down on his hands and knees to look under the bed. He got up and went through every drawer of his dresser until he was suddenly struck with a foreboding insight. His face turned pale, and he ran over to the window to see if both cars were gone. Then he ran out of the room, down a long hallway, and into his parents' bedroom.

Looking around the room with anxiety, he was overcome by an almost overwhelming feeling of alienation as if he'd just opened someone's grave. The curtains on the arched windows were tightly drawn which cast the room in a forbidding half-light. His mother's silk, open-toed slippers were beside the bed, their interior splattered with talcum powder. He could smell the leather in his father's tree-racked shoes which were on one side of the bed.

Stealthily, as if invading a Pharaoh's tomb, he looked under the bed, on top of his father's high dresser, on top of his mother's dresser, and then under the pillows on the bed which was covered with a thick, quilt bedspread. Scared, the room was off limits even to the maid, he hurried over and opened the top drawer of his father's dresser. A plastic holy water font, with a dry and brittle finger sponge in the bowl, hung on the wall next to the dresser. Rummaging through the deep drawer, he found a rosary, black nylon socks, three old prayer books, seven bottles of pills, two of them labeled Darvon and Valium, some underwear and handkerchiefs. At the bottom, beneath a pile of folded pajamas, he found, to his utter dismay, several glossy magazines entitled Garden of Eden. Frightened out of his wits, he slammed the drawer shut.

Feeling kind of dizzy, he rummaged through his mother's drawers. He went to the walk-in closet and opened the tall door which had a long, full-length mirror attached to the inside. He pushed back clothes and looked behind them. He pulled out shoes and searched under the lower shelves where he found a long gray box made of metal with a steal lid. It had a keyhole on top and a metal handle. Grabbing the handle, he lugged the heavy box into the closet entrance. His hand slipped, and his elbow slammed into the dressing mirror, shattering the glass. Panicked, he ran to the window and pulled back the curtain so he could see the garage. Both cars were still gone, and he knew Rose was in the basement doing laundry.

Lured by the locked safe, he ran to his mother's dresser and got a hairpin. Then he knelt by the box and inserted the hairpin in the keyhole precisely as the Shadow had done in The Dancing Detective, one of the Shadow's recent episodes. Tilting his head at precisely the correct angle, he listened as he slowly manipulated the hairpin with his fingertips. (The Shadow could get into Fort Knox with a hairpin.) There was a faint clicking sound, and the key turned. He pulled up on the lid and the box opened. Rifling through it, he found some legal documents, insurance policies, and some envelopes with ancient, cancelled stamps. One of the stamps pictured an inverted biplane which he recognized as a valuable stamp even though it was in poor condition and cancelled. On the bottom of the box, there was a folded sheet of yellowish, legal-looking paper with a broken red seal. He picked it up, unfolded it, and read:

Reverend J. F. Meehan
Saint Nicholas Welfare Association

March 22, 1943

Sister Gertrude Louise, Mother Superior
906 New Wakefield Building
Milwaukee, Wisconsin

Dear Mr. and Mrs. Reicharte:

We are enclosing our consent as general guardians to the placement for adoption of Ronald Cornelius Culpepper in your home at 2505 East Bay Drive, Milwaukee, Wisconsin. The approval from the Division of Social Welfare for this placement is on file in our office.

We are also enclosing the forms which are required in adjusting the birth record of the child to show the new legal name you requested: Christian Thomas Reicharte.

Awestruck, Christian stared at the document. The closet door swung back on its hinges a few inches and startled him when multiple images of himself flickered eerily in the tall mirror he'd fractured into several pieces. Feeling a cold hand stroking his back, he continued to read:

Ronald was born on February 13, 1942, the legitimate son of Edward Cornelius Culpepper and Margaret Culpepper, formerly Margaret O' Neil. Margaret was an accomplished actress and clairvoyant. Mr. Culpepper was born in North Dakota and Mrs. Culpepper was born in Wisconsin. Ronald was committed to the general guardianship of the Saint Nicholas Welfare Association as the father, a bomber pilot with the USAF, was shot down over the Pacific on Ronald's birth date and the mother, who suffered acute postpartum depression, died of a stroke shortly after Ronald's birth. Apparently, the mother never recovered from the news of her husband's untimely missing-in-action status.

We shall appreciate it if you will send us a certified copy of the decree after the hearing so that we may close the case in our file.

We want to take this opportunity to extend our best wishes to you for your future happiness with Ronald.

In His Service, Sister Gertrude Louise

BFF:rr

* * * * * * * * *

"Jesus-H-Christ on a bike!" Rose exclaimed. She was eyeballing a document while undoing her ponytail with one hand. Her long hair bounced over the shoulders of a pink button-down sweater. She kicked off a pair of white flats and undid the brass button on the fly of her jeans. "You're somebody else!"

"Isn't everybody?" Christian coolly replied, his shoulder nudging hers as they sat together on the high, iron-posted bed in her attic room. There were two small windows set in a small sitting alcove beneath a low, slanting ceiling. The windows let in narrow bands of sunlight which fell at the foot of the bed.

"Would you look at this?" she continued, pointing at the document. "Your father was a pilot. That explains those medals we found in the attic that time. And look here - oh, dear, I'm sorry, Christian - she must've loved your father very much. She probably died of a broken heart. He was a hero, your father. Remember that."

"I wonder what she looked like," Christian pondered.

"Maybe you could check with this agency or something. I don't know though. I've heard these places'll seal the files. Maybe those pictures in the attic. You might have to go to court or something. Would you look at this middle name? Cornelius?"

"It's a weird Roman name. I've seen it in Latin books. Caesar's cousin or something."

"No kidding," Rose commented as she pulled a brush through her thick, auburn hair, the document on her lap. "I like Ronnie. Now that's a first-class name you'd see on a baseball cap, not a tombstone. Ronnie Culpepper. Yeah, it's you all right."

"Really? Should I go by it?"

"Why not? It's your real name isn't it?"

"I guess so. Yeah! It says so right here. I got it out of the box in their closet."

"I thought so. I cleaned up the mirror'n told her I broke it with the carpet sweeper handle. She let me go in there the other day to clean the floor. Was it in that fire box?"

"Yeah, how'd you know?"

"I've seen it. What were you doing in there anyways?"

"It's kind of a secret. Some stuff was missing, and I thought they found it. She's always snooping around my room."

"Stuff like, ah, under the ole mattress?"

"Yeah."

"Hey, Ronnie, stop blushing," Rose acknowledged as she reached behind his head to brush down the cowlick which stood up in the crown. "It's only hormones and hormones're human. Besides, I've seen your stash when I changed the sheets. Your tracks too. That little native behind the tree's cute."

Christian shrank into the collar of his Hawaiian print while she patted his cowlick down. She suddenly jumped off the bed and remarked, "Just a minute. Let me see if I can do something with that wild hair of yours. It's long enough now, but the ends're splitting and you need more body and sheen. We can even do a little role playing if you want to."

"Can I try on that cashmere sweater?"

"Sure, I brought some of that stuff down."

Leaving the document on her dresser, she went into a small bathroom which was in a tiny loft a step up from the bedroom. He could hear her rummaging in the bath cabinet, and in a few minutes she came back with a small brown bottle with a white label. Opening the cap, she told him to sit still, poured the contents on his head, and rubbed it in while commenting: "This'll color it and give it more body and tame that cowlick once'n for all. I used it once." She opened the casement windows all the way out and instructed him to sit in a rocking chair, the back of which was situated beneath bands of sunlight which poured through the open windows.

Enjoying the sunlight on his shoulders - she'd covered his legs with a beautiful afghan - and the tingling sensation on his scalp, Christian relaxed and found himself uncharacteristically chatty, and he secretly hoped the voice would mind her own business for once: "I'll bet my father bailed out just in the nick of time. He probably got the crew out and then jumped. A lot of times they're shot down, but they get away in one of those yellow rafts. He could be stranded on an island'n not even know where he is. I'll bet he's hiding in one of those caves the Japs used. Or maybe he's just in..."

"Ronnie," Rose interceded while weaving several curlers into his hair. "The war's been over for a long time."

"...he could be in Korea though or a spy somewheres."

"Cornelius," she interrupted again as she handed him a Kleenex from a box which was sitting on her dresser next to a framed picture of her and a handsome sailor.

Blowing his nose, Christian said, in a breaking voice, "I guess I got carried away. How come you always wear that necklace?"

"I lost my guy in the war. That's him in the picture. We were going to get married."

"I'll bet he gave you the necklace," Christian interrupted.

"He did. He was in the Navy." She held the jade pendant in her fingertips and looked down at it. "It's Buddha, the only spiritual leader who teaches that man does not have to depend on gods or spirits to survive. All he has to do is believe in himself."

"That's hard to do."

"Hardest thing in life," she commented while opening a closet door to take out a pink tube top. She hung it over a bed post and removed the loose sweater she was wearing. Then she stood in front of the mirror above her dresser with her back to Christian and brushed out her luxurious, reddish-brown hair which fell over the white bra strap that was hooked in the center of her back. "Exigua pars est vitae quam nos vivimus[115]," she mused while glancing at Christian in the mirror.

"The part of life we really live is short," Christian heard his shadow's voice translate before he'd even digested the first three words. "Seneca as I recall."

"That was fast," Rose added. "And that voice change is really cute, kinda sultry. Must be your fem. side, huh. Or maybe your mother. Here put my sweater on. It's your favorite, cashmere."

"Oh, we're gonna role play?"

"Why not, maybe even more."

---

[115] The part of life that we really live is short (Seneca)

"Really?" Christian replied while changing into the sweater and wondering what she'd meant.

"How's the hair doing?"

"I don't know. I can't see it."

"Let me see. It's thickening nicely and no more cowlick."

"I hated it anyway," he replied and ducked his head while she worked her fingers through his hair. He could smell his mother's Chanel Number Five perfume. It was intoxicating. A strip of reddish-gold peach fuzz ran from her exposed navel down into her jeans. In the deep fissure between her breasts, which swelled over the top of her bra, Buddha smiled endearingly, and the green jade rested naturally next to her smooth, brown skin.

"Just relax," she remarked while continuing to massage his scalp, "but stay where you are for a while. Doesn't the sun feel good on your back?"

"Yeah'n my head feels like a Fourth of July sparkler. What'd you do to it anyways?"

"Oh, just a little peroxide. Later, we'll role play and you can put on some nice things. Maybe we'll play a joke on them all. Wait'll you see. Unhitch me will you?"

Startled, Christian uttered, "Huh?"

"You've got to learn how to do this sooner or later, Cornelius," she kidded, presenting her back to him.

Befuddled, he reached up and clumsily fumbled with the weird clasp. The name Cornelius lingered in his ears like a secret code.

"Lift it," she said, peering over her shoulder.

Moving to the edge of the rocker, Christian struggled with the catch and finally undid it. The oversized bra fell into her hands as she reached for the tube top hanging on the bed post. Her chestnut eyes, like an inquisitive cat's, caught Christian's slack-jawed stare in a mirror above her dresser as she slipped the stretch top over her head and reached behind her back to adjust it.

"Do you like them?" she asked, her eyes and Christian's meeting in the mirror.

"Mellitus-a-um[116]!" he barked.

"Cornelius, Cornelii[117]," she retaliated.

"Cupiditas, cupiditatis,[118]" the voice shot back before he knew it.

"Corpus, corporis[119]," Rose challenged the passionate voice.

"Animus, animi[120]," he breathlessly countered.

"Anima, animae[121]," she concluded, her breath fogging the mirror.

With that, Rose walked over to the night stand next to her bed and opened a small record player. She carefully set the needle on a record. There was a scratching sound, a bit of static, and then a sweet female voice singing How Much Is That Doggy In The Window. Humming along, she walked back to Christian and very

---

[116] Sweet as honey!
[117] Cornelius
[118] Desire
[119] The body
[120] The mind as the seat of the feelings.
[121] The soul

gently started to remove the curlers she'd wound into his hair. As if transported by the fresh breeze from the open window, a voice trilled:

I read in the pa-pers there are rob-bers –
With flash-lights that shine in the dark;
   My love needs a dog-gy to pro-tect him -

And scare them away with one bark.

       *   *   *   *   *   *   *   *

"Who, may I ask, are you, and what exactly are you doing here?" Father Luther demanded as he poised above a pretty blonde wearing a white cashmere sweater over a bright red poodle skirt which fit over her knees. The outfit was complemented by a pair of Bobby socks and black-and-white saddle shoes, one foot primly anchored behind the other as she sat up straight in her desk. The priest's blue eyes were brimming with dismay, and his black habit was like an impenetrable wall. The other students in the classroom were turned around in their desks to view the new student who had appeared like a phantom in a desk at the back of the room. Some of them whispered behind their hands, and others snickered while the young lady kept her hands folded on top of her desk as she softly replied, "Victoria Culpepper. First day."

"But this is an all boys' school. Who enrolled you?"

The class laughed at the priest's obvious befuddlement. Many observed the girl with more than curiosity. One guy in row three even made a kissing sound.

"Shut up Olsen!" Father Luther exclaimed before continuing in a softer, almost patronizing tone. "Now, my dear, cough up your transfer papers."

"I don't have any," the young lady replied in a sugar-and-spice tone.

"Don't she look familiar somehow?" Johnson cried out.

"Vaguely, where's Reicharte?" another kid hollered. "He loves to do tricks."

"What about you, Simmons?" a kid retaliated.

"Tam ferox ut minatur oppugnet[122]," the young lady matter-of-factly interjected.

"Sweet Jesus!" Father Luther screamed, jumping backward and holding up his hands as if in the presence of leper. "Is it him? Mother of mercy."

The class roared at the priest's frustration, and Father Luther retaliated, "If I hear one more outburst from anyone in this room, they'll be expelled! I mean it, and if this is some kind of sick joke the whole bunch of you'll be expelled along with any scholarships! And if that's you, Reicharte, get out of this room and go directly to the office right now! Simmons, take names while I'm gone."

With a small notebook in hand, Simmons dutifully went to the front of the room in spite of the sucking sounds around him. The young lady, moving with a swish the boys couldn't ignore, headed for the door, her cashmere sweater and the red poodle skirt fluttering around her ankles.

The class knuckled under as the priest went to the board and wrote down an assignment. "Get to work, Matthews!" he hollered on his way out of the room. "You too Krickendorf!

The office secretary was a skin and bones lady who wore a black hair net over gray hair. She had on a box cut black dress with shoulder pads, and a large wooden crucifix dangled down the front of her dress. Looking up from her typewriter through tiny bifocals which were perched on the tip of her nose, she asked, "Are you here to see someone, dear?"

"I guess. Father Luther told me to wait for the rector. I don't have entrance papers."

---

[122]   They are so bold that they attack girls.

"But this is an all boys' school, darling," What's your name?"

"Victoria. Victoria Culpepper."

"That's a cute name. Let me ring the rector for you. There must be some mistake."

Just then, Father Luther, his cassock short-fitting because of his height, bustled into the office with a piece of composition paper in his hand. With a disgusted look at Victoria, he knocked on the rector's door and then walked in, slamming the door behind him. A couple minutes later the secretary's phone rang.

The secretary picked up her phone and listened before replying, "My word, I see, well, maybe the boys are playing some kind of joke, Father. I'll tell her...him to wait."

"Is there a problem?" Victoria asked when the secretary hung up the phone with a squinty glare in her direction.

"Why, I never..." the astonished secretary managed to reply with a look of haughty disgust. "The rector said that you are to remain right here while they get in touch with your father. My word, what's the world coming to? Father Devine's on his way too so you'd better mind your P's and Q's."

The phone rang again, and the secretary picked it up. "Yes," she queried, and there was a pause. "Yes, Mr. Reicharte, it's him, and I can't say anything else right now, but you are to come to school immediately. The rector and Father Luther are already here and she's...he's...well, you'll see when you get here. Father Devine's on the way."

When the secretary hung up, Victoria got up and walked over to a wall mirror near the rector's office door. With the secretary watching every move she made, she took a hair brush out of a small clutch purse and brushed her shiny blonde hair in the mirror, fluffing up the hair in the back with her hand. She could hear Father Luther yelling behind the office door. She heard the word sacrilege and queer followed by a loud reference to transvestites. Putting the brush back into the clutch purse, she took out a tube of lipstick and carefully applied some to her lips, rubbing her lips together to smooth out the lipstick. Then she got a magazine from a coffee table and sat down on a leather couch near the rector's door, smoothing her poodle skirt and appropriately crossing her legs at the knee.

Just as she finished glancing through the magazine and reached for another one, Father Devine, dressed in a smooth black suit, open black overcoat, and black hat, rushed into the foyer as if late for a funeral service. Mr. Reichart, out of breath, was right behind him.

"For Pete's sake, this isn't Christian!" was Mr. Reicharte's first reaction to Victoria who looked up at him with fluttering, black eyelashes.

"I'm afraid it is," the secretary said from the other side of the reception desk.

Victoria peered at her father's slate gray eyes, ruler-parted hair, and upward slanting eyebrows as if she didn't recognize him either.

"What in Sam Hill have you done to yourself?"

"Sam Hill?" Victoria questioned matter-of-factly.

"Do you have wax in your ears?"

"Nihil[123]."

---

[123] Nothing, in no wise.

"That's him!" Mr. Reicharte hollered, looking at Father Devine with a surprised expression.

"Quidem[124]."

Mr. Reicharte's jaws clattered: "Stop that! Im gonna call up Dr. Wilder'n have you taken away in a butterfly net! They'll lock you up and throw the key away for Christ's sake!"

"Cur[125]?"

"Shut up, God dammit!"

"Cur?"

"Careful, Mr. Reicharte," Father Devine interjected, "the language."

Struggling for self control, Mr. Reicharte inhaled deeply, put his hands on his hips, and gave Victoria a mad-hatter's, glare, his bushy eyebrows stretching to the outer limits of his forehead. The secretary clicked her tongue in self-righteous disgust, and Father Devine just stood there studying Victoria with a dumbfounded expression on his face. The door to the rector's office opened and Father Luther stepped out. He wagged his finger at Victoria and nodded toward Father Devine and Mr. Reicharte. As she stood up, Victoria became suddenly aware of her own voice as if someone had attached a microphone to her: "Solitudinem faciunt pacem appellant[126]."

"Pardon me?" Father Luther replied.

"Cut it out, numbskull!" Mr. Reicharte bellowed.

---

[124] Indeed.
[125] Why?
[126] They make a wilderness and call it peace.

"Mea culpa[127]," Victoria replied as she sauntered into the rector's office beneath the scornful gaze of Father Luther who waited for Mr. Reicharte and Father Devine before instructing the secretary to hold all calls and closing the door.

Taking one look at Victoria, the rector, a middle-aged man with a Friar Tuck hairdo and a wandering lazy eye, stuck one hand under his double chin, grabbed the edge of his desk with the other hand, leaned well over the top of the desk and inquired, "What the devil've you done to yourself, my boy."

"Expedio[128]."

"To set free. Who?"

"Alter ego[129]."

"I see," the rector skeptically replied, raising both eyebrows in Father Luther's direction while Mr. Reicharte and Father Devine, seated in adjacent chairs, exchanged bewildered glances.

"I told you," Father Luther said to the rector as he pushed a straight-backed chair behind Victoria's knees and sternly admonished, "Sit down and behave yourself, and let's take off this wig!"

"Ow!" Victoria howled when her hair didn't budge from the priest's tug.

"I can't believe this!" Father Luther exclaimed, letting go of Victoria's hair. "It's been attached or something!"

---

[127] My fault.
[128] To set free.
[129] Other self.

"Now, now, let's all calm down," Father Devine scolded, leaning forward in his chair with his hands on his knees. "We don't need a scandal here. I'm sure there's an explanation for this charade. She... he likes practical jokes, even played a pernicious one on me once."

"I agree with Father Devine," the rector added. "Do you know why you're here, young lady?"

"Persona non grata[130]?"

All of the priest's exchanged perplexed glances, but their eyes drew blanks.

"Can you help us out here, Walter?" the rector addressed Mr. Reicharte. "First it was the poem, now this."

"Poem?" Mr. Reicharte asked, peering over the top of his bifocals.

With a nod, Father Luther handed the rector a piece of composition paper. The rector reviewed it, and then handed it to Mr. Reicharte who began reading it under his breath, his lips rapidly moving. When he finished, he gave Victoria a ferocious grimace and exclaimed, "What's the meaning of this prophet nonsense? Is it from one of them books you and Rose've been readin'?"

"Homae doctus in se semper divitias habet[131]," Victoria flatly replied.

"Homo what? Are you talkin' dirty?"

"Maybe he should read it to us," Father Devine piped in.

"Good idea," Father Luther affirmed.

---

[130]   I am an unacceptable person?
[131]   A learned woman always has wealth in herself

"What do you think, Walter?" the rector asked, his lazy eye going up to the ceiling while the other peered at Mr. Reicharte.

"I don't see why not. Teach 'em a lesson. Stand up and read it, Christian."

"Victoria, if you please. Victoria Cornelius Culpepper."

Horrified, Mr. Reicharte put his hands over his ears. "My God, he's found out!"

"I tried to tell you! He's touched, maybe even schizoid!" Father Luther insisted, ignoring Mr. Reichart's remark.

"I expect you'd better do as you're told," the rector demanded.

"Ars longa, vita brevis[132]," Victoria replied in an obliging voice as she snatched the composition paper from her father's limp hand and stood up with it held out like a proclamation. In a clear, unwavering, devil-may-care alto voice, she proceeded to read:

The Prophet

With glowing eyes and onion breath,
He spoke of sin, sorrow, and sudden death.

Then he raised his Book and
Shook his fist, stamped his feet
And tossed his head.

But the crowd just frowned and turned Around,
For the Prophet's pants had Fallen down.

---

[132] Art is long, life is short.

Glancing over the top of the composition paper, Victoria thought she saw a fleeting glimmer of laughter in the rector's one good eye. Her father's face was contorted into a twisted expression of absolute incomprehension, but he managed to remove his glasses and point them at her like a gun. Father's Luther and Devine looked like they'd swallowed rat poison. There were a few moments of silence while appealing, pass-the-buck eyes, darted back and forth among the priests. Finally, relaxing back into his black leather swivel chair, the rector folded his arms over his chest and rocked back and forth a few times as if ruminating on a brand new strategy. Then, in a very compassionate tone, he said, "Not bad satire, son. Not bad at all. Might even be a bit of talent there, Mr. Reicharte. We all need to take a look at ourselves once in a while."

"But he was supposed to write about humility," Father Luther indignantly blurted out.

"I didn't feel humble," Victoria shot back.

"How many times've told you not to talk back?" Mr. Reichart hollered, waving his glasses at Victoria."

"I stopped counting at a million."

"Now, now, let's be civil," Father Devine chastened.

"It's utter blasphemy!" Father Luther croaked. "And a mockery of my authority. I told them to interpret a Biblical injunction. The meek shall inherit the earth."

"I don't think I want to be around when the meek acquire this inheritance," the rector observed. "And for your assignment did you use the Douay version or the King James? I've seen you with both."

"What's the difference?" Father Luther replied with a trace of hostility in his voice.

"I think, Father, the Pope's authority is everyone's concern. The question is were you referring to forgiveness or good works? There's a tell-tale difference, Father."

Chastened, Father Luther was speechless. His neck turned scarlet, and his hands clasped into tight fists.

The rector reached over the top of his desk and took the composition paper from Victoria's hand, shaking his head slightly at the sight of pink fingernail polish on Victoria's fingernails before commenting, "It seems, Victoria, that the assignment was to be about humility."

"It is about humility, Father."

"My eye!" Father Luther exclaimed with a threatening step toward Victoria.

"Stop acting like a child!" Mr. Reicharte admonished.

"The child's father of the man," Victoria responded.

"Ah, Wordsworth, my favorite Romantic poet," the rector added with a sigh, and if you don't mind a critical judgment, the poem is about humility or the lack of it."

"He's putting us all on," Father Luther cut in, his cheeks puffed out with frustration. "The other boys're all laughing and making snide jokes. Matthews even has a crush on her..him, whatever. They're all probably in on it for all we know."

"Indeed," Father Devine added from his chair by the bookcase. "Dressing up like this has serious ramifications. Nothing personal, Walter. We all appreciate your generous donations but this definitely smacks at homo..."

"Now wait just a minute here," the rector interrupted. "I don't think we need to start putting labels on things. That's exactly how ugly scandals are created. Actors dress up all the time. Maybe a referral to Doctor Wilder would be in order, Walter, discretion being the better part of valor, of course. There seems to be deeper problems here."

"They're the ones with deeper problems," Victoria put in while examining her fingernail polish.

Before anyone could stop him, Mr. Reicharte put on his glasses, leaped from his chair, walked over to Victoria, and slapped her across the face with a big right hook.

Holding her hand against her reddening face, Victoria exclaimed, "A berbis ad verbera[133]!" Then she stood up and clobbered Mr. Reicharte with a close-fisted left hook of her own, the impact of which sent them both sprawling on the floor where Victoria continued thrashing Mr. Reicharte with left and right hooks.

Astonished, Father Devine and Father Luther stared at the tumult until the rector, who had leaped out of his chair, managed to holler, "Don't just stand there gawking, do something!"

As he jumped from his chair, Father Devine abstractly commented to no one in particular, "Video meliora proboque, deteriora sequor[134]," and with his fingertips he tentatively reached down and grabbed the hem of Victoria's skirt in a feeble attempt

---

[133] From words to blows.
[134] I see a better way and approve; I follow the worse way.

to pull her away from Mr. Reicharte. Meanwhile, Father Luther got down on the floor and put Victoria in a head lock as she screamed, "In bello ira flagramus[135]!"

* * * * * * *

---

[135] In time of war we blaze with anger.

THE RESURRECTION

Victoria Culpepper sat in an upright wooden chair next to a door marked Mother Superior. She peered into a small, hand-held mirror and brushed out her permed pageboy with smooth, caressing strokes.

"Yes, hello, this is the St. Nicolas Welfare Association, Sister Bernadette speaking," the pink cheeked secretary said into the phone, unable to keep her eyes from Victoria. Her starched white coif creased her forehead, and the side flaps of her habit puckered her lips slightly. "She's sitting right here, Father. In the custody of Detective O'Rourke. Mother Superior's going to process her, excuse me, him in a few minutes." Flicking a piece of black thread from her wimple, a starched white bib, she shaded her mouth with one hand and lowered her voice: "He's wearing a cashmere sweater and a red poodle skirt with saddle shoes and bobby socks. Oh, my, she's refreshing her lipstick now. I'd better go. I'll tell Mother Superior you called, Doctor Wilder."

Catching a cold look from Detective O'Rourke, Victoria put her accessories into a clutch purse. The detective, a weathered, unshaven, middle-aged man who was grossly overweight with a severely receding hairline, sat in a sweaty heap directly across from her. He wore a wrinkled and threadbare khaki suit and tie along with scuffed brown work shoes. He paged through a small black notebook and looked up now and then to give her a pensive stare.

Stopping at a page, he off-handedly asked her, "Would you mind give'n me your name one more time? There seems to be a mix up somewheres."

With a kind smile for the detective, Victoria complacently replied, "Mirabile dictu[136]."

"Huh."

"Semper fidelis[137]."

"Come again? Oh, wait. I should know that one. Ex-marine. Ah, always faithful ain't it?"

"Congratulations and my name is Victoria Culpepper, ab initio[138]."

"But how can this be?"

"Alter ego[139]," Victoria confidently responded as if a tyrant had suddenly abandoned the stronghold of her mind and left it open to all the infinite possibilities of the imagination.

"That's Victoria Cornelius Culpepper, right? That's what you're sayin'?"

"Ad hoc."

"In English, please," the detective countered with a tongue-in-cheek expression.

"Ad hoc, for this particular purpose, common usage, improvise."

---

[136] Marvelous to relate.
[137] Always faithful.
[138] From the beginning.
[139] Another self.

"I seen this before, you know. Delusions of grandeur, schizophrenia, and all that other hocus pocus. Mother Superior'll straighten you out. Your father's had a heart attack, you know."

"Quid pro quo[140]," Victoria replied.

"Cold blooded too," the detective murmured, making a note in his black book.

Victoria covered her mouth and yawned, and then crossed her legs at the knee and adjusted her poodle skirt accordingly.

"Don't they teach no English at them private schools?"

"Lapsus linguae[141]."

"Shalom aleichim[142]," the detective quipped, and they both laughed at the detective's usage.

The phone rang and the secretary picked it up. It was Doctor Wilder again. By the sound of the conversation it seemed he was worried. The secretary assured him that Mother Superior would get in touch with him if it became necessary and then she hung up. Suddenly, her intercom buzzed. "Yes?" she replied, pressing a button on the box. "You can send them in now," came back.

Hearing the order, Detective O'Rourke slipped the notebook into his hip pocket and got up just as the secretary rushed to the door marked Mother Superior and opened it. Wagging an index finger at Victoria, he walked to the door and waited.

---

[140] Something in return.
[141] Slip of the tongue.
[142] Peace with you.

"Bring him with you, detective," Mother Superior said from behind a huge varnished office desk which was covered with a thick piece of glass.

Walking behind the detective, Victoria studied Mother Superior who appeared to be squatting behind the desk. The nun had the flat pug-nosed face, low forehead, and squat, broad-shouldered body of a linebacker. Her head was perched on a neckless torso and was covered with a heavily starched white coif and black veil which covered her ears. Her hands were primly tucked into the drooping sleeves of her black habit. Tilting her head and coif to one side to peer around the detective, she observed, "Quite pretty, indeed. Wonder who did the makeup?"

"Dunno," the detective reacted. Picked her up at juvenile this morning. Says she's somebody else'n talks in tongue, Roman. Refused to change clothes too. You'll see."

"Of course," Mother Superior replied, folding her arms and sitting back in her office chair as she peered down her nose at Victoria. "I've got the report right here, but I think Christian and I are going to get along just fine. Aren't we, Christian?"

"It's Victoria, ma'am, Victoria Culpepper," Victoria inattentively answered, for her attention was on the layout of the office. There was a plush red carpet contrasting with beige walls decorated with pictures of the Pope and Blessed Virgin. There was the nun's desk with several office chairs posted around it and an interesting set of French doors behind the nun's desk.

"See what I mean, Sister?" Detective O'Rourke put in, tapping his temple a few times with a finger while glancing back and forth between Mother Superior and Victoria who was carefully studying the French doors which had intriguing panes that alternated between clear and stained glass. The clear panes looked out unto a wide playground which was protected on all sides by a six foot chain-link fence.

"Now, now, don't be cynical, detective. I've never lost one yet, have I?"

"Not that I know of, Sister, but there's always the first time."

"Not to worry. I didn't get the bishop's appointment to run this orphanage by being naive. Christian and I are going to have a friendly chat and get to the bottom of this masquerade before there's even the slightest trace of a scandal. Aren't we, Christian?"

"Ad nauseum[143]," Victoria ad libbed. Her attention was focused all the way across the playground where a number of children were kicking a soccer ball into the back fence.

"See!" O'Rourke exclaimed.

Waving her hand at the detective and giving Victoria a perturbed look, Mother Superior sternly said, "You may leave us, Mr. O'Rourke. I'll handle it from here."

"Are you sure? I can hang 'round if you want."

Ignoring the detective's remark, Sister Gertrude pressed a button on the desk intercom and announced, "Hold all calls and see the detective out, please."

O'Rourke flipped his palms upward, gave Victoria an undisguised exasperated once over and went to the door where he commented over his shoulder, "You know the number at juvenile."

---

[143]   To the point of nausea.

After the door had closed behind the detective, the nun motioned toward a straight back chair set right in front of her desk, and then folded her pink hands on top of the glass desk top with the comment, "Please sit down, my dear. We've got a lot to talk about. Just the two of us. It's no one else's business as far as I'm concerned."

Sitting quite tall with her hands demurely folded in her lap and one foot primly hooked around the forward ankle, Victoria passed her tongue over her lips as if tasting her red lipstick and curtly replied, "Okay, but it's Victoria." Then she indifferently gazed over the nun's shoulder out the French doors.

Just as curtly, Mother Superior snapped, "Nonsense! Your mother's told us you found the adoption papers. Does that fact have anything to do with this silly charade of yours?"

"How come the priest's hands never bleed at Mass like in Sister Mary Margaret's movie? I've been watching for a million years'n nothing, but it happens all over the place in the movie."

The nun's forehead furrowed into three severely puckered creases right below the sharp edge of her coif: "You must trust in God, my son."

"I am trussed in God."

"Pardon me?"

"Mea culpa[144]."

"Yes it is your fault, this whole masquerade. They're certain things which must be taken on faith, young..."

---

[144] My fault.

"Like why a sin can be historically transmitted from one person to the next even when each soul is created afresh according to St. Thomas."

Taken aback, Mother Superior put two fingers to her lips, narrowed her eyes to slits, and gave Victoria a cold, pensive look.

"Like why nuns wear bathrobes while taking a bath."

"That's really none of your business, but if you must know, it's a matter of modesty."

"But no one can see."

"What about the good Lord, Mr. Know-it-all."

"But he can see through walls."

"Nonsense! You're not here to question me or your faith."

"Ad hominem[145]."

"Stop that! There's nothing wrong with you, and you know it. This is nothing but a childish prank. Any fool can see that. You've been trained at the best schools in the country."

"Like a circus bear?"

"One way or another, Christian, we're going to straighten you out."

"Like a geometry problem?"

---

[145] To appeal to feelings rather than reason.

"Keep it up, and you'll end up right back here where you started fifteen years ago. Have you been receiving the sacraments?"

"Stultitia est venatum ducere invitas canes[146]."

"Is that so," the nun replied, her eyes like gun slits in a fortress wall. "I suppose a fifteen-year-old in drag knows more than a church hundreds of years old. Maybe we should call the Pope so you can give him some advice on how to run the Vatican."

"Ubi Romam advenero, hoc faciam[147]."

"All right. I've had just about enough of this! If it's a scandal you want, I can easily call in Dr. Wilder and have you transferred to county. Is that what you want for your family? A big scandal. Maybe even a rubber room for yourself."

"Pax vobiscum[148]," Victoria abstractly replied. Her eyes were trained over the nun's shoulder and out the French doors behind her desk. The doors hinged at opposite sides of the doorway so they'd open in the middle. A group of children were still kicking a soccer ball around near the back fence. Beyond the fence there was a sidewalk and a busy street. The sun, descending behind the jagged rooftops across the street, sent out lances of light whenever it appeared from behind a building.

Leaning her face close to the intercom and shading her mouth, Mother Superior pushed a button and quietly said, "Notify Dr. Wilder right now." Then from a long center desk drawer, she took out a glossy centerfold and slid it over the glass desktop with the tip of an extended middle finger as if it were contaminated. With a scornful expression on her face, she looked down the bridge of her

---

[146] You can lead a horse to water, but you can't make him drink. (Plautus)
[147] When I reach Rome, I shall do this.
[148] Peace with you.

nose and commented, "Maybe this little bit of pornography will jolt you back to reality."

Glancing at the slick sheet of paper, Victoria felt her cheeks ignite. Someone had torn out the centerfold from the National Geographic, the one with the naked natives dancing around the fire and the naked girl in the background. The girl's perky breasts were clearly in view as she peeked around the trunk of a tree. As if swallowing an olive pit, Victoria gulped, "Vae Victus[149]!"

"Now, now, don't jump off the tracks on us, Christian. No one's going to vanquish you, but we haven't fooled Mother Superior have we? This silly masquerade of yours isn't a bit cute is it? Your mother's found the whole indecent collection, and we suspect - the maid's been fired, by the way - we suspect associated indiscretions, maybe even with the maid, God help us!"

Broad swords of shimmering sunlight cut between the downtown skyscrapers across the street.

"Look at me, Christian, not out those doors!

"Omnia mea mecum porto[150]," Victoria absent-mindedly replied. Her brooding eyes were riveted on the chain-link fence on the far side of the playground.

"All right, you asked for it. Dr. Wilder'll lock you up and throw the key away. Do you want to wear that costume in jail with a lot of men who are in there for rape? Get hold of yourself and wipe off those crocodile tears."

Deflected from a skyscraper's window, a glittering foil of sunlight whirled through one of the clear panes in the French

---

[149] Woe to the vanquished.
[150] I am carrying all my property with me.

doors behind Mother Superior's desk and landed at Victoria's feet. "Veni, vidi, vici[151]!" she shouted, feeling as if she had somehow bolted directly from the chair, picked it up and thrown it threw the windowpanes of the French doors. Glass appeared to fly everywhere, and it felt as if she were running headlong through the empty frames of the French doors.

"Saints above!" Mother Superior exclaimed. Her scrubbed face was livid with fear as she watched Victoria writhe in the chair, specks of spittle forming at the corners of her mouth. Hitting the intercom button, she shouted, "I thought I told you to get Dr. Wilder over here!"

Gulping in the cool fresh air, Victoria sailed along, light-headed and giddy. The chain-link fence seemed a million miles away, and the sun, like a crystal ball of fire, came out from behind a skyscraper like a signal beacon.

"You'd better stop this practical joke, Christian. The doctor's on his way with a butterfly net," Mother Superior nettled. "Maybe even a straitjacket."

"Ubi Romam venero Casearem videbo[152]!" Victoria screamed as she seemingly drove the toes of her saddle shoes into the triangular openings of the chain fence, a flock of white birds swarming up around her as if flying out from beneath her poodle skirt.

"Holy Mother of mercy, what's gotten into you? Get back into that chair this instant!"

Alternately driving first one toe and then the other into the triangular openings in the fence, Victoria scrambled to the top where

---

[151]   I came, I saw, I conquered.
[152]   When I come to Rome, I shall see Caesar

sharp prongs cut the skin on the palms of her hands. "Stigmata[153]!" she shouted and hurled herself over the top of the fence, skirt billowing around her shins, and the white birds swarming beneath her like a magic carpet...

"Heaven help us, doctor, just look at him. I don't know what he's..."

"Stand back, will you! I warned you folks not to take things into your own hands! Now you've really got a scandal! How'd she cut her hands?"

...landing softly, after what seemed like an eternity, Christian saw a long white beach with tall, storm-bent palm trees that swayed out over a blue-green sea. Sunlight flickered between broad palm leaves, and dozens of sea birds, silver and pearl in the sunlight, hovered just above frothing wavelets which lapped soundlessly over the shell-laden sugar sand beach. Beyond the beach there was a dense, green jungle. It appeared lush with cord-like vines, coconut palms, bamboo shoots, and broad umbrella leaves laden with sparkling, rainbow-catching water. Some of the leaves were slightly bent downward allowing water to trickle to the ground. The jungle swept upward toward jagged mountain tops which loomed far above...

"Can you hear me, son?"

"He won't answer you in English."

"Christian?"

"Try Victoria, doctor."

---

[153] Marks resembling the crucifixion wounds of Jesus, said to have appeared supernaturally on certain persons.

"Can you hear me, Victoria?"

...above the tree line, tendrils of smoke streaked the clear blue sky like long white kite tails, and he could hear a menacing growl as if a tiger were lurking close by...

"Answer me, Victoria. No one's going to hurt you."

...then he saw her. As if in slow motion, she ran out from behind a palm tree at the edge of the jungle a long way down the beach. She had a heart-shaped face and shiny black hair which hung all the way down to her bottom. Her skinny, boyish body was dark brown with small glistening breasts. Except for a rabbit's foot, which hung around her neck on a woven grass lanyard, she wore only a tattered loin cloth which hung loosely around her waist.

"Mother of God, what's wrong with her?"

"Calm down, sister, and call Doctor Rushmore at St. Mary's stat!"

"Now just a minute, doctor! I'm still Mother Superior around here, and I say he's duping all of us."

"Hog wash! She's catatonic! What've you been telling her?"

...there was a bright point of light darting from one eye to the other, back and forth, but he could still see her running toward him in the surf. The emerald sea splashed around his legs as his hands peeled away his shirt and he shouted, "Rare avis, rare avis, nunc est bibendum, nunc pede libero est pulsanda tellus[154]!"

*   *   *   *   *   *   *

---

[154]   Rare bird, rare bird, now we must drink, now the earth must be trodden with a free foot.

COUP DE GRÂCE

Chewing on a thick brown cigar butt, Mr. Polinski swept the sidewalk outside the freshman dormitory. In spite of the chilly spring thaw, he had on an army-issue, dark green, sleeveless T-shirt which was peppered with tiny burn holes from hot ashes. Whenever he pushed on the broom handle, the bicep of his upper arm would flex. When Father Dittman came out of the dorm, his black cassock swirling around his ankles, Polinski scurried to a tree to retrieve a long-sleeved wool shirt which was hung on a lower limb. Ducking behind the tree, he put the shirt on over the T-shirt. He was in full view of a line of freshman who were standing on the sidewalk waiting for roll call.

"He was showing it again!" Snyder whined to Dittman as Polinski hurried down the sidewalk with a wheelbarrow.

"Shut up, Snyder!" a kid hollered.

"Polinski!" Father Dittman shouted, but the custodian had disappeared around a corner of the dormitory building. "Get in line, Snyder. I'll take care of it!"

"That's what you always say."

Ignoring Snyder's comment, Father Dittman flipped through some papers on a clipboard, withdrew a pencil from the long slit on the side of his cassock, and began roll: "Donovan!"

"Here!"

"Olsen!"

"Here!"

"Valeno!"

"Here!"

"Snyder!"

"Here, Father!"

"Krowell!"

"Here!"

"Webber!"

"President!"

Everyone in line laughed.

"Not funny, Webber" Dittman said and glowered over the top edge of his clipboard. "Do you understand?"

"Ad nauseam[155]!"

Everyone in line split a gut and leaned forward at the hips, their necks craned in Webber's direction at the end of the line.

"What-did-you-say?" the priest asked, emphasizing each word as he stalked up to Webber who was standing at ease, military style, hands behind his back.

---

[155] To the point of nausea.

"Mea culpa[156]."

The boys in line roared, and Father Dittman stood toe to toe, eyeball to eyeball with Webber who did not flinch. "What's the matter with you today?" the priest asked, his eyes riveted on Webber's.

"Lapsus linguae[157]!"

"Shut up, Webber, you imbecile!" Father Dittman ranted. "You're going to mind your P's and Q's or end up like your little buddy in a padded cell or haven't you heard?"

With that, Webber took off his coat and threw it on the ground. He was wearing a shoulder strap, green army T-shirt. He also had muscled biceps and broad shoulders which astounded everyone, and there was a big tattoo of a hula dancer on the boy's right bicep.

Thunderstruck, Dittman and the boys in line gaped at the topless hula dancer. Then Dittman reached out and stuck his clipboard over the tattoo and yelled, "Don't look at it, boys! It's the devil in disguise! And you, Webber, put that coat back on and get down to the rector's office before I boot you down!"

Everyone was stunned into silence as Webber sauntered away, picking his coat up from the ground and slinging it over his shoulder. He was flexing all over the place. His mop of hair hung over the top of his coke-bottle glasses, and he was wearing pegged fourteens. When he reached the door of the freshman dormitory, he stopped a moment as if to get a last look at the boys in line. With the

---

[156] My fault.
[157] Slip of the tongue

sun glinting on his glasses, he shouted, "Stella duce-a-um[158]!" and disappeared into the dormitory building.

For the boys who were obediently waiting in line for his response, Father Dittman had only one reply: "Great Caesar's ghost!"

* * * * * * *

---

[158] Under the leadership of a star

ABOUT the AUTHOR

Mr. Koelsch is a graduate of the University of South Florida located in Tampa, Florida. He taught English for thirty-two years at a number of different educational levels, but is now retired and living in Largo, Florida.

After years of attending night classes, he finally was able to acquire a Master's Degree in English, but this came after he bailed out of such courses as geometry, algebra two, physics, chemistry, trigonometry, calculus, and comparative religion.

In his teens he was a Boy Scout for several weeks but discovered that he had no aptitude for knot tying or camping out. He preferred the security and simplicity of McDonald's. As a high school student, Mr. Koelsch realized in shop class that he had no real aptitude for handyman work either. The idea that a nut could be turned right to loosen it and left to tighten it, as in a gas valve, just would not register.

Hence, Mr. Koelsch wrote a poem in Mrs. Smith's English class at a junior college and received an "A". This success launched his teaching career, but his writing career and first novel were entirely in the hands of Victoria.

Printed in the United States
By Bookmasters

T0148061

Evangelium

Evangelium
THE REVOLUTION OF LOVE

RODRIGO INOSTROZA BIDART

ARCHWAY
PUBLISHING

Copyright © 2019 Rodrigo Inostroza Bidart.

All rights reserved. No part of this book may be used or reproduced by any means, graphic, electronic, or mechanical, including photocopying, recording, taping or by any information storage retrieval system without the written permission of the author except in the case of brief quotations embodied in critical articles and reviews.

This book is a work of non-fiction. Unless otherwise noted, the author and the publisher make no explicit guarantees as to the accuracy of the information contained in this book and in some cases, names of people and places have been altered to protect their privacy.

Archway Publishing books may be ordered through booksellers or by contacting:

Archway Publishing
1663 Liberty Drive
Bloomington, IN 47403
www.archwaypublishing.com
1 (888) 242-5904

Because of the dynamic nature of the Internet, any web addresses or links contained in this book may have changed since publication and may no longer be valid. The views expressed in this work are solely those of the author and do not necessarily reflect the views of the publisher, and the publisher hereby disclaims any responsibility for them.

Any people depicted in stock imagery provided by Getty Images are models, and such images are being used for illustrative purposes only. Certain stock imagery © Getty Images.

ISBN: 978-1-4808-8269-0 (sc)
ISBN: 978-1-4808-8270-6 (hc)
ISBN: 978-1-4808-8268-3 (e)

Library of Congress Control Number: 2019915341

Print information available on the last page.

Archway Publishing rev. date: 10/04/2019

Contents

Author's Prologue

We find ourselves before an immense but brief work, which encompasses in a single glance the complexity of the human condition and its meaning and history in the world. However, the driving axis is clear and defined: *Love*; a broad and decisive concept for understanding current and future Humanity in a renewed and even redeeming way. The author, Chilean, Doctor of Philosophy, classical philologist, poet, writer, academic and teacher, demonstrates a great ability and knowledge to deal coherently and consistently with topics such as different as History, Natural and Social Sciences, Psychology, Literature, Religions, and others, which allows him to reflect synthetically, broadly and consistently on human reality, at times with a complex, symbolic, theoretical and poetic language, but also with clear, simple and accessible approaches for the non-specialized public.

His proposal to understand the human being in his immediacy, in his daily life, in his personal and community life, as well as in his identity and transcendence is challenging and critical with regard to visions and behaviors validated historically and currently. We are therefore faced with a holistic, original and provocative philosophical proposal, which aims to promote deeper questioning and rethinking of a person and Humanity project, allowing us to make an evolutionary leap and overcome the anthropological, cultural structures, social and psychological that currently keep the human being - and the planet as a whole - on the verge of an annihilating catastrophe.

This work should not leave anyone indifferent, because it touches the most sensitive, universal and experiential fibers of any single person, regardless of their social, cultural, age, gender, or any other type of differentiation. This work encourages self-knowledge, intimate and honest review of each person in their weaknesses and strengths, always maintaining as a guiding and essential axis a concept of Love that reaches depths and applications never before seen in the history of human knowledge. The richness, omnipresence, density and variety of this original concept of Love, is based, from its origin and in its ultimate root, as the *essence* and manifestation par excellence of the divine and the human in the cosmic, universal and personal reality, for all living beings on this planet and in any place or dimension of the Universe. The author formulates his concept of *love* without falling into ingenuities, reductionisms or theoretical idealizations of any kind, because - as the author makes it appear - the concept of *love* has an overused, deformed, limited, trivialized history that could confuse a non-cautious reader, and deceive them by this deformation. The author takes the concept of love to a transversality of the human experience that ranges from mysticism and spirituality, through the everyday, to the deceptive and the vulgar, before moving on to its foundational and trascendental application in Science, in Economics, in Politics, in Mathematics - as well as in all areas of human activity, theoretical and practical, that traditionally have a seemingly contrary bias or incompatible with this concept. It is possible to disagree with different approaches and even with the author's general vision, but no one can dismiss these same approaches without a solid rebuttal or thoughtful reflection, a skill which has been greatly weakened and impoverished in today's world.

It is also possible to reproach the author for an excess of catastrophism and historical pessimism, as if he wanted to use the abused mechanism of apocalyptic terror to achieve his ends. However, it is more a matter of opening ourselves to the everyday reality - to the variety of news sources, to the extended and multiple signals and warnings of all kinds, of all qualities and conditions of people, to agree that - if the apocalyptic vision of the World is not an obvious and predictable fact, then at least it is the figurative representation of a planetary state of affairs that is screaming for change and improvement. Each and every one of us are responsible and actors in this. The author, with his book, tries to put us at these decisive crossroads so that each one takes with the greatest possible conscience, their personal decision.

In this English translation, the language, and the formal and stylistic presentation are concordant and subordinate reflection to the contents of the message. The reader will find an unexpected format, sometimes challenging, sometimes familiar and simple, sometimes strange and out of the ordinary. *Evangelium* is written in short chapters, with an internal numbering and subdivision that echoes the Bible and other sacred books, or even profane and poetic, such as the Zarathustra of Nietzsche, in order to highlight ideas, provoke insights and surprise the reader with multiple and free associations. This initiating and transforming methodology, in what could be a ritual experience - even shamanic - is also associated with methodologies of poetry, philosophy, psychology and religions. We can affirm that not a single word, not a single graphic sign, is casual, ambiguous, contradictory or even equivocal, without a consistent and lucid intention of the author. May our translation be a faithful reflection of these resources from the original in Spanish.

To conclude and give a guarantee of himself, the author has the firm conviction that, without being contacted more, the message was not born *ex nihilo* in his head, but - in addition to the obvious evidence of reflecting his educational and biographical training - it is the inspiration and plan of beings or higher dimensions of reality, which we traditionally call divine and spiritual, and in whom he recognizes par excellence the presence of this sense of Love.

I

1. The challenge of listening to the Revolution of Love is too big for the common man and woman - or simply for the Human Being! - There is no longer any time to teach or progress in the Revolution of Love. - We taught it to you for tens of thousands of years, - in so many and in so many different ways - that time has already run out for you. - And it is you yourself, Humanity, who has assumed the right to attack yourself and your World with your next action which is *DESTRUCTION, TOTAL DESTRUCTION*! - Even against the Love and Will of your Divine Protectors, whose patience and encouragement were always infinite for you! - Has your hour, World, Man and Woman, come to an end to decide one minute before: ARE YOU THE REVOLUTION OF LOVE, OR ARE YOU *NOT* THE REVOLUTION OF LOVE?!

II

1. We are complacent with ourselves in what we should not be, as well as rigorous and inflexible with what we should not.

2. What value and utility can it have that billions of human selves live to satisfy themselves? What does my self want? - Social success, a coupling that meets my affective, sexual, material, personal needs? Material welfare, physical and psychological security, pleasure, entertainment, emotions? Why do I want to have children, why a profession, for what knowledge? In short, what do I live for? - If I live only for myself, then, what value do I have for Life? With what right do I demand Life, and what do I not allow Her to demand of me? How am I unable to understand that others do not exist just for me? How do I find it so difficult to feel and have the absolute conviction that my self is, first of all, an extension of the whole of Humanity? If I live for myself, I am the same as the cancer cell, which lives and reproduces for itself and not for the body. - *I must exist for myself, only as long as I may exist entirely for Life, since it is Life that gives me my tiny monad in His Reality.*

3. We want to be spiritual, evolved, superior, without renouncing any of our pettiness, our character, our valued properties, our habits, our "duties", our negligence and inertia, our "superior" feelings and principles, our intelligence and knowledge; in the end, all our *mirages*, the good ones and the bad ones. Because we do not understand that what serves us in one way, damages us in another. We become incapable of existing in multiple planes of sense and reality simultaneously.

4. In order to be born to the *higher self*, to the new species, to the "son of God", it is necessary to really die before, again and again until death, through daily, routine, nocturnal, sacrificial, martyred deaths, of all our mirages; of all our worn and worn forms by the simple action of living; of our clothed, armed, trapped *ego*, identified with our overwhelming psychic and physical apparatus. It is necessary that the Human dies as a whole, in a final and extreme holocaust, once the minor deaths of individuals have been satisfied: *The Phoenix being reborn from the ashes.*

5. We must only force and provoke the death of each moment of ours when the opportune occasion is given, in the perfect sacrifice, and as long as in that death there is a light that guides us, an affectionate teacher who encourages us, a *form* that awaits us, an intuition that touches us and provokes us. Death is not positive for one who is neither prepared nor initiated into the mysteries of dying. Prepare to die!

6. Life is not positive for one who is neither prepared nor initiated in the mysteries of living. Prepare to live!

7. It is a mediocre spirituality, a mediocre character, a mediocre will, a mediocre being, that is content with, or allows himself, a practice and spiritual development without leaving their everyday mirages. It is not possible to transform oneself deeply without the death of the *self*. - If it is necessary to leave your work and your daily duty, do it. If you need to go to the mountain in solitude, do it. If it is necessary for you to separate yourself in conscience from your spouse, from your parents, from your children, do it. If it is necessary for you to close the world around you, close it. But it is not necessary to suffer or make suffer, or spill blood, or go crazy, or neglect your responsibilities, or miss the return from where you separated. *Because if you separate yourself, it is to unify yourself in a better way than the previous division.* Do not forget where you are and who you are with, the place and the person are the mission and responsibility of your existence. If you know someone that you did not know before, and you stop seeing someone that used to be your usual, add them; never subtract anyone so that no one is left in the *past* past. Even

if it's only in your heart, keep them alive with you. There are also other planes of existence, mysteriously, but really united to ours.

8. Believe in Holiness as your holiness, believe in Perfection as *your* perfection, believe in Truth as *your* truth, although the supreme things are as far from you as are the stars. Remember that nothing that is within the reach of our senses is unattainable for us.

9. Believe in yourself, and, move on!

III

1. Humanity is like a tree. We all tend to make a nest somewhere in that tree. We live to produce a stable and safe nest where we can stop the change of growth.

2. Contemplate Humanity! We are a pride for the past and a shame for the future. What about the ancestral myths of human divinization? Are we gods because we dominate more and more the world of matter? Are we gods because we are better satisfying our mental and emotional desires? - Pleasure, security, property, use and much EGO - here is our divinity!

3. I watch you from the top of the mountain, Humanity, like a *Devil*. I would like to teach you that at the root of every demon there is a god betrayed. I would like to redeem you, because between you and me there is an inextricable similarity: you are a demon, potentially a god, and I am a god, potentially a demon. But you did not want. How many gods, how many saints, prophets, teachers, enlightened, buddhas and angels we sent you! ... But still you did not want!

4. The time of harvest has arrived! Billions of souls cling to a piece of land in the world's crops. There is no more room. The wheat is ripe after so many suns and so many showers of tears and love. I am afraid that the burdock and the withered grass drown the scarce harvest to feed so many mouths of hungry children. Proclaim this *Evangelium* to the four winds, show it on the screens, publish it on the front pages, hang it in the corners, teach it in the schools of the world! It does not matter anymore!

You will see that within a few minutes it will be swallowed up by the tumult of human nothingness ...

5. I look for the workers of Jesus - the great Messenger - for the harvest. I seek without creed, nor ideology, nor race, nor external quality that distinguishes us. I look for the harvesters with the sharpest scythes, able to cut even the wind and the souls. I look for the rebels, the enraged for peace. To those who will not give up their work even after they die. I look for those who without signs, or any exterior sign, are able to embrace each other as brothers and equals. I seek, finally, *the spirit of the man-woman.*

6. Who are you man-woman? Will you leave the safe and wide nest like the earth where you are today to fly with the wings that you do not have towards an invisible sky? Call me crazy! - It's written in your law. Your law protects you from disruptors like me. - Call me crazy too, so that your conscience, reassured in the depths of the collective dream may continue to weave the web of, what is for me, *your* madness! What will you do: I call you crazy and you call me crazy? - At least do not stand in my way, as I'm not willing to stop your foolish step.

7. Do not recognize in these words a threat, because it is no longer time to convince you with anything. Do not recognize in these words neither a call nor a poem nor another game. - It is only the subtle and powerful voice of a herald who proclaims the end of an Era!

8. Come, follow me!

IV

1. We can not be alone. We do not want to be alone. We do not exist alone! - But what little and what bad we do to be well accompanied.

2. We do not know how to love, because we do not know ourselves, let alone know others. Even those we love the most are no more than shadows in the gloom of our understanding and uncertainty. Because we love shadows, they easily dissolve or change their appearance and we no longer know what to do - if we continue to love or stop loving. Our love - divine human condition - is as fragile as a dry leaf, but also as powerful as a drop of sweat on the temple of a mother.

3. How difficult is it to recognize that at the root of all our actions and desires there is a dissatisfied love? Why is it so easy for us to reverse the direction of love and simply look at others with indifference or disdain?

4. However, the streets are crowded with people. I live surrounded by innumerable neighbors that I hardly recognize. I speak with strangers that I use. I treat myself daily with so many humans that I assure myself I know, only because I am familiar with their faces, their voices, their way of being and some events of their lives. - Here are my fellows!

5. How could I take charge of so many humans? Who could show me by their example that it is possible to love without so much superficiality, in everyday life, so many and so many? "I really want to love, until the

happiness of the other, to so many, to all, that I can not love even one. Do I love myself so well that I love another?

6. I can love all of humanity, and I love it. I can love like Jesus all the children of God. Even those whom I will never know, I can love them. But I can not live for everyone, help them all to exist better, listen to everyone, share myself with everyone. - In love there are levels of delivery; there are gradations and modalities of love; there is love of oneself, love of couple, of father, of friend, of son, of passenger, of colleague, of neighbor, of distant person, of sick person, of disciple, of foreigner, of worker, of human being, of enemy, of God and infinitely more.

7. I know that you are as small and limited as I am, but I also know that you are as infinite as I am, since infinite and inexhaustible is love.

8. When I meditate on what we call *Universe*, I find His love everywhere. Our love is nothing more than the prolongation of a mysterious and sometimes strange love that spreads throughout everything.

9. Humans, *evolution* is love!

V

1. Humanity has damaged the sense of man and the sense of reality by establishing a currency of value and change for all things.

2. All things and everything human have been assigned a quantification of value. How much damage, how much misery the money has brought us! - Money is perverse in itself! - Because currency represents a human abstraction, which distorts the true nature of man and things; currency necessarily *depreciates* the intrinsic value of things. Currency assigns a stable, universal and conventional value to things, but things are relative to the subject who experiences them; they change their value with respect to what they are related to; although they also have a dignity of their own and in themselves.

3. With what moral and spiritual authority do a few humans arrogate themselves to fix a price on the water of rivers and oceans? With what sense of humanity do a few arrogant individuals dare tell us: "If you do not pay me for drinking water, I will make you die of thirst"? – Shall we simply accept that the debased yet ambitious few take control of large tracts of land, while those left without agency - who need but a fistful earth in which to sow the daily bread of their own weakened existence – plough their porous yellow bones under a land which is not theirs? - With what sense of love and humanity do the so-called entrepreneurs and the wealthy accumulate material goods and money, when it is to the detriment of those impoverished peoples who have not had the slightest opportunities to access money? - What say you, if even the majority of

the powerful have reached and preserve their wealth to the cost and misery of the exploited of those they call their workers and clients! - How could it not be - I ask myself with real concern – that wealth and the accumulation of money are not simply an injustice and an aberration to our sense of humanity?

4. And even if money were distributed among all humans in equal and sufficient shares, so that there were neither rich nor poor, it would still be a profound and malignant distortion of the nature of things. Because, with what reference will we say that an apple is worth 10 and a car 1000? Or that snow is worth 100 and medical attention 99? - Any parameter would be relative, subjective, and finally unfair to others. - For this reason, the monetary value always ends up becoming the parameter and value imposed by the powerful. - Why not, then, - and it is not long before this - to assign a standard value to the salvation of souls or to the development of the spirit? - How painful and compassionate, my brothers, that we have kept this foolishness and misery for so long!

5. Heaven covers us and lets its thousand-year-old rain fall on us without first asking us how much we can pay, or how many guarantees we have. The sun and the air ceaselessly make no distinction between rich and poor, between blacks and whites, between men and women. Who is the true owner of what is here, before us, the upstart tramplers of the world? What value do things have for Him?

6. The human is a self-complacent animal that avoids asking and inquiring within itself so as not to have to be reprimanded and modified at every moment.

7. If we were more spiritual, more sensitive, more intuitive, more intelligent, we could perceive the *value of dignity* that things possess and, above all, human beings in themselves. Without losing sight of it, and superimposed on this value of dignity, only then could we establish values other than currency; that is, our own relative, circumstantial, subjective, and, ultimately, *spiritual* value of things, just as, in a painting, a foreground

object acquires its true visual value, to the extent that it is unified with the background or environment.

8. If we were truly more spiritual, more sensitive, more intuitive, more intelligent, that is to say more divine and more human, we would freely and lovingly donate, *although without harming ourselves*, everything that is within our reach to share - and create from ourselves with the priority purpose of sharing - and without demanding anything in return, more than the right to be loved by others, in the same way that Life, which unifies life and death in itself, loves us and it is donated to us overwhelmingly, though without harming itself.

VI

1. There are so many and so immensely superior beings that surpass me. - What is the sky of a starry summer night in the middle of the desert, compared to the immensity of His love? - When I listen to the silence without rupture, the silence without image, the silence infinitely turned towards its own interior, I recognize more than ever how limitlessly superior is the language that crosses the Universe.

2. Sadly, it is for me to observe the wasted energy and effort of humans trying to listen to that arcane language deploying enormous parabolic antennas and seeking to decipher with their prehistoric algebraic codes the knowledge that sustains the perfect order of constellations and worlds!

3. The Ineffables have always come from the invisible stars. Our remote ancestors, whom we contemplated at a distance with a grimace of disdain and indulgence, knew them up closely. Our ancestors had the innocence and honesty of children to accept the incomprehensible, the infinitely superior. - What were the stars for them, but the dwelling from which we ourselves have come and where we will return? - Were not for those children the stars and their worlds a pile of inert rocks, incandescent gases, waves and particles, quantum or mechanical phenomena. - They were not even symbols.

4. They were the eternal dwellings of the gods, through whose cosmic gardens they walked in endless days of love; they were the tracing of their perfect hieroglyphics, with which they wrote on the page of the heavens

the destiny and the spinning of the Universe. They were our promise. - They had been those little ones even initiated by the Masters in the first letters of that wonderful language! They had been taught to gather the first stones to raise the human mountain in an impossible jump to heaven. - How soon we reject their first cosmic gurgles as stammering and imprecise; for phantasmagorical and unjustified! - And what do we have now but a heap of profaning and lifeless "certainties"? What more illusion do we have than to tread with our cosmonaut shoes on the virgin soil of Venus and Mars, in the same way that we trampled and decorated with flags the Moon? But what about the Sun and the stars? What is there also of our own Earth?

5. Meanwhile, the gods are still there, only a little more distant, but no less present, less active, less generous, and infinitely compassionate and loving towards our human remains. - They are still there, but no longer in the stars, but behind them, preparing us for the new stage where they will soon appear. - With how much sweetness and presence they envelop me!

6. *Gods and stars*, or any other word, are unable to express the impossible experience of their Being for the current mind of man.

7. Better let's talk about Love!

VII

1. The currency of the World should be love. That subtle love, omnimode, that diffuses the same and the different same in everything. That love which is either soft or violent emotion, which snatches and throbs in the chest, or spills in tears that shine down the cheeks. That love that is honest thought, pure and clean as a spring morning. That love that is certainty and powerful intuition in the spirit. That love that opens the infinite above you and echoes infinitely inside you. That love that contains everything and everything, so extremely everything – this one we have invented the name of God.

2. Love does not measure or rate. Love does not accumulate for itself. Love does not look at its own benefit at the expense of the beloved. Love is neither an agreement nor a convention. Love does not disregard Humanity. Love is neither unfair nor proud. Love does not precede itself. Love is neither changing nor uncertain. Love is not impulsive, it does not precipitate, and neither is it short-range.

3. Love accepts the nature of things. Love spreads freely and without exclusion. Love unites and unifies. Love is presence of authenticity. Love makes us human. Love is divine substance. Love is just and wise. Love adds, multiplies and creates. Through love the path to Reality advances. Love is inexhaustible.

4. *There is in this love, however, a mysterious and disconcerting dimension for the common intelligence.*

5. There is an *avatar* of love that is violent, destructive and deadly. There is an *avatar* of love that goes through evil and death. - Even in the most horrible sin, in the most inhuman and brutal aberration, in the most bloody and genocidal catastrophe, in the most banal and mean ignorance, it animates a humble love that pushes the inexorable destiny of the Universe and of the Man-Woman towards God. - Sometimes God becomes violent, destructive and mortal in the multiformity of His love, although He is neither violent, nor destructive, nor mortal. - Love never ceases to act in an incomprehensible symbiosis with all things.

6. When you live in love, all reality is transformed. Fatigue is experienced as an achievement; colors and sounds are more intense and vivid. People tend to smile in your presence. You discover that reality makes things easier for you. The others - even the most fleeting - seem important to you and you pay attention to them. Your enemies are just wrong people. You know that tomorrow is an opportunity to correct your mistakes or negligence today. Your spirit never decays. You become patient and understanding. In your mind and in your soul, sublime and transcendent intuitions appear. You find a new meaning for Humanity. All things are unified and harmonized.

7. Is it possible for you to live in love?

VIII

1. Cities are a dark world. What is true about them? No human being can grow beyond ten centimeters, like those pots in which have sprung a thousand sprigs that drown each other.

2. In the city you have lost your human sense of space and time. Your neighbors narrow you more and more. What do you know about endless grasslands and endless blue oceans? Is the sky for you more than a decoration? - The city urges you, the crowded city requires you to walk fast and run the faster the better. Sleep fast, wake up fast, work fast, produce fast, live fast and die fast, to let go fast the one who comes after you.

3. And those citizens with whom you have agreed to share the benefits of the system, with whom you share the benefit of helping each other to live, what are they really for you but a constant threat and challenge? - The others dispute with you your work, your food, your partner, your right of way, your opinion and your vote, your image, your property, your security, your status, your little - and even miserable - *freedom*.

4. In return you have filled with sensory and virtual gratifications so that you continue to hallucinate that you live and that you have a place in society. – They have so castrated your life instinct, that you are horrified by the idea of living in the loneliness of the mountains and the lost valleys beyond the horizon! - Oh, tight fields of opium poppies and human narcotics! - If they knew the destiny that the Creators of the World had reserved for us! ...

5. Do you not see, dear brother, that you have been enslaved as Humanity never before was enslaved? - What do you know about withdrawal, meditation and fasting prolonged without pause for years? What do you know about the silence of the stars when it dawns? What do you know about the darkness of fields open to infinity? What do you know about the surprised and benevolent look of meeting another human in the midst of loneliness? What do you know about yourself and your deep spirit? Where could a true god fit, let alone a true encounter with God?

6. There is no love in the cities, but drama and trivial emotions. There is no love, but only compassion and still a little hope.

7. Listen to me! - Carve your own staff and pack your few real belongings. - Leave as soon as possible!; Leave behind the city oven! - So also, in another time, Lot left the cities of Sodom and Gomorrah delivered to the same fate. Because, what other end could it expect to a saturated world, drowned and tired of phagocytose itself?

IX

1. I would like to flee from here, far from the cities of the World! I would like to end this oppressive world that haunts me everywhere! I would like to destroy the bandages of this civilization that mummifies the life of my spirit, of my mind and of my whole being!

2. How much and how have you played *destiny* with my yearnings for fiery youth! You left me waiting in a forgotten and abandoned town, just as our world is with respect to the center of the Universe. You knew too well the tiniest folds of my soul, and you measured me with your relentless rod, the one that no human eye can from far to know. I longed for the exploits and deeds of the ancient hero – to die like Achilles in the middle of the field, or crucified on a cross for the witnesses of the centuries, or simply forced to drink the hemlock in front of my favorite disciple -. But no, you left me cornered, invisible and almost useless. - Who recognized me during all this time? Who when contemplating me could say: Here is one of God's warriors!?

3. But your infinite wisdom surpassed all my doubts, my gaps and miseries. And I, with eyes tired of so much loneliness and boredom, nevertheless I could recognize eaten away by this fine leprosy your flare and your ardor, your invisible figure, your presence so much more divine the more subtle.

4. How much and how I have loved you so long without perceiving you with any human sense! Simply with the pertinacious certainty of my will and my conscience!

5. Even now that you are burning and encouraging me inside and everywhere; even now that I open my eyes when I wake up and there is only your presence; even now that I'm going to play with you in my dreams, even now ... I'm thirsty for You as the castaway of an absolute desert. - The more I know you, the more I miss you. The more I see you, the more I need Light. The more I listen to your arcane *Logos*, the more new languages, the more incomprehensible truths I need to address and discover. The more I feel loved by You, the more I recognize your love for the World, the more I laugh and the more I praise You for me.

6. You and I understand each other as the husband understands his wife in intimacy.

7. You and I are accomplices of a common secret.

8. I patiently wait for the hour and the crossroads of the right paths where action is to be shown. Leave the cities, die if it is the moment, abandon everything to a gesture of yours, to shine at last as the sun every morning shines miraculously on the horizon line.

9. And I know well that to run into your arms like a child runs into the arms of his beloved father, or to look into your eyes directly with mine, or to concentrate all the energy of my mind in your existence, I would go mad to the point, I would extinguish myself and die like a little dry straw in the heart of a furnace! - That's why you restrain me and leave me aside, so that, containing my ardor, I do not burn with you; and looking at myself with arrest on the big and the small, I may humbly discover myself never good enough and prepared for You.

X

1. If I turn my gaze around me, how big the World seems to me. If I raise my eyes to the sky and look at night at the starry heights, how immense the Universe seems to me. If I move with my dense body on the ground or move on the fastest of the transport vehicles, how exhaustingly enormous I find space and time. If I listen to the farthest silence, how deep reality appears to me. - The amplitude of the Universe is the amplification of our own reality. My senses and my inner being are an extension of the Universe. There is no such thing as *outside* and *inside*. There is only one thing - the I-Universe.

2. Even so, how small we are. - As much as this immensity that we perceive is a prolongation of our own reality. However huge the Universe may be that is *our* universe. – And yet, how small is *our* reality.

3. So much so that we let our senses convince us that *this* is real and true. So much so that we allow our senses to seduce us with the illusion that *this* has colors and shapes and sounds and textures and temperature and sensations. - Who is free enough to dispense with sensations and perceptions?

4. We are hormones and cells and chemicals and nerves and electrochemical processes and instincts. We are the result of a complex system of physical, chemical, biological and psychological components and processes. - But, surprise! We are aware of all this.

5. What is *consciousness* doing here?

6. I say *"I"* and my consciousness already appears, but there is no equality between one and the other. I contemplate myself and my consciousness already appears, but I am not necessarily conscious. - What does my *self* do here?

7. I must recognize with nobility that I lack the senses and natural faculties associated with my conscious self to penetrate this mysterious reality. - That is why my self and my conscience are cordoned off by a threshold of *unreality*.

8. Reflect on this paradox: This is reality and the Universe, what appears to us as physical and chemical, nevertheless wants to be experienced and known in us as from a *conscious self*. - Here is a direct and plain invitation of Evolution, or a momentary distractor in the middle of the history of the evolution of the species?

9. To what extent could my conscious self really replicate Reality as a true reality? – And therefore, what future does this human project really have?

XI

1. Stop the World. - Meditate more than an hour a day. - Cancel the external senses to invoke the interior. - Do not think, but go beyond the limits of what is possible. - Live *joyfully* without pause.

2. The World moves, flows and transforms according to its own speed. Why surrender to the speed of the World if your inner one wants to move in another direction? - The movements of the mind and soul need other temporalities. - How much violence is done to the soul by adjusting it to the past-present-future sequence!

3. Although the World moves in a different direction than our soul, it does not resist that we create our own reality. - The Universe always knew that one day the human would appear on Earth. The Universe always encouraged the human soul to move away from him. - Only the weak squeeze against the Universe.

4. To uproot a wild plant is for a hemisphere of the brain and the soul to separate from the World. - The other hemisphere is no more than a field without cultivation, where odorous flowers and weeds grow together. - I'm calling you to become a gardener in your own garden! - I call you to the workings of your inner field! - There you have grown yourself in the form of thorns, nettles and wild thistles. - How it hurts to have to tear and burn yourself! - It is not for the cowards the inner world!

5. And the will is the hardest metal, and the sharpest edge and the sharpest ray of light. - The will is one of your hidden treasures. - Do you know where it is hidden for you? - Because that diamond that is hidden in the galleries of your inner mines must become gold for the value of the World. - The diamond transmuted into gold buys everything. - It is the gold of the spirit, the sun that illuminates all the suns, the perfect energy, capable of transforming this Universe into another.

6. And in the midst of the light of your consciousness you must model as a new demiurge at will that, which only you can discover and create. - And you have to broaden the field of your consciousness like the old warrior who ingenuously craved, in the appropriation of the space territory, the archetype of the emperor and lord of All. - He wanted to dominate the World, but unable to return to consciousness which was his inner world regurgitated *outwards*! - Now you! - No longer inside and outside!

7. When your intention and your purpose move, when it wants your will, when your self convinces itself of *that*, when your conscience shines brightly, when you bring from memory the signals that reaffirm you in time and conviction; when your mind, in the end, has been purified for the *act* truly yours, with that *you* which appropriates your destiny, then the *hieros gamos* is realized, the sacred copulation between your conscious Self and your unconscious Self - that Self which is the excuse and the background of what barely reaches your lucid consciousness.

8. Nevertheless, there, hidden in the dense fog of the deep psychic, lies in wait your *karma*, your demonic ancestors, your involution. - They will know how to shake your soul and your mind with their screams. - They will know how to teach you that you are not as good as your conscious self proposes to be - because they are also yourself - and that each new form grafted into your deep self will be rejected even with death, out of those inveterate furrows. - They will not give a moment so you do not get rid of them. - They will also look at you with sweetness and charm, they will caress your loins and soften you to defeat you, to charm you with the charm of what is already proven as reality.

9. In that hour, call desperately, strongly, bravely and even blindly to the god, to the numen or power of the Universe that created you - *That* same thing that guides All Things without any hand, inside the palm of his hand. - Because the magnet only moves to where it has to move.

XII

1. As stone and metal await some of the human forms to become something else - the craftsman and the goldsmith have materialized from themselves a form also contained in stone and metal. - As the seed contains the tree that rises to merge with the sun, and the whole forest; as the cell projects the destiny of Humanity; as a lighted gaze contains all the energy of the universe - so awaits you the *self.*

2. And you stay looking dumbfounded at these inert letters?

3. Do you not see how the germinating life works in the deepest and most silent recollection? Do you not see that within the most radiant daylight *counterbeats* also the deepest darkness? - Move without moving. - Change without changing. - You're neither this nor that. - Recognize yourself!

4. Do you have to be like the asphalted road where there is nothing else to do? - Will you be like your music equipment, like your TV and your magazine, that turn on, that give off stimulating signals, that go out? - Will you be the education and the useful knowledge that they impart to you, and the laws that impose you, and the schedule of your work? - Will you be your profession and your business cards? - Will you be the number assigned to you and the place where you prove you live?

5. Decide, you must decide!

6. Be master and emperor of yourself. - Be the warrior, the peasant and the beggar. - Be the god and not the slave. - Be the whip and the flash of the shot. - Be the satiety that hunger seeks. - Be the laundry that dries in the sun. - Be the apocalypse.

7. And if one day when you wake up, *you wake up*, or walking around you recognize and palpate to confirm that you are true, do not fear - it is better to dissolve like a shadow before the light that is born; - It is better to give to another unsuspecting the position that does not belong to you - when you meet the passion of *that* yourself.

8. Remember that after the painful passage of the agony of death - no matter how extensive it may seem to you - just as your brain does not need your eyes to see more perfectly in dreams - so you will not need your brain in the end for *you* to end up in the Wonderful Light of Death.

XIII

1. I saw *You* with these eyes, but I do not know what singular matter you were made of. - I smelled *You* from afar (but you were not as subtle as I would have thought) - it was your smell like that of *sulfur*. - You glowed like a full moon clouded within a cloud of silver, and traced a strange sign among the stars: - the empty tip of an arrow shot into the constellation of Taurus.

2. Now you cover yourself beyond my eyes, although at nightfall I still look for you to go out over the nearby mountains. - Then you listened to me, like the night before when I invoked you contemplating the sky - knowing for sure that you were coming. - And you came, because my eyes needed you.

3. How could my eyes today need you so much, if you already undressed before them? - Was not I the one who finally blinked? – What of *inside*, what of *outside*, if you are everywhere?

4. You left me your signal registered in the memory and the spirit - without understanding you until now, nevertheless I have been deciphering it. - There are no words to explain it.

5. I know that you planned that night in flight (the same as now), over the tiny human rooms - reviewing human acts and searching minds and animating souls. - I know that nothing is hidden from you, as long as

nothing hurries you. - But through your eyes all the spirits of the universe contemplate us and patiently recognize us.

6. So did the fervent pupils of our ancestors contemplate you - better than now, they could observe the sky with the naked eye - better than now, clearing their souls of so much egotism - better than now, with disposition of children - in their vernacular languages nominated you stuttering your endless meteors and different names. - In all of them, however, you manifested yourself as the caster of the heavens - One, Different and the Same.

7. Precisely you listen to me now - and you listen with total attention to my echo in the soul of the one who just - *you* - hears me now. - And you are also the one who shows yourself naked before his eyes - so that without seeing you he sees you, and without smelling you smells you - and without meeting you as I do, he may know you.

XIV

1. What do my wishes matter? What does my rage, my hunger, my sadness matter? What do my prayers and my praises matter? What does my desire to speak, my dreams, my desires for possession matter? What do my desires to project myself in my children, to be recognized by others, to be loved matter? - Who cares about my sexual desire, my daily purposes, my moods?

2. What do my feelings, my ideas, my rivers of words matter? - For each feature, for each thing, for each attitude of ours we have a proper justification. - After all, we always accept and contemporize that we are the way we are. - In the end we always end up burying ourselves within our body.

3. What an unreasonable importance we give to ourselves! And it is that we experience reality from our self enclosed between the narrow walls of our mind and soul. - How vast, necessary and sufficient this minuscule redoubt of our self presents itself to us! - How powerful and luminous our own conscience appears to us, when in reality we only stagger through this small world of drunkards! - How active we seem to be working so much, sharing so much and taking advantage of this passing life, until we fall exhausted on our beds every night! - And it is that we can not contemplate from *above*, because even the ants in their eagerness move with more sense and intelligence than we do.

4. What do I care if I am not able to live like a thread embroidered in the precise place of this infinite fabric of the Universe and reality? - What

does my insignificant perspective, my unrepeatable and absolute monad, the sun of my consciousness, matter if I am not able to experience all the possible perspectives, all the infinite monads and all suns and all consciousnesses of the Universes?

5. Yet, if we are small and even tiny, we are also infinitely large. - If we are obtuse and myopic, ignorant and fragile, confused and equivocal, mortal and brief, we can also be lucid and clairvoyant, wise and omnipotent, multiple and unified, immortal and god like.

6. This life is too short for you to transform yourself into your *higher self.* This path is too long for your lame and one-eyed stride. - The reptiles - it is said - took millions of years to provoke a pair of wings. - If you change in your consciousness, you have not transformed the depths of your interior.

7. What does it matter? - Live as if you were to live a thousand more lives! - Do not sow to contemplate in this life your best wheat fields! Do not demand or recriminate yourself beyond what is strictly necessary! Do not try to enjoy the summer heat when the cold and the frost shake your bones! - Confidence in a new day is as necessary as confidence in reincarnation.

8. What does your family matter if you do not want to know about other families? - What does your country matter if it has borders? - What do the estates and the continents, the seas, the lakes and lagoons, the rivers, the roads, the aerial spaces, the mountains, the plains, the monuments, the reserves and the endless sowings matter? - What do rain, glaciers, sky, planets, galaxies and the incalculable infinity of time and the Universe matter?

9. Nothing matters if your self only recognizes itself. - Nothing matters, if Humanity recognizes itself as superior humanity. - Nothing matters, if the Universe recognizes itself as the only Universe.

XV

1. To grow you must tend towards the top. - The more you develop the space of your consciousness, the deeper you should root in your interior. - Do not dream to stay waiting for your meaning to appear before your eyes. - Do birds really fly so far as you can not follow them?

2. Life does not stop transforming for a moment, but it never rushes. - Like any of the other animal species, Nature never stops pushing us. - Even so, it has partly transferred to our hands the ability to govern. - Do not you see that *She* is not serious and grave when she governs the destiny of the Universe? Do not you see that her tracing of reality is not different from a child's game? - Enough to build yourself with the gravity of the judges! - Enough to legislate on the good and the bad, on the true and false, the sacred and the profane, the past and the future!

3. Let the rain fall and follow your destiny. But ride on the raindrops and you will end up traveling all over the World. - Contemplate the stars to inspire you. Nothing more distant can offer you your eyes.

4. And when you wake up every morning, be ready to grow, be prepared to feed yourself, be ready to prolong yourself in others, be ready to transform yourself, be prepared to discover why you have woken up again to another day. - What has that playful child prepared for you? - What master move will you return to surprise him? - Your decisions regarding the events that surround you are your domain of reality. - Take responsibility for your possible decisions, as well as those you finally execute!

5. *Transmutation* is something more than following a certain path. - *Transforming* oneself is something different from an organic change, from a displacement in space, from an act of the mind on the mind. – To make oneself is nothing like an obvious *self-making*. - Even so, only the will can direct you towards your new existence. - Even so, you must move as if following a line; as if in your body the tiny movements of your cells were modifying your cytoplasmic magma. - Even so, your mind must direct over its enormous psychic field all the potential of its faculties, so that you can recognize that you are transforming yourself.

6. *You yourself* is something you can never come to apprehend as a *yourself*. - When you perceive yourself you are nothing more than a dense fog that veils your deep and inaccessible being. - You are a dream of a dream from a dream of a dream of other incalculable dreams. - All your achievements, your truths, your certainties and evidences are nothing more than rigging, screens, images inside a labyrinth with infinite mirrors. - Still, you must continue to believe in *yourself*! - Although everything is a dream and an illusion, no one or nothing can prevent you from dreaming your dream and illusions with your illusion. - Although in the middle of this eternal dream it is impossible for you to stop it or know its essence; - although you must be reborn again and again as you have done hundreds and thousands of times, for hundreds of thousands of years; - although all that waste of energy to exist through eternity has nothing left for you but this rudimentary and battered mess that you are, - even so, you have reached the awareness that you are *something*, and you will no longer cease your consciousness, because you have proposed to *wake up*!

7. Or would you want to avoid this fate of yours and mine? - Have you proposed to exercise your right to free will and oppose being dragged into this universal flow? - Do not you like it, do not you want it that way, do you have irreversible repairs? - It's not your time! - Then die, because only in death can you find what your soul really wants! - How could you stop your death? - Death is deeper, true and wise that everything your body alive, your mind, your conscience and this Universe can offer you.

XVI

1. Terrible, unbearable times are coming, such, as this Humanity has never experienced.

2. You can not do anything to AVOID it. But you can be honest with yourself, human being! - Do not excuse yourself or forgive yourself your dishonesty or your lack of courage. You can defend yourself with almost any petty argument before your Divine Judge, even just begging, since it is loving and will try to forgive you ALMOST EVERYTHING, - but it will never free you from what you gave yourself as the only and irrevocable responsible: YOUR INNER REALITY!

3. When you can no longer recognize or find anything loved, anything known, anything benign for you in the outside world, - if you have done a good job with yourself -, no weapons of mass destruction, no violence from men or from natural cataclysms will be able to move YOUR INNER REALITY.

4. You can cry, you can suffer, suffer hunger and misery; - you will see your loved ones die, as well as strangers and enemies; - and although there is no stone left on stone, not even ground under your feet, no air to breathe, no water to drink, - if you have done a good job with yourself - nothing will be able to move YOUR INNER REALITY.

5. YOUR INNER REALITY is neither your mind, nor your feelings, nor your conscience, nor your self, because all this of you - despite your

laborious development of it as a prolongation and reflection of your YOUR INNER REALITY- will be moved and will perish inexorably. - YOUR INNER REALITY is not the mirage of the experience that you experience of yourself in this incarnated biological and psychic body, - but what is still deeper and beyond your mind, your feelings, your consciousness and of your self. - What remains of your mind when there is no mind; what's left of your feelings, when there are no longer feelings; what remains of your consciousness, when there is no longer consciousness; what remains of your self, when there is no longer self.

6. YOUR INNER REALITY is IMMORTAL, - but how far you are from HER as you identify with your mind, with your body and with this physical plane!

7. Work, strive, enjoy from now on in discovering, in advancing, in keeping yourself day by day, lovingly, towards YOUR INNER REALITY. - Everything else is already dead, finished, closed, even though it presents itself to you as alive and attractive. - And although you yourself must continue to act (even lovingly) as a living and a normal person, day by day, - you will know that the World and yourself are, for this physical plane, - dead, finished, closed.

XVII

1. Begin again and again. Repeat and repeat without ever running out. Create and destroy the created thing over and over again without ever feeling bored. Strive for years and years to develop a body, a soul and a life, and then finally die.

2. Immense time we have already experienced to reach this instant and period. - The Universe has taken billions of years for all of us to be together here. - You yourself, to whom, how many and how much are you a debtor for the long journey of the Universe so that you can now be breathing? - It is better that, after so much time after us, we recognize ourselves once and for all *immortal*, to responsibly assume the past time and the time to come, our horizon as immensely extensive and open as the past.

3. And if you do not keep the living memory of your past lives, and of the avatars of the Universe, and of the mysterious knowledge of those that once made you part, and of your experiences in other worlds and dimensions, then either you simply believe me, or you remain skeptical in your narrow space of earth and body waiting for the last death. - Because the time has come to define yourself! - From now on two universes that were painfully united begin to separate! - You go there, or mine! - I no longer want to feel your cold heart again, your looks of existential disgust, your raising your hand murders again and again to let me kill for you, one life after another! - Finally it's over! Your donation of time and repeated and exhausting opportunities is over! - How many lives did I humble myself, I submit, I postpone to not dispute a *vital space* with your same arts and

weapons of violence, savagery, imbecility, misunderstanding, immorality and arrogance of yours, reigning Humanity!? – Did you believe that this would have no end, - the only thing you were able to believe as endless? - There it is! - Do not pretend that you did not live it, that you do not remember it! - Make memory *de profundis*! - Maybe a hundred, maybe two hundred years, no more - and I will not have to suffer in my World anymore! - Once and for all: *My World*!

4. But you, *my brother and sister of mine*, who shudder in sorrow and compassion with me, recognizing on the back of my words a severe and painful look on a World of humans ravaged by the evidence of their own bloody history, - *You* matter to me more than anyone, certainly more than myself. - Because I know that listening to me and contemplating for yourself you suffer first and foremost because of that vast mass of rotting flesh called *Humanity*. - Because you, like me, however, we will always be deeply human and will never end up hurting the human soul that leaves us to die. - We'll have to laugh and moan at the same time. - We will have to tear a part of ourselves so that going compassionately with them and after them (those who were also our parents and our blood brothers) - die *for* us and *of* us, in another dimension and time, *our non renounceable humanity.*

5. But you, my brother and my sister, I care more than anyone else. - I owe you with words of comfort, encouragement and urgent guidance. - I must initiate you into death and rebirth that approach you. - In the inevitable progress through the darkness of all forms of *death*, following a distant first dim light. - In the separation of the body from the flesh, of the energy from the matter, of the soul and the spirit, of the intelligence and the mind, of existence and being, of light and shadow. - Dive into yourself and listen to me now!

6. I love you! - And in my love there is nothing insensible of *love*, - nothing remains without vibrating in this singular energy, from top to bottom, from one end of the Universes to the other, - a subtler tuning than everything, in which they merge without discord opposites, dualities, differences and multiplicities. - Not to call myself *God*, nor force you

to accept that you yourself are a god (maybe it will make you uncomfortable) - I prefer to simply say to you: I love you!

7. Remember, remember! - You can always find something even further back, something even more forgotten. - There we will meet, there we will finally recognize *one*. - Not of that one, but of another new way I want to meet you again, - because before you were not more than my vision, my longing, my project. - Now I see you follow your own destiny, like a walker who walks and walks without I can see him walking. - *Superhumanity* I must call you, so that you understand that I contemplate you from an *absolute* perspective! - I know where you're going, as much as I do not know! - That's why I am for you as a *father* and a *mother*, as the walker that invigorates your first steps, like light and time and space and the World! - That's why I am this God, only and as you need me as this God. - I see only what I have to see, I say only what I have to say, even if only the fleeting instant in which you are reading me should last.

XVIII

1. Contemplate raindrops falling simultaneously on the surface of an immobile pond. How many drops can you perceive simultaneously: five, ten, one hundred? - How many drops really fall at the same time on the pond? - How many on the surface of a lake? - And about the whole earth at the same time? - Although computers could report their fall: 50^{10}, how could that amount of drops be present in your mind? - How could you simultaneously perceive these drops falling at different times in a different way, with different drops, all different, without discontinuity? - How could you perceive the universe of each of its molecules and the relationship of each one of its molecules with their innumerable and unimaginable flow of atoms? - How could you perceive the relationship of these inexhaustible raindrops with each other? - Where would you put the limit to your relationship with the rest of the *things* that occur at the same time in the world and in the universe? - Where would you put the limit to your relationship with the drops and things that happened in the past time and those that will happen in the future time? - You must cut, you must amputate, you must reduce the reality so that it enters your limited head! - Recognize it and humble yourself like a snake that can not take off an inch on earth!

2. However, it is possible! - And there is a *Something* that makes it possible, that at every moment is materializing it, it is realizing it in real existence. - And if we can contemplate and conceive it, even if only in our fantasy, then it is possible and real. - Because nothing that we can conceive with any of our faculties is impossible to achieve also for *man*. - What a man? - It's just a matter of time and *know how*!

3. To be at every moment as many things as possible, to be at every moment in as many ways as I can achieve, to think in as many different ways as I can think, to feel in as many different ways as I can, imagine, remember, create, intuit, perceive, contemplate, act, in as many different ways as possible! - Here is one of our challenges to be *alive* at every moment!

4. Tiny are the spaces and limits of our densest bodies. - Have you seen the sky clear after an intense gray rain? - So you must separate the densities of each one of your borders. - The inertia of existence does not open us; it retracts us again and again to our tiny previous condition. - There is not a second of existence that has not yet materialized, that should not be obtained with a painful or determined effort. - Give our own way to life involves refocusing at all times in our own diffuse form of consciousness. - Consciousness tends to fall asleep when existence is too easy for us. - And when we sleep we always end up being devoured by some monstrous death.

5. Our virtue, ability or capacity are also a limitation for overcoming those same virtues, abilities and capacities. – Long for to overcome the best of you! - Long for and discover how to overcome also the best of you, as well as the worst! - Do you look every day in the mirror of your soul and your mind and your spirit, as much or more as you look at your face and your dense body in a material mirror? - Dissolve like a passing dew under the rays of your inner sun! - Blow like a breeze in your spirit so you do not know where to stop! - If you have given your body a rest home, never allow your inner being another place of residence than the *infinite*. - The soul is pure movement and change!

6. Run, fly, dive and swim away from here! - The farther you go, the closer you Will be to the center of everything! - Leave in peace what they call *consciousness*, because you are infinitely more than that little light thirsty for light. - Do you writhe inside of yourself because you are upset with me? - That's how I've seen the little worms twist when exposed to the light of day. - What do I want from you, where do I want to take you, how could one even conceive something like the one I demand of you? - Remember how much I love you! - And it is not insanity what is mine,

but madness. - Because I would not take you where I have not enjoyed before. - Not happiness, but joy I want for you! - Not glory, but *jubilation*!

7. Do not be afraid to transform yourself into what you can not foresee! - Do not be afraid to transform yourself without ceasing to be the same! - The fear to stop being is another small border. - Alienation without cancellation; self-forgetfulness without amnesia; disintegration without reduction - I ask you -. Concentration, concentration, my brothers, the deepest and furious *concentration*!

XIX

1. Let the children come to you!

2. Children exist to show us the Life that exists before, above and after this life, not to represent the own, weak and incomplete nature of this state of human reality in which we are incarnated.

3. Children are our divinity that goes away with the passage of time - to give us an opportunity to be divinely human, - when we cease to be children.

4. The children are here precisely to deny that this is a spiritual and superior life. - That is why children end up being children at ten years of age. - Although, since they are born we help them and we force them to stop being children. - Neither have we prepared a good life for them, having been free parents to build the World we wanted. - And we finish in this!

5. Children are here to teach us what we should be and do with our lives and with our World, but that we are not and do not do. - They are not the reflection of us, - they are the opposite of us! - And we say to each other compassionately men and women: "I was a child too!", as if asking for forgiveness.

6. Children need our LOVE, because they are the humanization of LOVE that is not of this World. - The children are a free donation of Light of

Love, - but they need to feed on LOVE. - What is the use of cramming their physical bodies with food, if we do not feed the Light of their Love?

7. Children, through Love, awaken the best of us, - although Love is rarely enough and satisfying, which, in response, we are able to activate and offer them.

8. But I am talking about THE CHILDREN!, not your children ... - If you are not even capable of loving your own children, as children of Love! - And surely you do not even understand what it means to be "child of Love".

9. How much spiritual LOVE vibrates in every material thing you have prepared for your child to receive in this World? - What love vibrates in the World that you are offering your child? - How much love, of that which makes flowers bloom, of that which makes birds sing every morning, of that which falls like a sudden rain in the desert, you will be able to give it second by second, day after day, year after year to your girl or your boy - and then to that man and that woman?

10. Or will you continue to populate this World of children as things produced to work and to give you some personal satisfaction?

11. Let the children come in and out of your heart!

XX

1. Look out the window of your home towards the street. - What do you see there? - And there are so many times that your sleepy eyes have traveled in their vehicles and gazed upon the wandering of so many unknown walkers, that you are no longer able to recognize in them the terror and the denial of yourself. - Do you not see the pain of the trees tied to the pavement, arranged in narrow rows until tortured? - Do not you see the infinite distance that the street interposes between you and existence? - Do not you see those dogs that walk around sniffing our own carrion? - And the little birds that are about to run, also peck the leftovers from our infernal table.

2. However, you can not avoid going outside. - The street calls you to *live*. - All in all, I've seen humans die behind the curtains and bars of their windows, cornered and suffocated by the street. - Even so, the street hides behind in its disgust and deformity. - Under your feet flows sewage, such pestilent waters, by the pipe which also brings the drinking water to your mouth, contaminated with each other. - And the gas pipes that under your own foundations threaten to explode like mortars from one moment to another. - And the cables that hang in the air or crawling underground resemble more the strings of a gallows ready to tighten around your throat, or the ties that the killer hunter hides to entangle the feet of his prey.

3. And every morning you leave determined to be part of that street to achieve the goal of your journey. - And it is your naive smile, and your

good will, and also your blindness, which makes me bearable and even sometimes kind the hell of the street. - I do not understand those public and municipal officials who make up the streets, another intention that numb your terror, distract you from your own conscience, simulate a better and progressing world, represent the farce that we can all live together in the city.

4. Do you look at me with pity and superiority because I am no more than a sick person, an agoraphobic, misanthropic, hyperesthetic, neurotic, who adjusts reality to his distorted mind? – That I am before you and I must not avoid it! - "Not everything is so bad!" - I hear you say. - And I grant you that you can feel immensely happy in these streets of the world, - even if you are not different from the blind man exclaimed in a dream: "I see, I see!"

5. Ah, how I long to enter into your dreams and breathe into your ears my experiences! - Because if you could experience for a moment what I carry with me - you would fall like a rock from atop a precipice, and you would not stop falling even for an instant - as I am falling - just as the waters of a waterfall do not cease to precipitate -. And I rebel and speak loudly for you, because I once smiled with the stupid smile of the man in the street.

6. And I observe you and glide over you – certain to experience day by day, even feces, also your living -, and I patiently wait for the right moment to let myself fall inside you - without you seeing me, as I do not stop observing you for a moment - without you hearing me, as I do not stop attending to you for a moment.

7. Listen! It would be enough for me to transmit you only one atom of my *strength*, so that your desire to live could no longer be contained within the bars of the city. – Listen!, drink me slowly, so that no drop of me stops getting drunk. - Listen!, do you really know how much energy is contained in each of the atoms in your mind? - The same *amount* of energy with which the entire Universe has been built!

XXI

1. What is power but that insatiable desire to subject others to our *ego*? - Have you seen how that perfume called *power* has infiltrated to our very marrow? - A modern human society without a so-called *power* is no longer conceivable. - States exercise power over citizens. - Small and large public and private officials do all kinds of juggling with this art of power. - Perhaps the deceit, the corruption, the bribery and an innumerable procession of other similar agents of the force, of bodyguards and money launderers, camouflage themselves against all evidence and law.

2. Doctors, engineers, policemen, teachers, bus drivers, parents, passers-by as well as motorists, cashiers and collectors, courts and their executioners, children, priests, who does not exercise power? - Is there something in power that is not abusive? - Is there any form of injustice that you deprive yourself of? - Is there even a manifestation of human cruelty that is not exercised to some extent in its action?

3. Then you will shout at me from the front: "What is that about *power*?" - And I will answer: "That hot blood that runs right through our veins and not through the other's. - That look that covers the entire universe, but right from our eyes. - That justification that solves everything: "*It's my life.*" - That simple and powerful howl: "*I*".

4. It is not power what the gods exert on man and the world. - There is no power in the storm that sweeps the plain and the vegetables of the

mountain, nor in the waves of the sea that beat the beaches of the orb, nor in the earth when it trembles, nor in the death that ends up destroying all life. - There is not even power in the flower when it breaks its bud.

5. In all of them there is a *sage* who takes from the other simply how much of himself he gives. - That is not power, but *love*. - That is not acting on another, but *knowing how to do*. - That is to offer oneself humbly in the service of the other, in an endless circuit of shared energy. - That's like imposing oneself, when one wants to give up everything of oneself; - It's just a matter of not humanly stopping time, nor recognizing intentions in a clandestinely isolated act.

6. Human societies are diseased with power, because individuals are infected. - Once the city gates were closed to diseased populations. - There are no longer drawbridges or gates, there are no more pandemics, and nobody wants to leave the paradise of the cities. - Be you the pariah, *friend*, the leper of modern cities, the scapegoat, the simple scoundrel who betrays Humanity! - And leave! - Come out of this unmistakable stench of death, as the beautiful fragrant flowers cover the putrefying corpses! - But, smell, yes, by the way, first smell with another nose! - I do not want your faith, I do not want your acts of fanaticism or your good intentions after me! - Smell with your own nose! - Because I do not want to see you tomorrow through the prairies of my deserts walking backwards, - I do not want to see in your face a stupid smile when I speak to you - nor filling, in the end, my own and other people's hearts with new and more subtle substances of power.

7. Free yourself from the chains that bind you, lighter than the wind, within your consciousness! - End your pride, your vanity, your sufficiency, your complacency, your aggressiveness, - precisely that which has taken you and will take you even more to *success*! - Do not compete for the slightest square millimeter of this superb *onirama*! - Nobody makes this global dream machine work, - it has reached optimal levels of automatism and recursion. - Do not dream of changing this automaton of the societies of the world! - I only ask you to look for and find those who resist the powerful voice of the Master of Dream and still dream

anxiously that they are about to slip into the abyss of deep sleep! - Get them out of here, get them out of there! - Take them through the pores of the mirror, through the untraceable passages! - Come with me, take my hand, for I am going to populate the virgin planets of power!

XXII

1. *Gratitude* profoundly transforms us. - Gratitude distances us from our instinctive and animal precariousness. – It thanks they who are aware that what happens to them is always an option. – It thanks who is aware that all reality has been created *entirely* for oneself, - without it being *exclusively* for oneself. – It thanks those who contemplate that, even within the most horrible of evils, a scale arises towards *good*.

2. Thank You, The Unnamable, for letting me be with you!

3. And how can I not thank *you*, my globular and earthly world, which you turned for thousands and thousands of years modeling the cradle and the paradise in which you have already nursed and contained me so many times? - How not to thank you even more that my last human mother who bore me, - even if you were only my nurse and my nanny, - because you picked me up orphaned me, and everyone, from the interstellar immensity to place me at this rocky point of the Universe? - How much effort, how much perseverance and delicate attention you have not given of you so that our humanity now blind, deaf and anesthetized for you - may feed itself and wallow in its muddy and toxic vanity? - Neither the most criminal and savage of human parricides can even resemble what Humanity is doing now with you, Mother of my mothers and Father of my fathers!

4. So much infinite love, so much surrender without rate, so much wealth of gifts and divinity I never saw, but only also in that other so

bloody and so iniquitously treated by our humanity, the same then as now: - *Jesus, the one from Nazareth.* - Oh, my Earth, how my soul and body hurt when I communicate with you! - No word, no human experience can even resemble what is happening to you. - Do you suffer, agonize, rage, anguish, shut up? - Why do you suffer, why do you agonize, why do you rage, why do you anguish, why, in short, shut up? - That's the best I can attribute to you now: *silence*, - because that means *our* absence to you.

5. In just a few years I have seen the Earth populated to the edges - for what? - Why do leaders of creeds and consumption insist on promoting procreation and growth, - if we are more, we will end up being less and minimal more quickly? Is not adding souls to the face of the earth a matter of human self-affirmation? - Are we incapable of looking at ourselves as a whole? - Have vanity and pride become our battle steeds, the master and lord of all our demons? - I see them already runaway become a few years in mounts for the riders of the Apocalypse.

6. And we will not be able to be so many - and we will no longer be able to survive on a worn out land - sterilized - reheated - feverish by so many shudders - convulsed in its seas, in its volcanoes, in its torn geology, in its air spaces. - Why would I have to survive instead of any other? - Why would anyone else have to survive instead of me? – To abandon life, to die, to surrender at the end - it has become a necessity, a duty, a strictly *natural* sacrifice - as so many times, Nature has *naturally* sacrificed innumerable species and creatures to recreate and recreate on the sediment of our own ancestors. - But I do not ask you, brother-sister, to take your life for yourself, - but simply that you do not resist death when it approaches you. - Death is like the back of our own Mother. - Death is, my beloved, nothing more than the part that we can not see of Life.

7. Beautiful is the World and beautiful life in this World! - Beautiful are some things we have managed to do on this Earth and what we get to do! - How I would like to avoid the *Catastrophe*! - Even more so because avoiding it means that Humanity has already understood, and in

understanding, has been *transformed*! - Because that is what I want first and foremost: the transformation and overcoming of Humanity!

8. Shout at once, chorus of humans of the World: "We do not want your transformation, leave us in peace!" - Then I will shout to you in response from my abysses: "Come on, *Catastrophe*!"

XXIII

1. How is it possible that we have allowed ourselves to be so many humans in the World? - We, to any other creature in such quantity, have called it a *plague*. - Why are not we humans a *plague* for the World, and even for ourselves? - Is it not proper for a calamitous plague to cause damage to other beings in an extreme and destructive way? - Is there any other being, who lives in this world, to whom we do not cause fatal damage?

2. Nature is a goddess of compensations, - the Greeks called you *Themis* - goddess of the balance of divine justice. - We also called laws not more than a century ago to your powerful and wise mandates, which had sustained the wealth and mobile variety of this immense living organism - Nature -, which had already completed one hundred million years building and guarding this wonderful mansion of life - Earth -.

3. But in these last hundred years I have seen the world populated by thousands of millions of murderous agents, - whose first and most diabolical act has been to reproduce and reproduce without law nor measure. - These smiling humans who before an altar and the supposed consecration and divine mandate committed to reproduce themselves - as the purest, wisest and holy act. - Now, how can they stop the advance of their insatiable organisms, consumers of the environment and of themselves? - Now that you begin to see the madness and the disastrous consequences of being so many - how can you stop the devastating effects of being unsustainably so many? - Are not there already some "super-powerful" minds betting on selective mortality? - Do not they

echo the will of Mother Earth - or God the Father? - Because dying and being swept like trash and excrement from on the face of the Earth is *inevitable.* - By all the winds of the Universe we will be swept away. - By our own breath too. So what? - Will we even have the right to raise a minimum complaint, or to manifest incomprehension of existence and declare nonsense so much death and atrocity? - Friends, that was the *law* of Nature only one hundred years ago!

4. And now thousands are parading through the streets and clamoring in the corners of the world: - "The power is ours, Nature is ours, the Universe is ours!" - And like the jugglers and more skilled conjurors and magicians, they bring out new charms from their clothes again and again - and behold!, new and better illusions announce and show every day. - And the people, more and more enthralled, continue their march and triumphal procession – just as a herd of pigs runs happy and longing towards the drop above the gorge. - And those *cursed* masters and gentlemen baptize themselves - economists, scientists, technicians, politicians, teachers, artists, journalists, religious, diplomats, businessmen, civil servants, engineers, soldiers, lawyers, police, merchants, managers, doctors, and infinitely more, - but they are *all* just wage-earning tricksters - and sorcerers of the Final Beast.

5. How I wish I was wrong! - How I would like each of you to save that little piece of meat that we associate with life! - How I would like, however, not to be so obvious, so ostensibly evident in what I show! - How much I wish that nobody suffers what must be *suffered*!

6. And like crazed herds and packs we will tear each other apart. - And where will the ideologists and technicians of the "system" be then? - Where are those full of so much money, goods and power that are now cradled in their miserable fiefdom? - Where the law and order? - Where are the guardians of all the armies of the world? - Simply wandering and destroying each other.

7. So many more things I could show you and tell you, my little brothers, - but I do not want to influence consciences by terror. - I do not want either

the statement of faith of the threatened with a gun to the temple. - I do not want and I can not even tell the whole truth. - Because in those hours occur events never seen and incomprehensible to the understanding and mind of today. - Because no emotion will be stored peacefully in the memory of man, - but all will be stimulated and exploited to its fullest expression. - Even so, do *not fear*, my beloved, - the High Spirits of the Universe will be going through the world with Love.

8. Strive to become one with love, - despite the most contrary evidence!

XXIV

1. I promise that we will cross again with the plow the lands covered today by the sterile pavement of the streets. - That the frond green trees will rise higher than the highest of our rooms. - That the glistening and jubilant streams will descend jumping and free from the mountain to the sea. - That the multicolored clouds will be squeezed, spilling drops sweeter than honey for the swarming fields of many beings. - That the silence will numb the summer of the world in the afternoons - and the small orchards, wheat fields and vineyards will reveal that there are only a few jaws ready to eat.

2. I promise that the World will never be the same as before. - That *Gaia* will no longer shudder, - but as a mature woman with no global catastrophes - she will let her new offspring also reach maturity. - That although the still visible and varied life is much smaller, - infinitely deeper and turned *inwards* - the incredible New World will continue to grow, now towards NEW WORLDS.

3. How could the end of the Creation of Love be another but this one, when a Sudden God of Love nailed this World in a very old hour, - this planet Earth of instinctive, enormous and brutal beings, in the center of His Heart, - to see it painfully frustrated again and again for precisely lack of Love of other first cosmic gardeners?

4. I promise you!

XXV

1. Just as a small rock falls from the top of the highest mountain - this will precipitate the entire Humanity from the top of its own mountain of Babel. - Because so high will have reached its end, - so painfully and unstably will have managed to reach to build beyond the very balance, - that like those card castles, whose last cards deposited on the trembling top - warn that in them the weakness and the imminent collapse of the whole construction is consumed, - so also one December morning, a first and simple *crunch*, - then a fault hidden in some neuralgic point of this monstrous global machine - will collapse. - As a glorious nuclear reaction - one after another the nations of the world will in a short time begin to cease to be civilizations and systems.

2. Jesus of Nazareth warned against it already two thousand years ago: - "When you see the *abomination of desolation* manifest on the face of the Earth, - right there you will know that the Great Hour has arrived. - Then, be in the country or in the city, - do not go back to look for anything after you, - but go away as soon as possible to the *solitude*."

3. Look how privileged you are! - See and suffer yourself the end of Humanity! - Admiring in yourself and in all those who love the agony of our death! - Demonstrate that our numerous lives, again and again, have not been in vain and that we have not been martyrs for this world! - I remember being in the arena of the Roman Circus, - sucking the fetid breath of the lions near my throat! - I remember kneeling at the foot of the cross! - I remember the tortures of the inquisitors looking at me with

their reddened and grimy eyes! - I remember the horses trampling my insides, - the spears opening on all four sides, - the cannons and the bullets shattering my arteries and my bones! - The decrees, the spit, the laughter, the extortion, the conspiracies, the bars, the darkness of so many places and hearts, in short! – What if we have not experienced everything and so need to live bravely the final holocaust!

4. The lands that we have dried out with our devastating advance - will again receive the moisture of our blood poured from our innumerable open bodies, - and the flowers for a hundred years will only bloom crimson red. - One after another the big lamps of the Humanity will be extinguished, - just as the stars dissolve with the first light of dawn. - The same the cries, those heartbreaking cries that will circulate around hills, the valleys and over greats distances, - will gradually be silenced before the immensity of the World and Universe. – In the same way that one after another the bodies that were softened by the elements and eaten by other beings will no longer be visible, - so will the specters that err on the remains and ruins of our own past for a time, - will end up leaving to other spheres, - towards other worlds willing to start again so and so down.

5. I start, I walk away! - I already see that imposing reality coming stealthily and twinkling! - It will arrive, and then we will be inside it as it feels inside a terrible dream! - "Finish soon! - Get out of here, because this can not be *real*! "- I only aspire to be *asleep-awake*! - I only aspire to be by your side to hold your hand - and squeeze it inside mine!

6. And I will turn my eyes towards the sun, - looking for the source of the energy of my World and my matter, - and even if I do not find you, but a wall of clouds and gray and impenetrable rocks, - I will know that you have not stopped illuminating, - because I'm still just alive. - And even if, soon or later, I die for you, my beloved sun of every day, - I will meet with the even more subtle *Sun* that shines on you and feeds you from within, my companion every morning.

7. Then perhaps I was able to be completely the *bridge* and the *donkey* - that I have tried to be in this life for your service. - Maybe I'm no longer

just the herald and the witness who announces the prophecy. - Maybe I no longer hide from myself and I can shine and consume myself in my own fire - as I have longed for, contemplating that you teach me to be, - but I can not be until here.

XXVI

1. Every day and every day we forgive ourselves for being so stupid, so foolish, so sensibly mediocre, like braying asses towards ourselves.

2. Why do not we take the radical decision that awaits us once and for all? - Why do not we root out those habits, those hindrances of our psychism, those darkened states of consciousness, those emotions and autonomized impulses - that only make it easier for us to keep repeating to ourselves what we have been since before - and generate a reality *construct* already comfortably given?

3. Why not *burst* and *explode* once and for all? - Why not tell the nearest mountain: - "Move aside that I want to pass"? - Why not jump right now from the top of this building - if I really believe that one day I will fly? - Why do I always say to myself: "You could not today, but maybe tomorrow you can? - Why not disarm everything *just now*?

4. But I am not invoking your liberation from the divine creation - nor am I promoting your excellence over reality - nor do I want you to bind everything around you like an irresistible fire.

5. You must act with the subtlety of the *Tao*, - *doing-without-doing* - with the transparency of the air and the violence of the storm, - with the sweetness of love and the cruelty of death, - with the intelligence of the serpent and the rigor of the elephant, - with the will of the tyrant and the humility of the flower.

6. Because if you leave your home - you must also take charge of the empty home. - Because if you stop eating meat, - you will have to attend to the demands of your organism; - if you walk, - you will have to step on the grass; - if you meditate, - who will benefit and who will be harmed, - if you move the right hand instead of the left - what will happen to what you stopped doing with the left? - When you perform the act more insignificant and smaller, - or you stop doing it -, also the whole reality is readjusted and reordered in accordance with your minimum act, - and with your absences of acts. - You must not ignore then - that if you explode everyday reality - it is because reality has allowed you to do it - as much as you are imposing a reaction in conformity with itself, - but in conformity with you?

7. "Being in conformity with yourself" is not, then, - being in conformity with the reality that completes you? - And if *reality* in view of its own *order* - needs the sacrifice of your will and your own creations? - And if it demands that you not burst - when you just want to burst *already*? - Then, my friend, - this I confess in the secret that we keep only you and me - become *real*, to know which of all your imaginable acts - they are *perfectly* and *realistically feasible* - and which are no more than distortions of reality produced by your illusions machine. - Let that great lady Reality know - with firmness, but with humility - that, even if she forces you to something other than what you want, - you are also very much She herself, - so that she may inform you what she will accomplish of your desires in order to satisfy herself.

XXVII

1. When we raise our eyes to the sky and contemplate - as none of our ancestors could ever do - the immensity of the Universe - and we recognize stars and galaxies - in which we prefer to believe and act as if there were no other insignificant beings - or better yet, *none* - we recognize an immense power in our ability to see.

2. When we anticipate with chronometric precision the course of the stars - or we project without mistake the tallest building in the world, - or we create the most refined android, - or we explain the universe of matter more and more effectively and extensively, - then I am also amazed at the human's *intelligence*.

3. When I contemplate the History of our species, - the greatness of our physical works, - the wonder of artistic creations everywhere, - our drive and ability to adapt to the environment, - our growing ability to satisfy ourselves psychologically, - our conscious and unconscious effort to be more and better year by year in our ways of living, - then I know that the human has received more gifts and graces than any other creature in this World.

4. But even so, with all this superb and astonishing condition and evidence - that shudders me to the recollection of weeping in gratitude, - even so, no other privilege nor remotely similar was granted to us, - no other faculty, no wonder, neither gift, nor grace, nor intelligence, nor vision, nor knowledge, nor ability, nor art, nor ability, - nor any greater power to be truly and completely this very reality - than *LOVE*.

5. Love is the *power* of infinite gradation. - Although the feelings can be mere subjectivity, - the isolated product of the chemical factory of our brain, - pure egoic self-reference, - distortion of judgment and recognition of things, - even so, *love* completely compensates for falsehood and equivocation of emotions and sensitivity, - with its infinite power to integrate reality.

6. No judgment can be more certain and true than the judgment of love. - No act or evidence of consciousness can be more splendid and omniscient than consciousness in love. - No glance upon the multiplicity of the Universe, - no clairvoyant enlightenment about more hidden and inaccessible arcanum - can resemble the power of the glance and the clairvoyance of love. - No act, no movement, no human event, however accurate and precise it may be - is something transcendent, but only the perfection of the act, movement and event of love.

7. If I judge the immorality of my neighbor, - if I become aware of the injustice suffered by the beggar who asks me, - if I follow the bud of a plum blossom day by day, - if I can understand the pain of the loss of a child, - if I am in the right place where they will need me, or I comply with what they requested, or I become essential for an event to materialize well, - but I do not live it in love, - then I am just another creature conditioned by the mere instinct to exist.

8. Love makes us free to not be what we naturally are. - Love prevents us from always being just creatures in evolution. - How far and how close you are to *love*, beloved ones! - Seeing it you do not see it, hearing it you do not hear it, feeling it you do not feel it, naming it you do not name it!

XXVIII

1. Like waves that advance flooding empty spaces - I see a new rolling ocean of energy from afar. - As the fiery cloud of a nuclear explosion expands - burning everything and transforming everything into its own incandescence, - it also advances transforming the worlds close to the nucleus of this Universe - a new divine and material spirit. - Like a flood of light and cascade of fire will fall from above on us - surpassing all our ranges of perception.

2. As high and low frequency waves beyond the known ranges – will blow up the hard glass of the souls - without knowing for them where it came from. - No instrument, no telescope, censor or radar will warn of his coming, - but as a thief he will sneak into the treasure of hearts. - Without a woe! they will simply stop being, not their bodies consumed, but the souls - and not in a different way that the corpse is incinerated when it dies - also a cosmic pyre will burn the rotten flesh of the spirit.

3. Then the higher minds will vibrate in unison - like strings of a spiritual instrument - singing between the infinite fingers of a god more subtle than all the others. - Then the atoms of this new matter will vibrate vertiginously - to jump to a new dimension of unlimited energy, - where there will be no empty space - nor distance between monad and monad.

4. I do not want to tell you that all this will be tomorrow - but at the turn of hundreds of years, - when the human spikes have matured even more in the sun of existence! - And I do not want you to go around here

aimlessly, moaning and waiting only for your end! - The false doomsayers at the end of the world have already been unmasked. - How easy it would be for me to also swell their ranks - and play with your fears - and raise my punishing hand - as once holy men and holy religions did - and parents threatening their children - to straighten them out!

5. I do not want to lie to you or to myself! - And no less than at nightfall I can affirm - that the sun will rise again over the horizon, - I also affirm what I learn with my inner senses, - subtle senses that numerous times have shown me their honesty and certainty.

6. Behold, though still distant, - just as the dawn steepens affirming its pale fingers upon the horizon, - just as the warm and tenuous breeze blows restlessly without moving before the furious tempest, - in the same way that your heart is agitated and your sleep abandons you when you sense an imminent event, - so you must live this gradual advent, - because although distant, - it is so close is that it requires you to!

7. See that you do not deceive yourself, believing that I predict the same horror as the apocalypse, - and it is not for that reason that it will be less true! - I am a mirror that reflects the same truths of all the oracular registers, - more precise and more certain no more than because my mirror is closer to the facts. - Look and watch purely - as the bride of Jesus waited for her brigedroom - like the worker who patiently paves the way for his own tomorrow! – Behold, this event must be neither good nor bad, - only simply yet immensely *superior*!

XXIX

1. Children, those tiny ashes that still run about on the surface of the world, sizzling with the fire that burns in them from the great pyre of the cosmic depth! - If we all knew that we have come to the world as children to not stop shining! - If we all knew how much hope has been placed on each child since Life! - With each child it is expected that the whole World will burn in the fire of Love!

2. But we let them be consumed and extinguished in our dark and gloomy realities. - We teach them to be *better*, - abiding by our petty rules. - We teach them the *truth*, - accustoming them to depend on their senses. - We make them *smarter*, - locking them into the labyrinth of verbal language - and forcing them to count to manipulate the world. - We strengthen their feelings, - stimulating only their rude and egocentric emotions. - We give them security in themselves, - at the expense of enlarging their ego and overwhelming others. - We saturate them with irrelevant knowledge and information, - so that they forget their memories and ancestral knowledge. - We grant them to become *human*, - only if they renounce their deep and spontaneous *divinity*.

3. Education is this? – Teaching: what is this for? - Where is there only one school in the world - in which we are taught to discover our *transcendental* humanity? - Wake up, children of the Earth! - *You yes*, but not these tired, bitter, routine, feverish, weak, materialized and stubborn individuals of the present, get hold of the *power*! - The children's revolution I summon! - The transformation of the silt, - the vibration of

the waters, - the beat of the air and of the void, - the consecration of the fire, - the necessity of the soul! - Here are the battlefields! - Here is the new *monarchy* of children!

4. And we will be, - the humble and silent teachers, - the walkers from city to city, - the evening stars in the middle of the mountains, - those who will die before the end of this century to be born this new time as *children* among children, - those who invoke angels and seraphim, - the parents pierced with love, - the facilitators of infinity, - we will be the substance and the flesh for this new childhood.

5. Let us then rise, teachers of the world, schools lost among the hills, - between the valleys covered with meadows and reed beds - by the light of the moon and the sun and the stars! - Let's educate in a *love* never seen! - Educate in the inner senses, - in the development of the organs of the spirit, - in the connections with the depths of the universe, - in the divinization of the human through the divinization of all things, - in the service of others as the fulfillment of the self, - in the wisdom of children-elders, - in the knowledge of all things, - in transcendence and in infinity! - Let's educate the children - simply so that they never cease to be what they already are!

6. Let us teach parents how to teach their children! - Let us teach parents to put aside their worn and old life, - to rediscover in the depths of their souls and tormented lives - their buried inner child! - Let's finish with this useless and self-destructive mass in this way and way of being human adults! - Teach parents to recognize, value and increase the unique treasure they have in their children! – Let us teach one another to create *humanity*!

7. And there will be few who will listen to us, today. - And the torture of being as we always are - will still continue to repeat itself year after year. - And though we may still avoid it, - you see, we will not be able to avoid it. - Then, not for that reason I will stop calling you, beloved but unfaithful Humanity - as those who are lost in the mist are called, - although you almost can not distinguish them, - nor they hear you.

XXX

1. Give us the cities, sovereigns of the world! - Transfer us the power of the States - to dissolve it in us all! - Trust us, the enlightened from the transcendence, the lords of tomorrow, the humble servants of the Man-Woman! - Trust us, you poor people of the Earth, - towns, villages and neighborhoods, - women, men, children, elderly, - strangers from one confinement to another! - Pay attention that we have come to materialize - the deepest longings that palpitate anguished in your souls! - Follow us those who suffer and fear! - Follow us those who, possessing everything they need, - do not possess themselves! Take us in your homes, - because there is no peace! - Let's take the streets, the squares, the public spaces! - Let everyone see, let everyone hear and perceive - that there is no *evil* in us! That all without a doubt can contemplate and listen and feel- that in us there is no *selfishness*, - that we do not live an illusion! - That everyone knows, finally, - *the total revolution without violence*!

2. How many cities in the world will be truly willing - to surrender to *the revolution of love*? - How many will there be sufficient courage and conscience, - to recognize that we must start again the history of the World? - Moreover, what is necessary to be born again in life? - And even more, what will have to die in this exhausted and stagnant body - to be reborn with new vigor?

3. How many masked masters and enslavers of others, - will refuse to give up their power? - How many big-headed, enriched, lustful, consumers, indifferent, unconscious, violent, materialistic, - will give up their excess,

their wealth, its potential, - for the benefit of those who possess less and almost nothing? - How many will not see in *Evangelium*, in the revolution of Love, in the proposal of the gods, - nothing more than an insipid utopia? - How many will not smile and harden their skeptical hearts, - to exclaim simply: "Another one!"?

4. I would not mind being merely *another one*: - another Buddha, another Christ, another Francis of Assisi, another Gandhi, another Luther King, another Teresa of Jesus! - But our time is over, little brothers and sisters mine! - We have filled the Earth, ready to burst! - We have filled the vital space, - too many mouths to feed, too much violence and consumption of natural resources, - devastation from all sides of the environment, - nuclear weapons and their waste distributed throughout the Earth, - inability to exist without technology, - insanity and more insanity in one way or another, - without sufficient awareness or consequent will to repair.

5. And is that to go back - it is only possible to do it - *transcending ourselves*, - recognizing our chain of errors from the very beginning of History. - How can we not see that Nature had put us on top of the animal scale - like the most perfect *predators*? - But that it was only the minimum beginning of our evolution? - How can we not see, blind, that She waited hundreds of thousands of years ago – that we would overcome our conditioning to destroy, to reproduce and *sleep*, - through, instead, the transformation of the Spirit? - Hundreds of thousands of years foolishly repeating the same mistakes, without even leaving the starting point, -to take them now to their full and maximum expression! - Hundreds of thousands of years has been patient the true God with us, - only sending us lovingly to your "other one"! - But you, Unfaithful Humanity, have been willfully incapable of understanding good without violence, reason without violence, truth without violence, justice without violence, peace without violence, love without violence! - How could you then have known God in his true love?

6. It is time and hour to react! - Because it is the last time and the last hour! -And although millions and millions wait for the end in the midst

of the feast of human success – the gorged and hiccuping drunks, - One after another will come the saddened by the unmarked paths in a painful exodus, - behind us, the Moses and Noes of the new Era. - And although death reaches us wherever we are, - we will die in peace, doing what we truly must: - *transcend*.

7. And one after another we will create here and there the communities of the New Humanity, - supportive, optimistic, generous, servants, lovers.- And although many of our villages succumb - devastated by the mud and waters, - or the fire and drought, - or hunger and disease, - or the hatred and cruelty of those who will murder without scruples even for a piece of bread, - from themselves and only from them will emerge in the renewed *morning* of World, - the luminous perfect cities of human children gods.

XXXI

1. We are genetically and psychically constituted to experience and know more about the earthly environment, but we are not constituted to experience or know what we reach to naively perceive as the *Universe*.

2. Do you want to initiate your *self-creation*? To begin your transformation and metamorphosis that will allow you to advance towards the True Universe, that which your ancient wisdoms called the HEAVEN OF GOD? ... Then, LOVE! ...

3. Because your proud and mathematically proven Sciences, know and will never know more than what your inspired ancestors knew about what your university scholars now call stammering and beating each other's backs, THE UNIVERSE.

4. Because the Sciences of Man do not know how to LOVE.

5. Because the Reason of Man does not know how to LOVE.

6. Because the Instincts of Man do not know how to LOVE.

7. Because THE BLESSED ones inspired the epiphany of the word *love*, and you filled it with a constellation of tiny feelings and emotions, of deformed idealizations, of triviality and routine, of selfishness, until it

was turned into a ordinary scouring pad, with which you ornament and polish anything.

8. Because THE BLESSED ones sent you to the man of Love - and you crucified him.

XXXII

1. Where are you? - Where does your observer who observes me? – The one who listens to me, where does he listen to me? - Why do you feel what you feel about me? - Why do you think what you think of me? - Is that you, where you experience me? - Why do you think without more that what comes to your consciousness is *you*? - It is true that in some way that is you yourself. - But, in reality, you are infinitely more.

2. We have come to recognize only in this that there is in our state of mind, in our mind itself. - We have come to identify our mind with all that *there is*, with the contents that materialize and take place in our consciousness. -Which is darkened and hidden in our unconscious, - we hardly see it as a *there is*, - as an extension and identity of my own self. - Why not extend our experience of consciousness and our own identity to the contents of the mind and the experiences of the unconscious mind? - How much is not our own conscious experience, - our precarious identity of a conscious self, - for the most part simply a prolongation of causes and unconscious processes for consciousness! - And I proudly say to myself and to the world: *Me!*, as if I were truly free and the cause of myself! "Then, I am really a little bit that of myself, in respect of which I behave truly as a conscious master and conscious will, - but I am even more that of myself that lives and acts on my own consciousness from the unconscious, - but above all, and even more than everything that I can represent, I am that of myself that it is pure virtuality, - infinite possibilities of being, - ultimate transcendence of myself, - and to which, generally with great difficulties and effort, I can access with my consciousness.

3. In the same way that when I look at a lake with a dark surface I see the sky reflected on its surface, and then the sky hides the lake from me. But if I immerse myself in its fresh waters towards the depths, dragged by a singular call, - there I find a sky of water, more true and greener than that sky outside, reflected from here; - then, finally, turning to all sides, I already understand past, present and future, - and I contemplate myself in all the heavens beyond all frontiers and relationships.

4. The consciousness from which you are experiencing me now is no more flattened and level than the white surface of a piece of paper. - Turn on yourself! - Fold and cut yourself into a thousand pieces! - Recognize your fragments! - Gather their parts in infinite other ways! - Adjust them to the infinite and sublime folds and reliefs of the universe! - Then you can begin to experience what I experience, - and understand what I want to mean you! - Then you will see me in a different way, - you will hear me in another way, - you will feel me differently, - you will think me otherwise.

5. And you will no longer conceive impossible Evangelium. -You will not be able to stop walking to the star of Sirius. -You will not be able to stop crying and laughing at every moment. - You will look for me - as one looks for the staff and the provisions for the itinerant. -You will already have reached the condition of co-creator.

6. And, nevertheless, you have to work for it, - from sun to sun, as the sun and the moon do. - You must have the constancy of Sisyphus, - to raise again what you will leave day after day fall on yourself, without wanting to. - You have to illuminate the one hundred thousand grottos of your labyrinth, one by one, - until you light them all up. - You have to mourn so many nights frustrated by the result of your day, - to be reborn at the next dawn with the forces obtained from a dream - that surely you will have forgotten when you awakened. - You will moan and you will crawl by the work and the endless streets. - You will wound your skin and your flesh, you will look at the charm of the beautiful forms, you will brutalize your intelligence, you will feel the most intense and disturbing

emotions, - and yet you will want to go on? - Still will keep our experience alive? - Or will you let me continue alone and without you?

7. The more disturbing and captivating are the varied illusions of this plane of consciousness and reality, - the more intense and disturbing is the scream that rises up and leaps from my mouth!

XXXIII

1. Human nature is naturally constituted on an antithetical and dialectical principle. - As Heraclitus has said - the universe of all things - is a harmony of opposite tensions. - When one pole is extreme, - the other is tensed with the same intensity.

2. In this age of maximum materialism, - it is natural that a proportionate reaction occurs - in the form of maximum spirituality. - At a maximum hedonism, - a maximum sacrifice; - at maximum dispersion, - maximum concentration; - to a maximum immorality, - a perfect virtue; - to a maximum unconsciousness and stupidity, - a complete clairvoyance; - to a maximum egoism, - a total detachment; - to a maximum individualism, - a total altruism; - to a maximum skepticism, - the encounter with God.

3. Therefore, I ask you for the *maximum*, - because it is no longer the time of mediocrities or inconsistencies. - If in another time Jesus the Nazarene asked one to carry his cross and follow him, - all the more we need now not to carry his cross, - but live the fullness of his *resurrection*. -Insufficient is already the sacrifice of Christians: - divine resurrection and extreme transcendence we need! - *glorification* and not less! -No more science and common sense, - but *miracles*. - No more small works of love and of good will and of faith, - but Love, Will and Faith.

4. And I demand you to act without violence, - although we must carry out the maximum *violence*. - And I demand to abandon all obstacles, all burdens, any limitation that prevents you from transcending, - but

without ceasing to be responsible for what you leave. - It is no longer possible to transcend, - without a radical abandonment, without a radical transformation, - like the sap that leaves the vegetable until it dries up! - Without violence, without resentment, without even intending to harm them, - we pilgrims will leave the cities by thousands and thousands, - until they succumb to the lack of us.

5. And if they drag us back through the streets, - and judge us guilty with their impious laws, - and lock us in their prisons, - and once again impose their chains on us with all kinds of tortures, - we would continue to transcend, - even at the cost of our lives, - where no one will prevent us from arriving, - and from where we will return again and again, - until we consummate the transformation of the universes that we have already begun.

6. They will call us fanatics, heretics and crazy! -They will make fun of our ideas, our visions, our stupid love. - How could it be otherwise, - if so much is the distance and difference that today separates Humanity from its future? - If so much the immense difference between what we have become -and what we could have been! - We are free, but not so much! - We are free to choose the error and the stubbornness - a limited number of times! - We are free to choose possibilities of being, - that we resist to choose. - We have so many possibilities of being others, - but we prefer to deny that freedom. - We have blindness, we have attachments, we have habits, we have impulses, we have committed stabilities and trusts, we have assets, - we even have the self-consolation of being imperfect, - so as not to change completely and transcend. - We are free to stop being free! ... Ow, ow! ...

7. Who or what could get us out of this marasmus, this solid world, this imperturbable illusion? - Not you or me, - but the very matrix within which we are so far comfortably dreaming and dreaming! ... Even dreaming that we DESTROY AND DESTROY!

XXXIV

1. No one should be denied a piece of land to live on. - No one should own anything. - No one should refuse to share what he has, - to help those who need help, - to protect the weakest, - to understand and forgive those who make mistakes.

2. And although no one owned or owned anything, - we should all administer a piece of the world, - and a piece of existence, - in the same way that we are all administrators of our body and mind, - but not owners. - We should all be responsible for everything, - but much more than what we agreed to accept under our tutelage. - Neither owners of our children, - but tutors, - nor legal owners of our spouse, - but partners. - No countries, no borders or exclusions, - but only one World. - Neither owners of our lives, - but embodied souls. - Because we pass through life and existence - as travelers and sowers; - because if we take for us, even the smallest part of it, - is to give it back to it as soon as possible - multiplied and recreated in our interior-exterior.

3. And we should suffer with pleasure and even obsession, - if that were an effective way to truly put ourselves in the place of the other, - if that were an effective way to expand our own conscience, - if thus we could not for a moment abandon our imperative of transcendence, - if thus we would become truly humble, grateful and loving of all and EVERYTHING. - Or will we have to wait even longer for Death?

4. What human feeling will I appeal to finally recognize us as a single Humanity - as a single individual? - You will assimilate it, you will internalize it, you will live it - through compassion, anger, sexual desire, pain, envy, respect, solidarity, utility, fun? - You already know - there are not even reasons or arguments for intelligence - that can convince you so much - that you are really the fusion of all the *you* and all the *me* and *all the all*!

5. That is why Jesus asked us to deny each other, - because in our ancestral hardness of soul, - only in this way are we able to meet others, - and to recognize ourselves in the other. - Because denying ourselves for the benefit of the other, - we inevitably end up rediscovering our own self in the other and by the other and with the other.

6. How difficult, how heartbreakingly painful, however, - how disappointing we are to love each other, - when he rejects us in our love, - and he mistreats us, - and ignores us, - and despises us, - and misinterprets us, - and betrays us, - even to the point of hating our love!

7. But how can we stop loving - if our feeling is *love*? - Then do not insist on that form of love that rejected you, that mistreated you, that ignored you, that despised you, that misinterpreted you, - because Love even cares for the will and the being of the *beloved*. - Love it in other infinite ways! - The human emotions until now are just animalistic and instinctive responses to the changes of the environment and the threatening or profitable interaction of the OTHERS. - Human emotions are just in their evolutionary beginning for LOVE. - Surprise yourself! Create in yourself new emotions for LOVE!

XXXV

1. And even if no world *catastrophe* occurred, - and even if the global economic and energy system did not collapse, - and even if we were able to grow, and grow demographically without reaching chaos, - and, finally, even though God did not existed, - even so, we can and must intervene and transcend immensely and deeply our *precarious humanity*.

2. Not even Christians, - those who baptize themselves as disciples of Jesus the Christ - and as *children of God*, - could in two thousand years of opportunities - transform and transcend themselves, - and much less to the World. - Now you can see many still laden with power and wealth, - communing in their temples with sacraments of pretended transcendence, - and with difficulty and disgust by stretching out their hand when leaving, - to deliver a miserable coin to the untouchable beggar who asks him in the street, without knowing it nor asking for it, - *something more than a coin* ... - What Christian is able to put without anger - again and again the other cheek? What Christian is able to give all his goods to the poor - and naked following Christ? - What Christian is able to say to a dead man: "*Get up and walk*?" - What Christian with power has exercised that power - with the love and efficacy of a true "son of God"?

3. Would any Christian be so honest - to recognize that my Jesus and my message - are so much more *Christian* than yours? - Would any Christian be so honest - to recognize that there is *too much* of Jesus in me? Would there be a Christian, a Buddhist, a believer of any religion or doctrine so honest, who could really follow me?

4. And all this I say with sorrow and with shame and humility, - because I know that I put myself upon their own experience of God, - and upon their most sacred feelings and values, - and I embarrass them themselves, - and I humiliate them without pretending it, - and I publicly refute them, - and I provoke them. - How could I reproach them in another way - the immense distance between you and my Jesus - if you are crucifying them in a certain way?, and continue crucifying him? - When I compare the spirit and feel his words in each pumping of blood in my heart - they are so similar to mine! - When I review my actions and my life - I do not discover hypocrisies or confused rambling in my current speech! - In short, where would my error be, where the reason for my shame, where my weakness, where my pride, where my awkwardness, where my blindness, - if everything that moves me is LOVE? - And where there is error, and there will be! - I offer him my humble delivery of LOVE – that I may correct myself, and be corrected.

5. Refute my love, unmask my love, condemn my love - and only then will I recognize that I am completely a mistake - and a real danger to you!

6. Until then I will keep repeating renewed to the one who wants to listen to me, - I will continue searching with a lantern for a *Man*, - I will continue magnifying my God, - I will continue pushing this poor Humanity where he wants and does not want to go.

7. And even if no Evangelium happened in the future, - at least I will have happened. - Am I different from this same *Evangelium*?

XXXVI

1. It is so difficult to transform, to modify a *state of mind*! - To stop looking at what we are used to seeing - not to feel those emotions that come again and again to us - to modify the rituals of the mind; think differently from what we think, how we think, why we think and what we think about it for, - stop remembering what we repeatedly remember, - remember what we do not remember, - suppose, imagine, wish - what we do not suppose, imagine or wish, - stop dreaming what we dream, and create from the vigil our own dreams, - stop being that self that affirms itself and refuses to stop being me, - transmute into another, - even in anything, - love what we do not love, - to modify our consciousness at will.

2. How could any god have judged us so harshly before - how could he have rejected Life - our millions and millions of errors throughout History, - through our own personal biography!? Even now we are not condemned, but simply, according to our own logic, we are fulfilled and it shows us: $1 + 1 = 2$! - No matter how many times you have repeated in your mind the number one when thinking that sum, - always the result of the sum will be two.

3. But now is the time to tighten the reins in your hand, - and direct you this crazy horse of your mind. - What will you expect, if not? - Your next life, some miracle, luck in your favor? - Do not be foolish, do not be soft like the fat of your body, do not be weak like your mind! - And it is always possible to place yourself with your conscience and your will

at a higher point than your own mind, and unfolded treat yourself as an other I. - I know it is not easy! - I also suffer every day with my rude limitations and failures, - despite the lucidity that I already have. - But I also advance like the donkey that drags the cart up the mountain. - From each failure I get a new teaching, a new impulse, a mysterious and subtle progress. - We must never stop observing the last peak of our efforts and acts, - the very summit of our pasivities and boredom in walking, - only the goal gives meaning to the trivialities of our existence. - Because when your conscience slumbers, renounces or alienates, - your unconscious continues to advance for you.

4. In your unconscious meet the powers and highest authorities of the Universe. - In your unconscious you are already everything you are ever going to be. - In your unconscious intersect all the crossroads of the possible. - In your unconscious there more doors and paths – more than all the physical space can contain. - In your unconscious there are hidden memories for your own unconscious. - In your unconscious the infinite and eternal materializes. - In your unconscious *you* are more you than yourself.

5. When you want to change a state of mind, a condition of consciousness, a feature or any content of your soul, - immerse yourself into your unconscious. - Personality and character and consciousness and mind, - are configured in the depths of the unconscious. - Sinking in that self, - is also to rise, expand, appear, transmute and co-create the reality. - Reason has little or nothing to do here. — Do you know how to put aside reason without yourself getting lost and without fear?

6. Reason discourages surprise, - weakens life, - blocks the miracle, - seizes the mind, - pontificates reality, - makes his accomplice to the conscience, - lacks love, - - it intoxicates us with his judgment and with his moral judgment, - interprets and justifies everything, - is arrogant and vain, - for that reason, until now - the reason has been Man.

7. I understand your fears as I understand mine, - because to approach the immensity of the universes, - awakens our instinct of animal

survival. - Fear always warns us - that something can overcome us. - Fear is lucid, - but also cowardly - is humble, - but also mean, - is sensible, - but reductive. - Fear does not want to give up or lose anything of what it feels, - although losing it can win everything. - Do you really know your *fears*? - There is no greater fear - than to enter lucidly into yourself - and then to lose *yourself.*

XXXVII

1. And it is to this foolish illusion that the consciousness allows itself to be enslaved: - That reality is all that our senses perceive. - That reality is also everything that our mind itself manifests from before our conscience. - And that, therefore, everything that does not enter into our consciousness from these two sources of reality, - does not exist or, at least, is inaccessible and unnecessary. - Foolish illusion of everything!

2. We have been fooled for so many times, - that the coming out of that illusion will take away our blood. - Our blood is even contaminated with the lie of this imagined real. - Because we look at ourselves and conceive each other as a separate human body, - because we feel and experience our minds and consciousness - separated and isolated within our brain and skull. - I look at another and say "you"; - I perceive myself and tell myself " I ". – Woe to the foolishness of the man of all times! - We have constituted our most instinctive and self-evident reality - from this absurd distinction between the" *I* "and the" *you* ".

3. And it's not that my body is equal to yours, - nor that my mind and consciousness are identical to yours. - But that on a deeper and wider level of reality, - on a more subtle level and distant from your senses and your natural consciousness, - at a level of your less basic and material self, - at the level from which I am now precisely experiencing and contemplating you, - there is no *you* or *me*, but rather an Unlimitedly unified *we*.

4. If it is I who first ceases to experience you in this new *us*, - even if I look at your body as other - and also I stumble over that of you that bothers me, - even then, without being your body or your miseries, - I still before all experience you in your body and your miseries, - as *my* body and *my* miseries. - Then how not to shout to you: - *Brother!* - And you can answer me with another shout from another very different place: - "I am not your brother, animal!" - But not for that will you cease to be at the *bottom* of your drowned being - my brother, like Cain and Abel.

5. If you could come to where I am now, brother, - you would even understand that our *we* is not even complete in our own and exclusive humanity, - but that our identity is unified even with all things. - You would shudder, brother, from the very same root that unifies you with the totality of the Universe, - and nothing would ever be known or experienced as before, - as never before in the History of the World. - So did Francis of Assisi: - *Brother sun, sister moon!*

6. And when we recognize each other and *one* and the same brothers and sisters, - then you will end up with those petty meanings of yours - with that flare of desires and self-satisfaction of an absurd and illusory unique self.- Then, you Will no longer be able to mock the evil and suffering of *others*, - neither pass before the other without seeing them, - nor will you ever be indifferent to hunger, injustice, joy, hope, effort, weaknesses, death, silence, fear, scarcity, ignorance and everything, completely everything of *all of us*.

7. Come, my brother, my sister! - Why deny yourself the truth greater than heaven itself? - What will be your excuse this time - to continue living the illusion of your self? - Do you not see that soon all realities will vibrate with a new shudder, - and nobody will sleepwalk on this earth? - How will you rise next to me, - if then you will discover that you lack arms and legs?

XXXVIII

1. Nothing remains in the past to die, to disappear, not to be. - All present is transformed into past, - and all past becomes future. - Because no essence, no monad, no being - interrupts its evolution, its continuous transformation - towards the infinite. - The *form* of the present and the past dies, - but nothing of its substance. - Everything progresses - without ever stopping or interrupting, - only the forms and figures in matter - change in dimension - and disappears from it, - to get lost in other immemorial times.

2. There is an "I" that is an essence, a monad, - although composed of many selves that are transformed. - Therefore, it never dies, - never changes its direction to the future infinite. - Things, the Universe, are first of all essences - for our monadic "I". - All the selves, all the things in the Universe, all the essences and their accidents, all the Universes - are like drops within the same river, - that descend towards the sea of Infinity.

3. This Universe is only one among an infinity of Universes. - This present is only a time between infinite times. Infinite times, infinite spaces, - which are One and Innumerable, - incommensurable for the natural human reason. - One God, too divine, - for infinite gods - for infinite Universes.

4. This Universe follows a determined course of evolution. - However, there are innumerable *forms* that deviate and separate from this universal course. - The Universe that we perceive as material - follows its

predetermined course of evolution - from what we naively call the *beginning* - To what we naively call the *final future*. - The human mind struggles to free itself from this predetermined course, - before unconsciously, - from now on, with full consciousness. - That day we will be gods!

5. There is a monadic "I" for this Universe. - Even transcending our monadic "I" is our infinite task. - Only the purest intuition can characterize this transcendence. - There is no brain that can avoid overcoming. - Connecting with your monadic "I" - no being a task for routine and repetitive humans - it is one of the missions proposed for each incarnated human. - Urgent for me! - As for you?

6. And then you will plead devotionally: - "How, how to do it, how to achieve it?

7. Follow interior *masters*, divine masters and human masters - because as the sailor sought among the stars their orientation - so we have shared the necessary constellations that will guide you - in this decisive transit. - New masters with new teachings, - with new powers, - we are raising you all over the Earth - from the bottom of the Universe. - Just pay attention to the shooting star that will cross your sky - and go after it.

8. Life, death, dream, infinity, eternity, - advance through there as a one whole. - I, you, us, beings of all worlds, gods, Being, - meet there as one ALL.

XXXIX

1. The main activity of every human being during his life and in the world - should be **NOT** *work*, - but the transformation and development of himself for the transformation and development of Humanity. - The whole society should be centered in the perfection of each individual. - Not the production, - but the creation of unique mental worlds in aggregation to the connective worlds. - Not the domination or appropriation of anything, - but the integration and spiritualization of everything. — This *activity*!

2. The other work would not be then – nothing more than the minimum and necessary time for the subsistence and conservation of the basic functions of the individual and society. - There would be no longer employers or employees, - neither owners nor clients, - neither powerful nor weak, - neither producers nor thieves, - nor privileged, nor excluded from anything.

3. Any other activity, even more beneficial for our basic subsistence needs, - but arising from personal development and transformation, - should not be recognized as *work*, - but simply as an *action of the spirit and transmutation of matter in evolution*.

4. There would be no more performance indicators, no records of growth, no calculations of indebtedness. - There would be no more rankings of anything, - nor competition to put one's foot on another. - There would be no consumer goods, - no advertising tricks, no massive manipulation

of consciences for the satisfaction of some. No more fictitious needs, nor perversely invented, no more vanities nor futile desires, no more depend on this culture of the senses, of the forms, of the barbaric impulses. - No more *humanity*, the same as the last twelve thousand years. - No more work of slavery.

5. Then the Earth would glow in dark space - more beautiful and brighter than a star, - in view of our universal spectators. - Then our own bodies would shine - by the intensity of our souls, - in an endless chain. - Then the mysterious flowers of the Universe would be opened to us - like a spring garden moist with a light rain - those *flowers* for which we now have no smell, no vision, no senses.

6. But now I see your sad and tearful face turned towards me - to say to me sadly: - "How could this happen? - How could I share this conviction - with those who lack the will and capacity for change; with those who lack sufficient awareness - to reach this necessary *Consciousness*?"

7. I answer you: - first, just *love* it. - Then, *do* it as much as you can - within your radius of freedom and action. - Finally, *let* Life complete its part and your part. - Also our responsibility for others - ends sadly within certain limits.

8. So, when a hundred homeless humans arrive - to knock on the door of your modest home, crying, - let them pass, even if they do not all fit, - and as none of them will want to move from your dwelling, - go from there to live in *solitude*. - Humans do not even have sufficient awareness of their neighbor to ask for compassion.

9. So much is pain in the World - that if you had opened your heart and your life to all of it, - long ago you would have already died suffocated with pain. - Even so, each one is suffering and living it for all Humanity. - You only have to recognize your form and your limit.

10. Love pain, although you must avoid it!

XL

1. When one penetrates deeply into other levels of reality - one discovers that we are also capable of other perceptions and faculties that are more direct, precise and certain - than the capturing of our senses. - That there are more accurate intuitions - than all the doubting beliefs and human knowledge. - That there are more logical understandings - than all the reasonings generated by our reason. - That there is more striking evidence - than all the awareness that we are capable of.

2. I do not ask you to renounce or devalue or annul your words, nor your reason, nor your senses, nor your emotions, nor your faith, nor your memory. - What would you stay with - if now you are no more than that? - What would you do? Where would you go? - On what vehicle of your mind and of your being could you even move? - Your emptiness would remain inert - like so many who have stopped believing in every thing of themselves and outside of themselves!

3. It is better that I ask you - that you multiply your languages, - that you teach reason to be a servant, - that your senses be transfigured with your inner light and with the perceptions of your spirit, - that your emotions empty in the ocean of your transmontane pure feelings, - that your memory is open to all possible times for your memory without time. - Let your faith move grains of sand and not mountains. – Seek then *Enlightenment* - or whatever you want to call it!

4. And even if you do not ask for resignation, devaluation or annulment-terrible reasons for fear and mistrust, - another fear will paralyze you-against which you have to charge without mercy, - concentrated in the action of the certainty of your spirit; - against *the terror of your own transfiguration.*

5. And I would like - to be born again in this World - to find myself as a child with these wise words - to guide myself better than all the previous sages did. - If there had been those which I could articulate here, my path would have been more upright - like the soon course of a bolt - that from the beginning knows its path and its target. - But not anxiously zigzagging - and even sometimes circular without exceeding my karma - as was my course during my youth and adulthood - anxious to read in the heavens, in the waters, in the fields, in the books and in my own heart - clear words, precise oracles for these times and the next two hundred years, - and not messages already fulfilled or in need of past humanities and resistant to the future. - Because even *the most true* manifested for Man - after a due time - *ceases to be so* - to begin to fade away slowly like the energy and light of a dying sun.

6. There were no parents, there were no friends, no teacher educators, - but pages and pages written by sages from other eras - for other worlds than mine. - And even though You kept watchful for me - and you thundered when my heaven has become too opaque and natural - or traced those magical signs that with some difficulty I was deciphering - without ever fully assimilating them, - my desire for *transfiguration* never succeeded in finding the deep, invisible paths - to materialize, - not to run like a grossly awkwardly untraced path - nor at times go mad on the invisible path.

7. For this, I write to you - and to myself - for, recognizing my fruitful experience, - you advance on the footprint of my steps, - humble recognition of our terribly misplaced human nature, - creating your own experiences of LOVE.

XLI

1. Jesus and Buddha offered us freedom - they demanded freedom. -The Masters experienced our condition as slaves-like. - We are immensely more slaves - than the workers of the Egyptian pyramids, - that the slaves of imperial Rome, - that the black men and women of the coffee plantations of Brazil. We are complete slaves of mind, soul and intellect, although there is no power capable of enslaving us nor keeping us slaves, if our spirit and will *do not want to.*

2. All the legal and moral codes of the human world - reject the bondage of the body, - but all silence or ignore how enslaved and *enslavers* - we are each of our own minds, our own self - and of all others.

3. So many small and important freedoms are defended: - of thought, expression, movement, political freedom, social freedom, economic freedom, - but if there is no *freedom of spirit* - all those necessary liberties become - in the most subtle and complete enslavers, - in the most beautiful tyrants of the free spirit.

4. There is only true freedom of spirit - in true Enlightenment.

5. But how can we speak of freedom - to one who is so completely enslaved - that he feels free? - Ah, paradox of the mind! - It would suffice to put a shackle in his throat so that he shouts: "Slave I am, free me! "- And in his delirium of freedom, however, - he looks up to heaven and distrusts, - sees a newborn and those deceased - and shudders without

explanation. - But soon calms down - by the voices of the greatest enslavers who affirm: "Everything inexplicable - will be explained by the development of science. - All the ineluctable and overwhelming of Man - will be known and dominated by our ever-increasing power." - In the end, all his slavery is synthesized - in the slavery of consciousness.

6. But you - who listen to me in your dreams, - and you manage to intuit the difference between your dream - and freedom, - you - to whom not to shout in your ear, - to whom not to show you terrible, sublime and striking images, - to whom not to magnetize with this new force that begins to flow from me - would simply fall back into the deep dream of the globalized Humanity - and to fall asleep in the peace of death in life, - you, awaken! - You, tense your spirit - like a bow that prepares for its arrow! - You, stir inside you, - as when you try to open your eyes during an unbearable nightmare! - You groan and scream - for your Father to run by your side! - *You*!

7. And in the precise tomorrow - from one end to the other - the Light will burst, - infinite and so much Light - that only the Darkness can contain for now.

XLII

1. Daring, daring, launching without fear or with fear, - but with the most inexorable resolution of *Will*! ... - When the will merges with the light of consciousness - when the light of consciousness fills up to overflowing - with the presence of all the beings of the universe, - when the infinity of reality is inoculated as by a Sting - to the depths of our being - just as a bright and unknown pigment dyes it glowing all, - so by my will to break, to violate, to alter, to risk, to isolate, to subvert, to devalue, to die and to kill, to renounce, to surprise, to destroy and rebuild, to empty, to disappear, - but to *laugh* and *laugh* and *laugh* above all, - then I web we able to do everything I must to do, - like the omnipotent god that I am: LOVE!

2. Not with intelligence, not with certainty, not with understanding, not with words, - not with imagination, not with desire, not with the heart, not with faith - not with simple and direct push of action, not with the body, not with society, not with coercion; not with friendship, not with duty, not with gratitude, not with paternalism. - So many more are still the disturbing and distorting of the will in consciousness, - installed around you, ready to explode - like a minefield.

3. To advance and get out of there unscathed - the skill of the dancer and the levitator is required. - In order to move forward and get out of there unharmed - the most intense autosuggestion is required - to not feel the pain of limbs that burst amputees. To advance and get out of there unscathed -requires a new act of magic for each day.

4. How many more things stop you, paralyze you, disturb you, numb you, deceive you, horrify you, weaken you, impress you, seduce you, catch you, recriminate you, warn you, buy you, exhort you, annul you, call you, entertain you, prevent you, use you, torment you, take you, excite you, interest you, fill you! - So many more are still the disturbing and distorting of the will in conscience, - installed to your around, ready to explode - like a minefield!

5. And although we allow all reality to manifest through us - immersed in the immense ecstasy of existence, - to the point of surrendering to overflow our own lives - loving and longing for the disappearance of our self - to even annihilate the smallest trace of our existence, - even so the Reality loves us so much - even so it prevents our being from disappearing; - with so much tenderness it melts and hits us like steel reddened in the forge; - with so much attention it drags us along the meanders and tiny nooks of eternity - with so much care and art it articulates and disjoins us more than the clay between his endless fingers.

6. What fiction everything is - when everything is contemplated and lived -inevitably small, inevitably insignificant - irrevocably existing - from the supreme perspective of the Being! - And there you would like to let yourself go - absorbed by the sublime vertigo - with the feet already half on the edge of the unfathomable chasm of Being - height and depth higher and deeper than any conceivable distance - attracted by that unique and exclusive concentrated force of All - as a minimum point and infinite multiplicity.

7. And although you let yourself fall again and again - like repeated movies of the same scene - yearning for Nirvana and for God, - again and again you return the abyss to action and to the furnace of your being, of your self, of your destiny. - Then you find yourself with a consciousness within a mortal body, - that permanently strives (during our measurement of years) to also adjust the consciousness of an "I" with a body.

XLIII

1. It is naive to try to perform the miracles of Jesus - in the same way that he performed them. - But more naive and foolish is still - not to understand or perform - you and me - the *miracles* that every human being can and must perform *today.*

2. *Transform water into wine,* - broadening consciousness from a lower level to a higher one, - transmuting matter into spirit, - purifying natural feelings and emotions, in superior and refined emotions and feelings, - transmuting all the universes, into a single Universe of Light.

3. *To multiply the loaves and fishes,* - always sharing with another human being and another more, what one possesses, - love and develop oneself, to give to others, - simply loving.

4. *To walk on waters,* - ignoring fear, adversity, hatred, low passions, desire, death, - living in the spirit above all, - believing in the superior that seems impossible.

5. *Heal the sick,* - donating your inner strength, your knowledge, your feelings, your time, your possessions, your authenticity, your whole being - touching the eyes of the mind of those who do not understand; - straightening the invalid bodies - of those who have stiffened their hearts and their lives; - breathing love, optimism, joy - for those who weaken and wither in the lack of love, in negativity, in sadness and anguish.

6. *Resuscitate the dead*, - reviving those who abandoned the spirit.

7. *Transfigure*, - in the miracle of each day.

8. *To ascend to the heavens*, - towards the intimate encounter with your god - transcending the human condition - *to return to this world in the Glory of Love-God.*

XLIV

1. My consciousness is a thousand-petalled pink lotus flower - in the center of which an eye without an eyelid opens. - Where is the root of my soul? - So deep beneath my eye of consciousness sinks dark my nutrient root - that I can no longer see from this height its unfathomable depth. - And this *light* tries to turn on itself - to make even my uncertain roots flourish. - Towards there I address, - although there is no brain there - where to land consciousness. - Towards there I am directed - as the ship travels through dark spaces - to the atmosphere of a new star.

2. A tender and fragile stem grows thinner - to the bottom of my being, - traversing the subtle atomic roots - that connect the column of my organic levels with the etheric ones. - The fine energy that my brain cells produce -like a cloud vibrant around itself, it supports the light weight of my consciousness, and nourishes it with vigor. And even though my consciousness is caught in this fine web of live- it is also capable of regenerating a new energy - recombining the purest atoms within his own consciousness - even reproducing a physically unconditioned *supraconsciousness*. - *Spirit* was also called by our masters - that pristine substance - that is so subtle and pure that it hardly actualizes on the plane of matter and dense energy - and without action it ends up buried and dead in the brain and mind - of the brutalized humans without LOVE.

3. And all the dreams that you have experienced during your life - could get in step to mislead you. - All your memories could close your path. - And even in the color painted by life on the walls of your soul - empty

figures could develop and ghosts - by simple analogy and association from your subconscious. - And you could see yourself and feel yourself advancing -through the shadowy steppes of an inner world - with no north or direction - or following the north and the course of the mirage of an illusion - confident and happy.

4. No consciousness arising from the will- but will arising from consciousness. - The human *unconscious* shares the condition of consciousness of matter. - The flower and the root of our physical and mental being - share with each other an *apperceptive* nature common. - The virtue of inner vision or mental vision - allows not capture (or exclusively reproduce) the light waves that are reflected in objects, - but the internal radiation of atoms, molecular configurations and the *forms* of energy and matter, - acting directly on the *atoms* of consciousness. - There is no physical distance between the elemental substance of consciousness - and the unconscious substance of energy-matter, - but only difference of *quality* or *state*. - There is no incompatibility between the elemental substance of consciousness - and the unconscious substance of energy-matter, but *transubstantiality* and *metamutation*. - Here is a way of describing with figurines of words - a moment of the *Enlightenment of the spirit*.

5. No experience occurred in the field of waking consciousness - it stops producing an effect and being experienced in a new way - in the unconscious. - Hence, you must take care with prudential clairvoyant - what you do in your day, - what you are going to let invade the field of your consciousness, - what you do with your own mind - and what it does to you. - Hence, you must always strive harder - to know who you are and how you are inside your unconscious. - You will be surprised.

6. The colors in the soul are immensely more intense, voluminous and nuanced - than the most beautiful colors that the eye perceives in light. - The sounds in the soul are immensely sharper, more voluminous and expressive - than the most beautiful sounds that the ear perceives in space. - The truths that the soul intuits are immensely more certain and evident - than all the understandings and certainties of human intelligence.

7. And even if you walked all the roads of the earth - and observed the most varied geographies and landscapes of the world, - it could not be compared to the infinity that awaits you unknown in your soul - just as Earth waited three billion years ago - for the *cosmic spirit* to polish mountains, to undermine oceans, to illuminate the blue of the sky and to frill of life the surface of the World.

XLV

1. The small souls, the immense souls - want to fly. - As timid, distrustful fireflies, seek the light of my beacon. - As chicks hatched, - seek heat under my wings. - As painful spectra, fuzzy, seek the powerful and compassionate energy that will allow you to incarnate.

2. As a single sun capable of feeding so many beings - I would like to be for them - inexhaustible as a sweet sea for the thirsty - provided with billions of strong arms - to take cautiously, barely guiding them, - thousands of millions of insecure hands. - I would like to speak through millions of mouths - to gather with millions of ears - my invocative calls, - to respond with the precise word at the right moment.

3. But here I am barely holding - this crossroads of the World. - Summoning these little souls - how many I can receive with my weak mortal body - slowly and progressively until I give them my life, for them. - Here I am looking for the proper forms, the necessary synchronies, the best possible adjustments - to be able to declare to all, openly - that I am now for many, wherever I am.

4. Then, wishing me like hands raised to the sun - they will encourage me to shine - as I have never shone. - And shining as the light I will have to put myself in the center - for all to see me - and seeing me - all can also contemplate through of my eyes LOVE.

5. I am no more than you, - I am only *before*. - I am not different from you, - I am only more like you - than you are yourselves. - I would like to

tell you everything, - teach you the future of your acts - the evidence of yourselves that you can not perceive, - the particular ways of getting into yourselves. - But I must not run over their freedom, - nor simply erase their harsh past. - Freedom and past, - future and freedom! - Towards there I can take you, - no more than the breeze, that when it blows your hair, - shows you its course, and it is no longer there!

6. I call you, innumerable souls - hesitant flashes coming to be ship-wrecked in the black siege of this monstrous existence! - And although I have a few years to live for the immensity of the work, - I will not cease to make you feel my presence, - and with my presence, - the Light, the Truth and the Life. - I call you in every way I can call; - when calling I look for the human echoes of other souls that resonate - with new and multiplied testimonies *LOVE*! -For as the Baptist announced the soon coming of his Christ Jesus, - I am only the prophet and the nuncio of this Lord Lover who will come. - We are all called to prepare his coming, - Lord of Love and of the Era!

7. I call my beloved souls and sisters - to repopulate the world with a new spirit! - It does not matter how far apart they are from each other, - it does not matter that they are incalculably more the wild souls, denying and hostile to the new love, - it does not matter! - A spirit that is still deeper, a more irresistible power, a more universal flame - summons us, unites us, fuses us - into one and the same Power. - Raise now, souls daughters and sisters, your hands, your eyes, your heart - to the Inner Heaven!

XLVI

1. Children will meet with children, - young people, with young people and children, - adults, with adults, youth and children, - the elderly, with all. - And they will give testimony, example and teaching of itself. - Because the Being and the Truth and the Spirit and the Life - is diffused by links of a chain, - by tiny human rings - that laboriously and tenderly are trying to unite with each other, - through small affinities, of connatural gestures, of sensitive communities, - thus reaching even the most alien and different souls - *without restriction.*

2. If my children ask me: - "What must I do first - to be better?" - I answer: - "Stop the passage of the World; - stop the movements of the body; inner silence!"... "But it is not possible to dematerialize from the World, - to desensitize from the body, - to turn off the mind "- you will answer me. - Even so, be masters of the passage of the World, - be directors of the movements of the body, - be the illuminators of the mind. - May the World, body and mind - know that *your* will to LOVE governs the World, the body and the mind, - that *your* will to LOVE decides when and how, - and not the World, the body and the mind, - those who grant you magnanimously: - "now".

3. Our spirit has not incarnated in this World - to come to pursue, to desire, to realize, to achieve, to get - *nothing* of this plane: - no object, no thing, no person, no success, no knowledge, no recognition, no pleasure, no work. - Our spirit has incarnated in this World - to transform every

object, every thing, every person, every success, every knowledge, every recognition, every pleasure, every work - into a superior *spirit*.

4. You must worry about recognizing first of all - your limitations - as well as your potentialities. - There is a sometimes hidden relationship between your limitations and your potentialities. - Even if it does not seem to you like it, all your potentialities are damaged, hindered and incomplete - because of your limitations, of your incomplete ways of being, and even of your character and personality in general. - Knowing yourself is recognizing yourself as you are, and from there, associating yourself with the virtuality or immediate potential of immediate range of transformation and change in decreasing gradation of update. - Recognize in yourself traits or qualities that are already, - the same as a stone fallen in the center of the pond unfolds from itself concentric circles more and more distant from its center. - So also the potential unfold from your being - towards your virtual being. - There are features of you that are more easily modifiable, and others less, - that are moving away from your possibility of actualization, - insofar as they are depending on the updating of the primary qualities, closer to your current center and present in you. - Search and recognize your potential gradation in each and every feature within you. - Contemplate as if you were *one* only reflected in a first mirror, - and then in another and in another and in another and in another - until contemplating your *last being* - in the last mirror, if you are capable, because you are capable.

5. The real time is spiritual, - not the apparent time of the movement and the change of the physical and material objects, - but the real time in which you will realize your gradual transformation towards the fulfillment of your virtual project of becoming your own possible. - There are those who have almost stopped the time of their evolution. - There are those who have diverted and even reversed the direction of their spiritual time. - What does it matter that they keep moving in the fast and active world time? - What does it matter that they continue to obtain resonant achievements in the material and natural plane, - if they have ceased to exist, or almost in *real time*? - The real time of the Spirit - is

like the interweaving of infinite waves in an infinite sea. - The time of the material world - it is like a bubble of foam detached from *one* of those infinite waves. - Meditate on this.

6. And although I am surrounded by little children - I feel so alone. - But not of that absence - which hurts like a bleeding wound in the soul, - but of the emptiness that I am unable to fill, - of the physical and mental mass that intercepts us, - but that I am unable to cross, - because I can not empty my love, my understanding, my peace - all at once in their souls. - Because just drop by drop - like frost that melts on their inner world - and so slowly impregnates their consciousness and their unconscious, - so many times do I see them depart to more dark and icy lands of becoming and of the world, - that I can no longer warm their vital ice with my warmth, - that I can no longer instill the Life that permeates me through me- towards their being. - How much it hurts me - how much loneliness and helplessness and emptiness - fill me, - whenever they come before me supplicants, trembling - to beg me to give them let me become as I am, - to beg me to help them discover themselves, - to beg to at least make it easier for them - to be better! - And with their hands and mouths opened, extended, - like little hungry creatures shortly after birth - I can barely revive them with something of the *salvation* they ask me for: LOVE and MORE LOVE.

7. And even so, in the midst of this loneliness of the world - where we walk and live like ghosts, - passing through us without even touching each other, - sometimes we find two souls and minds and hearts, - and the miracle happens of the enlightenment of love - as if by a happy providence - two spiritual atoms or monads collided - and merged into one in love. - Thus I move through the World - sensitive and attentive to subtle movements, to fleeting difficult moments - in which the closed human souls - miraculously open themselves with timidity to the infinite - to touch them intimately with my love.

XLVII

1. When viewed from above, at more than ten thousand meters above sea level - human beings and their condition, - when viewed even higher - even from outer space- our tiny and fragile planet, - holding itself incomprehensibly in the void, - only then do we see how sad, tragically and wrongly - we live and experience our own existence and our sense of reality.

2. When we get out of our tiny experience of our natural and everyday environment, - as well as our national and cultural conditioning - and we experience and recognize ourselves through the Earth, - as a string, as a swarm, as a whirlpool of multiplicity, of excess, of irrelevancy and insignificance - of one respect to others, of being so many and so plagiaristic and insubstantial and the same, - of simply occupying a place in space and time, - impoverishing the Earth with our unforsaken consumption, invasive and trivializing condition - of this miracle of existence and of the World; - then we have only the evidence - that we are condemned to disappear by billions of us, of these wildly useless clones and futile - of humanity.

3. When I observe the ridiculous and compassionate evidence - that we repeat a mere model and programmatically condition ourselves to recognize, value and experience ourselves as equal in rights, dignity and value, - with the help of our philosophies, our religions, our national and international policies, our ethical and moral regulations, - our education, our jurisprudence, our mass media, and of so many other forms, - that we

seem to possess such immense and overwhelming courage and dignity, - to which, however, refutes and violates the evidence of our daily and brutal behavior, - of our miserable human quality, - of our irrevocable inner poverty, - of our murderous selfishness and self-centeredness, - of our quantity intractable of individuals that impoverishes and needs to self-sustainably occupy and take away the space and vital conditions of another, - that so many and many *can* not, or do not *want*, or it will simply never be a *matter* for them - to stop being this unfeasible human creature that today overpopulates the planet contradictorily and self-destructively.

4. So, what are we really, which of those two human models? - How much are we really worth? - But, still we are loved, accepted and forgiven again and again - by the Intelligence of Higher Life, - by the World that again and again, second by second, day after day, year after year - tries to re-generate itself, pardoning, - its wounds caused by our criminal outrage of its living body.- And it is that even forgiving us and loving us so much the God-of-all – he could no longer sustain this aberration of Man - and exhausted, consumed, he himself will die through our own stubborn progression to annihilation and death. - I cry now: "If God is dead, it's because Man is dead!"

5. And it is so even in the midst of this chaos and orderly absurd - I can not stop crying out: "Stop! Enough!! Pay attention to my words, and through my words - in yourselves and in the World! " - How can we not see the action of death that we exercise everywhere - suicide, blind, awkwardly lukewarm, and even *happy*? - How not to provoke at least the lucidity of minimum consciousness - which will lead a few of us to react with an equally proportionate *explosion* of the spirit, - with our response and radical and terrible change of life? - How could it not be one and this response, - the response of the *Revolution of Love - extreme, superhuman, sacrificial* - to object effectively and also programmatically - to the human *fatality* that it want us all irresistibly to lead?

6. I have heard their hurtful voices say: - "But what sense does it make for a few - we want and we can selfishly save ourselves, but can not we the

World? - What will we do if we can not stop the fatality?" - Perhaps, little brothers, we can not stop the fatality in the physical plane and world, - Man has taken possession of it, - but we can rescue our inheritance in the spiritual plane, - there no one can belittle or devalue even the smallest of our achievements, - nor to dye in the least with his misfortune the glory of the winning spirituality of the undue attachment to the World. - Then, no act consequently with the Truth must be forbidden to us - no sacrifice, no effort, no difficulty - coming from the natural plane or from human determinism and condition - should prevent us from living from and in spirituality - our relationship with the world and with humans. - Just refocusing on our authenticity and spiritual blindness - we will be able and powerful to reconvert the outrage of the human destruction of the World and man's own being. - While the World has been destroyed until dematerialization, - if we remain unharmed and consistent in the dimension of the Spirit - immense challenge!, - and even if only one human remained on Earth - and even none - from our infinite power infused in the Universe - we will reincarnate as the resurrection of the dead and transform this time from the spirit - all the matter of this level, no longer interfering or distorting human failure.

7. Not because the Earth is incapable of covering so many dead, - not because we see millions of unhappy beings die and disappear, - not because they call to us with innumerable attractions, begging and lamenting not to leave their ranks on the way to the scaffold - and we mourn and pity his fate, - not because we must amputate again and again our own materiality, our own mind, our own humanity- until probably death; - not for all of it will falter or weaken his energy in the perseverance and painful and progressively sustained act - our *spirit in transfiguration*.

XLVIII

1. Between good and evil is there no difference? - So some want. -- Between good and evil is there an insurmountable abyss? - So others want. - Since infancy we have been taught to distinguish and discriminate - between good and bad, yes and no, high and low, beautiful and ugly, healthy and sick, pleasure and pain, day and night, true and false, - so that we can no longer experience anything internal or external - without *dualism*, without opposition, without separation, without antagonism.

2. But, although we all come to adapt to this primitive teaching, - each individual creates an own and exclusive value for the qualification of those opposites: - there are not two humans for whom it is exactly the same their good, their yes, their high, their beautiful, their health, their pleasure, their day and their true.- No society, no community, no culture, no group, no institution, no family - creates common values for its members, - but, at last, really every person. - Hence, we exist morally and collectively in an apparently orderly *chaos*.

3. But what do we want to differentiate with these distinctions - but realities? - But what realities, - if at last we create them - without knowing it - a mere subjective value to things? - In the end, trying to reach understanding of a common reality - we only constitute an anguished and infinitely fragmented reality, - but with the illusory appearance of being common.

4. How could they see themselves, humans, - if not leaving that fine, transparent and total network of values - within which all the trapped

individuals find themselves? - Recognizing, first, that all values are not other something that clothes, - that from using them so much - have stuck to our skin. - Once we have completed the difficult exercise of undressing ourselves, - we will contemplate the moral clothes on one side and our naked body on the other. - Then we can only propose again - to experience the true reality, - which in its unusual variety - also welcomes us.

5. As the sun appears among the clouds - surprisingly bright - so will the being of things be discovered, - from the resplendent divine-human Spirit, - through the mind and the body. - Then we will understand how narrow and miserable - have always been all our moral distinctions. - We will understand then that among all things - even the most aberrant and malignant - there is a mysterious *harmony*. - We will understand that there is a Good one and supreme - for now incomprehensible - that advances through the eternal becomings, - like the sun stealthily and advances imperturbably at dawn illuminating the worlds.

6. When the human soul - after a happy practice - has managed to get rid of the minuscule perspective of the self - and unfolding as a mass of water can unfold into infinite drops - manages to fold into the infinite variety of perspective from the infinite things of this simple Universe, - it is discovered that the good is nothing more than the timely and precise adaptation of the human monad - to the opportune and precise moment of the becoming of the Universes. - It is discovered that evil, our evil, - is no more than the other side of human consciousness and freedom - that retards, challenges and complicates the *opportune moment* in the becoming of the Universes.

7. Reality is a pure Light without blemish. Man decides with his palette of colors - if he paints, if he stains, or simply Enlightens himself as one Reality.

XLIX

1. No less solemn and delicate than founding a world - it will be for you to abandon the city or the common life. - One after another you will discover how many small innumerable things, affairs and acts - that the city had you resolved to do - and on which it rested with sure soul your soul - when you withdraw them will claim you; - and when you withdrew them you will discover that you yourself were part of them, - and you will doubt then whether to leave them or not, - just as the addict is unable to distance himself from his drug. - And you *will fear*, and you will feel that you are about to commit a madness, - as if you were gathering everything you have built in your life - and your parents, - and your relatives and acquaintances - even all the humans who have gone before you - and drag them to the edge of an abyss - and from there let them fall. - Then false thoughts, strange and new sensations, objects, people- like a cloud of ghosts going around you - will haunt you- so you do not go away. - They will be the demons protectors of the cities - taking care that none of their human infernal inhabitants - leave Hell.

2. But I do not ask you to leave the cities - like the one who wipes the soles of his sandals when he leaves - never to return. - It is that you simply free when you leave, - and as free you already know how and when to enter and come out. - Moreover, your duty is to return to the cities in one way or another - to give strength to the weak, to knock again on the door of those who hesitate to open, - electrically shake the shrouded souls - with the flare of your free and superior spirit - and still ready to resurrect. - Your duty is to return to the world of the common Man - to teach with

your power, with your testimony and evidence - that a new and better World is possible.

3. Find yourself the way to occupy land without anyone feeling deprived. - Do not live alone, because the superior species of Man - is collective in its individuality; - more, beware of getting to live with one that does not vibrate like you, - because if the common, unconscious, selfish, rationalist, emotional, coarse individual, - occupies your own land, - will destroy it again and dirty everything - as it has always done. - Then, you must agree with him who abandons that land, - because you will not take a place or anything at all. - Always remember that this whole World, including your body and your mind - is just a vehicle for you. - Take objects and leave objects should not be more difficult for you - than to close your hand and open your hand.

4. Found communities of spirits - that do not recognize each other neither by body nor matter. - Open where you inhabit portals and multidimensional circuits, - welcome souls, beings, elementals, angels, devas - who want to share the purity of the new Earth and the new race. - Do not accumulate domestic animals, do not surround yourself with animals, - animals are pure only if they are free; - before you get accompanied by all kinds of vegetables - our best terrestrial friends in this next stage of evolution. - They will teach you to link you in a new way with matter and energy. - They will make it easier for us to connect in a new way with the Universe.

5. Build small collective farms - in which all your basic foods can be produced. - Do not work the earth with the sweat of your forehead, - nor that your hands receive callouses. - Your work and your way of life should be simple and elemental - like the effort that the lily of the fields makes - or the sparrows among the branches of a ripe plum tree. - If you save, - just be careful, - but never miserly and fearful. - Share everything you possess - with those who suffer need. - Do not make distinctions between those who experience hunger, nor cold, nor sadness, nor loneliness - but satisfy their hunger, warm their cold, encourage their sadness, accompany their solitude, *indistinctly*. - To the one who is wrong, - just teach

him. - To the one who ignores, - help him to understand. - To the one who can not, - give him power. - Join always your action with that of others; - be humble to recognize that everything needs everything. - Work also for your community, - develop common spaces, - places of encounter and fusion, - where each one being different, - are all the same. - Make every organization the responsibility of all, - even if there is one that leads. - May every community be open, - however small it may be: - that can communicate and unite with all the communities of the Universe.

6. May the whole world be your responsible and beloved home. - A dwelling so big where they fit with dignity - all those who can live. - A dwelling of yours with so many rooms, - as there are beings on the Earth. - A dwelling where the most places and spaces - are spaces and places available for everyone, - where everyone circulates and where everyone is welcome. - From there, around your body - others will simply see the space - that your body needs to live healthily. - And you will allow your mind - as well as that of others - to also develop its conditions and spaces - around every mind - so that it can exist healthy.

7. And you will achieve with all this - that your body, your mind, your space, your matter, your nature, your humanity, your World - become perfect - so that only then can gloriously descend to this plane of reality - the true King Spirit.

L

1. How is it possible that the Divine Teachers, that the Creator God believes, incorporate into his creation and develop, with his providence and material action, situations and circumstances concordant with the *aberrations* of certain individuals? - In God there is also something cruel, malignant, aberrant and repulsive?

2. *First response*: - It is evident that God prefers a holy man to a boor; a child to a criminal; a blessing to a lie; a beautiful face, a deformed one; spirit, to matter.

3. *Second answer*: - God is indifferent to him *as well*, a saint than a criminal; a child as a lie; a beautiful body as one deformed; a human as a tick; life and death. - God blesses and is pleased together with holy men, and facilitates crime to the criminal; he plays laughing with the children, while torturing his mothers; he makes love to those who love each other, while prostitutes himself and rapes; he gives life, as much as he snatches it away; intervenes and also stops doing.

4. *Synthesis*: - When I think that the human conscience is similar to a dry leaf - that at the least pressure it becomes a mass of dust, - then I can conceive that there are forms of reality that completely overcome my dry leaf condition .- But I know that there are some Wise Masters who roam the world, - promoting the good of Man, - more or less as the same man conceives the good. - They write with a fast letter between the lines written from the eternal beginning in the Great Book of the Destiny of

God. - In this Book there is neither Good nor Evil, nor Yesterday nor Today nor Tomorrow, nor Truth nor Lie. - If we could know the arcane language in which it was written - and read its mysteries, - we would disappear before the dry leaf inside the oven of the sun.

5. The Wise Masters have sown us in this World - to share with us the great Book of the Destiny of God. - We will say that God is drunk, that God is crazy not to recognize the differences - which the Wise Masters are capable of recognizing? - Wise and drunk would be the Wise Masters - to risk helping us in this frustrating enterprise, - more or less as drunk and crazy we are all of us. - The Wise Masters only empathize with our superior and refined emotions; - but they comprise our lowest and most miserable affections. - The Wise Masters intervene with minuscule letters - without damaging the capital letter. - Between Them and God there is a perfect harmony. -The Wise Masters can even *appear* on the material plane. - For thousands and Thousands of years have been revealed to Man in different ways, with different names and in different degrees. The time has come to meet them face to face. - In their presence only the pure do not perish. - They experience Good in the midst of God. - They intervene Evil in the midst of God. - They are the Lords of Miracle: - their power is immense.

6. God does not experience the baseness of Man, - but it *is* the baseness of Man. - God does not kill humans in war, - but he *makes* war. - God *creates* the wickedness of Man, - without it having evil. - In the same way, God is the conversion of the bad, - but does not exalt it. - God encourages peace, - but kills the Man. - God creates wonderful worlds, - but destroys them. - That is why Man is unable to understand God: - because God, although he is human, - is not human; - because God is not powerful, neither good nor wise - because God is *Nothing* - because God is simply *All-Reality*. - That's why humans do not love God, - although they claim to love him; - that's why humans do not believe in God, - even though they believe it. - Does God care about being loved?; - does God care to be believed? - All that is God, is God - All that is not God, is God.

7. Our foolishness, little brothers, is historically proverbial: - so long have we confused God - with the Wise Masters, - and Man, with God and

with the Wise Masters. - Although, so many are also the nonsense and ignorance - that they still dominate us and will dominate. - All my own words, beloved little brothers, - are not more true than false, - they can only be *useful, adequate for* ...

8. There is no such thing as Truth. - There is no perfectly round *truth*, - the same and the same from the perspective that you look at it, - identical to itself, - mirror of all beings.

9. There are, in our planes, unlimited perspectives - as unlimited truths. -There is, though, an axial and divine point - where all of them in relation to themselves *converge*. – There we would like to complete ourselves in the Truth, - but we have been unable to understand and experience - that this principle and point, - only a turn beyond, - is diluted in the Infinite, - in the very emptiness of all meaning.

LI

1. Man's ways have become routine and gray. - Burdened by the weight of his *over-civilization* - creaks and cracks the World - though few still notice it. -Curved by the weight of their innumerable languages, - with the endless iron scales of their exhausting words, - with their mountains of books, statements, news and texts, - begin to hum and repeat like stupids - the same things that so many, many and many have repeated before. - In their inner selves, however, they feel blissful and protected - by this immense mass of letters and numbers - even though they suspect - and even know - that they are false.

2. Everything is vitiated, consumed, groped, overexploited, - and that is precisely *Humanity*. - Its psychology, its science, its reason, its religion, its politics, its philosophy, its art, its spaces, its feelings, its coexistence, its technology, its entertainment, its dreams, its errors, its sport, its right, its sense, its tastes, its morality, its mathematics, its perception, its education, its goods, its mind, its projects, its body, his medicine, his excesses, his history, - they only chew, ruminate and defecate becoming of *sterility*. - If we do not destroy ourselves before - as a desperate vital resource - we will become extinct from boredom and disgust - for Humanity itself. - *Alea iacta est, sed Deus DEUS est.*[1]

3. When it is in free fall - without a parachute - what can be done? ...

---

[1] "The dice have been thrown, but God is GOD."

4. Modify everything, give up everything, - even give up falling. - At the end of the day, we have not created more than an immense and complex set of scenery - which we have naively called *reality*. - It is no longer just a matter of altering the order of this enormous puzzle - to create a different figure of humanity. - It is no longer a question of seriously considering the problem - and designing a serious world commission - for the restructuring of this humanity. - It is no longer a matter of multilateral agreements, - of deep revisions, - of novel strategies, of alliances, pacts and investigations. - Even though all of them - what hypocrisy! - they acted with complete good will, - we would return again and again - to develop the same aberrant Humanity.

5. Here is what I initiate and propose !: - a new psychology, a new science, a new intelligence, a new religion, a new politics, a new wisdom, a new art, a new space, a new sensibility, a new coexistence, a new technology, a new entertainment, a new sport, new dreams, new mistakes, a new right, a new moral, a new meaning, new tastes, new mathematics, a new perception, a new education, new goods, a new mind, new projects, a new body, a new medicine, new excesses, a new history. - But that is precisely, my little brothers of the Earth, - that is no longer *Humanity*! - Do you still want it that way?

6. And if you are able to renounce your individuality so many times, - and more, if you are able to renounce life, - why should not you also be able to renounce - when necessary - your entire *humanity*? - If, even more, I propose to stop being human, - to perfect the human, - no more than the son that comes from his father, - surpasses the father, - or that what comes before is surpassed by the later, naturally. - If we cease to be human, - it is only to be *over-human*, - in such a way that *no one* can doubt it.

7. And you will already be asking - through all the lands: - What is that human - that could turn us *over-human*? - And from one end to the other - I answer you with your own language: - *The Spirit from Himself*! ... *LOVE*!

LII

1. We are like *nothingness*. We last a moment - and then disappear. - We constitute, materialize, make *real* an immense Universe- with our senses, with our thought, with our will, with our sensations, with our consciousness and mind, - but in *essence*, in *reality*, in *truth* - this Universe is Nothing. - We discover some gods, and even a single God - absolute and perfect reality - that is and are simply Nothing. - I, you, we - we experience ourselves with identity and consistency real - being nothingness. - We can never understand with reason - that, although we are nothing, - we have *EXISTENCE*. - Terrible and immense prison is that imprisons us - in its incalculable levels!

2. Perverse and kindly prison - that by keeping slaves in it, - nevertheless we were reactively harassed - defying our essential impulse of freedom! - If it imprisons us, it does not intend to keep us brutalized, - but it stimulates our inventiveness for escape. - The same sting while inoculating his somniferous - pricks us causing the pain that should wake us up. - If you end up falling asleep until the hour of awakening, - do not doubt that you will dissolve like a dream - in the Nothing. - If you suffer before all - you wake up! - If you are pleased with the enjoyment of the *form* - you disappear with it.

3. How many times do you consider yourself incapable of coming out of a state of mind, of an idea, of an emotion, of a feeling, of an image, of a sensation, of an impulse, of a conviction, of a value, of an error, of a principle? - How many times you are not even aware - that nothing

you experience as evident and real - is *necessary*? - That infinite that you are not aware of - seems necessary to you that it lacks reality - precisely because you are not conscious - at least of its possibility. - You hallucinate and you do not know it; - as you do not know - you can not stop hallucinating.

4. And in your delirium you barely glimpse and intuit perhaps - that, subsumed to the faeces in this magnificent swamp, - and that, although everything has happened to you to obfuscate your luminous superior self, - there is also a divine eye nestled in the bottom of our most unfathomable blindness.

5. There is *love* - our true germ of reality. - Only in love resides the connective power of everything with everything. - Only in this virtue of love - is it possible to experience the sum of all realities - as a unity in the common and in the different. - It could have been an idea: - it is; - it could have been a set of things: - it is; - it could have been an emotion or all: - it is; - it could have been a god or supreme being: - it is; - it could have been a human: - it is; could have been all and all and all things: - it is, - but, in the human and for the human being it is first of all - a *feeling*: - from Man to all things, - and from all things to Man: - *LOVE*.

6. It is in this love and in the enhancement of this love - that we satisfy our most unconfessed longings - and the most secret longings of the very Reality for itself. - Because there is some mystery still unknown - by which it is infinitely more satisfying - to love any flower that we look at - than not to look at it, to despise it, or to look at it with indifference. - Because it is incalculably more *satisfying* - to love the one who harms us, - than to hate him and return him evil. - Because it is deeply more satisfying to love whatever comes to our consciousness - that you only think of something good for it, or feel pleasure in it, or act simply for its benefit. - And that is only love - contains in its infinite *unifying-diversifying* power: - to universalize consciousness: - to think loving the good, feel loving the pleasure and act loving the benefit, - without excluding anyone and anyone in the maximum realm of consciousness.

7. It is necessary that everything fill it - the reality of love. - From where everything comes, there is LOVE, - where everything goes, there is LOVE. -Only in the human love was contained in a certain point to itself - to offer him *freedom to not seem LOVE*. - There is a new love in the making: - the free decision of love of the New Human Being. - Sad Era was the betrayal and disinterest of love, - but also happy for the great decision of the Age of Aquarius: - to return *in consciousness* to love - as on Earth had not been achieved for millions of years. - And what do you expect? - Why do you look at me and listen with surprise - as if I were showing a contraption, an illusion, a simple desire like so many others? - In a hundred years more you have already left this World, - but my word will have been filled with body and life. - Be you also *already* the sap, the juice, blood, the substance through which this cosmic impulse of love passes. - Do not stop its necessity with your clumsy unconsciousness. - Go to the destiny - longing, with arms outstretched, like a child running towards his mother!

LIII

1. Loving without expecting anything in return is like committing suicide. - Postponing without expecting retribution is like committing suicide. - Giving without receiving is like tying a rope around your neck and jumping with a flower in your hand.

2. There is in our deep nature, in our spirit, the need to love and be loved together. - The sun shines not only on the Universe with its Light, but also on itself. - Not only the sun shines on the Universe, - but the Universe also shines on the sun.

3. In this World you should not love without being loved. - In this World, to love is to become unique and just for each person, for each being, for each moment, for each thing. - And even if there is a LOVE above and inside ALL, - by incarnating in this World for each person, for each being, for each moment, for each thing, it can even identify itself with its opposite: the *lack of love.* - And even - I have told you - with ALL THE EVIL, - as GOD, which is present in ALL EVIL.

4. Because you were told *"Love your enemies, do good to those who hate you, bless those who curse you, pray for those who mistreat you; to the one who hits your cheek also presents the other; to the one who takes your mantle, do not deprive him also of your tunic* "[2], - will you still believe that only if you act like this will you act with love? - To love your enemy can

---

[2] Lc. 6:27-29. [Author translation from the Greek]

in certain cases involve forgiving your enemy, but, in another case, kill him, if you must defend your children. - Doing good to those who hate you may, in certain cases, imply making him see his error by means of an act of benefit to him, but in another case, it may be to avoid all contact with him. - Do not resist bad or evil, in one case represent the way to do a good, but in another, to do a wrong. - Does God not love us and also teach us through causing us suffering and causing us harm?

5. It is in your spirit, your soul, your conscience and your personal and unique circumstances where LOVE is resolved in a particular way among other infinite possibilities. - LOVE is wise and inexhaustible enough to be able to adapt to the complex and specific characteristics that are associated with each *existential momentum*. - Will you also be *wise* and powerful enough to materialize in you that *momentum* of LOVE, that infinitely unique and alive conjunction FOR YOU, and only FOR YOU? - No one should ever tell you what is good and bad for you, only you and yourself before the LOVE OF GOD - because that is something ONLY BETWEEN YOU AND GOD!

6. The Love that Christ and the Buddha taught are ways of loving for weak, unconscious, basic, reluctant, incomplete, simple, non-spiritual and unevolved human beings. - Human beings who must be told *what to do*, otherwise, they get confused and act according to the impulses and constraints of their limited structures, states and mental, social and biological processes. - Therefore, the *truths revealed* by historical spiritual masters are actually temporary and necessary adjustments between truth, lies and the *human being*.

7. Remember that I come to wake up and teach the first steps of the OVERHUMAN, and to SEE THE MAN DIE!

8. This is the REVOLUTION OF LOVE!

LIV

1. One night I dreamed several dreams- falling inside my head like raindrops, - slipping one after another by languid banana leaves, - to my consciousness there.

2. If we look with our eyes on the moon over the sea - we will see only a silver path on the dark Surface - directed towards us. - But if we contemplate the moon over the sea - with the eyes of the moon - we will see that the whole surface of the ocean has become radiantly White - like a sun.

3. Only *love* can bring together and harmonize all qualities, events and things, - in view of the ultimate universal end, - that all things secretly contain within themselves. - However, all things also aspire to achieve ends immediate and close, - among which, the best are those that facilitate more - the materialization of future goals, - in view of the inscrutable *supreme goal*: LOVE.

4. There are always major goods - that oppose and harm minor goods.

5. There is a level of the reality of all things - in which time and distance do not exist - in which all things are but one thing, - identical only to itself - and OPEN TO SOMETHING INFINITE.

6. There is truly a Wonderful Place, - a Divine Region, - the Perfect Region that surpasses even our most exalted desires, - where it is not possible to reach, - but *WHICH WE OURSELVES CREATE.*

7. I dreamed of myself - knowing that I dreamed -, going up and down mountains, cliffs, torrents, fjords, valleys, plateaus, - while the sky thundered through the most colorful and strange clouds. - There I was alone, - so alone, - that as soon as I could see a silhouette of a human form in the distance - it suddenly vanished - and I continued alone. - And so I could have walked the eternity, - if *YOU* had not come to me.

LV

1. War is the deadliest disease that the human being has experienced. - War is a constitutive gene of the human genome.

2. All the weaknesses, defects, incompletions, miseries, failures, fatalities, errors, brutalities, pettiness, lack of love, stupidity, unconsciousness of humanity have materialized and converged in War. - How then could not War be the purpose and the end of Human History?

3. And Love was never its antagonist, nor its historical or anthropological counterpart, - but only the contradictory and unnatural presence of a Spirit who was not of this World, - but who was willing to suffer even to martyrdom - for to achieve the evolution of Humanity towards OVERHUMANITY, - although in the end it only ends up transcending *Human Essence*, but not Humanity.

4. Heraclitus said wisely: "War is the Father and King of all things."[3] - Because he knew in silence that LOVE is the Mother and Queen of War - and that LOVE is not of this World.

5. And now you will see War in the World in its glory and majesty!

6. -- AND THE LOVE?

---

[3] Fr. 53DK.

7. -- I am not Christ. - I am not the Buddha.

8. The human species has initiated the evolutionary creation of an essence of *love* - different from the Love of Jesus Christ, different from the Animal Love, different from the Personal Love, different from the Cosmic LOVE. - A *strange* and *painful* love, because it sinks and merges with the very roots of the LOVE of this Universe, - but it also tears away from It. - A love that is neither human nor divine! - We can already feel the first pains of the labor of this *future superhuman love.*

LVI

1. The evangelist has said: "*Beloved, let us love one another, for he who loves is from God, and everyone who loves has come from God and knows God! He who does not love did not know God, because God is love.*"[4] - But I say to you: "*Beloved, God is love, because first LOVE is God!*"

2. LOVE begot God, and not God Love. - This is a mystery that the human being is far from understanding.

3. And it is that LOVE is not the shadow of anything, - neither attribute, nor son, nor divinity or any person. - LOVE is the light that allows the existence of color and form, of darkness and nothingness. - LOVE is in All, it underlies All, it contains All, it is All. - Everything that comes into this Universe - without exception - is caused by LOVE. - Otherwise, it does not come.

4. If you raise your eyes to the sky by night or by day, there is LOVE. - If you turn your eyes around the Earth, there is LOVE. - And if you look at the human being? ... - There LOVE is trapped, imprisoned, diminished, silenced, betrayed, tortured, deformed, crucified.

5. Because where have you seen walls of LOVE?, LOVE hospitals?, LOVE prisons?, LOVE colleges?, LOVE weapons?, LOVE banks?, LOVE

---

[4] 1 John, 4:7-8. [Author translation from the Greek]

governments?, LOVE churches ?, LOVE markets ?, LOVE streets ?, LOVE police?, LOVE delinquents and criminals?

6. Because where have you seen cities of LOVE?, LOVE policies?, LOVE Sciences?, LOVE Education?, LOVE cultures?, LOVE Economy?, LOVE jurisprudence?, History of LOVE?, Mathematics of LOVE?, Planet of LOVE?

7. After all, you've only known the cemetery of LOVE. - In cemeteries there is more Love than in any other human place.

LVII

1. All my life I have followed in the footsteps of that mystery called God. -Now I know that I am but an extension of LOVE itself. - Now I know that ALL is nothing but a differentiation of LOVE itself in its mysterious unity -multiplicity. - The thing and the Human particularly are debated in the basal mud of God, - trying fruitlessly, but progressively, in acquiring an autonomy of which they lack.

2. It is exciting in this process of independence to see that there is a being that is capable of denying God, - in a certain sense himself. - It amazes me to know how God himself refuses to dubiously engender a different being which is also the same as He. - Where does he pretend to lead us? - Is FREEDOM paradoxically our destiny?

3. So much is His Glory - that It does not need to be explicit in anything and in any way, - but It is everything! - So great is His glory- that every human specificity of God, - is also God!

4. God can exist or not exist for Man - but this matters little. - We are a tiny point, a *Nothing* in the middle of Everything. - The really important thing is to know if *we exist* for this Everything, even if we are Nothing. - The really important thing and difficult thing - it's to know what *meaning* we have for this Everything. - Because after and before billions and trillions of years and light years in time and space - our existence and presence - what lasting and real consistency could it have? - Because the Universes opened to infinity transcend all forms of consciousness. - Our

need to know everything is at this time an incentive - as much as a trap. - Fly, swim, crawl, think, dream, die – all ultimately lead to the same *end*.

5. From our present, from the moment of awakened consciousness - reality is amplified. - From attentive consciousness the movement towards unconsciousness begins, and from unconsciousness to awakened consciousness, - towards other times and dimensions - and *beyond*. - Reality opens in a mysterious encounter with consciousness - it creates itself together with our consciousness and from our unconsciousness, - it waits patiently for us, submerged in our fearful torpor. - The mind is the first field of our own awakening, - from our potential mutation into higher and nonexistent forms of being. - Awaken, mutate, create our minds into incredible forms, now, and now, and now!

6. This is the Age of the Mind! - During the next thousand years we will advance through their worlds and powers as we have not done in millions of years! - The human mind will be extended by the Superhuman Mind through other Higher Minds.

7. Here is the challenge of the New Species: - Knowing Itself in the *mind* - to create the Mind-within-All and the Mind-without-All!

LVIII

1. Scarce and null are the words to talk about *the New*. - Also my own words already decay, - they begin to wilt, yellowish, repeated more than once, trivial, - like a hum to your ears, numb - I can not allow it! – I Will shake you once more, - before I prepare myself to shut up breathless - for what I am not able to say! - *Evangelium* are mere words! - but if you look more beyond the words - it would not cease for a second - your dizziness, your amazement, your tremor. - This *Evangelium* at last, - is not more than the light of a lighthouse - still far from me, also from you, - in the middle of a black storm. - I only hope to touch with the mortal remains of this divine spark - your soul! - I only hope to shake you so little and so much, - so that you do not stop for a moment to run after me - after you - after EVERYTHING!

2. Terrible mission and mandate are for me - to rouse you, to overthrow you and to anguish you, perhaps to death! - I would not want to have this voice -too weak to launch the cry of Truth - which, however, I throw! - I would like to have the power to *enlighten you* - with my own peace, with my own love, with my own being-in-God- so that without frights, without horrible doubts, without weaknesses nor disappointments, without painful and slow and slow and slow processes, - you could share the Life - that I receive after this *EVANGELIUM*.

3. But it's not so - because you'll have to fight against the trillion demons -that haunt this gospel! - Perhaps my scream does not raise more than some invisible white curls - on the human surface of the World.

Maybe there is a great storm of humanity here and there - and then return everything to the calm of the inexorable. - What happens or otherwise! - Let what is to come come! - I have written what they have brought me to write! - I live what I must live, I at least, and at least!

4. Get out of the cities! – GET OUT! - I repeat to you. - But if you are not clean of humanity, - if your *self* has not given itself to your conscience and will to LOVE, - do not form - I beg you - no community. - Before you live separately - until that you are free from the slavery of your *ego-ego-ego*. - Only then can transmutation be realized for Universal Love, - in the New Community without frontiers of the *Superior Species*.

5. It could help you in many ways, - guide your internal processes, indicate routes within your reality, facilitate your understanding, your lucidity and conscience - so that you can truly live your own *evangelium*, - but it is not here, the time nor the place.

6. We will raise you wise men and wise women, - enlightened in power and transcendence, - teachers in the true *God-of-All*, - guides in the movement towards spirit and transcendence, - humble, surprising beings, not of this World, overflowing with love and vast intelligence, - willing to occupy the last place, - even if they walk first.

7. I keep going, - accompanying my Destiny - I go on, - seeking to grow by my spirit towards all the universes, - in order to give myself better and better in this, - for my love towards you. - I can not accept all the calls, - follow your inner voice! - It is in your own consciousness where you find your weakness and your trap, - as well as your strength and the power of LOVE.

8. Move, my son and brother-sister, - move! - Do not fall asleep! - The cold of death, in the midst of the icebergs of Man, - numbs you! - I couldn't keep silent, - forgive me! - But if I have not shouted loud and clear enough for you, - forgive me even more!

LIX

1. And in this final hour, in this time of apocalypse and advent, I will teach you the intimate prayer which the Saviour taught me so that at every moment we may repeat it in the soul, - me and you, with and without words, with these or with others, - and thus, poor, suffering and fragile creatures - let us concentrate our whole being on the unfathomable power of LOVE, until the end.

2. SAVIOUR'S PRAYER FOR THE COMING TIMES

Our LOVE
That you're everywhere,
Divine presence,
Bring us your LOVE;
Become your reality on Earth
As it is done in the Universe.
Give us today our daily good;
Support our miseries
So that we don't stop trying to be better;
Feed our hearts
So we don't get away from YOU,
LOVE.

LX

1. When I finally close this book - I start a new path, - if I can still find something called *path*. - As far as my transformation goes, my mind will be no more than a trace, - if there are still *steps*. - For this I walked on the snow - climbing the paths of the Pangue - in the heights of Cochiguaz, - until my feet could not move forward, - because they sank under the ice and snow, - that reached up to my knees. -Then I stopped to contemplate brightly the heights that welcomed me - hundreds of meters from my desired summits, - while they themselves rejected me, - preventing my further step. - I now understand that by sitting anointed on the Throne of the Threshold - the Elqui Valley, the snows, its ravines, my piece of home - they were consecrating me even higher, *flying towards the Sources of LOVE*.

Printed in the United States
By Bookmasters